SINFUL
HARVEST

Books by Anitra Lynn McLeod

WICKED HARVEST

DARK HARVEST

SINFUL HARVEST

SEXY BEAST VII
(with Kate Douglas and Shelli Stevens)

Published by Kensington Publishing Corporation

SINFUL HARVEST

ANITRA LYNN McLEOD

APHRODISIA

KENSINGTON PUBLISHING CORP.

http://www.kensingtonbooks.com

APHRODISIA BOOKS are published by

Kensington Publishing Corp.
119 West 40th Street
New York, NY 10018

All Kensington Titles, Imprints, and Distributed Lines are available at special quantity discounts for bulk purchases for sales promotions, premiums, fund-raising, and educational or institutional use.

Special book excerpts or customized printings can also be created to fit specific needs. For details, write or phone the office of the Kensington special sales manager: Kensington Publishing Corp., 119 West 40th Street, New York, NY 10018, attn: Special Sales Department. Phone: 1-800-221-2647.

Aphrodisia and the A logo Reg. U.S. Pat. & TM Off.

ISBN-13: 978-0-7582-3535-0
ISBN-10: 0-7582-3535-6

First Trade Paperback Printing: February 2011

10 9 8 7 6 5 4 3 2 1

Printed in the United States of America

For Mouse, who loved to play with words:
vesta, zanti, beater balls, bonerific, kissy woman . . .
I feel your loss to this day
and yet when I think of you,
I can't help but smile.

1

What Kerrick missed most was his hair.

Women loved his hair, and he loved women. A lack of locks would certainly curtail his flirting. All he had to do was tilt his head so that his golden hair fell across his green eyes and women couldn't help but reach out to push the strands away. When they did, he'd capture their wrist and kiss the palm of their hand, which inevitably led to kissing their lips. His signature move worked every time. Of course, he didn't need to flirt with the women he would encounter today.

As Kerrick entered the Harvest room, he barely noticed the elaborate decorations or the paintings of his predecessors. The sacrifice table riveted his attention. Hundreds of beautiful women adorned in finery lay supine, all of them waiting for him. Below his codpiece, his cock was hard and ready. He didn't miss the hair down there so much, as shaving made everything seem bigger. Sadly, he couldn't feel a thing. He was as rigid as the blade at his side, but *estal* oil blocked all sensations. A drink called *umer* would keep him hard but unable to orgasm. The nasty burnt wood taste of the elixir still lingered at the back of his throat. Had he known all of this, Kerrick might not have bothered to become the Harvester. What fun would there be in claiming the virginity of all the young women in the land if he couldn't feel a damn thing?

Of course, it was too late to turn back now.

After the last Harvester had selected his bondmate, Kerrick stepped forward, claiming the right to proceed in his place. None of the other recruits challenged him. Kerrick was newly arrived, but he'd been in training his whole life. Even seasoned recruits were not as muscular as he was. Nor did they possess his skills. For a moment, two or three considered challenging him, but in the end, they shook their heads and moved aside. They'd decided a fight to the death wasn't worth it. After a hasty indoctrination, the magistrate took him to the massive double hung doors of the Harvest room.

"Tell me now if you're going to select a bondmate so that I might ready the next Harvester." Ambo Votny seemed annoyed and flustered. "You're the third Harvester this season, and I'd rather like to stop running back and forth between here and the training rooms."

Kerrick assessed the elderly, rotund man. Several chins quivered as he spoke and exertion flushed his skin a deep, bluish red, as if his entire being cried out for air. Underarm stains ruined the grandeur of his silver uniform. One more pass from here to there would probably result in the man's death. Kerrick longed to take Ambo's position as magistrate, but killing him with exercise probably wasn't the best way to get there. Besides, Kerrick would need more than a brief stint as the Harvester to garner enough pull among the elite to ascend to such a powerful post.

Calmly, Kerrick insisted, "I have no intention of selecting a bondmate this season or next. I will be the Harvester for as long as I can."

Ambo released an overwrought breath. "Thank the gods!" He flicked his fingers at the guards. "Open the doors."

Several places down from the north end of the table, Kerrick spied his first harvest. His boots boomed on the Onic tiles as he strode toward her. Freeaal! The damn things sounded like a stampede of boulders! He tried to walk softer, but his stride made no difference in the pounding of his boots. Several of the women noticeably flinched at each booming echo.

When he reached the first sacrifice, he took a moment to assess the woman who would be his initial harvest. Her round, ebony face was serene, as if she didn't mind waiting most of the day and half the night for him to arrive. Her fine features were cute rather than beautiful, but her eyes were the most amazing mix of brown and green. When he placed his hands upon her knees and parted her thighs, she smiled up at him with such joy he couldn't help but smile back. Her yellow-green robe slid off her legs, exposing slender thighs and her tender sex. Glistening drops of *estal* oil clung to her tight, brown curls. Out of the many pheromone-laced scents in the air, he pinpointed hers and breathed deeply. Only the truly innocent women had such a compelling essence.

In Cheon, he'd been careful to keep most of his conquests to the iniquitous women, those too jaded by love to take his flirting beyond a fleeting tryst. The innocent ones always broke his heart, for they believed they could tame him no matter how many times they'd seen other women fail. Always, they thought they were different. He'd flirt with them, he'd tease and torment their beautiful bodies, but he'd leave their virginity intact.

Frustrated when this lovely virgin's scent did nothing to his cock, for it was utterly without sensation, he took another deep breath to consider later when all the drugs had worn off. Hers was a scent he would never forget. Gently sliding her forward, he placed her left foot on the hilt of his sword and lifted her right foot up, so that her leg was almost straight against his bare chest.

In the ancient words, Kerrick said, "By might of the blade I claim that which belongs to me."

With a lilting voice, she returned, "I freely give myself to you."

Her gorgeous gaze held steady with his, as if she would brand herself into his mind. In that moment, he wished he could do more than just speak a few words and follow the exacting rules of the ritual. He would like to know her name, her history, what touches she liked, and which she didn't. Women fascinated him. Sadly, his duty limited his contact. With a sigh, he lowered his hand and slid the codpiece aside. Thick and numb, his cock sought the heat of her sex. He tilted his hips forward and plunged fully within. *Estal* oil eased his entry but deadened all tactile sensations. He felt slight pressure, and she apparently felt only fullness, for she didn't even wince. He withdrew, lowered her leg, and helped her from the table.

Her *astle* robe swirled around her calves as she exited. With the ritual complete, she was now a fully recognized citizen. One thrust took her from child to woman. She could now own property, bond with a mate, and have children. To celebrate her new standing, her family would likely shower her with gifts at a huge feast.

His *paratanist* approached. Hidden behind a beige robe with an enormous cowl hood, his personal servant tended to his needs. At the moment, she cleansed and anointed his cock for the next sacrifice. When she finished, she bowed and backed toward a small niche in the wall.

Kerrick wondered what the robe hid. He knew she was a woman, but as to age or appearance, he had no idea. Idly, he wondered what would happen if he pulled her hood back to examine her face. During his hasty indoctrination, when the magistrate introduced him to her, he warned that Kerrick couldn't touch her, only she could touch him. Right after, Ambo shook his head, and said, "Don't touch *it*, a *paratanist* is a sexless servant, nothing more." However, the truth was out. The servant who caressed him so intimately was a woman. As to why Ambo seemed to have such a grudge against her, that was as big a mystery as what she looked like. Kerrick thought of violating the rules, but then decided soothing his curiosity wasn't as important as remaining the Harvester. He wouldn't do anything to jeopardize his position.

Turning his attention back to the sacrifices, he lost himself in the sheer multitude of women. Tall, short, thin, heavy, all different skin colors from the palest milk to the richest ebony and every shade in between. Their eyes went from small and glowing pink to enormous and black as night. Slender noses, wide noses, pug noses. Sweet smiles, shy smiles, lusty smiles. All were beautiful in their own way. Each was unique, special, and memorable. Even though he couldn't feel anything, it didn't matter. He was their first. They would never forget this moment, and neither would he. Pressed into the pages of his memory, each lovely lady would be his for a lifetime.

When he reached the south end of the table, he almost slumped with relief. He'd enjoyed every moment of his first Harvest, but the act of cleaning and oiling his shaft so many times would undoubtedly result in some rawness tomorrow. Still, he felt an enormous sense of accomplishment. Whenever he completed a task he set himself, he felt a rush of pride that he'd proved his father wrong. Kerrick would make something of himself. Becoming the Harvester was just the stepping-stone on his way to becoming the palace magistrate.

His *paratanist* knelt beside him, cleaning and oiling his shaft yet again. Perplexed, he pointed out, "There are no more women."

In a droning, sexless voice, she said, "You have sacrificed all the virgins, now you will mate with the Harvester."

Mate? Kerrick considered all the ramifications of that particular word. Moreover, he was the Harvester. Kerrick considered himself a kinky guy, but mating with himself wasn't quite what he had in mind, not after a day of denied orgasm. Then he realized she was speaking of his female counterpart. In all the tales he'd heard about the Harvest, he'd never heard that the male and female Harvesters mated afterward.

"I won't be bonded to her, will I?" He better not be. His understanding was that he would remain the Harvester until he chose his own bondmate or a recruit challenged him in a fight to the death.

"You will find your satisfaction with her rather than by my hand." Finished cleaning him, she applied a thicker oil over his entire genital area.

Did he detect a note of disapproval in her tone? Digging deeper behind her words, he asked, "So, the male and female Harvesters haven't always mated after the Harvest, then?"

"You will be the first in thousands of seasons."

Was it just his imagination or was feeling returning to his shaft? Her light strokes were causing zinging pleasure bolts across his entire body. To distract himself, he focused on what she'd said. "Why am I the first in a long time?"

"I know not. All I know is the living god decreed this return to the most ancient of prophecy."

Kerrick had a feeling more questions would only prompt more questions. Life within the palace was a source of great gossip within his region of Cheon; however, he had no first-hand knowledge of anything. For all he knew, everything he considered fact wasn't. As he allowed his *paratanist* to undress him, he began to realize he might have placed himself into a position of forced servitude. He'd always thought the Harvester had power and a certain level of freedom. After this his first day, he was beginning to realize he labored under strict protocols, rituals and apparently, appeasing a living god.

Of course, it was too late to turn back now.

Once she'd stripped him bare, his *paratanist* slathered oil from his head to his toes. Sensation returned to his form followed by curious warmth. His balls felt heavy and full. If he didn't find release soon, they would ache unbearably. When he questioned his servant, she admitted the oil counteracted the *estal* oil and *umer* drink. This was to encourage him to mate.

Such longing possessed his body he didn't think he needed any encouragement at all. When he saw this woman, he'd have to refrain from mounting her without preamble. Within him burned a need to bury his shaft and thrust until climax released the knotted tension in his body. He wouldn't just mate with her; he'd fuck her in a frenzy of lust. Briefly, he wondered what she looked like, but decided it didn't matter. He'd jump anyone right now to take the edge off. Besides, if female Harvesters were notorious for anything, it was their astonishing beauty.

Deeming him sufficiently oiled, his *paratanist* led him to the double hung doors of the Harvest room. As she pushed them open, he wasn't sure what he was expecting, but certainly not what he saw. Hundreds of people lined the massive hallway. Deep jewel-toned clothing proclaimed them high-ranking members of society. As he followed his servant, they eyed him critically but remained silent.

Crazy, wild, or dangerous stunts had always appealed to Kerrick, but he'd never been on display like this, not nude, hard, and filled with raging desire. Without the drugs to cushion him, the unique smell of each woman he passed heightened his need for release. Clamping down hard on his cravings, he wanted to order his *paratanist* to make haste, but he didn't dare speak. He worried that if he did, they would have to start all over again, and he didn't think he could bear one more moment of delay. His tormented body needed satisfaction now.

Endlessly the hallway went on and so did the spectators. He had no idea what the population of the palace was, but it seemed all of them were jammed into this corridor. Men and women alike ogled him. His bouncing, swollen cock seemed to command their attention. If questioned in detail, most of them would not be able to describe his face, but they could illustrate every feature of his genitals. And it wasn't just the women who showed lustful interest. Several men licked their lips and slid a hand down to grasp bulges between their legs. What his grandfather said was true; the elite were a lusty bunch.

At an elaborately carved Onic door, his *paratanist* paused and placed her hand against a metal plate near where a doorknob should be but wasn't. The door swung open. Ducking inside, Kerrick breathed a sigh of relief to be away from prying eyes. Dust swirled in the air, causing him to sneeze and wonder if they'd only recently cleaned this place. If the Harvesters hadn't mated in thousands of seasons, it made a kind of sense that they would have to renew the chamber where they mated, for, of course, they wouldn't just fornicate in some back room. This wasn't sex for the sake of pleasure; this was sex for the culmination of an ancient prophecy.

Kerrick followed his servant down a long, dark stairwell. At the bottom, another *paratanist* waited beside a smooth metal door. His *paratanist* nodded to the other one and simultaneously they placed their hands on the door. When it swung open, they motioned him inside.

"*Noganth a nogonth,*" he said, using what he thought was the classic battle cry of the Tandth people. Roughly translated, it meant to have glory, one must have guts. Or perhaps it was no guts, no glory. He couldn't remember exactly as he'd spent his time on Tandth racing down ice-shrouded mountains on a single piece of carved timber. Afterward, he'd burrowed below thick animal furs with lusty natives. Usually three of four robust women at a time joined him. What they lacked in amenities, they more than made up for with generous hospitality.

With a deep breath, Kerrick stepped into darkness.

As the door closed behind him, lighting crystals flickered to a soft, golden glow. Upon a circular bed, which took up almost the entire circular room, lay a woman. Clinging *astle* sheets of the blackest black he'd ever seen molded to her long-limbed body. Her hair, also black, teased around her regal face, then blended into the covers so that she appeared to lay entwined in her own tresses. Apparently, they didn't shave the female Harvester bald. Without conscious thought, his gaze wandered to the juncture of her legs, and his penis throbbed in response. Covered in downy black hairs or bare, either way, he couldn't wait to uncover her *sasalan*. Literally translated, the Plenetin word meant "secret treasure." He took a deep breath and all he could smell was her. Rich and sweet, her essence caused hunger to gnaw at his belly and balls. He wanted to taste her, then fill her. Sheer force of will was the only thing that held him back from pouncing on the bed, yanking the covering away, and mounting her. So provocative was her essence, she stripped all others from his mind.

Her skin complemented the blackness of the room, making her seem paler than she was, but he couldn't quite place the tone of her skin. Not white, but not caramel, more like between the two, like the color of the *noisseur* tree: white with a hefty dollop of brown mixed in. Truly, she possessed lovely skin. What he could see of her face and arms was flawless. Her hands were large but finely boned with delicately tapered fingers. Short, no-nonsense nails spoke of her practicality, while her twice-pierced ears spoke of her boldness.

Slowly, her gray eyes opened, pinning him to the spot. He'd never seen such a cold gaze. In that very second of considering him, he felt she'd probed his history back to his childhood, judged him as unworthy, then dismissed him entirely. If he had hackles, they would have bristled. After meeting thousands of women in his lifetime, he'd never encountered one who so utterly disdained him.

Her eyes went suddenly wide as she sat up, exposing stunningly perfect breasts. Not too big, not too small, with sweet caramel nipples that begged for his mouth. Balanced between them was a necklace with a black stone. When she noticed the direction of his gaze, she yanked the sheet up.

She didn't speak, which was a shame, because he longed to hear her voice. Would it match the regal cast of her face and the prim set of her mouth? Gods forbid she had an annoying voice like Creea, who had the face of a goddess but the voice of a cat-erwauling animal in heat. The only way he'd been able to abide Creea's company was by keeping her mouth busy. Turned out she was a natural at oral pleasure. Once she wrapped her lovely lips around his cock, she wouldn't stop until she drained him, and he could hold back for a long, long time.

Kerrick realized he could say something, but what would he say? "I'm here to mate with you" sounded silly. "I'm going to fuck you until my aching balls explode" was more accurate, but crude.

In the end, he settled for a simple statement of fact. "I am the Harvester."

Her eyes narrowed and she clutched the sheet more firmly to her chest.

He wondered if her *paratanist* had told her what was sup-posed to happen here. Although a big bed and little else should have made the point clear, she might be like Lakoo, who was gorgeous but vapid. The simplest question often left Lakoo scratching her head. However, one didn't need to discuss the imponderables of the universe while tussling between the sheets.

"Does your neck hurt?" she asked.

If possible, her voice was lovelier than her face. Rich and thick like fresh cream, comforting as it poured over him. Hers was a voice he could listen to all day. However, the question left him baffled until he remembered that he didn't have his hair anymore. Without a thought, he'd canted his head to drape his golden strands across his eyes. How was he to thaw out this chilly lady when he couldn't even use his best move?

"Depends." Stepping to the foot of the bed, he grasped the edge of the sheet.

"On?" Her knuckles turned white as she gripped the thin fabric that shielded her from his gaze.

"What we're going to be doing." She was no match for his strength. When he yanked sharply, the sheet flicked off the bed and pooled on the floor. Now he had an unfettered view of her form. Long arms crossed over her breasts as she drew her legs up, tucking them beneath her, but not before he saw tight, black curls on her mound.

"So, you're not shaved there. Good." He climbed onto the bed and crawled toward her like a hungry beast. "I find that right as a woman reaches climax, a good tug on her hairs can prolong her pleasure."

Her brows drew together as her lips parted on a shocked exhale. She curled up at the head of the bed, as if she tried to get away from him, but there was nowhere for her to go. He found her modesty charming, especially after she'd willingly taken the virginity of hundreds of males. Each movement he made closer caused her to shrink back, but then her face lost all expression as she lowered her arms and slid down the bed onto her back. She changed from disgust to submission without missing a beat.

Curious at the abrupt transformation, he inquired, "Tell me your name."

"What does it matter? Just get this over with." She closed her eyes, settling back as if in sacrifice to him.

Never in his life had he forced a woman to his bed, and he wasn't about to start now. Even though just the smell of her was causing his cock to twitch, he was not a randy boy in heat. He was a connoisseur of women. If he had to suffer anticipation for another while, he would, especially when his ego demanded that she must want him as much as he wanted her. He wouldn't allow himself to be a trial to be borne.

"I want to know your name." He trailed his fingertips along her calf, marveling at the smooth perfection of her skin.

She jumped, then visibly forced herself to relax. "If I tell you, will you just get on with this?" She sounded as flustered and annoyed as the magistrate had been earlier.

"Of course," he said, even though he did not intend to do so.

"Ariss."

"A lyrical name that suits your royal bearing. My name is Kerrick."

"Kerrick?" She frowned, narrowing her eyes, examining him more coolly than she had before.

"You've heard of me?" Perhaps he wouldn't need his hair after all. She wouldn't be the first woman impressed by his legendary exploits.

"Hardly." Ariss didn't roll her eyes; she somehow managed to roll her entire body in contempt. "Do you know what a kerrick is?"

With a seductive grin, he asked, "A devastatingly handsome man?"

His charm was lost on her as she stared at him over the bridge of her long, straight nose. "I'll tell you once this is over." She said it as if that would be enough to motivate him to leap upon her and finish quickly.

He frowned. Did she think him a simple peasant?

Curious as to why she wished to hurry, he teased his finger up from her calf to the spot just behind her knee. Most women found a light touch there stimulating. Ariss didn't. With a sigh, she parted her legs, shoving his hand out of the way, and lifted her arms over her head. Again, he had an image of her in sacrifice to him and wondered why she saw him as such a chore.

"Why are you in such a hurry?" he asked, breathing deeply

of her scent. With her legs now parted, he could almost taste her sweetness. As tempting as her offer was, he refused to rush. Stubbornly, he vowed to drag this out until she begged him for release. As much as his body clamored for climax, his ego bellowed louder for satisfaction.

"I've been waiting most of the night for you. I just want this over with so I can return to my rooms." Her tone upbraided and enticed him all at once. Considering her expressionless face, he doubted she thought much about him at all since she was asleep when he found her. Had she rushed through her Harvest just as she wished to rush through this? Never in his life had a woman been indifferent to him. Although, usually, they met him under circumstances other than a forced tryst. Perhaps the fact she had no choice irked her. But it wasn't as if this was his idea. He was only doing what the ritual demanded.

"I'm sorry I made you wait." Lifting her hand, he kissed each of her fingertips, pleased when her eyes widened. "I didn't want to rush my sacrifices." Turning her hand over, he placed a closed-mouth kiss to the center of her palm, reveling in how she inadvertently parted her lips. "Had I known such a beauty as you awaited me, I might have missed some in my haste." He breathed the words into her palm, then kissed the pulse at her wrist. Her fluttering heartbeat told him she wasn't completely immune to his charms, despite the expressionless cast to her face.

"As if you remember all of them," she accused, drilling her eyes into his as if she could ferret out the truth with her gaze alone. He'd never encountered a woman who shifted moods faster than the swirling sands of Vernama.

"But I do remember each and every one." He angled his face earnestly up toward hers. "I memorized not only their faces, but also their very essences." If he were an expert at anything about women, it would be in knowing their individual scents.

Each woman bore her own unique bouquet. Blinded, he would be able to tell each woman by smell alone.

In a challenging tone, Ariss demanded, "Tell me about the one in bright yellow."

Kerrick considered for a moment, flipping through each woman in his mind. It didn't take him long to assess her game. "Your sister." Just the thought of taking two sisters on the same night aroused him beyond the excruciating pain he was already in. "Her nose was similar to yours, although she was not nearly as beautiful as you."

Ariss' eyes went wide with surprise that he remembered, but his compliment slid off her as if she were ice. When he lifted her other hand to kiss her fingertips, she said, "You don't have to do all of this. Much like her, I have no choice."

The comment wounded his pride. For a brief moment, he thought of leaping upon her and doing as she asked—banging away until he climaxed. A deeper need helped him realize it was the fact that she was forced into this that truly bothered her. Good. He preferred women who forged their own way and didn't just let society dictate their actions. Sadly, he couldn't do anything about their circumstances. All he could do was try to make this as enjoyable as possible.

"I don't have a choice, either, but that doesn't mean I wish to hurry." He kissed up her arm until he maneuvered himself beside her on the bed. "Just because we didn't select each other is no reason not to enjoy being with each other." Tenderly, he kissed her shoulder. "You are a beautiful woman, Ariss. The thought of leaping on top of you and pounding away is revolting."

Something about what he said excited her, because for a brief moment, she lost her mask. Simmering passion rose to the surface of her gaze, then vanished into cool gray without a ripple. Was that her secret? She had a furtive desire to be overpowered? Kerrick wasn't opposed to such rough couplings, but not for a first encounter. Besides, he wouldn't dare act on such an impulse unless he was very, very sure his aggression would be well received.

"Is that what you want?" he whispered against her shoulder. "Do you want me to yank your legs apart, spear you with my cock, and buck against you like a man possessed?" He nipped her flesh, causing her breath to catch against parted lips. As if in battle with herself, she primly composed her features, compressing her lips as she readied a sharp retort. Before she could respond, he cupped her face, turning her head so that he could kiss her lips. In direct contrast to the harshness of his words, he kissed her tenderly. At first, she kept her lips firmly pressed together, denying him entrance to her mouth, refusing him such intimacy. After repeated soft nibbles along the edge of her mouth, she parted her lips, almost against her will, allowing him to slip his tongue inside. Her taste was sleepy sweet, seductive. As he slid his tongue against hers, she groaned into his mouth, then followed suit, exploring him as thoroughly as he explored her.

In all his life, he didn't think he'd managed such a perfect kiss without using his hair. When she turned into his embrace, he mentally congratulated himself for breaking the first layer of ice. However, he wasn't finished yet. In spite of her small show of pleasure, she still maintained a controlled aspect to her countenance, almost as if she couldn't bear to show passion. He'd heard of ice queens—those women who disdained love and sex as utterly beneath their elevated selves. He'd never bothered seducing one, as he feared what lay at the center of the glacier. Now, he wanted to know what made Ariss turn a cold attitude to something she so desperately craved.

Capturing her firmly in his arms, he kissed her more deeply until he had tasted every bit of her luscious mouth. Pulling back, he grasped her hands, lowering them alongside her body.

"Lovely skin, sweet as heavy cream." He kissed her face, her neck, and across her shoulders. Below him, she writhed, as if offering up her breasts. Since he knew that's where she expected him to go, he refused. His first lesson in seduction was never being predictable. If a woman knew where he would go and what he would do, he had lost the element of surprise. And he knew that every woman loved surprises.

Kerrick released her hands so that he could angle up to kiss and stroke his way along her body. From her sensitive sides, to the curve of her belly, to the swell of her hips, not a bit of her exquisite form escaped his attention. Everywhere he looked or touched, he found perfection. No scars, no marks, every flawless bit compelled him to speculate she'd either led a sheltered life or had access to a most skilled surgeon. He couldn't think of another woman with such faultless features.

Each press of his lips or fingertips caused painful awareness in his own body. When he did finally achieve orgasm after this seemingly endless day, it would be spectacular. Already moisture leaked from the tip of his throbbing cock from just touching her. Forcefully, he turned his mind away from his needs and on to hers.

When he glanced up, her face was a mixture of denial and control. Why was she still trying to maintain her facade of indifference when her body clearly felt otherwise? Was she ashamed? How could a woman who competed against so many other women to become the Harvester be so . . . He searched for the word. When he found it, he understood. Naive. Ariss may have knelt over hundreds of aroused men, but she'd never taken a lover into her arms. In a strange way, she was a virgin. That's why her scent was so captivating. Her essence was experienced and innocent all at the same time.

Sliding up the bed to lay beside her, he kissed her again, this time noticing how tentatively she kissed back, as if she weren't sure she was doing it the right way. Her guileless response confirmed his suspicions and increased his ardor. Ariss was exactly what he'd been looking for his entire life; a wonderful combination of modesty and lust all wrapped up in a flawless female form.

As he continued to kiss her, he cupped her breast, causing her to arch into his caress. Her breast filled his palm perfectly, as if they were designed for each other. Her caramel nipple peaked invitingly, and he lowered his head to pull the turgid flesh between his teeth. Once secured, he flicked his tongue across the captured tip.

She hissed and clutched his head, pulling him closer, encouraging him to open his mouth and draw the tasty bud within. Her wanton reaction pleased the hunter inside himself, but moreover, it compelled him to try to lift her higher. His pride demanded he have her wild with want by the time he plunged into her depths.

Back and forth, he switched from nipple to nipple until she quivered below him. Such silky skin she had, rich with the flavor of *valasta*. Never had he encountered a woman who tasted of the sweet cooking spice, but now he would never get the taste from his mind.

"Please, just finish." Her breathless plea only compelled him to go slower. He sensed something more dire than a need to be away as fast as possible. Was it a hint of fear? Did she worry that she would actually enjoy his ministrations? Is that what caused her slight show of panic? What harm could there be in sharing physical pleasure?

Carefully, he slid his hand down her torso, then stroked the wetness of her mound. The idea that many men had plunged within only to withdraw without satisfaction excited him. Was she sore or, like him, had the *estal* oil cushioned her? As he continued to tease his lone finger up and down the slick wetness of her sex, she did her best to remain indifferent but couldn't quite manage to maintain her aplomb. Her pupils dilated while her breathing hitched.

"One little finger can be so seductive," he murmured, swirling his fingertip around her hooded clit. "After all of those hard cocks plunged inside you without touching you here"—he smoothed his finger over the tight nub—"this must be a relief, to finally get this straining bit of flesh some attention." Repeatedly, he traced his finger down and around her now-slick passage, then up and over the hood of her clit. When he finally slid his finger straight up, pushing back the hood, making direct contact with her swollen clit, she involuntarily lifted up. For a split second, her carefully controlled face wasn't. Pure lust exploded from her expression. Just as quickly, she forced the mask over her features again, but he had seen the truth.

Determined to expose the untamed woman inside, he continued his delicious torment despite his throbbing need. His cock envied his finger, pulsing with a demand to exchange places. Slowly, carefully, he fondled her sex until her pulse danced wildly at her throat and her breath hitched in small gasps. The closer she came to release, the more she tightened up. From her toes to her forehead went rigid, as if she refused to release control.

"Relax, Ariss," he encouraged softly, teasing his breath to her ear.

"I can't," she whispered in an agonized gasp. Almost on the verge of tears, she added, "If I do, I'll fall apart."

"I'm here to hold you." He pressed his body the length of hers. She gasped when she felt his cock, hard and hot, against her hip.

"Put it in me," she begged, her eyes closed tightly against the truth of her need. "Please, please just put it in me and finish."

A surge of agonized longing swelled him impossibly tight. Her words were innocent and wanton all in the same breath. Before he could comply, she pushed him to his back, straddled his hips, grasped his shaft, and lowered herself onto him. Shocking heat enveloped his cock, causing him to gasp in surprise and clutch at her hips to steady her atop him. Never had a woman taken such forceful command of his body.

Wild with abandon, she rocked atop him, her breasts bobbing as she rode him hard and fast. Clutching her hands to his chest, she dug her fingertips in to steady herself against the movement of her hips. As she angled forward to press her clit against him, her hair cascaded over her face, hiding her from his gaze. When he reached up to push the silken strands away, she swung her head to the side, covering her face again.

Stunned by the swift and sudden change from reluctance to enthusiasm, Kerrick watched her as she writhed atop him, desperate for release. Stroke by stroke, he saw flashes of her face revealed. She kept her eyes firmly closed, her features straining with need. Ever more firmly she pressed into him on the down stroke, until she caused the bed to give below their weight. Her limbs were slender but stronger than he thought. He could overpower her, but why would he? Having a woman use him for her pleasure was possibly the highest compliment he'd ever been paid. His ego swelled to epic proportions. Besides, it wasn't as if she were hurting him. The way she shimmied her hips around on his shaft was beyond pleasurable. Hers were not the practiced moves of an experienced lover, but those of a lusty virgin caught up in overwhelming passion. In that moment, in the fury of her need, she took him back to the first time he'd coupled with a woman. He'd been frantic and eager, more enthusiastic than knowledgeable.

As she rocked, she stroked her hips back, rubbing her clit along the oil slick of his pubic bone. Low, keening moans, quiet at first, grew progressively louder. Tighter and tighter her passage clutched around his shaft. Faster and faster she rocked her body atop him. Desperate to hold back his climax, Kerrick closed his eyes to think of anything other than her, but such a trick did him no good. Daylong denial placed him in dire need, causing him to erupt within her on a strangled groan.

Ariss tossed back her head and emitted a cry of victory. As she leaned forward, she caught his gaze. Pride, satisfaction, and triumph—she was pleased with herself for making him climax first!

Shocked and somewhat embarrassed, Kerrick reached between their sweaty bodies, sought out and then ruthlessly stroked her clit. She tried to turn away, but his other arm held her securely against his chest. Struggling only helped him by moving her bud more firmly against his body and fingers. When she climaxed, he uttered a growl of satisfaction.

Slumping forward, she buried her face against his chest as she milked the last of his orgasm with the walls of her sex.

He waited a moment for her to recover, then asked, "What's a kerrick?"

2

Ariss heard him speak, but his voice seemed terribly far away. Pleasure created a haze in her mind, permeating her with peaceful satisfaction. When her *paratanist* had anointed her with *estal* oil and forced her to drink the *umer*, she'd almost blurted out the truth of what her parents had done to her, but some little voice in the back of her mind begged her to use caution.

None should know of her shame.

For the next season, she would be blissfully out of their reach. She knew she would have to see them at official gatherings, but her day-to-day life would belong exclusively to her. Perhaps she could allow herself to indulge in her ultimate fantasy of leaving Felton and the palace behind to live in the *galbol* tree forest. The one and only time she'd confessed her deepest dream to her father, he'd peered at her with his pinched-up face, then called her a fool. If she hadn't darted away, he probably would have slapped her for good measure. So long had her mother and father preached their ways, their needs, and their longings, Ariss felt she was simply an extension of them. She wasn't a person in her own right but a creation to be used by her parents. Buried deep in a seldom-visited place in her mind lurked the girl she once was, the little girl who greeted each day with joy and anticipation. It had been a long, long time since she'd been that bright-eyed, exuberant child.

Below her, Kerrick's breathing returned to normal as his penis softened and slipped out of her grasping sex. She would never forget her first glance of him. All oiled and muscular and dangerously male as he stood proudly naked at the foot of the bed. In her semi-awake state, she thought him half man, half animal, especially when his nostrils flared as he caught her scent. Dark green eyes, the exact color of deep forest shade, pinned her more effectively than any weapon. Only by sheer force of will had she not riveted her attention on his penis. Deftly, she'd kept her gaze on his face while using her peripheral vision to consider the great heavy shaft between his legs. Shaved of all his hair, there was nothing to soften the view of his arousal. Oil glistened golden light upon his sex as if magic touched his mighty cock. She wanted to see him grasp it in his fist and stroke his hand up and down the length in a slow show of dominant male aggression. Just imagining such a moment caused her sex to weep in response.

Ariss blamed her *paratanist* for her reaction, for it was he who had removed the numbing *estal* oil and replaced it with something that warmed her flesh and returned sensation to her body with tingling awareness. The remarkable oil he had used destroyed whatever her parents had forced her to consume and place upon her person. For the first time in ages, Ariss felt her body. Her eyes had widened at Kerrick, but not at anything he'd done. Her shock came from the fact that she could feel the sheets upon her skin and cool air upon her nipples when she sat up. Even now, the slightest puff of his breath raced tingles along her flesh.

When he'd crawled up the bed toward her, she had pulled away, too terrified to let him touch her, and thus enslave her to him. If the silken sheets could cause her body to writhe in bliss, his touch would be beyond her. Somehow, without her quite knowing it, he maneuvered himself close and kissed her. She had no idea how that happened, but the contact caused a series of explosive meltdowns in her body. When her maids had dressed her for official functions, she was so numb she could not even feel the makeup they placed upon her lips, but she had felt every texture of Kerrick's lips. When he had slid his tongue inside her mouth, she almost cried at how many sensations assaulted her. However, when he'd placed his lips upon her tender nipples, he almost propelled her to orgasm. Desperate for more, she'd grasped his head, holding him firmly to provide her deeper pleasure. When he'd hesitated about penetrating her, she'd leaped upon him in desperation to feel his shaft thrusting within her slick and aching sex. So long had she been numb, that to feel everything, suddenly and fully, overloaded her senses and sent her on a glutinous frenzy to feel more. She wanted to mount him, to suck him, to bite him, to kiss him, and to feel him do all those same things to her. Hunger made her ravenous and washed away any shame.

In her hyperawareness, she felt every ridge, every vein, every sinful inch of him invading her. Sinful, for such a rich pleasure must surely be a violation of her parents' rigid view of such matters. When he'd added his talented fingers to the already overwhelming sensations, she'd almost screamed and curled away. The feeling was too intense to bear, yet she was desperate for release. For so long she swore she would rather feel constant pain than heavy numbness, but the gods finally heard her prayers, and rather than torture her with pain, they rewarded her with the most sublime pleasure. Reborn in that shattering moment, she'd lifted her face to Kerrick, proud and triumphant that finally, finally, she was not isolated within the prison of her body. His touch freed her. As soon as the waves of pleasure passed, she worried that his touch would now bind her. Once was not enough. She'd barely recovered her breath and already she wanted to ride him again. And now she understood her parents' admonitions against such encounters and why they'd taken such drastic steps to protect her.

Sex wasn't just sinful; sex was addictive.

During the Harvest, she had felt nothing as she lowered herself over the sacrifices. Each boy became a man as she took him within herself. Most seemed eager to have the ceremony complete, but a few trembled below her. Two cried as she knelt over them. She longed to comfort them, but she couldn't. All she could do was speak her sacred words, "By the power of my beauty I take that which belongs to me." In turn, each of them answered, "I freely give myself to you." When they did, she would stand above them, her legs parted, then slowly lower herself onto their stiff shafts. She wasn't sure what kept them endlessly hard, but she knew, like her, *estal* oil deadened any sensations. Not that she had felt anything in years, which was why her encounter with Kerrick had so possessed her.

Shocked by her own frantic behavior, she felt a blush heat her cheeks as she continued to doze atop him. Perhaps if she didn't move, she could lie here forever. However, holding still took more and more of her focus, for deep inside her sex burned a longing to feel him again. To feel the thick hardness of him sliding inside, parting her lips around him, welcoming him within the sacred depth of her body.

Her *paratanist* said she must mate with Kerrick but offered no advice beyond that. Did it matter how many times they mated? Ariss considered what Kerrick had been through; he had plunged into woman after woman without satisfaction only to find his pleasure with her. Would he be capable of another encounter? Her parents had deliberately kept her ignorant about not only the mechanics of sex, but the practicalities as well. Ariss was certain she could go repeatedly, but she didn't know if he could.

When she had finished harvesting all her sacrifices, she'd breathed a sigh of relief. With that part over, she now had the next season primarily to herself. Or so she thought. When her *paratanist* undressed her and began to rub more oil on her, she questioned the reason for his actions. In dulcet tones, he informed her that, according to the most ancient Harvest prophecy, she would now mate with her male counterpart.

Stunned, Ariss had followed her *paratanist* with shaking steps. When she had first exited the Harvest room, shock had rendered her numb again; members of the elite lined her path. Their critical eyes seemed to touch her every private place with curiosity and, in some cases, mocking. When tears threatened to blur her vision, she deliberately lifted her head, thrust back her shoulders, and kept her attention on a spot far down the hall. If not for her servant's plodding steps, she might have run in panic. As it was, his slow pacing forced her to live up to her nickname; they didn't call her Rhemmy for nothing. They compared her to the frozen wasteland of Rhemna, for she too was cold, indifferent, and her icy gaze could strip the heat from a man within moments. The first time she heard the name she had cried, but then it gave her strength, purpose even. She would become hostile and frigid. So cold would her heart become that no amount of heat would thaw her frozen feelings.

Only when she was alone did she let her tears fall.

When she had finally made her way to the mating room and found the circular bed empty, she breathed another sigh of relief, but then fretted under the sheets. What would her counterpart look like? Would he be an animal as some said? Male Harvesters were notorious for their size, their strength, and their battle prowess; they were not known for looks or mental ability. How would a man like that be as a lover? Violent? She shocked herself when the image of him using her in an attempt to sate his insatiable hunger caused a deep, fluttering excitement in her belly. But what if he were a tender warrior; a man who took out his aggression on other men so that he could bestow only the most caring touch to his chosen? This image, too, caused her body to react with an unnamable and untouchable longing. Ariss had fallen asleep wondering and waiting.

Now she knew he could be both aggressive and gentle. She'd spurned him by rote, as she had been taught to do, and it was easy to maintain her disinterest when her body truly felt nothing. Without the protection of powerful drugs, she'd been overwhelmed by her response to him. She wanted all of him at once. A massive storm swept along her, making her frenzied and crazed. She wanted his hands, tongue, and cock to minister to every need within her tormented body.

Tentatively, she lifted her head and glanced at Kerrick.

He flashed an arrogant smile bursting with male pride.

Did the conceited creature truly think her reaction was about him and him alone? Unwilling to disturb her comfortable perch atop him, she curled her head back down, resting her cheek against his chest.

"Now that the moment has passed, you are shy again." He stroked his fingers through her hair, teasing the strands and his fingertips over her responsive back. The texture of her hair was softer than the most expensive *astle,* but his fingertips brought the sensation of the strands flowing across her skin to a new and exquisite height.

When she purred in pleasure, she realized her sensitivity had not worn off. A new dread washed over her. If she allowed herself to wallow in physical pleasure, she would only be more tormented when she must return to the control of her family. For the sake of her own sanity, she had to end this. Now.

Coolly, she said, "I mated with you as my position decreed." With that, she slid from him to the edge of the bed. Before she could stand, he maneuvered himself behind her, wrapped his arms around her torso, and pulled her back into his lap. Their oil-slick bodies slid together in a most erotic fashion, which only exacerbated her fears of addiction.

"How dare you take such liberties with my person?!" She pushed at his massive arms, then realized the folly of engaging him physically. "Unhand me at once."

His laugh infuriated her and allowed her to realize that she would never become enamored of his touch, for she could not stand him! No doubt, he was from one of the barbaric outer regions where men laid claim to property by using their brawn and not their brains.

"Unhand you? Honestly?" He nuzzled her neck. "After what we just did that seems rather dramatic, don't you think?" The heat of his body permeated into her, lulling her, as his touch calmed her instinct to run. "Especially when your body clearly wants to be handled."

Tenderly, he cupped her breast, caressing the nipple between his forefinger and thumb. Her body betrayed her, for her nipple instantly hardened under his attention. That one tiny sensation caused ripples of pleasure across her entire form, especially deep into her greedy sex. She would have bolted, but he captured her earlobe with his teeth, drawing the sensitive flesh into his mouth as he continued to tease her breast.

"In all my life I've never met any woman as responsive as you."

That she could believe, for how many women could he have known who had been forced to consume body-numbing elixirs for half their lives? She didn't blame herself for her reaction. How could one who'd been numb for so long resist the sudden beauty, the absolute dangerous attraction of physical pleasure? All her parents had done with their machinations was ensure her compulsion by withholding what most considered normal. Every day those around her knew the comfort of soft fabrics, the shock of cold water, the sensual bliss of a lover's kiss, where she literally felt nothing. Like a woman half asleep, Ariss awoke to pleasures beyond comprehension and simply didn't know what to do with her own natural reactions.

He growled as he kissed his way along her neck. "Stop fighting me, *tanata*. Let me show you just how good it feels to surrender."

The word alone caused a fight within her. Surrender of what? She couldn't give herself to him, not the way most women gave themselves to their chosen mates. Involuntarily, she tilted her head to the side to dismiss him with harsh words, but her movement inadvertently gave him greater access. When he bit the tender juncture of her neck and shoulder, she startled back, pressing her bottom against him. He lowered his hands to her hips to settle her against his dangerously muscular frame. Ever so slowly, she felt him harden, until his penis dug into her flesh, seeking the heat and wetness of her acceptance.

Somewhere in the back of her mind, she heard a little voice saying that one more time couldn't hurt. One more time with him taking control and pinning her to the bed with not only his strong body but also his wicked, piercing gaze couldn't hurt. Very likely, he'd called hundreds of women *tanata* with that exact same rumbling seduction, but who cared? For now, he was hers. If she chose to think so, she could consider him a reward for a Harvest well done. Best of all, her parents never had to know.

Conflicting her innate longing was the other voice, the louder voice of her parents reminding her of why she'd become the Harvester. She had not competed against all those beautiful women to take the virginity of hundreds of men. A clear purpose filled her mind, focusing her attention, fighting against every wave of physical pleasure Kerrick wrought. Her only purpose was to select a high-ranking man as her bondmate. Her heart clutched in fear when she wondered whom her father would select. She already knew the choice would not be hers.

Her father would demand she pick a man who would bring prestige and money to Yellow House.

"Let me go," she begged breathlessly, even though she honestly didn't want him to. She wanted him to ignore her pleadings, toss her back on the bed, and then rut with her like an animal in mindless heat.

To her shock, he not only let go, he actually levered himself off the bed, using his body to lift her up to her feet. The loss of his heat shocked a wave of tiny bumps along her flesh. Wordlessly, he turned her to face him. His eyes penetrated into hers so deeply she stopped breathing and simply stared up at him.

"Don't say one thing when you want another." His rough voice washed new heat over her as his gaze held steady. "Mating games and courtly flirting have their place, but not within the bedchamber. Here you should be explicit about your needs, as I refuse to guess."

On a deep breath, she opened her mouth to upbraid him for his impertinence, but he shook his head side to side, effectively silencing her.

Lowering his voice and his brows, he held her pinned, and said, "Don't fling your anger at me. Tell me what you want, Ariss. Not what someone *told* you you should want, not what you *think* you should want, but what you *actually* want from me." He lowered his voice. "Because we both know you want something."

Words escaped her. How could she convey her most primitive longings to him when he was looking right at her? Exposed, she closed her eyes and tried to step away, but she bumped into the edge of the bed. She spun away from him, and that's when she breathed in the scent of the room. Their combined essence filled her lungs, shivered her body, tightened her nipples, and contracted her passage. All at once she overreacted to just the smell of sex they'd created. A deep, insatiable longing for more caused her to turn back and face him. She realized just how big he was when she had to arch her neck to lift her face level with his. She was tall for a woman, but he was taller, and much, much broader. Naked or not, he ate up the room with his presence.

Without pride or anger, he stood watching her, his hands held loosely at his sides. Muscles coiled around his chest, his hips, and his legs—power held barely in check by the thin membrane of his skin. Still hard, and pulsing ever so slightly, his penis drew her gaze inexorably down. Hundreds of women, her sister included, had reclined passive for his possession. Only she had climbed upon him to use him as she saw fit. Why then couldn't she find the words to tell him what she most desperately wanted now?

Repeatedly, she opened her mouth only to close it when her embarrassment grew stronger than her lust. Part of her thought he would sense her distress and make this easier for her, but for whatever reason, he refused. Still as one of her mother's garden statues, Kerrick simply watched and waited. Anger gripped her. He knew what she wanted, but he had to humble her first. Kerrick must have heard the rumors about her, and he had to prove to himself that he alone could melt the cold one. However, when she considered his face, she didn't sense that within him. He stood waiting, watching her speculatively, but not with condescension.

More conflicting thoughts and emotions held her in thrall until she realized that she never had to see him again. Why not ask, or even demand from him, exactly what she wanted? It mattered little what his motives were, for even if he told everyone he knew and the information got back to her parents, she had only done what her position demanded. By the ancient prophecy, she must mate with him. When the night was over, she would return to her private rooms and never lay eyes upon him again.

Courage borne of knowing there would be no repercussions

straightened her spine. Primly, she settled on the edge of the bed, her hands folded together in her lap. Using her coolest gaze, she assessed him from head to toe, pleased when he didn't withdraw but actually preened under her consideration. In the end, she brought her gaze to his.

"Wrap your fist around your cock."

A new heat filled his green eyes as he palmed his still growing erection.

"Stroke your hand up and down." Ariss leaned back on one arm, watching him through heavy-lidded eyes. Just as she'd thought earlier, his masculine hand wrapped around his straining need was the most arousing sight she'd ever beheld. Aggressive and dominant, he proudly stood before her and did precisely what she asked. All the muscles in his arm moved in concert, flexing around strong bones to provide relief to the swollen member in his hand.

Even and precise, he continued to glide his hand up and down the full, wicked length of his cock. When a pearl of moisture trembled at the tip, he quickly palmed it, drawing the moisture down his length to provide a smooth ride for his next stroke. Over and over, he slid his hand along his shaft, his eyes riveted to her.

Ariss fought the urge to lick her lips. Instead, she lay back on the bed and lifted one leg, parting her thighs so he could barely see between her legs. Deliberately, she gave him just enough of a view to whet his appetite. With the same purposeful ease he used on his shaft, he moved his gaze from her face to her hips, then back again.

"Stroke it as if you were thrusting into me." Commanding such an aggressive male excited her. For this moment, she could pretend he was a servant she used strictly for her pleasure.

He combined a growl and a groan as he held his tightly clenched fist to the tip of his cock. Holding his hand steady, he thrust his hips, as if he penetrated his hand, just as he would do to her. His entire body strained forward as he forced his thick cock into his unyielding fist.

Ariss almost felt that invasion between her now-trembling thighs. Before, she'd leapt upon him so quickly she'd not had time to savor that moment of penetration, but this time she vowed that he would go so slowly that she would writhe and beg him to hasten his pace. However, she already knew that he wouldn't hurry. A man like Kerrick would savor her passionate pleas, drinking them up like rare nectar.

A muscle twitched in his angular jaw when he gritted his teeth. Was he finding it difficult to maintain his composed facade? Sweat beaded across his forehead, gathering into a trickle that flowed into his golden brows. As it tumbled down into his eyes, he flicked his head. In slow motion, she saw a bead of sweat fly through the air and land on the sheet next to her. On a deep breath, she tasted his aroma—pungent, captivating, and undeniably male.

When she glanced back, he'd forced his cock halfway into his fist. His attention was now riveted on the space between her thighs. Ever so slowly, she reclined and then parted her legs, giving him a most teasing glimpse of exactly where he wanted to be.

Kerrick growled low in his chest as a snarl twisted his handsome features into something wild. Long lashes lowered across his gaze, shuttering some of the intensity, but not enough to hide his untamed hunger. Now, he couldn't take his eyes off her fully exposed sex. Silky black curls did little to hide her from his view.

Breathlessly, she ordered him to kneel between her legs.

Cock in fist, he dropped to the floor and stared up the length of her body. His breath, harsh and fast, rushed along the tender skin of her inner thighs.

"Remember how you told me that one finger could be so seductive?" Ariss teased her hand from her waist, to her hip, then across the juncture of her thigh. The closer she came to her mound, the faster his breathing accelerated. When her middle finger hovered over her sex, his gaze was so intense that nothing short of divine intervention would have pulled his attention away.

What she intended to do was oh-so-naughty. Her parents often preached against such self-indulgent self-pleasuring. Of course, Ariss had never bothered to try; with her numb body, such would be an exercise in futility. However, now she could feel everything. Having Kerrick watch her self-exploration only added to her wicked thrill.

"One finger, sliding down." She moved as if to touch her open sex but at the very last instant, she used her hand to part her thighs.

His disappointment was audible and caused a shudder to run through her body. Below the edge of the bed, she imagined he still held himself tightly, but he did not move his fist, for she saw no echoing motion in his arm. Heady with the power of keeping him at bay, she stretched her legs up until they pivoted on her pointed toes. With both hands across her waist, she slid them down her hips, then between her legs, pushing them open, spreading herself wide. Exposing herself fully to his view was utterly reckless and oddly empowering.

Kerrick licked his lips as a muscle twitched in his arm.

"How badly do you want to be inside me?" she asked, arching her brow. Playing the part of a wanton was more exciting than any of her fantasies had ever been.

A growl laced his laugh. "As badly as you want me there."

"Perhaps I'm content on my own." Without warning, she slid her middle finger down between her slippery nether lips, then teased her opening with a slow, circular motion. Contact caused her to gush anew. She parted her legs even wider. Long nights had passed where she'd cried over her need to soothe herself with pleasure, but the numbness never let her. Now, with the elixir and drugs removed, she felt the very texture of her fingerprint against her swollen sex. Reveling in the sensation, she wished to taunt him as much as she wished to tease herself.

Between gritted teeth, he said something in a language she did not understand, but she gathered the gist of it when she saw his arm flex as he tightened his fist around his cock. How much longer would he be able to resist? He seemed barely able to keep himself back as it was. Such aggression held in the balance by her word alone was thoroughly intoxicating.

Lowering her other hand, she parted her lips, releasing her clit from its hiding place. Bit by bit, she brought her other hand up to stroke softly across the exposed little nub. A shower of sparks blinded her and caused her body to contract and pull in, curling her into the cushioning of the bed. A violent orgasm hovered just beyond reach.

"Lift up, Kerrick. Come forward just enough to place yourself against me."

He did as she bid, nestling the very tip of his cock against the tender opening of her passage. For a long moment, they held there, gazing at the other, each trying to hold back until the other gave in to their wild longings.

"Say what you said before." Kerrick lowered his hands to the inside of her thighs, then down to cup her bottom, as if holding her ready and open for him.

After a pause to consider exactly what he wanted, she remembered her breathless unheeded plea from their first encounter.

Whispering, she begged, "Put it in me." Right after she said the words, a blush burned her cheeks, but she refused to drop her gaze. As unsophisticated as her phrasing was, it nonetheless excited him, given his groan of appreciation and the way his nostrils flared and his pupils dilated. His entire face and body surged forward with need. In that moment, Ariss realized she didn't have to be the perfect lover; all she had to be was herself. For whatever reason, her lack of sophistication intoxicated Kerrick.

In an imperceptible increment, he nudged forward, but he'd not entered her, he'd only placed himself more snuggly against her now-trembling opening. Suddenly, she didn't want to have this battle of the wills with him any longer. She wanted him to plunge forward and fill her in one mighty thrust.

"Take me the way you take your harvests." Ariss tried to lift her legs into position, but he stopped her by widening his elbows as he continued to hold her bottom in his hands.

"You are not my sacrifice," he said, his voice so low it was almost inaudible. "I will not take you in a mindless ritual." He moved forward, then back, as if seeking permission to enter her, his penis knocking at her passage for access. Rolling his hips caused the head of his cock to part her lips as it slid relentlessly toward her clit. Contact caused another shower of sparks and the breathless moan of his name. "That's it, Ariss. Say my name. Tell me again what you want me to do."

A thousand dirty words paraded through her mind, but all she could say was an echo of what she'd said earlier. Whispering so softly she almost prayed he didn't hear, she said, "Put it in me, Kerrick."

A delicious form of torture ensued, where he would slide up to stroke her clit, then down to wedge just the tip of himself within her opening. Maddening. Blind in her need to feel him finally stretch her around his shaft, she angled her body up, intending to wrap herself around him, thus pulling him down on top of her, but he moved back with a chuckle, yanking her fanny to the edge of the bed.

"Say it again."

Over and over, she asked him, begged him, until her voice rose to a fervor pitch. Just when she thought she could stand no more, he thrust forward, filling her, completing a circuit within her body that caused every nerve to awaken simultaneously. Howling like a wild creature, she tightened her legs around his hips to hold him deeply inside. After a bite of pain from the sudden shock of him plunging within, all she felt was wondrous fullness. Every bit that stretched to accommodate him felt wonderful, magical, and unforgettable.

"You are lovely in your surrender, Ariss."

His words fell against her like tiny drops of rain, soothing her fire while he held steady, ready to stoke her flames even higher. She wanted him wild with need and thrusting frantically, but he only cupped her bottom, holding her snuggly against him. When she drew her gaze up to his face, she found his eyes intensely fastened on her, not on any particular part of her body, but on her as a whole. Kerrick watched and considered, waiting for something, but she had no idea what.

Confused, she parted her lips to ask him why he hesitated, and in that very moment, he withdrew ever so slowly from her captured heat until he was utterly without. She exhaled a disappointed groan that changed to a startled gasp when he lowered his face to breathe out a hot, moist breath against her clit. Smoothly, he lifted up, moving his hips forward, only to glide back in with the same measured stroke. Over and again, he rolled against her, filling her, withdrawing, breathing.

Kerrick moved like rushes in the wind, nodding and bouncing back, giving and taking, building the energy within her until she thought she would fragment. Ariss caught his rhythm and echoed it with a subtle lifting and lowering of her hips. Heat built along her flesh, fusing into molten fire at the very tip of her clit. If only he would touch her there, she would explode, but he didn't. Only his hot breath gave the frustrated flesh any attention at all.

When she lifted her hands to touch herself, he swore, "If you do, I'll stop."

Regretfully, she lowered her hands to her sides, considering why he would care. Then she understood that he wanted to torment her beyond her perceived ability to withstand. What shocked her most of all was that he cared very much about her pleasure. Of course, he sought his own, as any person would, but her satisfaction meant even more to him than obtaining his own. To him, this wasn't about simply achieving an orgasm; this was a dance. A dance at which he excelled. Ariss could almost feel his hand at her back, gently guiding her along the necessary steps. When she fumbled, he pretended not to notice and simply continued into the next round of complicated movements.

"You like to watch, Ariss. You made that very clear earlier, so relax, and watch me."

His voice was low and softer than the silken sheets at her back. Releasing the tension in her body was almost impossible, but she did her best to let go and simply watch him. As she gazed at him, his shoulders went back, pride enlarging his muscular body. She realized she might like to watch, but he clearly enjoyed being watched. Kerrick loved being on display as the object of attention. As she considered him, the first thing she noticed was his intensity. His eyes never closed, not all the way, and his thick lashes couldn't hide his flickering gaze that moved over her, seeking and exploring every nuance of her reactions. Every movement from the lifting of her brow to the parting of her lips to the clenching of her calves drew equal attention. He kept his thrusting pace leisurely, his movements graceful, but his exertion showed in the beading of sweat along his bronzed skin. Without hair to give guidance, the sweat gathered and ran willy-nilly along his flesh, even down his arms and along his hands, which slipped his grip of her buttocks. With his control slightly lessened, her body moved more fluidly against his, changing the beat, causing him to dig his fingertips more firmly into her bottom, but eventually he slid his hands out from under her and placed them low on her waist, so the great span of his palms almost encompassed her hips. Holding her this way afforded him tremendous control, but still he kept to his even pace, watching and waiting.

Slowly, his thrusts took on a sharper edge, a more powerful plunge, and each time she could feel him press against her nub with almost enough sensation to release the building tension. Almost enough. So close and yet so far that she realized he knew just how much pressure to give to keep her on the edge, for each time it was barely too little. Just enough to hold her simmering. Quite suddenly, she realized she was practically gnashing her teeth at him in frustration.

His smile could have wooed an acolyte from her goddess. Tauntingly, he asked, "Have you never been teased, Ariss?" Before she could answer, he withdrew and placed his face above her sex. His hot breath only caused her to writhe uncontrollably. "Tell me your deepest, darkest secret."

"Why do you wish to talk?" She lifted her head to glare fully at him, then dropped back on the bed so she could glower at the ceiling, exasperated. "We are here to mate, and that's all that we should do." His silence prompted her to lift up so she could consider him again.

Patiently, Kerrick knelt between her legs, watching her the way a hunter considers prey that has already been trapped. He had her, he knew it, but he still considered that there was a part of her that might elude his prowess. "Tell me." His eyes delved deeply into hers, frightening her, for his scrutiny was such she felt he knew the truth of her. All the truth of her existence including the horrible shame of what her parents had done. Terrified, she pulled her legs together and tried to slip out of his grasp, but he would not let go.

"We are done," she insisted, even though her body clearly wasn't. Painful heat, a fire ready to spark into an inferno, flashed between her legs.

He shook his head slowly side to side, his eyes never leaving hers. "We have only just begun." At that, he lowered his mouth, placed his lips around her clit, and sucked the trembling flesh into his mouth.

Ariss almost leapt from the bed. She had only ever heard of such perversion, but to actually see someone perform such a lewd act, especially upon herself, immobilized her. What shocked her even more was how *good* his ministrations felt. He didn't bite or chew upon her, only gently sucked her nub between his lips, then laved it slowly with his tongue. All the while, he looked right at her.

Her shock astonished him, given the way his eyebrows climbed at her reaction, but then he tilted his head as if intrigued.

So dazed, she told him her secret heart. "I want to live in the *galbol* tree forest."

Rather than the mocking she expected, he stopped his lusty work for a brief moment to flash her a satisfied smile, then continued to torment her with his lips, teeth, and tongue. Green eyes considered her anew, delving into deeper secrets as he continued to lick her in a most intimate fashion. He seemed to wonder if she would make him stop, and for a brief moment, she considered doing so, but in the end, she realized she didn't want him to. Somewhere inside she knew that Kerrick would quit if she demanded he do so, but she had only this one time with him, and although what he did was disturbing, it was also utterly delicious. Her shock and shame fell away under a tide of sensual bliss.

At first, he used the slick underside, then the rougher textured topside. Her eyes rolled back in her head as she let her lids settle, blocking him from view so that she could focus on simply feeling what he did. Somehow, not looking at him removed the sting of shock. Hot, wet, and delicately textured, his tongue moved across her clit as if the two danced together and her nub was the shy partner. His talented tongue had to coax her bud to push back the safety of her fleshy hood and allow her partner to examine her from top to bottom. Kerrick seemed to enjoy the dance, as he never tired of easing the flesh away every time her bud retreated.

Glorious sensations built in her body, focusing her attention to that one tiny bit of flesh that he held in his mouth. Within moments, the flames grew higher, hotter, and she squirmed below him. Strong hands cupped her hips, holding her down, which only allowed her to wriggle harder. To better his angle, she lifted her legs and placed her feet against his shoulders. She could not stay still, not when her body screamed for release. Her efforts were not meant to dislodge him, for she didn't want him to stop, but she simply couldn't quit moving. Then, with one quick flick, he caused the showering sparks to dance along her vision and her body, surging her up from the bed as she pressed against his shoulders with her feet.

Kerrick released her beyond sensitive clit and captured her ankles, straightening her legs as he rose up and slid his cock within her quivering passage. He did all of this so smoothly she scarce knew what was happening until she felt him stretching her around his throbbing shaft. He growled and again said something in a guttural language she didn't comprehend. More sparks enveloped her as she tightened around his thrusting staff. Kerrick increased the tempo, working himself deeper into her with each powerful thrust.

When she opened her eyes, the look on his face held her enthralled. His head was back, the strong column of his throat taut with barely leashed bellows. Sweat covered his heaving chest, while his arms strained from the act of holding her up for each mighty plunge. Animal heat, untamed lust. In that moment, he was a beast using her to sate his longings, which caused her to experience another series of shattering sparks.

When Kerrick bellowed, thrust forward, and clutched her hips in a forceful grip, she knew he'd climaxed, too. He gulped breath and fell against her. Sweat slick, his skin felt cool against hers. The smell and texture flickered the very vestige of a memory, a memory she realized she wasn't supposed to have.

Before he could say anything, Ariss slid from beneath him and rushed toward the door. To her utter relief, the heavy door swung open, allowing her to make her escape.

3

Ariss was gone before Kerrick realized her intent to flee. Exhausted, he flopped facedown on the bed. His cock twitched, releasing the last of his climax against the bedding. He would have gone after her, but just the thought of running with his still-spurting member jouncing between his legs made him cringe. With a shake of his head, he rolled over and placed himself more fully on the bed. He trained his eyes on the glowing ceiling crystals.

What was wrong with that woman? Never, not once in all his vast experiences, had he ever bedded a more intriguing combination of frightened virgin and wanton *yondie*. True, most of those he'd been with had either lost their virginity to a man long before him, or if they were from planet Diola, they'd willingly given their virginity to a Harvester like him during the Harvest ritual, which surely, Ariss, as a native Diolan, had done.

However, one moment she was passionate beyond words, so eager for pleasure her greediness fairly oozed from her pores. In the next breath, she quivered below him, holding her breath, her eyes widening with shock, especially when he'd taken her tender clit into his mouth. Her eyes rounded along with her mouth into perfect little O's. He'd almost pulled back, for he misread her reaction as revulsion, but then her brows settled over those cool gray eyes of hers, turning them smoky and lustful.

Rather than pulling away, he'd delved in deeper, enjoying the musky essence of her scent, and the way she could only fully enjoy his ministrations with her eyes closed. Such conflicted directly with how she'd enjoyed watching him handle his cock. How could she enjoy watching him doing one thing but not another?

Considering, Kerrick couldn't think of another woman who'd ever asked that of him, not quite like that, where he was to masturbate with her simply observing. Most women wanted him to pleasure them so they could watch, not watch him pleasure himself. Something about that moment had intrigued and aroused Ariss. He needed no more proof than that of her stiff nipples. When she'd parted her legs, ever so slightly, he'd seen further evidence of her arousal.

Gods, and the scent of her!

He shook his head as if to dislodge her essence. Ariss smelled so wonderfully delicious he wanted to consume her utterly. It was more than the simple essence of *valasta,* which any woman could put into a cream and place upon her person. No, her scent was something intoxicating. No perfume or potion he'd ever encountered had such a compelling effect on him.

Kerrick would have done anything to please her.

With a start, he realized that was what blossomed the scent to its full richness: pleasure. When he did things that aroused her, her scent intensified. When he did things that shocked her, the scent faded, but as her surprise gave way to bliss, her luscious essence returned even more powerful than before.

Kerrick considered the glowing ceiling crystals for a long

time. He thought back over the women he'd bedded, all of them lovely and special in their own way, each of them pretty, perfumed, perfect in form and dress. Even Otana, a flame rider from Cuearcy, who wore only mannish peasant clothing as some kind of protest against the treatment of her sex. Even Otana was perfect in her garb, for it suited her. Besides, Otana only wore the style of the great unwashed. Her peasant clothing was fashioned of expensive fabrics and doused with even more expensive perfume. At best, he would call her mode of dress a costume, but Kerrick could not imagine her in anything else but billowy pants and a tight-fitting blouse. Still, not one of his many conquests had ever ensnared him with a scent, manufactured or natural. Ariss was unique in that sense.

Moreover, her secret wish was to live in the *galbol* tree forest. She had confessed to him as if she thought he would burst into laughter and mock her endlessly. He found it a sweet dream that would probably never happen. But her confessing the truth to him was telling of her character.

Another thought occurred to him, something darker and more disturbing. If his *paratanist* gave him drinks and oils to effect some change in his person, such as endless hardness or the deadening of sensations, could she not also do something to him that would make Ariss' scent more compelling?

Kerrick had never heard of such a thing, but who knew what secrets those at the palace held? By the prophecy, he must mate with Ariss, so why wouldn't they do something to him to ensure his compliance?

An ironic laugh escaped him then, for they needn't have bothered. One look at Ariss and he was ready to mate with her. Cold gray eyes or no, she was devastatingly beautiful. From her slender limbs, to her silky hair, to the curve of her high cheekbones, he didn't think any man would need much inducement to take a tumble in the sheets with such a lovely bit of female pulchritude.

He sighed and dropped his hand to his belly. Below his palm, his stomach rumbled in protest. Too much time had elapsed since his last meal. Not that he'd call what they'd served him in the training rooms a meal. Kerrick wouldn't have fed such dreck to his worst enemy. Undercooked vegetables, meat of questionable origin, and no spices at all wasn't food so much as it was slop to feed the mass of men. It certainly didn't help that they turned the glop out into one long trench in the center of the tables. Still, Kerrick had taken his portion of the best of the worst, then stood back watching the others fight over the remains.

Frowning, he wondered why, in a place of riches like the palace, they would allow those who trained to serve them in the highest ritual to suffer such indignity. Surely, they could afford to feed the potential Harvesters decent food. Undoubtedly, there was some reason for such degradation. Perhaps the act of fighting for nourishment allowed only the strong to flourish. Not that his complaint would change anything. Kerrick had a feeling that here, time moved at a different pace. Palace inhabitants had riches and technology that far surpassed the outer regions, but they still clung to ancient rites and rituals that he would call anachronistic.

The other worlds he traveled to that were rich with technology proudly displayed it. Some worlds were still a bit backward but even on those worlds, they had modern amenities for wealthy travelers. Only here, on Diola, was technology hidden, as if it were shameful. Kerrick's father kept his fleet of spaceferries well away from the population in Cheon. Far on the outskirts, where only the duskdogs played, had Kerrick been able to hide himself away on a ship to make a name for himself somewhere other than Diola. Two days after he'd undergone his Harvest ritual, Kerrick left Diola. Ten seasons later, he'd returned.

Movement caught his eye. His *paratanist* glided into view

and bowed. It seemed to be what she did to get him to ask her a question, for she couldn't speak unless spoken to. Idly, he wondered how long she would stand there, quietly waiting, but he decided it was cruel to torment one bound to serve him. He had quickly grown annoyed of her speak-only-when-spoken-to rule because he worried that if he didn't ask her the proper question, he might miss something important.

In deference to that, he asked a simple, "Yes?"

"I will lead you back to your rooms."

Apparently, he'd overstayed his welcome. "I don't suppose I get to cover myself?"

"There is nothing for you to wear," she said simply, her head bowed within the covering of her beige robe.

Kerrick ran his hand over the silken sheets but decided against taking them. He didn't want to violate some obscure protocol by hiding himself from view. Hopefully, the hallways would now be empty. As soon as he stepped from the mating room, he realized there were even more people crowded into the wide hall. Poor Ariss. What had it been like for her to dart between the thick rows of thrill-seeking elite?

Kerrick didn't mind the attention at all. In fact, he purposely performed stunts and competed in dangerous sports for notoriety, although not while he was naked. When he'd asked Ariss if she'd ever heard of him, he was genuinely curious, for many had. However, he should have remembered that without any kind of media technology on Diola, even those in the palace would have no clue about anything outside their little world. Ariss couldn't have heard of him, for there was only word of mouth here and he'd never performed any of his feats on planet Diola.

Well, bedding all eight of the Grandier daughters had been quite a feat, but he seriously doubted his father, or their father for that matter, had bragged about his accomplishment, especially when it meant he'd gone to his Harvest ritual anything but a virgin, and so had two of the Grandier daughters.

Kerrick considered the people lining his path, eating up his nude body with their hungry eyes. If this was all they had to get adventure from, they had sad lives, indeed. They should try the deadly game of velto on Isela Five. Forty men clad in fabric uniforms with minimal padding chased a bladed disk across a large circle of ice. The only protection they had from the spinning puck of death was their metal sticks. Kerrick had almost lost two fingers from miscalculating the path of not only the puck, but of one of his teammates. As soon as he'd taken his share of winnings, he'd fixed his fingers and moved on.

It seemed he was always moving on.

The farther away from the mating room he got, the more the thick crowd of people began to thin. His *paratanist* kept her small, even steps slow and he began to wonder if this parading through the populace was part of the ritual. He wouldn't have minded so much but for the fact he was bald, flaccid, and utterly exhausted. This display had been much more fun when he was hard and primed. At the moment, he just wanted to get somewhere private.

A long time later, they reached a set of massive Onic doors. A carved pattern swirled in the grain of the wood, but he hardly had time to consider as his *paratanist* ushered him within.

"Now this is more like it."

Simple in design with sparse furniture, the massive main room was all black, burnt umber, and rich browns. A bathing unit of polished Onic tile and warming crystals took up the entire north wall. Golden lighting crystals lined the ceiling, giving the room a beautiful glow. While he stood taking it all in, his *paratanist* moved to the bathing unit. She activated the warming crystals, set the water jets to the correct temperature, and then motioned him near.

Kerrick had never allowed another to bathe him, but if such were part of his position, he had little choice. Gingerly, he stepped below the spray and instantly felt his tension slipping away. Hot water pounded along his body. His *paratanist* didn't even push up her sleeves; she simply grabbed a bar of soap and began smoothing it all over his body, heedless of how water splashed on her robe. Her hands were small and delicate, which made him feel massive, and a little uncomfortable.

"How old are you?" He couldn't bear the thought of a child having such intimacy with him. Of course, he hadn't thought enough to ask earlier when she'd been cleansing and anointing his penis for the Harvest.

"I am twenty-three seasons."

A sigh of relief escaped him when he realized she was only five seasons younger than he was.

"How long have you been a *paratanist*?"

"Since birth."

She answered as she always did, with a matter-of-fact tone and an utter lack of interest in why he asked. Kerrick waited a moment, thinking she would fill the silence with an outpouring of information, but unlike most women, she remained steadfastly silent. She truly only spoke when spoken to. Worse, she remained completely emotionless while doing so. This was not only odd, but also made reading her in the conventional sense impossible.

The only time he'd sensed any emotion in her voice was when she'd spoken of him mating with Ariss. She'd not seemed to like that idea. Her tone had sounded contemptuous that he would find satisfaction with Ariss rather than by her hand. He wondered why she would care, then thought that maybe she simply wanted to masturbate him to see what it was like. He didn't know a whole lot about her station, but from what he'd gathered, she had spent her entire life shrouded in her robe and learning about the Harvest prophecy. Serving the Harvester was the highest honor a *paratanist* could obtain.

"Do you have a name?" he asked as he leaned down so she could wash his head.

She hesitated for so long he doubted she would answer, but finally, in a somewhat stunned voice, she said, "I am called Fana."

"Fana. It's pretty." He wondered then what lay hidden behind her flowing robe with the enormous hood.

"It's a name."

It was clear there would be no point in flirting with her, as she took everything he asked or said literally. "Do you know what a kerrick is?"

"That is you, is it not?"

He sighed. "Yeah, as far as I know. I just heard someone say it might be something else." Ariss had left before he'd been able to press her for an answer. And damn it all to the nothingness, but he really wanted to know what she thought a kerrick was. All his life he thought his name was in tribute to his great-grandfather, but since he'd never met the man, Kerrick had no idea who or what he'd been named after. Although, he couldn't imagine his father or his mother giving him a ridiculous name, not unless they didn't know it was ridiculous. Maybe Ariss was only teasing him and there really wasn't another meaning to his name at all. Besides, it wasn't as if her name wasn't a little funny: Ariss sounded exactly like heiress, and fitting for someone with her haughty demeanor.

Kerrick shook the water off his head and wished he could fling that perplexing woman out of his thoughts as easily. It wasn't without regret, though, that he tried to forget about her. She was intriguing to say the least. Sadly, they would have only that one time together. He hoped she had enjoyed herself, even if some of what he did shocked her.

Fana took her time washing him, but not with any kind of lustful intent. As far as he could tell, she simply performed her functions. Fana soaped his cock with the same clinical movements as she had during the Harvest. If she did stroke him to climax, she would probably make the same mechanical movements, and he couldn't imagine how that would stimulate him to orgasm. He didn't get hard. His prick felt so raw and drained he feared he'd never become aroused again.

Once Fana finished with him, she rinsed him, dried him, slathered him in oil, and then handed him a black loincloth that he slung around his hips. The slinky *astle* fabric felt wonderfully soft against the pain of his abused genitals.

Next, she addressed his rumbling belly. While he sat at the head of a long wooden table, she brought platter after platter of seared meats, puffy breads, and vegetables smothered in rich sauces.

Now here was a meal fit for a Harvester! Even on Tapring, after he'd won the orph challenge, they hadn't managed a feast as grand as this. So much food crowded the area around his plate he didn't know where to start. Rather than put the food on his plate, he ate directly from the platters. Kerrick stuffed himself until he thought he would burst.

When he yawned hugely, Fana drew him to his bed. The last thing he remembered was flopping into the black bedclothes face-first.

Kerrick woke in an unfamiliar bed to even more unfamiliar surroundings. It took a moment for him to remember he was in the Harvester suite. He sighed and stretched his hands over his head, then immediately drew them down to his genitals. Pain unlike any he'd ever known throbbed in his balls and along his shaft. Gingerly, he removed his loincloth to find his skin raw, red, and slightly inflamed. If he didn't know better, he'd be in panic that some virulent disease had infested his crotch. But he knew this was from all the rubbing, oiling, and thrusting of the Harvest, not to mention what he'd done with Ariss.

Annoyed that she was almost the first thought in his mind, Kerrick swore that would be the last thought he'd give her today or any other. His encounter with her would be his last, and now he could turn his attention to the multitude of women within the palace walls. Of course, he'd have to wait for his crotch to recover before he made any amorous liaisons. Still, that would be the best way to ingratiate himself within the power structure of the elite. As he'd confirmed last night, they were a lusty bunch. Providing them with pleasure could assure him many votes when he pushed to become the magistrate.

As Kerrick limped gingerly to the basin and took an even more gingerly pee, he considered his painfully abused genitals with a sigh. How had the other Harvesters dealt with this sad aftereffect? He didn't think he would suffer any permanent damage; however, the next few days were going to be unpleasant, to say the least.

"Fana?" he called out for his *paratanist*, thinking that she would know of some balm to soothe him, but she didn't answer. He hobbled over to the bathing unit and perused the bottles of oil. Not a single one had a label. Considering where he intended to put the stuff, he was reluctant to experiment.

Frustrated, he glanced around his massive main room. There had to be a way to summon his servant. He found an odd button, near the door, almost at the point farthest from him. With a growl, he shuffled over to the door and pressed the discreet black button several times in rapid succession. After a long moment, where he stood hunched over, considering the swirling pattern in the wood, the door flung open so fast he didn't have a chance to get out of the way. The hunk of wood hit him squarely, sending him careening sideways. He landed with an ungainly plop on the floor because he'd curled around to protect his genitals.

Howling in pain from the jostling, he looked up into the expectant faces of four palace guards.

"Where is your attacker?" one guard asked, sweeping his gaze around the room while holding his *cirvant* at the ready in his mighty fist. The other three took up positions around Kerrick, protecting him from all sides.

"Attacker?" Kerrick stood with as much dignity as he could manage. Then he understood that he'd pushed some kind of panic button, not once, but several times. Chagrined, he mumbled, "I was trying to call my servant."

One of the guards laughed, but the one who'd asked the question frowned darkly, abruptly stopping the laughter of his compatriot.

"That cord, over there." He pointed. "Pull it once and your *paratanist* will come. This button"—he thrust his sword at the black button beside the door—"will summon palace guards."

Embarrassed beyond words, Kerrick nodded his understanding.

As they left, he heard one guard ask another, "Did you see his puffy red—"

Kerrick slammed the door closed before he finished speaking, then hobbled over to the cord. He gave the rough rope a sharp tug, then released it. Within a few moments, Fana entered, or at least someone in the very same type of robe entered. If ever someone wanted to kill him, all that person had to do was send an assassin wearing a *paratanist* robe. But he knew it was her when, true to her station, she walked right up to him and bowed, waiting for instructions even though his distress was clearly, painfully obvious.

Annoyed, he held his arms wide, his palms open, and asked, "Do you see anything wrong?"

"Your penis appears to be irritated," she said in her calm, slightly bored manner.

"Irritated? It's practically on fire!" He paused for a beat, thinking she would respond. When she didn't, he groused, "I'll bet you wouldn't be this calm if this were happening to you."

Calmly, she replied, "I don't have a penis."

"Oh, for the love of—just get me something for it, would you?"

Dutifully, she retrieved two bottles of oil from the bathing unit, mixed them together in her palms, and then slathered them over his genitals. Pain melted away under her touch. A dull numbness set in. At any other time, the feeling would have been dreadful, but now, it was bliss. Finally, he could feel something other than his tender crotch. Sadly, that's when he noticed how sore the rest of his body was. Muscles he didn't even know he had ached from overuse. Even after the most demanding sports, he didn't feel this wrung out.

"Had I known being the Harvester was this difficult, I wouldn't have bothered." Kerrick had honestly thought slipping his cock into hundreds of beautiful women would be a dream come true. He had no idea that the sheer physical demands would be such a nightmare. Thankfully, he only had to perform once each season, so he had plenty of time to recover from his debilitating exertion.

"I was told many men would think the position easy, also that they might try to shirk their duties. Part of my duty is to remind them of theirs."

"What duties?" Kerrick hesitated to ask. Was he wrong in thinking he had the rest of the season off?

"There is training, which is, of course, your primary duty. You will also be required to attend official palace functions. Then there are the Harvest festivals, rites, and rituals."

All his plans of bed-hopping in the palace and then planet-hopping during his downtime seemed to be slipping from his grasp. With a feeling of dread eating up his belly, he asked, "I can't leave the palace?"

"No."

She said it as she said everything else: simply, matter-of-factly, just so blithely he wanted to scream. She said one word that completely changed everything. His grandmother had once told him that he should look before he leapt, cautioning him against his propensity to find trouble in the most innocuous places. As Kerrick stood there, contemplating his sentence, he really wished he'd slowed down long enough to listen to his grandmother. If he had, he wouldn't be in this mess now.

As Fana moved off to the kitchen, Kerrick watched silently, his genitals numb, his body aching, and his mind awhirl with panic. He hadn't stayed in one place for longer than a cycle. They expected him to stay here for the next nine.

Of course, it was too late to turn back now.

4

Ariss hardly saw the crowds of people lining the hallway. She followed her *paratanist* back to her room in a state of shock. With his help, she bathed, ate, and then curled gratefully into bed. She didn't even bother to take in her new surroundings. Bigger issues consumed her.

Something sparked in her mind when Kerrick had fallen against her, his skin cool and slick with sweat. A brief memory, more a picture than anything, filled her mind. A man with dark hair and darker eyes, his head tossed back. That was all she had glimpsed, but the vision was enough to cause her entire body to rush with adrenaline. She had no idea who the man was, or what he meant to her, all she knew was his face, his agonized face. Sleep offered her no relief because she dreamt of the man, but only that incremental moment captured in time.

She awoke wondering who he was, what he had meant to her, and what the agony on his face could mean. When she focused on remembering, fear gripped her so tightly she almost lost her breath. Had he hurt her? Was that it? Somehow she knew that she had known this man during her life before the palace, but other than that, she drew almost a total blank. Was this mysterious man what her parents had paid a fortune to strip from her mind?

Ariss rose and immediately regretted it. Even though her black sheets were the softest *astle,* they chafed like rough-textured rocks against her tender sex. Her *paratanist* had left a bottle by her bedside. When she'd asked, he'd informed her that she would want it come morning. She couldn't see his face, but she'd sensed he smiled ruefully as he spoke.

Tentatively, she opened the bottle, sniffed, and then poured a drop onto her fingertip. Smoothing the oil over her thigh deadened sensations. The feeling of numbness was one she was unfortunately familiar with, but this wasn't as deep or as utterly deadening as what her parents forced her to consume and spread upon her person. Carefully, she poured more of the oil into her palm, then rubbed it onto her sex. Numbness replaced the pain. She was able to rise from the bed, but her body felt drained of energy. From her hips to her ankles hurt, probably from squatting down so many times. Between her legs, at the most tender part of her inner thigh, she found more pain, so she slathered that area with oil. The more she moved, the more she discovered little aches and pains. In the end, she covered her entire body with the oil, then slipped on the robe her *paratanist* had thoughtfully left at the bottom of her bed.

With a sigh, she considered her new living quarters. Everything was black, burnt umber, or dark brown. The black was befitting her as the Harvester, for only a Harvester could wear black. Her family color was yellow, but from now on, even when she returned to them, she would wear black. Such would be a welcome change, as the particular shade of yellow her family line wore made her look sallow, as if she were perpetually ill. Black matched her hair and brought out the gray of her eyes. She frowned. What did it matter what she looked like? Her family had already mapped out the rest of her life. Refusing to dwell on them, she moved to the far wall and pulled open the drapes.

Tandalsul, the twin suns, poured bright, golden light into her rooms. She stood, soaking up the heat. After a quick glance around to ensure that she was alone, she opened her robe. The oil captured more heat, penetrating into her flesh, then into her muscles. When she heard her door open, she yanked her robe closed and spun.

Her *paratanist* entered and bowed.

"How are you?" she asked for a lack of anything else to ask. It had taken her a long time yesterday to realize he only spoke when she spoke first. When he'd been given to her during her indoctrination, he'd not come with a set of instructions and she'd been too overwhelmed by everything to ask. Never in her wildest dreams did she think she'd actually win the Harvester competition.

"I am fine, Harvester." With that, he moved to the kitchen to prepare her morning meal.

She had tried to get him to call her Ariss, but he'd refused, saying that such violated his sacred duty. He shook his hood-covered head when she asked after his name. He begged her to call him *paratanist* and nothing else. Ariss had been raised with servants, mostly the deliberately bred *serbreds,* but she'd never liked treating another human being as lesser than herself. Her sister, Darabelle, delighted in tormenting them, especially the younger handsome boys who cared for father's prized Cuearcian mounts. So fascinated was Darabelle with handsome boys, that Ariss wondered if Darabelle had made it intact to her Harvest last night. Not that it mattered so much these days, but Ariss took pride in knowing that she had come to Chur a virgin.

Another frown darkened her face, for she wasn't as sure of that fact as she had been before she'd remembered the man with the agonized face. Had she had sex with him? Was that why her parents stripped him from her memory and forced her into chemical numbness? The more she dwelled on trying to uncover the truth, the more her head ached. In the end, she pushed the thoughts away.

Now that Harvester Chur Zenge had ascended to a demigod, having been sacrificed to him was a mark of prestige. All she really remembered of her Harvest was lying there, freezing, buried under a pile of autumn leaves because Darabelle had hidden the sacrificial robe. Other virgins had used the same technique, though they usually did so to hide their family line. For good or bad reasons, they did not want to be associated with their family color. The use of nature's bounty was entirely fitting for an autumn Harvest. Ariss hadn't cared about concealing her family line; however, Darabelle was convinced that Chur would choose Ariss just to get his hands on the wealth of Yellow House. Ariss suspected the truth was something else entirely; Darabelle didn't want Ariss to be attractive for her Harvest. Darabelle didn't want any of her sisters to be more beautiful than she was. When the sacrificial robe magically reappeared a week ago, just in time for Darabelle's Harvest, Ariss had confirmation of her theory. She was also certain the robe would once again disappear before Imosa or Lissak could use it.

Not that any of it really mattered. So many things that were of vital importance to her family were beyond Ariss' understanding. What did it really matter who wore the family robe? If their father weren't so insufferably frugal, they might each have their own; however, Radox Tunima decreed the robes a "wasteful indulgence," and that was the last of that.

If a Harvester were to choose one of the four sisters, Ariss doubted what they were wearing would make any difference. A Harvester selected a virgin because of lust, or longing, or some kind of magical spark that told him this woman was the woman for him. Ariss couldn't imagine any man making the selection based solely on the color the woman wore. Considering how many variations there could be in the same color, it would be ludicrous to choose that way unless he had memorized the exact shade.

Yellow House alone had over two hundred unique shades designating rank within the House. Her family, as the highest rank, wore the brightest, most vibrant yellow; however, the next family wore a shade only slightly different. Oftentimes, the only way to see the difference was to compare the colors side by side, a fact that her mother despaired endlessly. Byss Tunima despised being mistaken as a member of Fenning, the slightly lesser family in Yellow House.

Ariss knew that as a Harvester, she could have selected a bondmate from her sacrifices, but few female Harvesters did, mainly because the offerings were boys and not men. In theory, her actions brought them into manhood, but as she knelt over them, she didn't sense a sudden transformation within them. Perhaps, too, women were naturally attracted to older men, just as men seemed to prefer younger women. Unlike the male Harvesters, who must select their chosen from the sacrifices, a female Harvester could choose any free man within the palace.

A furrow deepened over her brows. Something about that sparked another memory. Why would her only being able to pick a man from within the walls of the palace matter? And not to her, but to her parents. She could hear her mother whisper, "This will put an end to any hope Ariss might cling to . . ." But the harder she tried to focus on the memory, the faster it slipped away, until she wasn't sure whether it had happened.

Ever since her parents' friend had visited, Ariss' memory was so confused she didn't trust any of it. She knew the woman had done something to her mind, but Ariss couldn't remember what. All she knew was that the woman had taken some of her memories. For a long while, she hadn't even realized that much, but the littlest things, like rain dripping off a leaf, or the swirling pattern of dust in the wind, caused snippets to surface and plague her until she slowly unraveled the barest bit of the terrible truth. Her parents had paid a stripper to remove her memories. That much she now knew, but as to what memory the woman stripped, Ariss still didn't know. However, the man with the agonized face was certainly a part of what was stolen from her.

Her *paratanist* placed several platters on the table and Ariss settled herself in her chair even though she wasn't that hungry. To be polite, she sampled a little of each dish, but mainly she examined her beautiful new living quarters.

The main room was massive, filled with simple but high-quality furniture. Plants cascaded from the ceiling, pedestals, furniture—just about every available space held a plant of some kind. Some were the palest of green, while others were so dark they were almost black. The effect was as if she lived in the forest, which she found infinitely comforting. What made the room stunning was an elaborate sunken bathing tub along the north wall. She'd barely paid attention to it last night, but now she considered how much time someone had spent fashioning the unit so that it appeared crafted by nature.

Smooth, polished stones, most likely from along one of the rivers that led to the Valry Sea, were fitted into the wall, so that when water ran for her bath, it rolled over the rocks like a waterfall. The sunken tub was carved from one large piece of black stone, probably from the Onic Mountains. Faucets and knobs, crafted of polished gemstones, lined the topside of the tub rim so that she could recline fully yet still reach them if she desired. How had she soaked there last night without really seeing any of it? Her vision of the man must have disturbed her deeply for her not to give the bathing tub much consideration.

Her *paratanist* had already had the tub ready for her last night. Warming tiles below the bath kept the water hot because she had felt their heat penetrating into her back as she sat within the perfumed water. She knew she would have suffered a lot more aches and pains today if she hadn't had the long soak last night.

Distracted, she didn't notice that her *paratanist* hovered next to her chair. Ariss tilted her head and lifted her eyebrows inquiringly. Statue still, he stood beside her. Baffled, Ariss finally remembered the harsh rules he operated under, and asked, "What?" in a more abrupt way than she normally would have.

"If you are finished with your meal, we will make our way to the *lantis.*"

Unfamiliar with that word but afraid to reveal her ignorance, Ariss nodded and rose from the table. Dressed only in her robe, she followed him out of her rooms and down the hallway. At least today, the hallway was relatively clear of people. Only a few palace guards stood here and there along their path. For the most part, they ignored her and her servant, as they seemed to expect their presence in the hallway. At least someone knew what was going on. For once in her life, Ariss would like to have the security of knowing what would happen next. For the next season, she would be at the mercy of the prophecy and all the rites and rituals crafted by her ancestors over five thousand seasons ago.

They walked for a long time, but then, finally, her *paratanist* stopped at a doorway hung with black fabric. Lifting up one edge of the cloth, he extended his hand, ushering her within.

Sweet perfume filled her lungs as she ducked inside a spacious but cozy room that was oddly similar to her Harvester suite—all black, umber, and brown, with smooth tiles and a multitude of green plants. A young male acolyte, clad in a flowing white robe, took her hand and led her to a padded table. When she tried to lie on her back, he softly informed her that she should lie down on her belly. At the head of the table was a small hole for her face to settle into. Once she was in position, the acolyte removed her robe with deft but precise movements.

Uncomfortable with her nudity, Ariss barely had a moment

to press her body into the padded bench before eight sets of hands began to stroke her. From the back of her head, to her shoulders, to the small of her back, to her buttocks, to her thighs, and her calves—all were touched and pressed by multiple sets of hands. Soft music of woodwinds, chimes, and low bass notes vibrated through her, as if she were part of the composition.

Unsure of what they expected of her, she tensed, waiting for instructions. Soon she realized all she had to do was relax and let them ease the thousand pains in her body. Never in her life had she felt so aware of herself and yet so relaxed. To her astonishment, she fell into a wakeful slumber where her thoughts and dreams mingled.

Again, she could see the dark-haired, dark-eyed man in profile, but this time there was movement. His head hung low, his long, rough-cut brown locks obscured his features, but then, in slow motion, he flipped his head up, flinging his hair back, exposing his face to the light and his tormented features to her gaze. His lips peeled back into a grimace, exposing straight white teeth. He clenched his angular jaw as tightly as his eyes, causing the tendons on his neck to stand out.

Her sex gushed with sudden arousal, shocking her. How could she find pleasure in another's torment? Who was he? No name came to mind, only startling feelings of stimulation.

Awakening.

That was the one word that summed up everything she felt about this man, but she had no idea what kind of awakening he represented. When her thoughts drifted away from him, she didn't fight. Thinking of the mysterious man gave her a terrible headache and conflicting feelings of arousal and shame. Much like what she felt last night with Kerrick. When her thoughts focused on him, she forcefully pushed them another direction.

Tumbling like rough water, her thoughts turned back to the

Harvester competition. Half a cycle ago, her father had informed her of his decision that she would compete. Ariss had almost laughed, but the seriousness of his face and her father's complete lack of humor cautioned her to silence. No daughter of an elite House had ever lowered herself to compete in the contest. There were no rules against them competing, but Ariss knew whether she won or lost, she would become a social outcast. They would see her entry into the pageant as a desperate bid for attention. Mocking jests would follow her wherever she went for the rest of her life. Her relationship with her peers was strained enough without adding this to her list of blunders. Already her contemporaries found her odd, cold, and as Janda of Violet House said, "Perfectly strange." Not that Ariss blamed them. What else could they say about someone with part of her past a mysterious blank?

The other high-ranking daughters of the Houses gossiped and chatted endlessly about all the myriad parties associated with palace life. Ariss had nothing to say. She'd spent her whole life in Felton, a small but prosperous region along the Onic Mountains. They had dances and such there, but nothing like the opulent celebrations hosted by the empress.

One day, without warning, her father decided the time had come for them to take their rightful place within the palace walls. Ariss left behind everything she'd ever known, including some of her memories. When she asked her mother, she turned away, always in a rush to go somewhere. Her father just peered at her down the length of his sharp nose until she retreated. Three of her sisters cast her baffled looks, unsure if she were joking or not. Darabelle laughed, calling her a silly child who wanted attention. Whatever memory her parents removed, her sisters had no knowledge of it, or someone had removed the memory from them as well. Shortly after they'd arrived at the palace, her father had come up with the scheme of having Ariss enter the Harvester competition. The timing was so odd that she honestly believed entering her into the contest was the sole reason he'd moved them to the palace in the first place.

Typically, only women from the outer regions, those with enough beauty to either win a local contest or catch the eye of a recruiter, were allowed to participate in the Harvester competition. Somehow, her father cleared her entry with the palace magistrate. Revulsion had swept chills across her flesh when she'd met him. The palace magistrate, Ambo Votny, had small, furtive eyes set in his rounded face. His multiple chins quivered when he spoke, and he had the most disgusting habit of picking his nose and wiping it on his silver trousers. And the way he looked at her, with a dirty kind of hunger, made her want to bathe in the hottest water with the harshest soap, as if she could wash the slime of his gaze off her person. Just what had her father promised Ambo to get him to allow her into the competition?

A desire to argue with her father rose up in her, but she clamped her mouth shut and hid behind her frosty exterior. Quarrelling with her father served no purpose. He would have his way. He always did. Radox Tunima ruled his Home with absolute authority and a brutal intolerance to defiance. Casting her out would not be his solution, for then others would know he could not control his own. Ariss knew this because she had actually sought to push him into that most harsh decision, but he refused to let her go. As soon as she had arrived at the palace, she wanted to return to Felton. She thought that if she embarrassed her father enough, he would send her back. Instead, she only solidified his determination to use her to make an alliance that would likely line his own pockets. As the Harvester, Ariss could choose any free man within the palace walls. She was certain her father had someone in particular in mind. Her only question was when would he reveal his choice?

Ariss had spent the last quarter cycle in the training rooms, surrounded by other hopeful candidates. All day and most of the night, they preened before the floor-to-ceiling mirrors, trying new hairstyles, makeup designs, and clothing. When they weren't perfecting their physical appearance, they practiced singing, playing an instrument, composing poetry, or dancing, because if two of the hopefuls were close in scores, they would have to compete in all areas; only the one with the greatest number of skills would triumph. In the final contest, a panel of judges, composed of the magistrate and others in high authority, would select a winner to harvest the males who came of age.

Ariss had a distinct advantage in that she was already accomplished in all five areas. Rather than practice or preen, Ariss had spent her time gazing out the lone window and into the gardens ripening below. She would rather be there than anywhere. Only surrounded by living things had she ever felt serene. Being boxed in by the unforgiving chilliness of the stone palace made her feel cold and constricted.

She returned to the present with a jolt. Eight sets of hands turned her upon her back and set to rubbing and stroking the front of her body. Her protest was lost amid her moan of pleasure. They knew just where she hurt the most. Strong hands stroked lightly along her breasts and the inside of her thighs, but not to stir her desire. Lust was not within them or at least they didn't show passion. Then again, it was difficult to assess what lay under their flowing white robes with her eyes barely open.

Ariss wasn't sure, but she didn't think they castrated the male acolytes in the palace. Not like what they did to the *actratos* at home. Those poor young men were snipped during childhood to preserve the sweetness of their voices so that they could sing the praises of the gods. Personally, Ariss found high, soft voices emerging from full-grown men disconcerting.

With practiced precision, these acolytes massaged her tension away. The only part they didn't touch as deeply as she wished was her neck. When she lifted her arms to remove the necklace that the magistrate had placed upon her during her inauguration, they gently but firmly returned her arms to her sides.

"You cannot remove the *parastone.*"

Curious, Ariss fingered the polished black stone. It seemed heavier than it should for its size, and rather than reflecting light, the stone seemed to drink in brightness, not in a sinister way, but as if it craved the light and could never receive enough. Ariss felt no fear in wearing the strange item, but, again, she'd been too overwhelmed at the time to ask about its purpose during her induction ceremony. Honestly, she'd thought it was purely decorative.

"What does it do?" she asked.

The acolyte, a young man with thick black hair and the softest blue eyes, tilted his head curiously to the side. His hand trembled as he reached out to stroke a finger across the surface of the stone. In the most reverent tone she'd ever heard, he said, "It announces the creation of the *paratanist.*"

Devotion shone from his masculine features in such rich detail, she felt he'd literally touched something divine. Moreover, she was baffled as to his meaning and, again, too embarrassed to ask.

5

"You can't hide in here for the entire season."

Kerrick regretted letting his handler, Sterlave, inside the Harvester suite, but it was too late to slam the door in his face now. Damn that the thick door did not have a peephole. He never knew who was on the other side until he opened it and then it was too late. Kerrick silently vowed to himself that from now on, he simply wouldn't answer.

"I haven't been hiding," Kerrick snarled, "nor have I been staying here for the entire last cycle." After a breath, he complained, "Remember? Your bondmate, the former empress, removed me from my rooms to accommodate a visiting dignitary. Something that has, apparently, never happened in the history of Diola."

Before Sterlave could answer, Kerrick moved away from the main door and stood gazing out at the snow-covered land below. His breath condensed on the glass, blocking his view, but one swipe of his fist wiped the mist away. If only he could remove all of his problems with such ease.

"Kasmiri did what she had to do." Sterlave defended his

bondmate with his calm and controlled voice, lifting his head so his short brown hair caught the glow of the ceiling crystals.

Kerrick considered his own reflection in the glass; his head looked about the same, but his close-cropped hair was startlingly golden. He looked the way he did as a boy when his mother, frustrated by trying to keep his hair free of tangles, would simply order the maid to shave it off altogether.

Sterlave was the Harvester before Kerrick for a grand total of thirteen sacrifices. Kasmiri, the daughter of Empress Clathia, was Sterlave's thirteenth harvest. Sterlave claimed her virginity and claimed her as his bondmate all in one thrust. No wonder Ambo had been so vexed; in the same Harvest, Chur Zenge had selected a bondmate, and once Sterlave became the Harvester, he too selected his chosen. Ambo must have breathed a sigh a relief when Kerrick didn't select one of the sacrifices as his bondmate.

"Kasmiri's intent was to accommodate another, not inconvenience you." As always, Sterlave used his pacifying voice. It was the exact same tone he used to cajole Kerrick into engaging the recruits in training exercises. Once Kerrick recovered from his bout of tender crotch, he'd done as his duty demanded and marched off to training. If he was going to be the Harvester, he was determined to be the best Harvester ever. Such worked better in theory rather than practice. Kerrick had thrown down his *avenyet* in disgust after three sessions. For good measure, he'd kicked the wooden double club before he'd stomped off.

To be honest, Kerrick wasn't upset about Kasmiri moving him from his rooms, or his boring schedule of eat, sleep, train, repeat. What infuriated him was that something historical had transpired and no one would tell him the details. All he knew was that Empress Clathia had died, which made Kasmiri the empress. A bunch of villagers had surrounded the palace to worship Chur Zenge, and somehow, for some reason, within a mere quarter cycle, Kasmiri had relinquished her throne and now lived as Sterlave's bondmate. Had Sterlave not selected Kasmiri during his very brief stint as the Harvester, the magistrate would have crushed Kasmiri under the stone or exiled her to Rhemna. How and why all of this had transpired was what Kerrick wanted to know. Damn Diola and the planet's lack of any kind of massive media. Word of mouth did him no good when Kerrick could only speak to his *paratanist*, his handler, or the other men in the training rooms; all who knew less than he did. Well, his handler Sterlave knew everything, but he was the most closed-mouth *tandgref* Kerrick had ever met.

After his three visits to the training rooms, and one brief discussion with Sterlave, Kerrick returned to his rooms a bitter, frustrated man. Why oh why hadn't he listened to his grandmother and learned more about the Harvester position before jumping blindly into it? She swore that one day his impetuousness would be his downfall, and she'd been right.

"You've been returned to your rooms." Sterlave closed the heavy Onic door behind him. Rather than settle himself at the couch, Sterlave kept to his feet. Probably in deference to not messing up the furniture as sweat and grime covered him from head to toe. Heavy muscles bulged along his arms and legs, causing a streak of envy within Kerrick; if he didn't do something, he would lose the body he'd worked so hard to obtain. "And surely, you've recovered from the Harvest by now."

Sterlave's words were slyly challenging, causing Kerrick to glare out at the winter blanket that smothered the land. Kerrick wouldn't mind the snow so much if he could be out in it, but he was forbidden to leave the palace. The longer he stayed cooped up inside, the more he felt himself shriveling, not just physically, but mentally and spiritually. Kerrick needed to be outside. Once, he'd tried to sneak out, but four burly guards, the same four he'd inadvertently summoned by pressing the panic button, had hauled him right back in. Kerrick had gulped two deep breaths of fresh air before they'd surrounded him. Now, his only recourse to get fresh air was to stand out on his tiny balcony. He considered rappelling his way down, but he didn't have any rope, and tying the bedclothes together only worked in the tridees. *Astle* was a slippery fabric that wouldn't hold together no matter how he tied the knots. Worse, it wouldn't give his hands decent purchase. Once he went over the railing, he'd scream his way straight to the ground. If he survived, he wouldn't be enjoying fresh air, or walking, anytime soon.

To add insult to injury, it wasn't just that he couldn't go outside, he also couldn't go anywhere within the palace that wasn't on his strict schedule. With four guards constantly on his ass, Kerrick hadn't been able to sneak off for a tryst, either. Not that he had anyone in particular in mind, but never had he been confined to such a limited existence. Like the men who made religion their life, Kerrick had been cut off from all the pleasures in the world. The difference was his exile wasn't voluntary. Well, it was in a way, but he never would have become the Harvester had he known. He wondered if they kept lovely Ariss caged, too. Had he known she would be his last for the next nine cycles, he never would have let her run off so soon. The thought of not knowing the touch of a woman for nine long, lonely cycles was something he tried desperately not to think of. By the end of it, he and his right hand would become very, very intimate.

"I've recovered just fine." Somewhere behind the clouds, *Tandalsul* blazed, but the gloomy black-blue puffs effectively blocked the light. Dark skies echoed Kerrick's dark mood. If he'd known the truth about being the Harvester, he never would have bothered to return to Diola. Becoming the magistrate and having power over his father simply wasn't worth this. He almost uttered a bitter laugh, for he'd thought this way would be the easiest and fastest way to power.

"If you're in good health, then why do you refuse to train?"

"Because it's boring!" Kerrick whirled around to face Sterlave.

"My training ground was the mountains I climbed, the waves I rode, the ice I skated. What you do is pointless." Already Kerrick felt his body turning to flab. He needed to be active, outside, not slamming away with a bunch of sweaty grunts in a smelly, old training room with a handful of weapons he had no idea how to wield.

"Pointless?" A smirk lifted up one edge of Sterlave's mouth. "I would think the upcoming challenge would give the training a clear purpose."

"Freeaal," Kerrick whispered to himself as he closed his eyes. Hesitantly, he asked, "What challenge?" Would the surprises never cease? If nothing else, he should have paid more attention to the tales his grandfather told. Every night at Grandier's Crown, the local tavern, his grandfather would sit in a place of honor and tell stories about the ancients. Kerrick had always been a little too interested in chasing the skirts of the Grandier daughters to listen with full ears.

"Right before the next Harvest, any recruit can challenge you in a fight to the death to become the next Harvester." Sterlave paused, a frown drawing his brows down between his golden brown eyes. "Surely, you understood that when you stepped forward to take my place, that the fight would have been to the death."

Kerrick slumped and banged his head softly against the glass in time with his words. "Stupid, stupid, stupid. I am a stupid, stupid man." Bracing his hands against the glass, he pushed himself back and shook off his overwhelming dread. "I thought that was only when I stepped forward to take your place. I thought that when they issued challenge to me later, it would be a fight to the first, like in the orph challenge." On Tapring, the orph challenge consisted of ten separate events, one of which was the crossing of blades.

"A fight to see who draws first blood?" Sterlave didn't openly laugh, but Kerrick sensed it took him quite an effort not to. A man who fought to the death would see a fight to the first as almost womanly.

"It's the only kind of weapon fighting I've ever done, and only with a guarded blade." The slender blade used in the fight was not only dull, but had a small rubber guard placed just below the pointed tip, so that any blow would only draw blood, not truly wound or kill. The tiny point would give his opponent little more than a deep paper cut. Sadly, even with that, it wasn't Kerrick's best event. More often than not, he received a nick in his arm or chest.

With a few steps, Sterlave was at Kerrick's back, peering at him through the reflection in the glass. "In eight cycles, you will face at least three challengers that I know of. They will pick the weapon. You will pick your stance." At Kerrick's baffled expression, Sterlave explained, "You can choose either a defensive or offensive posture."

"But they get to pick the weapon."

Sterlave nodded.

"And they all saw what I can do with those weapons."

Again, Sterlave nodded, but with more reserve.

Glumly, Kerrick whispered, "I'm a walking dead man, aren't I?" Kerrick's skill with the unfamiliar weapons had been less than impressive. In fact, to be honest, his pathetic attempts had been so comical that several recruits openly laughed at his ineptitude. He'd thrown down the *avenyet* in shame, not fury.

All his life it seemed everything physical came easily to him. Everything, that is, except handling weapons. Bare-handed, Kerrick was amazingly skilled, but put something in his hand, and suddenly, he would do more damage to himself than to an opponent. His father called him *tandulfi*, or two left hands. Just thinking of the jib caused Kerrick to grit his teeth. He'd intimidated the recruits with his impressive size and unbelievable arrogance when he'd taken the post from Sterlave. That trick would only work once. Now that they knew the truth, he wasn't going to be intimidating anyone. Every recruit in the cells was probably salivating at the thought of taking him on.

Sterlave canted his head to the side. "If you cower in your room, you most certainly are, as you say, a dead man walking. If you stop acting like a child and train, you most definitely will have a chance. A very good chance, if you faithfully follow my advice." Sterlave clasped his hand to Kerrick's shoulder. "I'm your handler, and I intend to see you succeed. However, the choice is entirely up to you."

With that, Sterlave strode to the main door.

"Wait," Kerrick called.

Sterlave turned and without prompting, said, "Kasmiri relinquished her throne because her father was not an official empress consort, which made her illegitimate."

Kerrick's eyebrows climbed. "Clathia was unfaithful to her consort? I always thought it was the other way around." Clathia's consort was notorious for bedding damn near every woman in the palace. His exploits were so legendary that Kerrick had heard about them all the way in Cheon.

"Apparently, it was mutual." Sterlave sighed. "Now that you know, does knowing change anything?"

"Not really." Kerrick shrugged.

"Then why did you need to know so badly?"

"Because I'm curious." Knowing the history of those in power was an important tool in rising through their ranks.

"And knowledge is power." With a small chuckle, Sterlave shook his head. "Seems to me you are just interested in gossip, much like women and servants."

Kerrick would have bristled at the insult, but there was no way he was taking Sterlave on in a fight, verbal or otherwise. If anyone could help him get through the challenge, Sterlave was that man. Calmly, Kerrick returned, "What you call gossip, I call information."

Sterlave narrowed his eyes. "And what could you possibly do with this information?"

"Who knows?" Kerrick shrugged.

Both men turned when the door creaked slowly open. Kerrick's *paratanist* entered, bowed to them both, and then entered the kitchen to prepare his midday meal.

"Will I see you tomorrow for training?" Sterlave placed his hand on the doorknob. Tension only heightened the sheer power of his body. Kerrick could look down his nose at the training all he wanted, but Sterlave proved whatever the instruction method was, it clearly gave results.

"Considering my choices, I'll be there early and stay late." Kerrick would rather suffer the laughs of a thousand men than certain death by one. He might be lazy, but he wasn't a fool.

Sterlave smiled. "Half the battle is just showing up."

"Right." Kerrick turned his attention out the window to watch snow drift lazily from the clouds. "Because if I don't show up, there can be no battle."

"Which would make you a coward." Sterlave's voice cut deeper than any snide aside Kerrick's father had ever made.

At that, Kerrick turned, fire in his gaze. "I may be many things—lazy, unskilled, foolhardy—but nobody, and I mean nobody, calls me a coward." In the last ten seasons, he'd faced challenges most men wouldn't dream of taking. They didn't call them death-defying sports for nothing. How ironic that his exploits had cumulated in the most deadly sport of all.

Sterlave flashed him a contemplative smile. "Show up and prove me wrong."

Determined, Kerrick lifted his head, squared his shoulders, and said, "I'll be there." As soon as the door closed, Kerrick hustled into the kitchen, and asked, "Where did you say those practice weapons were?"

Silently, his servant left off her food prep and glided across the main floor to a small closet off his bedroom. When she opened the door, crystals bloomed to full brightness, revealing various clutter and several weapons stacked neatly on the floor or leaning against the wall. He hadn't even touched them, yet already he felt them slipping from his grip.

"You will not have time to practice this night."

Kerrick let out a long-suffering sigh. "And why not?"

"This is the eve of a new cycle." She said it as if it should have some meaning to him, which it didn't.

"And?" he prompted, not really sure he wanted to hear more. Gods, he probably had to perform some disturbing ritual with bloodletting and the consumption of raw animal parts and, gods forbid, naked dancing. He shuddered. He was a horrible dancer, and gyrating naked probably wouldn't help matters one bit.

"Tonight you will mate with the Harvester."

"Really?" Kerrick breathed a sigh of relief as a smile wiped away what had almost become a perpetual frown. "Maybe things are looking up." His smile faded and his face fell when Fana remained very still.

"What?" he asked, trying to keep frustration from possessing his tone. Couldn't he have just one nice thing happen to him? Honestly, he wanted to know what he'd done to anger the gods so much that they now gloated in punishing him at every turn.

Hesitantly, Fana asked, "You want to mate?" Her question was a cross between repulsion and shock.

"Of course I do!" So far, he'd only been celibate one cycle of thirty-six days, but still, he hadn't gone this long without sex since he was young. Just the thought of being with Ariss rather than his own hand caused his penis to twitch in anticipation. "Don't you?"

He couldn't see her face, hidden as it was by her enormous cowl hood, but he felt her utter horror at his question.

"I am forbidden!"

With that, she retreated to the kitchen, leaving him to stand and wonder. Fana touched him intimately, prepared him to take the virginity of hundreds of women, and yet they forbid her to have sex? Kerrick shook his head. The more he learned about the Harvest prophecy, the less he liked it.

6

Ariss took a deep breath and pushed the door open. Kerrick sat on the edge of the round bed. When he saw her, he trailed his gaze from her feet to her face, but showed no outward reaction. Neither delight nor disgust crossed his features.

Had she known she would have to mate with him every cycle until the next Harvest, she might not have behaved so wantonly the last time. Just thinking about what she'd done caused her to blush. She had hoped to assess his feeling toward her by his expression, but he remained remarkably expressionless, which only prompted her to put on her mask of indifference. Two could play this game. However, she had a feeling he was far more adept at the masquerade than she was.

Ariss made a great show of closing the door behind her, which gave her another moment to consider him from under the sweep of her lashes. The first thing she noticed was his hair had begun to grow back. Golden ceiling crystals caused his head to positively glow. She felt an overwhelming desire to run her fingers through the short, spiky strands. Too, the bright blond made his eyes even more impossibly green. Hunter eyes. Eyes that even in his relaxed state seemed to delve right into her very soul. His body was not as oiled and bulging as it had been last time, but still, he was impressively large. Strong, sleek, seductive. Short, shiny blond hairs now covered his arms, his chest, and his legs. She didn't dare try to look between his legs, but she imagined hair was returning there as well.

"Ariss," he said, nodding, his voice somewhere between commanding and condemning.

"Kerrick," she returned, inclining her head slightly. Did he know the truth? Nervously, she fingered the black stone about her neck. If he didn't know, she wasn't sure how she would tell him, or even if she should. Perhaps what he didn't know couldn't hurt him. Not until it was too late, anyway.

Smirking, he patted the space next to him on the bed.

Head held high, Ariss approached. "Didn't they give you a robe to wear this time?" She clutched the tie of hers as if the flimsy fabric could protect her from him and the needs simmering inside her own flesh. If she thought she hungered for him before, that craving was nothing like the ache she felt now that she had seen him again.

He flicked his head toward the floor. "With what we're going to be doing, I didn't think I'd need it."

Ariss gulped at the fire in his eyes. How could green seem so menacing? "Did you see all the people in the hallway?" To her, it seemed every inhabitant in the palace filled the space just to see her stride toward the mating room.

Her heart pounded when Kerrick stood. All male and sexy and smiling, with his penis hard and heavy and within arm's reach. Gods help her, all she had to do was lift her hand and she could cup that silken shaft in her palm. Night after night, she'd dreamt of doing just that, and now to have him so close she could almost taste him . . . To stop herself from touching him, she clasped her hands together.

Kerrick considered her joined hands for a moment, then leaned over, placing his mouth right next to her ear, and whispered, "Holding on for dear life or holding on to your dignity while you can?"

Confused by the insult, Ariss took a step back. Kerrick caught her about her waist and spun her so that she faced toward the exit. Again, he put his mouth tantalizingly close to her ear. "There's the door. Are you going to run like you did last time?"

Ariss drew a deep breath to retort, but his scent filled her lungs. He smelled of the forest. Of living green things and dangerous animals. She wanted to do just as he said: run. But her legs were too weak and there was nowhere to run to. No matter her own fears, she had to perform her duty. Deep in her secret heart, she admitted that she wanted to complete her obligations.

During a dream, when the image of the tormented man in her flashbacks overlaid the image of Kerrick, she realized what the memory was her parents paid such a high price to remove.

"I ran not because of you, but because of my parents."

Kerrick held very still, listening intently.

Desperate to explain, Ariss haltingly said, "When I was younger, I caught one of our servants masturbating." She knew she blushed when she said the word, but thankfully, Kerrick wasn't looking at her. "He was older than I was by at least ten seasons. He had dark hair, dark eyes." She pictured him so clearly in her mind despite the fact she couldn't remember his name. "He was mysterious and rough-hewn. Watching him aroused me, even though I was a bit too young to fully understand what I was seeing."

Kerrick said nothing. He held her to his chest, listening, as if understanding her would open up entire new worlds for him. She'd only been with him twice, but already she'd told Kerrick more about herself than everyone else in her life combined. He knew secrets of her heart that she swore she would never tell anyone. Somehow, in some way, she felt secure with him.

"My mother caught me just as he climaxed." Ariss remembered his head tossed back. What she thought was a look of agony on his face was actually ecstasy. "When I witnessed his release, the most exquisite joy filled me." After a breath, she added, "My mother slapped me so hard she bruised my face for a quarter cycle. Mother, in turn, told Father. He immediately fired the servant." What she didn't tell Kerrick was that her parents had filled her with body-numbing chemicals to suppress her natural lust. "Then, just to be sure, my father paid handsomely to strip the memory from my mind." She took a deep breath. "Last time, when you masturbated for me, the feelings I felt brought back fringes of that memory they paid to have stripped." Softly, she added, "That's why I ran away."

After a very long time, Kerrick asked, "Are you ashamed of what you felt watching him or watching me?"

"No." That was the simple truth. "I enjoyed every moment."

"Do you want me to stop touching you?"

Her desperate need made the answer ready to burst forth, but she maintained a modicum of modesty. Softly, she whispered, "No." She turned her head slightly, wanting to kiss him, but unable to do so. "I don't want you to ever stop touching me."

He gave an almost imperceptible sigh of approval.

When Kerrick slid his hands across her waist, then down to cup her hips, she whimpered. When he yanked her back, pressing her against his erection, she gasped and clenched her eyes tightly closed. In a way, she'd felt she'd now given him permission to do whatever he wanted to her. Her heart raced wondering what that would be.

"Once I healed from the Harvest, all I thought of was you.

Did you know that, Ariss?" His voice was sultry thick with erotic accusation.

She shook her head, causing some of her upswept hair to tumble down and tickle along her back.

"Endless dreams of my cock plunging into your heat." He pressed her against him, so she had no choice but to acknowledge his straining need sliding against the fragile fabric of her robe. "I'd wake so hard I'd hurt, and all I had was my own hand to relieve me." Once he'd settled his shaft between the cleft of her bottom, he let out a short growl of satisfaction. "My hand that you watched stroke my cock." He nipped her earlobe as he slid his shaft along the *astle* wedged into the cleft of her bottom. "So I slipped my hand under the covers and imagined your cool gray eyes watching me, noting each and every caress I made to try to give myself relief. Relief from the torment you inflicted."

Behind her closed eyes, she saw him stroking himself for her, then the way he'd forced his shaft into his unyielding fist. Her shiver caused him to chuckle and blow hot, moist breath across her neck.

"Did you dream of me?" he asked, nuzzling his lips to the most sensitive spot on her shoulder.

She didn't answer, but her soft sob gave the truth away. How could she not have dreamt of him? He was stunningly handsome, and he did things that evoked feelings she'd never allowed herself to even think of.

"Why do you deny yourself?" Deftly, he untied her robe, teasing his fingers along the parted fabric, widening it slowly until the edges hung from her now-thrusting breasts. Each time he moved his hand along her flesh, he came tantalizingly close to touching her nipples but never quite managed. The wait, the breathless anticipation of his touch, had her alternately gasping, then holding her breath until she was dizzy.

"I'm not supposed to want this, to want you. I can't—"

He didn't let her finish. He lifted his hand to her chin, turning her head just enough so that he could kiss her lips. His move was aggressive. His palm against her face was utterly possessive, but his kiss was softer than feather down.

"I don't want to hear excuses," he growled against her mouth. "And I won't wait for you to make up your mind. We are here to mate, and that's exactly what we are going to do."

Kerrick pulled the robe off her shoulders and slid it down her arms. She thought he intended to strip her last shred of protection away, but he gathered the fabric around her wrists, wrapping the garment so that he bound her arms behind her.

Ariss couldn't find the breath to ask what his intentions were, and a part of her was secretly thrilled, because now, he had taken the choice away from her. Let him do as he wished. There was nothing she could say or do to stop him. Whatever the consequences of this encounter, they were now beyond her.

"I know you've never been bound," he stated, his words blowing warm against her neck. "Are you afraid?"

More strands of black hair fell along her back when she shook her head.

"Not brave enough to admit what you want, but you'll submit yourself to my control. You are a perplexing woman, Ariss. One I will know in every way by the end of this season." He moved back, taking his body heat with him, leaving her to shiver in the chill air. His words confirmed that he knew they would mate seven more times, on the eve of each cycle, until the next Harvest.

Her nipples, already straining for his touch, were now even more painfully hard. If he didn't caress her soon, she thought she'd go mad from longing, which undoubtedly was his intention. The walls of her sex wept for him, clenching so tight she feared she'd die if he didn't fill her soon. Such emptiness inside caused her to hang her head and bite her lips to hold back desperate pleas.

Clearly accustomed to control, Kerrick took his time perusing her bound form. Ariss kept her head down and only watched him through lowered lashes. Carefully, he removed the clip that kept her hair artfully piled on top of her head. Still damp from her bath, the moist strands caused tiny bumps to wash across the surface of her flesh when they tumbled down her back.

Even though she and Kerrick were separated for a cycle, and she'd had time to become re-accustomed to the world of physical sensations, she still found herself ensnared by him, as if he made her feel everything for the first time. The texture of fine fabrics, expensive cosmetics, rich unguents and potions—none of it was as powerful as his touch. However, what struck terror into her fragile heart was how his gaze alone caressed her most strongly of all.

"Such skin you possess. Smooth, soft, and surprisingly sensitive to the smallest stroke." Kerrick traced the tip of his finger from her earlobe to her neck, pressing against the fluttering of her pulse before trailing his devastating finger down the length of her arm. "Oh, Ariss," he whispered, "I don't believe I even have to touch you."

She held her breath, stunned that he realized what she'd thought only moments ago. She wondered if he could read her mind, but she held perfectly still, waiting. Kerrick leaned close. And then, in the most incredible display of mastery, he used only the subtle feel of his breath to touch her. He murmured words in some language she didn't comprehend, but she didn't need to. They were shameful words. Sinful words. Rough and seductive words. Again and again, he muttered wicked terms that described what he would do to her in the most vulgar way. She didn't have to understand the language to find his naughty speech passionate and undeniably arousing as the words flowed over her skin, more powerful than any touch.

"You've always been such a good girl." His mouth now hovered above her right nipple, his breath tormenting the straining flesh. "You've always done exactly what everyone told you to do."

Panicked that he again knew a truth without her telling him, Ariss shuddered and opened her mouth to deny his accusation, but all that emerged from her parted lips was a tremulous, "Yes."

"Yes," he mocked, tilting his head up so he connected to her gaze despite how she kept her head lowered. One second of those hunter eyes drilling into her caused her to flush and look away. Kerrick cupped her chin and forced her to look at him before he said, "But deep inside you've always wanted to be a bad girl."

Quicker than she could blink, he swiped his tongue across the tip of her nipple, causing her to hiss and automatically move forward, as if to force her nipple in his mouth.

With a mocking chuckle, he moved his head away. He'd anticipated her reaction.

"You want to do wild, wicked things. Sinful things." He blew a short, sharp burst of air across her moist nipple, causing the fragile skin to contract so tightly the sensation bordered on pain. "But you don't know where to start."

Skillfully, he breathed his way between her breasts to her belly button, and then lower until he whispered right across her mound, "That's what I'm going to show you." Slowly, he slid his tongue across the throbbing tip of her clit. Before she could react and thrust toward his face, he gripped her hips with his massive hands and held her still for another delicious swipe. "I'm going to teach you how to be a very, very bad girl."

Ariss knew she should protest. If nothing else, she should at least make a token objection. Nevertheless, when she parted her lips to deny him, all that emerged was a wanton, breathy sigh of surrender.

Smoothly, he rose and faced her. "Look at me, Ariss."

Upon a fortifying breath, she lifted her head and met his gaze.

"Have you ever had a man's cock in your mouth?"

He asked the question so nonchalantly that, for a moment, she thought she misunderstood. When his shocking question registered, she felt her mouth and eyes widen into perfect little O's of surprise.

"Judging by your expression, I'd say the answer was no."

How could he expect her to do that? It was bad enough she'd allowed him to do such a perversion to her, but how could she do the same? With a quick glance down, she wondered how such a thing was even possible. His penis was large. Trying to wrap her lips around his throbbing shaft would be impossible.

"You needn't look so terrified. I promise, it won't hurt either of us." He smiled, then grasped her shoulders in his strong hands. Ever so carefully, he lowered her to her knees. He wasn't forcing her so much as guiding her, but Ariss felt powerless to resist.

A new kind of awareness flooded her. Trepidation, because she'd never done what he suggested, but she was terrified she'd do it wrong and possibly hurt him, which she was loath to do. Moreover, a simple curiosity to try what she'd always been told was disgusting, amoral, licentious behavior only added to her conflicted feelings. All those wicked admonishments only compelled her to want to wrap her lips around his cock just as much as they made her want to turn away.

Between their bodies, his penis was what made him utterly different from her. She could not describe the rapture she'd felt when he placed his mouth upon her sex. She wanted to give him the same pleasure. Undoubtedly, many women had done this for him, so the sensation would not be a novel one for him, but she would take him into her mouth just to watch his face and see if her ministrations affected him the same way his did her.

Casting her gaze up the length of his massive frame, fully aware of her bound arms behind her, she considered how strangely sinister his shaft seemed from her position. Kerrick was enormous, a wall of muscle looming above her. His cock was so hard that each beat of his heart caused the heavy shaft to twitch slightly. Darker blond stubble grew along the heavy skin that cradled his balls, lightening as it dusted his groin, then lightening even more down the length of his legs.

Trailing her gaze up to his face, her heart skipped a beat when she saw the intensity of his expression. Suddenly, she felt awkward, ashamed, but terribly aroused. Kneeling below him, she felt so small and innocent, a wayward woman brought to his feet in payment for some unknown crime. Towering above her, he was a symbol of lust and knowledge, a wicked master ready to extract punishment for her wrongdoings. What if he demanded more than she could possibly give, or worse, laughed at her feeble attempts to please him?

After a fortifying breath, she whispered, "How do I start?"

Something shifted in the confidence of his gaze, something that opened up just the tiniest sliver of vulnerability. "Start slowly." He stepped forward, bringing his penis close to her lips without forcing her. She would have to bridge the distance between them and show him that she was willingly his servant.

Ariss angled up on her knees and kissed the darkened tip of his cock. Immediately, she drew back and looked up at him. He stood mindfully still, his face lowered to watch her without mocking or mastery. If anything, his face betrayed the depth of his anticipation. And then she knew what other dreams he'd had. Not just dreams of her watching him tease himself, but of watching her performing this very act. She knew when she glanced into his feverishly bright eyes that never left her face.

Emboldened by this knowledge, Ariss moved forward and placed an open-mouth kiss upon his cock, giving him just a taste of how hot and wet the inside of her mouth was. She doubted he'd ever held so statue-still in his life, almost as if he thought if he moved, she would stop. Ever so slowly, she parted her lips wider and drew him within the hot hollow of her mouth.

His nostrils flared as he drew in a deep breath and whisper-hissed a vulgar word.

Coyly, she pulled back, making her eyes innocent. "Am I hurting you?" She knew she wasn't, but she wanted to understand his reaction, for surely, this wasn't his first time.

"Gods, no." He breathed the words out. "It's never been like this." He shook his head, causing the light to scatter beautifully in his short-shorn hair. "With you, everything is different, more intense." He seemed genuinely shocked by his reaction, which pleased her immensely, and gave her the confidence to continue.

Playfully, she lifted his penis with her nose, sliding it down until again she held him balanced at the entrance of her mouth. If he didn't breathe soon, she feared he would pass out. When she parted her lips in a kiss to his tip, he gulped a breath and held it. As she slid her lips down his shaft, he gulped more air, then released his breath in short, panting bursts.

So entranced was she by his reaction that she suddenly realized how unique was the texture of him—soft skin over hardened flesh. Not too hard, more like a new sponge wrapped in velvet. And so alive. The deeper she took him, the more she felt the pulse of his body, the need rising up within him, their combined attention on this singular bit of his body only intensified the tactile sensations. What she'd always been told was a repulsive act was beautiful in the trust he granted. He didn't force her to pleasure him; he trusted her enough to let her hold between her teeth the most fragile, vulnerable part of him.

When she looked up, she caught his gaze, shuttered under his lashes to hide a defenselessness that almost brought tears to her eyes. He would never admit the truth, but Kerrick needed this. It wasn't about lust so much as it was a show of trust on his part and a show of acceptance on hers. He wanted to make her a bad girl, not because she wanted him to, but because he desperately longed to corrupt her. Something about her innocence sparked a craving in him that she only now began to understand. Just as she let him bind her, he let her command him, for if there were power in either of their positions, that power belonged to her, even though she was on her knees. With one bite, she could emasculate him. However, that was something she would never do, not when she had taken such pleasure with him.

Carefully, she took him deeper and sucked gently, just enough to cause tension against his already taut skin. She had to angle her head far back to avoid scraping her teeth along him, which also brought her face directly into the light and his gaze. He reached out and cupped her cheek, teasing his fingers along the shape of her lips wrapped around him.

Without words, he begged her to hold still so that he could slowly thrust into and out of her mouth. While he moved skillfully, letting her feel pulsing power against her lips, she also felt tension coiling tighter and more powerfully in his muscles. Drops of moisture fell against the back of her tongue, salty and luscious, unlike any flavor she'd ever tasted.

Greedily, she sucked harder, wanting more, longing to feel him lose his valiant struggle and explode within her. To taste him, to feel that shock of his flesh rhythmically pumping caused her to clench her thighs so tightly together that she climaxed in a sudden shocking burst.

Tremors caused her to release him with a gasp.

Kerrick realized what had happened and lifted her up into his arms. "Wrap your legs around my waist." When she did, he plunged into her still-quivering passage.

Another orgasm trembled through her, clenching her around him as she held still in his arms, breathless and overwhelmed that she could do nothing, not even hold on as her arms were still bound behind her.

Three strides and Kerrick had her pinned to the wall. Balanced there, her hands finding some purchase on the rough-textured stone, he thrust into her so deeply she cried out. Pleasure and pain held her in thrall, freezing her tongue from saying she wanted more or begging him to stop.

Murmuring her name, he slid his arms against hers, clasping her bound hands with his, holding her steady against the wall and the power of his body. Now his arms cushioned hers from the unforgiving hardness of the rock. Kerrick surrounded her and within the comforting barricade of his flesh, she was safe.

"Such passion in your mouth, such pleasure from your lips." Tentatively, he kissed her, so lightly did he press his mouth to hers she scarce felt him.

"I wanted to taste all of you," she whispered.

Groaning, he kissed her harder, but still with erotically light pressure. He did not move the rest of his body, only his mouth made delicate love to her. Worshipfully, he kissed her, as if her mouth were the altar and he was a plaintive priest seeking absolution. Hesitantly, he stroked his tongue to hers, as if asking permission, which she granted by sucking softly to bring their mouths closer together. All the while below, buried inside, she clutched at his shaft, squeezing him as he held her prisoner in his arms.

"Ariss." Her name was a whisper-hiss against her mouth, a curse and a prayer all at once.

Without thinking, she asked, "How could anyone call this sinful?"

Kerrick leaned back, a frown furrowing his brow. "This is not a sin, *tanata*, and anyone who claims that it is must be doing it wrong." He pressed his forehead to hers and peered right into her eyes. "This with you is nothing short of divine."

Blasphemous words that would send her mother into a faint, but they lifted Ariss up. She would use them as a mantra to wipe away the shame her parents had tried so desperately to instill in her.

With his arms holding her securely, he kept his forehead to hers as he rolled his hips, circling his shaft within. Each pass rubbed his stubble across her clit, bringing her back to the edge of climax. All the while he held her gaze, determined that she would not close her eyes and hide away this time. Not that she wanted to. The intensity of his gaze added another layer of intimacy to their act, one that was both fantastic and frightening.

"Ariss, it is not enough to have you only once each cycle," he whispered, as if he feared someone listening in. For the first time, she considered the room. Round with impossibly tall ceilings that faded into shadows while a cone of black hung from the center with lighting crystals adorning the edge. What hid in the shadows above them? Before she could ask, Kerrick insisted, "We must find a way to meet outside of here."

A new surge of pleasure tightened her passage. To meet him somewhere, furtively, hands seeking, mouths working, his cock so hot and hard and plunging into her slick passage . . . another climax rocked her, compelling his, causing him to capture her mouth and kiss her as deeply as he buried his cock within her sex. Liquid flowed inside her and now she knew it was too late. She couldn't turn back from her plan. If she told him, he would never forgive her. For surely, the fact that he willingly filled her with his seed meant that he didn't know the truth of her duty.

7

Kerrick refused to let Ariss go. Behind him, he heard a soft *snick* and knew the exit had been unlocked. Once they mated, they were free to go, but he didn't want to leave. Not yet. Not when he wanted to do so many other things with the beautiful woman in his arms. Once his *paratanist* told him he would mate with her tonight, he'd carefully planned everything he intended to do; however, once he'd laid eyes on Ariss, all his plans crumbled to dust. Suddenly, everything wasn't about his need to climax. One whiff of her scent caused him to focus everything on her.

Things he'd only questioned before he now knew with certainty. She was an innocent. He knew that deep down to the wicked part of his heart. She came to him this time perfectly clean of all other essences, so hers shone through. Her scent was shy, pure, and untried, but hidden below it all was the faintest note of yearning. Whether she knew it or not, Ariss wanted what he offered. Deep inside she craved what he could give her. Once she accepted all of herself, she wouldn't be a bad girl so much as she would be a dangerous woman. A woman who knew her wants and wasn't afraid to achieve them was truly powerful. He didn't understand why, but he wanted to be the one to peel back the layers and transform her into the woman she was meant to be.

Teasing his wanton words over her sensitive skin had driven him wild with desire. Telling her the truth of his darkest wish, to turn her into a bad girl, was almost his undoing. So prim, so proper, so unlike the women he routinely seduced, she ensnared him without even knowing. But then to have her bound, on her knees, his cock held between her luscious lips . . . Just thinking of it caused him to shudder and twitch within her silky passage.

She moaned and nestled her head tighter in the hollow of his neck and shoulder.

All he could hope now was that he hadn't pushed her too far too fast. He'd wanted her to test her perceived limits, to see for herself that a lifetime of indoctrination was wrong. Sex wasn't evil, or dirty, or shameful, or any of the other condemning words the zealous believers used. Kerrick remembered well how those in Cheon had viewed his lustful ways. They called him hurtful, hateful names that he'd decided to live up to. He became exactly what they said he was. Only much later had he learned there wasn't anything wrong with his behavior. He never forced a woman, and he never lied to them about his intentions. They flocked to him because of the air of danger he possessed, but also they knew, upfront, what kind of man he was.

Kerrick imagined Ariss had suffered under similar misguided fools. Only when he'd gone beyond the small-minded world of his village and out into the immense universe had he realized how backward his home planet was. Out in the vastness there were entire worlds devoted to pleasure and races of beings that prized the expression of love above all else. Diolans used the derogatory *barsitas* to describe people from another planet, but Kerrick called them by their proper names: Cuearcian, Tandthian,

Tapringinan, Vernamian. They would look upon the Harvest prophecy as the quaint ramblings of ancient fools looking to control their people. If not for Diola's strange abhorrence of technology, the ancient ways would have died long ago. But here, everything moved at such a slow pace, even change had been frozen in its tracks.

"You can put me down," Ariss whispered against his neck, shifting uncomfortably in his arms. He feared that if he did, she would run for the door. Of course, if he kept her bound, she wouldn't be able to run anywhere . . .

Kerrick cradled her in his arms as he carried her to the bed. Once there, he lowered her to the edge, placing himself on his knees. She'd had her arms bound behind her for a long time, but he wasn't quite ready to release her. He couldn't stand the thought of not seeing her again for another cycle. Not if he had to slave away in the training room and suffer the snickers of the other recruits. If only he could find solace in her arms each night, he thought he could bear anything.

"Will you meet me?" He spoke softly, right to her ear, leaning over on the pretext of untying her hands. He didn't know if anyone listened to them, but he suspected they might. How else would they know when to unlock the door?

"Kerrick," she began, but stopped. She waited for a long time, her panting breath hot against his ear. "Untie me first."

"Please," he begged. "Ariss, we must find a way."

Weakly, she nodded. When he freed her arms, she wrapped them around his neck, holding on as if she thought this time *he* would run away.

Damn the rules. He wasn't going to leave until they came and tore him from her. Gently, he maneuvered their bodies on the bed until they lay entwined. Ariss clung to him so tightly that he realized she truly was afraid to let go.

"Tell me," he asked softly, nuzzling the sensitive space between her neck and shoulder.

"I don't want to leave." Her voice was almost a sob as she tightened her arms around him, clinging with a desperation that touched him deeply.

"Me either." He breathed a soft sigh onto her skin. "I think as long as we're mating, so to speak, they will leave us alone."

At this, she pulled back and considered his face. "You're not angry about being forced to copulate with me?"

"Copulate?" He laughed. "There's a word I don't often hear." He kissed the tip of her nose. "No one is forcing me to do anything. I want to copulate with you." Their first night together he had suspected his *paratanist* had drugged him to find Ariss irresistible, but he didn't believe that now. All by herself, Ariss compelled him. Nothing he or anyone else did would change that.

"Fornicate?" she asked playfully.

"Closer. Try"—he came very close and whispered to her lips— "fuck."

She laughed. "Fuck." As she said the word, she blushed. "You'll make me a bad girl yet."

"It's going to be a difficult challenge, but one I am uniquely suited for." Again, he drew near to her mouth and said, "Fuck just sounds hard and nasty, doesn't it?" He knew how to swear in a hundred languages, but that particular word always excited him. Just hearing her say it caused his erection to return.

Nodding, she trailed her fingertips over his face, then down his chest. "Cock," she said, grabbing a handful.

This time he laughed. "Another hard and nasty word." He placed his hand upon her mound and said, "Cunt."

She winced. "That word is so vulgar."

"Is it?" he asked, teasing his finger between slick folds. "What word would you prefer?"

Playfully, she squeezed his shaft, and said, "Give me some choices."

He gave her several, and each time he named another word to describe the enchanted place between her lovely legs, he plunged his finger deep inside her beautiful cunt. He was just getting to the Cuearcian terms when she clutched his shaft a little too hard. He cautioned her, but knew he would never be able to concentrate with her fondling him, so he had her lift her hands above her head, letting him continue his recitation of terms while finger-fucking her into a frenzy.

"That's it, lovely Ariss. Lie back and let me tell you more luscious words to describe this glorious place." Now he slipped another finger inside her, which she acknowledged with a deep moan and the rolling of her hips. The closer he pushed her to the edge, the more she moved, wild and wanton and desperately craving the culmination. Just as she came close, he pulled her back.

"Kerrick, please, this tension, this tightening, I can't bear it." Her breath was harsh, gasping, her body covered in a sheen of sweat, but she was not where he wanted her, not yet.

"But you will bear it. You'll lie there and take everything I have to give." His words were harsh, but his voice was softly threatening, whispered right to her ear. "Now, repeat after me."

Each time he said a vulgar word, she repeated it, then he would thrust his fingers deep and rub his thumb across her now hard and greedy little clit.

"That's it, Ariss, what an excellent bad girl you are."

Her whimper surged desire straight to his cock. He'd wanted to watch her climax, but he couldn't hold back his own burning needs. All this talk of naming her sex had him dying to feel her slick cunt wrapped around his cock.

When he pulled his hand away, she grabbed for his wrist, begging him not to stop, not now when she was so close. And there, just briefly, was a flicker of anger in her gaze. Perhaps some day, when she was more secure, she wouldn't beg but demand he finish. That day was not today, but it wasn't far off, either. Still, he should take advantage of his power position while he could.

"I'm not going to stop." He lifted her up, placing her on her knees. "I'm just going to do more."

Balanced on her hands and knees, Ariss turned her head to look back at him. Her cool gray eyes were smoldering like coals ready to spring to life. Her mouth was parted prettily, almost begging him to again thrust his prick between those sultry lips. As much as he wanted to, there was something more profoundly erotic he wanted to show her.

With a wicked smirk, he parted her cheeks.

Her eyes went wide and her lips drew apart in denial as she tried to move forward. However, his hands were strong and gripped her buttocks firmly. Without a word, he lowered his face and placed his tongue against the puckered skin between her cheeks.

Her reaction was a surprised sound followed by a long drawn-out moan of pleasure. Carefully, he teased his tongue around the delicate skin, reveling in the way she now tilted her hips, lifting her bottom, encouraging him to continue. Gods, she had a beautiful ass. High molded cheeks, smooth skin over taut muscles, and tiny, almost imperceptible dimples on either side.

"Do you like this?" he asked, making sure to ask the question so that his breath moved across her now fully awakened flesh.

"Yes." Wonder made her voice soft.

Kerrick had never known of this particular activity until a woman on Tapring had done it to him. His shock and disgust had fallen away when he realized how sensitive the skin there was, and how astonishingly good teasing that responsive flesh felt. The woman had opened his mind to a whole new range of sensual bliss that he now wanted to share with Ariss.

He knew she was ready for more when her whimpers deepened, and she clutched the silken bedclothes in her fists. Kerrick kissed his way up her back until his cock pressed against her now-dripping cunt. So excited had he become he knew it wouldn't take long for him to climax. He didn't want to go too fast, so he didn't enter her, he just held steady at her passage while he teased his finger to her bottom.

"Do you want me to put it in you?" he asked playfully, knowing she wouldn't know if he was talking about his cock or his finger.

After a brief hesitation, she whispered, "Yes, put it in me."

Slowly, he slid his finger inside that tight channel, causing her to arch back in welcome. Her fearless response, her stunned willingness to try, amazed him. He longed to give her even more. Holding steady with his cock to her passage, he slipped his other hand around her hip to smooth his fingers over her clit. Ariss bucked her hips up and down, riding the alternate motions of his fingers.

Kerrick watched her hands grasping and releasing fistfuls of the bedclothes, signaling her pleasure and a clear desire for more.

"Are you a good student, Ariss?"

She nodded her head in time with the movements of her body, never missing a beat of the erotic dance she performed with his hands. At that moment, he wanted a mirror on the wall so that he could see her movements from the side. She must look spectacular with her body making sinuous waves, and her black tresses obscuring, then revealing her face. He could just picture her expression: her lips pursed, her eyes closed, and then her lips parting to emit tremulous moans of hunger.

"Tell me the dirty words you learned today."

Softly at first, she named them in whispers, but as he continued to torment her, her voice grew in volume until she chanted them proudly and almost musically. Then her tone took a darker edge as she hissed the words between clenched teeth. The words enveloped him, compelling him to the point he couldn't stand anymore. Without warning, he plunged his cock deep into her. He'd never heard a sweeter sound than Ariss' bellow of acceptance. The walls of her passage clutched him, the temperature blazing around his shaft. So snuggly did she grip, he wasn't able to thrust for a moment. She captured him and held him, possessing him and showing him that, yet again, he did not have total mastery over her. Pleased by her swift progress, he altered the stroke of his fingers, forcing her to shift her rhythm, which allowed him to thrust deeply in time to her uplifting bottom.

Together, they created a new pace. Each time she rose up, presenting her bottom to him, she would groan a sultry chant of encouragement. Each time he plunged deep, ramming his cock fully into her, he would growl an animalistic snarl of possession. Moving as one, they reached closer to the edge. When he fell over, climaxing and thrusting out of sync, she too succumbed, tumbling down into bliss as she lost her strength and collapsed on the bed.

Before they could even recover, four guards entered, yanked Kerrick to his feet, tossed his robe over him, and hauled him away. The last he saw of Ariss was her reaching out to him. And damn it to the nothingness, but he forgot to ask her what a kerrick was.

8

The two palace guards didn't touch her, but they ensured Ariss returned to her rooms without any detours. Once there, she shrugged off her robe and headed for the tub her *paratanist* had thoughtfully filled. Within moments, warm water frothy with bubbles came up to her chin. Angling the pillow behind her head, she closed her eyes and replayed her time with Kerrick.

Even though the water was wonderfully hot, she shivered at how he made her feel. Kerrick evoked such strong feelings, and not just physical sensations; he said things that made her crazy with desire. She tried to understand exactly what it was about him, but she couldn't put her finger on anything in particular. He was terribly good-looking, with a physique any man would be proud of and any woman would want to explore, but he was also intelligent, emotionally sensitive, wickedly clever, and possessed a wild sense of humor. He also had a smile that could charm anyone. In the end, she decided the sum of him aroused her.

Even when she thought she couldn't do as he wished, that

his desire was too far removed from what she could comfortably endure, he proved her wrong. All the dirty words she spoke went through her mind, each causing its own little ripple of excitement first in her brain, then in her body. She laughed a little at how in one night he'd changed her vocabulary forever.

A deeper tremor caused the bathwater to splash beyond the edge of the tub when she thought of his tongue . . . there. Never would she have even thought of such a thing, and when she realized his intent, she'd automatically pulled away, but then when the contact came . . . bliss. How could something so sinful be so pleasurable?

Her eyes blinked open at the thought, for who was the one deciding what was immoral? If anything that felt good was evil, then all of sex had her destined to spend eternity in the nothingness, right along with everyone else. So far, everything she'd done with Kerrick was pleasurable beyond words. Did that make it wrong?

Confused between what her parents preached and what she had now discovered on her own, Ariss decided she simply couldn't trust her parents, not in this matter or any other. Once again, they proved to her that they did not have her best interests at heart. Behind her on the table lay the proof of their selfishness, not to mention the shocking depth of their greed. Placing their own daughter in bondage bothered them not at all, for in their minds, she was their possession, and they could do as they pleased with her.

Ariss had hoped her *paratanist* would have removed the shameful thing, but he'd probably not known what to do with the dress, so there it stayed, spilled across the table in glaring silver condemnation.

Another series of shivers caused the bathwater to splash, but this was not a tremor of lust, this was a quiver borne of dread. How could her parents have done this to her? When she'd first seen the dress, Ariss had been delighted by its beauty but puzzled by its color. Her family color was yellow, her color as Harvester was black, so who would send her a silver dress when only the palace magistrate wore silver?

And that's when her heart sank. The small card announcing the gift only confirmed what she already knew. Ambo's skittery script praising her as his soon-to-be bondmate caused her stomach to clench and her eyes to water. Tears tumbled as she tore the note to shreds and tossed it away. Now she understood everything her parents had done in the last few cycles.

Coming to the palace wasn't about securing their place among the elite; taking residence here was the first step to getting Ariss into the Harvester competition. Ambo helped, because once she was the Harvester, her parents would force her to select him as her bondmate. He could have taken her as a mate without all of this subterfuge, but a magistrate needed a bondmate with prestige, and the only position with greater prestige than the Harvester was that of empress.

Once she bonded to Ambo, he would, in turn, reward her parents with access to those who could buy their products for use at the palace. Already they provided *estal* oil and the herb used to make *umer,* but her father often complained that the palace should buy his raw material to make *astle.* Out of everything the palace used, *astle* was the most profitable item, and the palace used the fabric in great quantities. Her father swore his thread was superior to all others, and finally he'd found a way to get the palace to buy from him.

All it cost him was his eldest daughter.

Ariss stepped from the tub and dried herself mechanically. Ambo was seventy seasons. All he could offer her was money and position; two things she cared nothing about. He couldn't love her, for he didn't know her, and gods only knew what he would do to her in his bed. Rumors of his disgusting practices of combining food and multiple partners had reached all the way to Felton. Once she'd seen him, in the flesh, she'd been immediately repulsed by his weight, but he only made matters worse when he picked his nose, wiping the mess on the side of his silver uniform. His sparse hair had been a tangled mess atop his head, and his furtive eyes had crawled over her, undressing her, molesting her, before finally settling on her breasts. All through the brief encounter, where he ostensibly conversed with her parents, he'd kept his eyes riveted to her chest. Ariss had then understood why her mother insisted she wear the low-cut yellow gown. During the brief chat, she stood there feeling like meat on display in the butcher's window. Several times, Ambo licked his lips, as if slurping back the drool that would surely fall if he did not mop up.

Ariss tried to imagine the bonding ceremony; her resplendent in the silver dress, its color matching her cool gray eyes, and then Ambo, his uniform wrinkled, covered in dried snot swipes, his florid face wet with sweat. She covered her mouth with her hand to hold back a sob. Almost of its own accord, her hand trailed down to the necklace. Against her palm, the stone felt warm and heavy, reminding her that her fate was not sealed. If she dared, she could change the world and avoid the trap her parents set for her.

Across the room, her ghostly reflection mirrored her stance, shocking her with the dejected shape of her pose. Automatically, she straightened her shoulders. She wasn't beaten yet. Standing around crying wasn't going to help matters one bit. Determined, Ariss tossed her towel by the tub, slipped on her robe, then settled herself at the table. Again, her *paratanist* had thoughtfully left a small snack for her under covered platters. He said he had served the last ten Harvesters, and she believed him, because he anticipated even the smallest of her needs.

She selected a bowl of creamed *nicla*, a large portion of seared *aket*, and several slices of dark bread. To persevere through this challenge, she would need her strength. What she had to do was not something she ever would have deliberately chosen for herself, but she selected the path that was the lesser of two evils.

No matter what, she couldn't bond to Ambo. Now that Kerrick had shown her the unimaginable pleasures of the flesh, she couldn't bear to even think of trying such things with Ambo. She'd rather toss herself from the balcony than suffer one night in his bed.

However, her other option would be the downfall of an innocent. One who didn't even understand what her true duty was. Kerrick's ignorance certainly *would* hurt him. Ariss felt awful about taking advantage of him, but what else could she do? She had two choices, neither one honorable, but this choice at least gave her the possibility of having a successful bonding. Kerrick would be furious when he found out, but she hoped that with time, she could prove to him that they could work together. She hoped and prayed that maybe he would understand.

Ariss knew her parents would not relent, and if she defied them by choosing a man other than Ambo, they would likely reveal the subterfuge in getting her selected as the Harvester, which would end in her execution. Despite her protests, none would believe she had entered the contest without prior knowledge of her assured success. Ambo would likely walk away unscathed, as he had in several other scandals. Ambo had a knack for escaping punishment for his misdeeds, probably because he had been the magistrate for so long that he knew secrets about everyone. This, in turn, made the voting body of the elite reluctant to cast their ballot for his inquisition, for what if those secrets should inadvertently tumble out during the harsh questioning? In that defiant scenario, only Ariss herself would suffer. She shook her head, knowing that was not the path for her.

However, if she followed the other path, her parents would have no choice but to accept the inevitable outcome. How could they protest if she fulfilled the extent of her true duty? For surely, they didn't know the Harvester obligations had changed so drastically, or they never would have forced her into this position in the first place. No matter what they said, the populace would not listen to them, for Ariss would have given the people the ultimate goal of the Harvest prophecy: a true *paratanist.*

Chur Zenge had turned the prophecy back to its most ancient obligation: a child born of the male and female Harvesters, and carried directly by the female Harvester. Her and Kerrick's child, once grown, would rule beside the empress and have as much power as she. Out of all the rules, rites, and rituals, this was the definitive purpose. The ancients had believed this child would be strong, beautiful, and possess godlike powers.

Ariss took a deep breath, worried to have so much heaped upon the child she hadn't even created yet, but who knew what truth there was to the prophecy? Perhaps there was some magical aspect that she did not understand. Her and Kerrick combined might be bigger than each apart. Somehow, she doubted that, but she refused to let that stop her, for her only other alternative was to bond to Ambo.

Curious as to where the *paratanists* had come from prior to this return to the most ancient way, Ariss had spent several evenings pouring over the Harvester tome she'd been given during her inauguration. There, in a rather nondescript passage about the benefits of daily bathing, she had discovered the awful truth. Prior to this Harvest, the male and female Harvesters had their sperm and eggs combined, then placed in a *tanist.* Such sounded innocuous enough, but then, they ritualistically killed the poor woman to retrieve the issue, which were isolated from society and became *paratanists.* Ariss' very own servant would have come from such a terrible scenario. She wondered if he knew the truth of his birth, then decided not to tell him if he didn't. Telling him served no purpose other than hurting him. In this instance, ignorance was truly bliss.

Ariss sighed. Kerrick seemed as oblivious as everyone else did about the new duty placed upon her. She had not known until she'd asked her *paratanist* about the stone around her neck. In even more reverent tones than the acolyte, he explained that the *parastone* would change color when she became pregnant, thus foretelling the coming of the *paratanist,* the first true and proper *paratanist* in thousands of seasons.

Her initial shock fell away to furious speculation. If she became pregnant, she would automatically be bonded to Kerrick. No longer would she have to worry about Ambo. Together, she and Kerrick would raise their child. What would happen to that child in the future was of profound importance to her. She did not want her child used as she had been, as a political tool, but all that she would deal with later. To save herself, she must fully mate with her counterpart.

Kerrick enjoyed the mating, as most men would, but he didn't consider all the ramifications of the word *mate.* Another pang of guilt assaulted her conscience. She should tell him the truth. Ariss was not one for lies and subterfuge, for she felt she was doing to him what her parents had done to her, but she wondered what good confessing would do. It would ease her conscience, but would it really matter? They didn't have a choice; they had to mate. If he chose not to mate with her, they would punish him, and probably extract his semen, anyway. One way or another, they would try to impregnate her.

Her *paratanist* wouldn't discuss exactly how they would punish Kerrick, but his silence made her think it would be something horrific. Essentially, Kerrick would be refusing to carry out the Harvester duties. If another man wished to mate with her, he simply had to fight and kill Kerrick, and he would become the Harvester. Ariss didn't want that to happen. She didn't want Kerrick hurt.

"Oh, who am I fooling?"

She wanted Kerrick.

Every insufferable, arrogant, and so blatantly self-assured-it-bordered-on-delusional bit of him. Something in him called to her so strongly she couldn't deny it. Question it, yes, and endlessly, yes, but refute it? No. Besides, if she refused the new Harvester, she would suffer a similar fate. They wouldn't kill her, but they would either force her to mate or exile her, and then replace her with the next woman in line. The magistrate himself would burn a brand of shame on her forehead and then send her to the frozen wasteland of Rhemna.

Therefore, she and Kerrick must mate. Of the nine times they must mate, there was always a chance she would fulfill the prophecy and conceive. If she didn't, Ariss didn't know what she would do. Her gaze drifted to the balcony. Was it high enough? If she jumped, she wanted to make sure the drop would kill her, not just wound or cripple her. Deliberately, she pulled herself from that line of thought; not all was lost yet. She still had time to fulfill the duty placed upon her slender shoulders.

Once she finished her small meal, she pushed away from the table and settled into bed. Sleep eluded her. Curled on her side, she held the stone in her hand, pressing it firmly against her skin. Ariss fell asleep praying that when she awoke, the black would have faded to leave a clear stone behind.

Morning came, filling her room with dazzling brightness. Her *paratanist* had silently entered and opened the heavy drapes that would have blocked the twin suns. After several days of clouds, *Tandalsul* emerged, bouncing brightness off the fresh layer of snow with blinding intensity. Before she'd even pried her eyes open all the way, she leapt from bed and rushed to the mirror.

Disappointment slumped her shoulders when the stone remained black. Seven more times for them to mate. Seven more chances for her to become pregnant. She knew how fragile pregnancy could be. Women sometimes waited a lifetime without success.

Her frown faded slowly when she realized she might have many more chances if she dared to be a bad girl. Kerrick had made her swear to meet him, and she'd automatically refused the idea because she didn't want to be caught and perhaps punished. But now, if doing so increased her chances of pregnancy, how could she say no?

The only trick would be in eluding the guards. She wasn't certain, but she believed they lurked near her rooms to ensure she didn't leave and none but her *paratanist* entered. Getting past them would require skills that she didn't have. As she considered the frozen land outside her rooms, a plan formed in her mind.

"Well, he said he wanted me to be a bad girl. I'll show him how sinful I can be."

9

Kerrick expelled a great whoosh of air when he hit the mat again. He'd lost count of how many times Sterlave had knocked him off his feet.

"You must anticipate your opponent's moves." Sterlave twirled the *dantaratase* in his hands, then quickly tossed the slender staff from hand to hand. "Get up."

Using his *dantaratase* to balance his exhausted body, Kerrick pulled himself to his feet. "Can't we go back to bare-handed wrestling?"

Sterlave scoffed. "You already know how to do that. Training is about improving on skills you don't have." He feinted the staff left, then right, then attacked on the left. Kerrick blocked the blow but barely and clumsily. "Clearly, you don't have any skill with this weapon at all."

Offended by yet another rude remark, Kerrick moved his staff from hand to hand, then tried a great, sweeping arc at Sterlave's feet. At the last moment, Kerrick lifted the staff and poked Sterlave in the belly.

"Better!" Sterlave said, brushing aside the thrust of the staff.

"Just when I thought you were hopeless, you surprise me and actually land a blow." Before Kerrick could smile proudly, Sterlave rushed on, "A tiny blow that wouldn't hurt a child, but still, it's better than nothing."

Kerrick wanted to wipe the smirk off Sterlave's face. He wanted to throw the *dantaratase* on the floor and fight barehanded. Kerrick controlled his anger because he knew that if he let it out, he would have no control at all. Flailing wildly at his target would only open himself to attack. That had been the first lesson Sterlave taught him.

"Never approach an opponent in anger. When you are unfocused, you give him all your power. Approach only when your head is clear and your body is calm. Only in this way can you prevail." Sterlave had delivered his little speech over Kerrick's gasping body. On his back, in agony on the mat, Kerrick had stayed there, listening, hating his handler, but acknowledging the truth of his words. Kerrick hadn't said anything only because he'd had no breath left with which to speak.

Even now, his pride still smarted from Sterlave's blows. With careful precision, Kerrick continued sparring with Sterlave, who clearly held back from his full power with the slender staff. As the day progressed, Kerrick managed to block blows with greater accuracy and landed a few more. His strikes lacked any real power, but at least he was making progress. And the mocking of the recruits had died down considerably.

The snickering had reached a peak the first day when he'd been working with the double club; no matter how hard Kerrick tried, he simply couldn't swing the *avenyet* with the same precision as Sterlave. Blow after blow to his padded midsection resulted in louder and louder chuckles from the recruits. Dark glares from Sterlave lowered the volume, but even he couldn't stop them entirely. That's when they'd switched to barehanded wrestling; there, Kerrick showed off the true power of his body, and those who were laughing stopped. When they'd grown bored and drifted away, Sterlave had switched to another weapon.

Day after day, Kerrick made minute progress. At night, he suffered his humiliations by thinking of Ariss and the next time he would meet her in the mating room. At least in sex he wasn't a clueless buffoon. There, he knew exactly what he was doing. He couldn't wait to indulge the very depth of his needs upon her. Already he planned for the night when he could take her in his arms again. Ariss utterly amazed him. Open, willing, eager even, she embraced him with a passion that astounded him.

A blow to the side from the *dantaratase* pulled Kerrick out of his thoughts and back to the training room. Repeatedly, he and Sterlave crossed staffs until Kerrick's forearm ached from dampening the vibrations.

Sweat covered Kerrick, dripping down into his eyes, but he shook it off, determined to knock Sterlave to the mat at least once. When he saw his chance, he took it, swinging his staff in a fast and furious arc at Sterlave's feet. To his shock, Sterlave jumped at the last moment and blocked the forward momentum of the swing with his staff. He then flipped Kerrick's staff up, which, in turn, knocked Kerrick to the mat. Kerrick didn't even bother to get up; he just rolled to his back, panting weakly as he again considered the heavy timbers that held up the ceiling.

Sterlave's face popped into view. "You never had a chance." Sterlave tilted his head to the side. "Did you know that right before you attack, you tighten one eye down and lift the brow of the other? A clearer message you could not send to an opponent."

Kerrick had started to believe that Sterlave possessed some extrasensory ability, for he always knew what Kerrick would do. Now Kerrick understood that he'd been inadvertently conveying his every move with his facial expressions. He would have rolled over and bashed his head into the mat saying "stupid" several times, but he didn't have the energy.

Sterlave smiled. "I know my method seems harsh, but I doubt you will ever again forget to comport your face during training from this moment on."

Kerrick nodded, knowing that he would always remember to keep careful control over his entire body during sparring events.

Sterlave offered out his hand and Kerrick gratefully accepted. He pulled him to his feet, then clapped him on the back. "Rest up, for tomorrow we start with the *avenyet.*"

Even though he wanted to groan, he didn't. Quickly, Kerrick learned not to give away anything he was feeling inside, because an opponent could use simply everything against him.

With as much dignity as he could, he made his way back to his rooms. His four guards shadowed him at a discreet distance, whispering on things Kerrick couldn't hear and didn't care to. He speculated they discussed his skill, or lack thereof, with the weapons, and he'd had enough snide remarks from Sterlave.

Once ensconced inside his rooms, he pulled the cord for his servant. With her help, he bathed, ate, and then dismissed her for the night. Kerrick didn't want an audience for his practice session. Out of the closet, he pulled the slender staff. One way or another he was going to master his lessons and prove that he was worthy of being the Harvester. Kerrick was in the middle of an overhanded twirl strike when the main door opened. Curious, he placed his staff upright, tip against the floor. His *paratanist* entered, then closed the door.

He set the staff aside and straightened his loincloth. Kerrick knew he should be used to his servant's odd silence by now, but he still found her speak-only-when-spoken-to stance more than a bit disconcerting. At times, he felt her gaze on him, as if she considered him in some way that was not entirely complimentary. Ever since she'd asked him about his desire to mate, her speculative consideration seemed to occur at greater frequency. Gods knew what she was thinking. When he asked, she mumbled quietly to herself and hurried away.

"Did you forget something?" he asked.

Fana walked toward him. She stopped a handspan away, stood silently for a moment, her head lowered, then dropped to her knees.

"What the—" he began, but cut himself off when she reached for his loincloth. She tugged on the fabric, making her intentions pretty damn clear. "Whoa!" Madly, he clutched at the slippery *astle*. "Oh, no, no, you don't need to do that."

His mind whirled. She'd told him she was forbidden and he really had no desire to find out if that were true. For the first time in his life, he wanted one woman. The knowledge shocked him, for he'd made no official declaration to Ariss, but his gut reaction was that he would be with her, and her alone.

Now he was stunned on two levels: one, that Fana had apparently decided to give sex a whirl; and two, that his visceral reaction was to be true to Ariss. Never in his life had he been faithful to any woman. Three times he'd been forsworn, and three times the bonding never happened because he couldn't keep his penis in his pants.

"But I thought you wanted me to be a bad girl?"

It took a moment for the voice to register through his panic. "Ariss?" Abruptly, he stopped struggling to keep his clothing on. One sharp yank and she had him bare. With the timelessness of a dream, she tilted her head back until the cowl hood fell away. Cool gray eyes met his. After flashing him an insolent smile, she parted her lips and slipped them around his cock, drawing him into the heat of her mouth. Having her do this to him while she was dressed as a *paratanist* was the most arousing and unbelievably kinky thing he'd done in ages. Possibly ever. It was like throwing down with an acolyte in the temple.

"You naughty, naughty girl."

Slowly, she twirled her tongue around the tip while cupping his shaft with her palm. Clearly, she'd been thinking about doing this to him, because she tried new and wonderful techniques that had him hard within moments. However, what really aroused him were all the wild fantasies running through his mind. Ariss was the vixen and the virgin with her devastating, sultry innocence. On the verge of an intense climax, he pulled back. He didn't want the evening to end so abruptly.

Concerned, she glanced up at him. "Did I do it wrong?"

"Gods, no." He laughed. "You're doing it a little too well."

With a smile, she pushed the hood off her head until it spilled around her shoulders. Somehow, the bland beige that should have looked horrible on her didn't. She seemed almost regal as she knelt there on the floor, her eyes shining and her lips wet and slightly parted.

"How did you manage this?" Not that he really cared. He was so happy to see her, she had barely started to answer when he scooped her up into his arms and kissed the breath right out of her.

"Stop!" she said, playfully pushing him back. "This won't be any fun at all if I'm not breathing."

"So you came here for fun, did you?" With a few strides, he tossed her on his bed, then leapt next to her, taking care not to injure his erect penis. Rolling over, he framed her face with his hands. Finally, he had something he knew he was good at. Confidence filled him. He might fumble with weapons, but he never fumbled in bed.

"You are an amazing woman." Softly, he kissed her nose, her lips, and her chin, utterly impressed with her creative problem solving. "How did you even think of this?" he asked, running his hands along the *paratanist* robe.

Twice he'd tried to meet her, but both times his guards stopped him, marching him back to his rooms with unrequited lust. As he had predicted, Kerrick became ever more intimate with his right hand. Quickly, the romance faded and he began to resent his lover, Mr. Fist. Sure, he was always there, but he only knew one position, and he didn't kiss.

"The idea was the easy part," Ariss said, working the tiny clasps of the robe apart. "I noticed that no one ever paid my *paratanist* any mind. He could wander the halls of the palace without question." She paused for a moment, denying him more than a glimpse of her upper breasts. "Did you know that they are untouchable? To even brush against a *paratanist* accidentally could result in death."

Kerrick didn't know that, but he remembered how Ambo cautioned him not to touch his servant. "During my inauguration when Ambo presented me with Fana, he made a point of informing me I wasn't to touch her."

"At least yours gave you a name; mine insists I call him *paratanist*." Ariss shook her head, then continued, "The hard part was securing his robe."

Kerrick had a sudden flash of her servant tied up naked in her rooms. He frowned. "What did you have to do to get his robe?"

One sleek brow rose over a cool gray eye. "Are you accusing me of something untoward?" She batted her lashes with teasing innocence.

Frowning, he considered then rejected several answers. In the end, he decided silence was the best response.

With a laugh, Ariss said, "I very cleverly spilled something on his robe, and in my genuine sorrow, I followed him to the supply room so he could retrieve another. Where, of course, I snagged one for myself."

"Clever girl." In a hurry to see more of her exquisite skin, he attempted to help her with the clasps, but his fingers were too big and clumsy. He did his best not to let his frustration show; he'd never had a problem undressing a woman before, no matter what she wore.

Ariss pushed his hands away. "Naughty girl, bad girl, clever girl; you realize I'm not a girl?" She finally got the last clasp separated but didn't remove the robe as she waited for his answer.

Considering her curves, he said, "Believe me, I know." He winked and gave her a practiced leer. "But bad woman doesn't sound nearly as sexy as bad girl. See, the second implies innocence corrupted."

"Well, that explains it." She lifted up so she could slide the robe off her shoulders, revealing that she wore nothing below, nothing but that peculiar black stone necklace.

"Should I call you a bad boy?" she asked mischievously.

Distracted by her lovely form, he hesitated before answering, "Most definitely." He managed to refrain from pouncing on her in a state of high lust. Kissing his way across her shoulder, he murmured, "You should do everything you can to corrupt me even more."

Impishly, she stopped him from dipping his head to her breast. "Why would I waste my time?" Lifting his face to hers, she dropped her gaze to his erection, and said, "I do believe you are quite fully corrupted."

With a laugh, he fingered the *paratanist* robe lying on the bed. "Maybe next time you can steal an acolyte's robe. Think of the games we could play with that."

Her mouth dropped into a perfect little O of shock. When she recovered herself, she flashed him a disapproving frown and said, "You *are* a bad boy."

"The worst," he agreed, sliding his hand up to cup her breast and gently tweak her nipple. After considering her response, he blurted, "I love when you do that," then immediately regretted what he'd said. Never, ever did a practiced seducer of women use that particular word in the bedchamber. He was making mistake after mistake, almost as if he'd never done this before.

Perhaps his ineptitude in the training rooms was rubbing off on his other skills.

"When I do what?" she asked, warily considering his face.

Smoothly, he dropped the panic from his gaze, kissed her nose, and said, "When I do something you enjoy, like giving your sweet caramel nipple a little twist, your eyes go very wide with shock, then narrow into speculative slits of encouragement."

Without a thought, she denied his claim with a sharp, "I do not." She practically *tisked* at him while shaking her head in denial.

He rubbed her nipple between his forefinger and thumb, eliciting the exact same response. Watching the pleasure surge through her caused the strangest reaction in his body; somehow, her enjoyment literally became his.

Once she realized the truth, her brows lowered and she frowned, but she wouldn't meet his gaze.

"What?" he asked teasingly, glad she hadn't noticed his slip in using the word *love*. He'd thought he'd fully banished that particular troublesome word from his vocabulary, but apparently not. "Are you upset that you do it, or that I noticed?" He read more than just Ariss' physical response; he could literally read her scent. Pleasure erupted from her flesh in a burst of *valasta*, which only made him want to give her more. "Lovely Ariss, you work so hard to keep your face immobile, probably so you don't convey anything, but when I surprise you, your emotions are very clearly displayed."

Her fear was genuine, probably borne of the same fear he'd had in the training rooms, because when someone could read your true feelings, they could use them to hurt you. Instantly, he understood and sought to reassure her.

"I would never use what I know to hurt you, Ariss. Only to give you even more pleasure." He swore it directly from his heart. Carefully, he lowered his lips to her breast. Capturing her nipple in his mouth, he placed a soft kiss to the straining bit of flesh.

For a moment, she tensed as strongly as she had in the mating room during their first encounter. Ever so softly, he continued to tease her, not rushing, simply enjoying the feel and taste of her, easing her with his meanderings. No way would he rush her now, not when she'd come so far in becoming the woman she was destined to be.

Sighing, she released the tension in her body and whispered, "I trust you."

Fear trickled in like an unwelcome pest. She trusted him? No woman could trust him beyond his fleeting desires. Kerrick continued to tease his lips, teeth, and tongue over her body, but his mind was a universe away. Trust was the first stepping-stone to danger. Once she trusted him, she would come to care for him; then she would make the inevitable slide into loving him.

Kerrick couldn't let Ariss fall in love with him.

He couldn't return her affections, not fully, not in the way she deserved. He wanted to transform her into a woman of passion, but not a woman who was in love with him. In order for him to succeed in securing the position of palace magistrate, he had to be the Harvester for more than one season. He had to prove himself not only a man of raw physical power, but he had to capture the fleeting fancies of the elite. Charming them, cajoling them, creating an almost mythical persona for them to *ooh* and *ah* over was the only way he would succeed.

Kerrick knew he was charismatic, but he needed more than one season to ingratiate himself with those in power. He couldn't wait for the first official palace function so he could begin the laborious process of securing their favor. No matter what he had to do, he would swallow his pride and do it. From fawning over ill-bred children, to praising passable goods, to seducing the fat, the ugly, or even the pathetically badly dressed—he would do it all to obtain the power of the magistrate. Kerrick vowed to remain the Harvester until he wrested the position from Ambo. Then, Kerrick's father would pay.

Just thinking about the challenges to come caused his erection to fade. No matter what he did or how he turned his thoughts, he couldn't get it back. Embarrassed, he moved away from Ariss. Never, ever had he lost his desire in the midst of a lusty romp. He didn't blame anyone but himself. He couldn't stop thinking about the bloodlust in the eyes of the other recruits. Given a chance, they would tear his limbs from his body and beat him to death with his own appendages. Turning his back on Ariss, he sat on the edge of the bed, his legs flung over the side, his toes digging into the thick carpet.

He didn't see her, but he felt her sit up as her movements tugged the bedclothes taut from the counterpoint of his butt.

She didn't speak and neither did he. What could he say? She had to have felt him go soft. He wasn't about to tell her the truth. No woman wanted to hear that her lover was just as frightened and vulnerable as she was. Women expected men to be men. To be strong and sure and so secure that nothing broke their stride. He'd always known that he wasn't real to his lovers; he was the sum total of all their perceived notions of masculinity. To date, he'd always played the role well. The difference was that this time he was gambling with his life.

In all the dangerous sports he played, he never felt vulnerable, for he always knew the risks before taking part. At any time, he could withdraw with no repercussions. Well, perhaps a bit of damaged pride; but in this, the game of the Harvester, he'd leapt in without fully understanding the rules. He simply couldn't back out. He had to fight or die. Kerrick exhaled a slow, deep breath and slumped his shoulders.

Silently, Ariss slid off the bed. From the corner of his eye, he watched her pull the robe on and redo the tiny clasps. He made no move to stop her until he saw the tears held tightly in check spill over and track down her cheeks. The truth was written all over her face; she thought his lack of interest was her fault.

His shoulders slumped even farther. He might be a selfish man, but even he could not hurt her newly forming sexual self-esteem like that.

"Ariss, wait."

Lifting her nose, she strode toward the door. "Don't bother. You'll have another chance to humiliate me at the beginning of the next cycle."

She was fast, but he was faster. As she wrapped her hand around the doorknob to twist it open, he covered her hand with his. "I'm sorry." Two words he rarely said. Sometimes he might think them, but he didn't often speak them aloud, especially not to a woman. One of his rules of seduction was that he had to be willing to watch each woman walk away. Not apologizing for a real or perceived slight was a guaranteed way to get his lover to leave. If she refused, she'd silently agreed to take the relationship on his terms.

Ariss yanked her hand away and took a proud step back. "I don't want to play your game." Anger placed two high red marks upon her cheeks and turned her tears to glistening fury. Her black hair tumbled around her shoulders, tangling up in the edges of the robe's hood.

"Game?" he asked, yanking his loincloth off the floor and wrapping it around his hips. The last thing he wanted was to have an argument while he stood with his penis dangling about.

"Why else would you make me go through all of this, then cast me aside? I'm just a game to you!" She gritted her teeth and took a hissing indrawn breath. "That's it, isn't it? You had to make the cold one grovel. You just had to prove to yourself that I would risk everything to slip into your bed." She shook her head in a gesture that said she was angrier with herself than with him. "I hope it was worth it, because this will be the last time." She pressed her lips together, cutting off her speech. With jerky motions, she gathered her hair and tossed it down the back of her robe, then yanked the hood over her head.

"It's not a game!" Kerrick hadn't realized how irritated he was until he bellowed. Rage shivered through him, seeking an outlet.

10

Ariss flinched back at Kerrick's outburst. With one big step, he advanced on her, capturing her arms with his massive hands. Rage caused him to tremble and turned his forest green eyes dangerously dark. Fear caused her to shake within his grip. Mesmerized, she watched a lone bead of sweat tumble down from his forehead to his temple. Even with her quick breaths, she smelled and tasted the sharp, bitter tang of his fury.

Baffled, she held still and wondered why he was so enraged. He'd been playing a game with her, not the other way around. Why was he so upset she'd caught him out? It was almost as if he stole what should be hers; she should be the one fuming and snarling, not him. Quite suddenly, she realized she was alone with a man twice her size. A man strong enough to do anything he wanted to her. A man who stood blocking the only exit. . . .

He drew a deep breath and shut his eyes, forcefully calming himself. His grip on her upper arms lessened slightly. Ariss stood very still, unwilling to do anything to infuriate him anew. From this angle, the ceiling crystals scattered light across his short blond hair, causing it to glow, almost as if the gods themselves bathed him with their glory.

With all her might, Ariss prayed that they would reach inside and calm him where she could not. Just as quickly, she realized they would not hear her calls, for she had debased herself with her licentious behavior. Apparently, her parents had been right all along and lust only lowered her. Why would Kerrick want her anymore when he'd already thoroughly had her? Just as her mother always said, "Men are about the hunting, not the capturing. Once they capture you, there is nothing more for them to do but sate their lust and walk away." Byss had tapped her wrist where her mark of bonding, a small yellow dot, showed her commitment to Radox and Yellow House. "Bear the mark first, then enter the bedchamber."

Of course, Ariss was at a distinct disadvantage in that she had no choice but to submit to Kerrick, for that's what her duty demanded. She winced when she realized she never should have come to him; he should have walked through the nothingness to get to her. She wasn't much of a capture if she willingly came to the hunter. Ariss didn't have the luxury of berating herself for her foolishness, not when he was so irate and so near.

She wanted to move farther away from him but didn't dare. Anything she did might attract his attention and for the moment, he stood very still with his eyes closed. It was best that he remain that way. His grip on her arms loosened a fraction more, but clearly, he had no intention of letting her go. She breathed as silently as she could, pursing her lips together and down so that even her breath wouldn't touch him.

When he squeezed almost delicately, she startled, lifting her gaze to his face. His eyes were open now, considering her as if he'd never seen her. Ariss stilled under his perusal, not even daring to lift her nose in practiced disdain. Deep within his eyes burned something she couldn't identify. Whatever it was had caused this entire mess.

"I'm sorry, Ariss." He caressed her upper arms tentatively, as if he were afraid that if he loosened his grip entirely, she would bolt. "None of this is your fault."

"I'd like to leave now," she whispered, terrified that she would stir him to anger again, but more afraid to stay within his rooms.

He winced at her words, lowering his head and breaking the intense eye-to-eye contact. "Let me explain first."

"I'll listen if you take your hands off me."

He let go and took a step back, firmly blocking the exit.

His hands left two warm, moist spots on her sleeves that she rubbed away. She straightened her robe, snuggling the hood around her neck. For a long moment, they stood at impasse, him barricading the door with his body and her eyeing the slab of Onic wood with obvious intent.

"None of this is a game to me." His voice was hollow, empty, almost devoid of emotion as if everything that had been simmering within only a moment ago abruptly drained away.

The fear she felt vanished, leaving behind a curious confusion.

"I wanted you here so badly, and then when you arrive, I make a mess of things." He glanced up, capturing her gaze for a brief moment before he looked away again. If he had longer hair, he would have hidden his eyes behind it, but the short locks kept his face fully exposed. "I wasn't upset with you, but this." Kerrick grasped the center of a long staff that leaned against the wall. As he brought it near, he fumbled, his fingers failing to find purchase, causing the staff to slip from his grasp. "Damn it to the nothingness, but this is what has aggravated me to no end!" He continued to fumble with it, his hand never quite gripping it firmly, almost as if someone had coated the entire length with oil.

Before it could fall to the floor, Ariss reached out, grasping the slender rod in one hand.

Kerrick's mouth fell open in shock. "How did you . . . ?"

Spinning it horizontally, she gripped the wooden staff firmly in the center, spacing her hands about the width of her shoulders. "It's similar to a *fleed*." At his frown, she added, "In Felton, the servants use a stick like this to herd the *astles*."

He frowned dubiously as if she were playing some cruel joke on him. "I thought *astle* was a kind of fabric?" Suspicion turned his voice bitter.

Having been on the receiving end of several spiteful jests, Ariss understood his distrust. "*Astle* is a fabric, but it comes from an animal, an *astle*, which has a long, silky coat that generates the fibers used to make the fabric." Ariss rocked the staff from side to side as if gently tapping the bottoms of the six-legged animals. "They are docile creatures, but they can wander great distances in search of roots and bulbs."

He watched her moving the staff with nothing short of pure envy. "Why don't you just keep them in pens and feed them directly?"

"If they are confined, they go bald, then die. Either they roam free or they cannot exist. It's one of the reasons why *astle* is so expensive." Something about that had always intrigued Ariss, causing her to feel a kinship with the pudgy little animals. Frustration had always met her father's efforts to find a way to imprison the poor beasts. The mindless beings had succeeded in eluding his grasp where she could not; she alternately admired and resented them. "When I was young, I would help gather them up for the harvest." With a sigh, she tapped the staff uselessly to the sides. "But once I got older, my mother refused to let me participate anymore." Lifting her nose in imitation of her mother, she mimicked Byss' haughty tone: "Proper young ladies do not indulge in such improper pastimes."

Kerrick laughed at her display.

"My mother thought my time was better spent learning dances, and musical instruments, and the fine art of flirting."

Hours of sitting in front of a mirror, watching her own reflection, washed through Ariss in a slow tedium. "But I also had to learn how to put a lusty young man in his place with a practiced frown." She flashed Kerrick her most proficient pouting frown of disapproval.

He clutched his hand to his chest as if mortally wounded. "That would certainly put me in my place."

His playful display touched her heart, but she had a feeling nothing would put Kerrick in his place.

They blinked at each other, suddenly aware that all the intense emotions had dissipated. They stood talking as if they were friends and not two people who just moments ago had been embroiled in a terribly intense situation.

"Why does it matter that you don't know how to handle this staff?" Rather than handing it back, Ariss continued to move it slowly back and forth, loving the feel of it in her hands and the peaceful memories it evoked.

"Because without that skill, I'm a dead man."

Ariss literally felt her heart lurch in her chest. "What do you mean?"

"If I want to remain the Harvester, I have to fight any recruit who issues me a challenge."

Relief flooded her, but she did her best not to let it show. If she fulfilled her duty, Kerrick wouldn't have to worry about remaining the Harvester. Once she was pregnant, they would bond, and the recruits would battle amongst themselves for the right to be the next Harvester. Somehow, though, she didn't think that's what Kerrick wanted to hear.

"What if I taught you?" she asked softly, expecting him to laugh and dismiss her proposal without a thought. What man let a woman teach him anything? Her father certainly didn't think women had anything to offer, other than children and a place to ease his passions. Time after time, Radox had made his feelings on the subject quite clear: Women had their place, and that was in the corner, quiet, until he told them what to do. He'd made his feeling so clear, in fact, that Ariss had no idea what possessed her to make such an offer to Kerrick.

"Would you?"

Stunned by his earnest expression, and the almost pleading tone to his voice, Ariss found words had escaped her, so she nodded, tugging her tangled hair up from the back of the robe. Moving to his side, she took a deep breath and planted the staff tip into the thick carpet, wondering where to start. When an idea came to her, she blushed deeply.

"What?" he asked, leaning near enough so that she could smell the tang of his fresh sweat. It really wasn't fair that he always looked and smelled wonderful. She spent hours perfecting her casual look where he just tumbled out of bed. She sighed. So it would probably always be. She better get used to it now if they were going to spend a lifetime together.

"I watched you fumble with this, almost as if you didn't know how to hold it, but when," she took a deep breath to steady herself, and lowered her voice by several degrees, "but when you touched yourself for me, your hands were sure, your attention riveted."

After a very long pause, where she didn't dare look at him, he asked, "Are you suggesting that I hold the staff as if it were my penis?"

Blushing furiously, she nodded. After a long note of silence, she glanced up at his face.

One eyebrow rose along with the edge of his mouth as he considered the staff that was several heads taller than he was. With a lascivious wink, he murmured, "You know, that might make me a little insecure."

Baffled, Ariss blinked in confusion, then rolled her eyes when she understood. "Be thankful your penis isn't that long. If it were, some enterprising soul would have captured you and sold you as a novelty slave to the empress."

His laughter surged a thrill of pleasure straight from her ears to her heart. In many ways, Kerrick was almost the exact opposite of her father, and most of the men in Felton. Even in a dire situation, he found humor. Kerrick laughed easily and openly, embracing himself, foibles and all. Ariss longed to find that effortless self-acceptance.

Kerrick wrapped his hand around the staff with practiced confidence, stroking his fist lightly up and down the smooth wood. Mesmerized, Ariss simply watched, her mind back on the first time they had been together in the mating room. Watching him handle himself had thoroughly aroused her. Something about the power in his arm, his focus on his own pleasure, the way his lids settled low, giving him an almost sinister appearance.

"I can do that for you again, if you'd like," he offered, leaning close so that his warm breath wafted against her ear.

She shivered and drew the hood closer around her neck and face. "I thought you wanted to learn?"

He made a small *um-hum* of agreement, then twirled the staff. "Well, bless Behdera's testicles!" Smoothly, he shifted the rod from hand to hand, his grip sure, the movement of his fingers flawless.

Ariss backed away, giving him room, which he used to swing and twirl the staff with graceful precision. He fought with a shadow opponent, twirling and thrusting his staff with movements that were almost like a dance. She marveled at the change that came over him. His smile was so wide it transformed his face. Each move he made caused his muscles to bunch and flex below his taut skin. The crystals danced light over the sprinkling of golden hair that covered his form. When he held just right, he literally glowed. She could not take her eyes off him. As she watched his hands, she felt her passage weep to feel those talented digits working so earnestly upon her tender flesh. At least now, she knew his seeming lack of interest had nothing to do with her; he was consumed with his inability to work this weapon. Of course, he was now fully focused on that and oblivious to her. With a sigh, she settled herself on an armless chair pushed back against the wall.

For a long time, Kerrick practiced, hardly aware that she watched. When he did notice her, he proudly showed her a complicated series of twirls and thrusts, and then set the staff aside. He moved in front of her, causing her to strain her neck to look up, but only for a moment, because he dropped to his knees, cupping her hand in his.

"You," he said, kissing the palm of her hand, "are the most amazing woman." Reverently, he lifted his intense gaze, pinning her where she sat. "You realize you have saved my life?"

She honestly didn't think she had, but if he wished to think it, who was she to say otherwise? "There are many ways to show me gratitude. Ways that don't involve words." She couldn't believe she spoke so boldly, but she wasn't sure how else to get him to wrench off her heavy robe and finish what he started earlier.

Wantonly, he teased his tongue to the center of her palm.

Melting at the thought of his tongue making the same movements along her body, she sighed, and tugged at the clasps of her robe.

Kerrick let go of her hand and pushed the edge of her robe up, exposing the length of her legs. Once he pooled the bulk of the fabric in her lap, he teased his fingers along the sensitive flesh of her calves, the tender back of her legs, then around so that his palms rested on her knees. Leaning forward, he placed a delicate kiss between them, then gently pushed them apart, all the while staring right into her eyes.

His gaze was so intense he almost stole her breath. Ariss grasped the back of the chair to hold steady. Against her hands, she felt two loops. When she glanced down, she saw two thick animal-hide strips on each side of the chair back. As Kerrick worked his way up her inner thighs, one luscious kiss at a time, she explored the curious devices, trying to determine their use.

When he pulled her legs forward, gently moving her to the edge of the seat, causing her to grasp for purchase, she suddenly realized the purpose of the thick loops. But what left her baffled was why a Harvester would have such a device within his rooms. Ariss fondled the thick animal-hide, her mind racing at how she could get Kerrick to sit in this seat. All thoughts fled when he reached the tender juncture of her inner thigh. Smoothly, he slid his finger up the length of her sex, his rumble of satisfaction clear when he found her slick and ready. His tongue followed the same route, causing her to lift her bottom off the chair so that he could find a better angle with which to lave her clit.

Over and over, his tongue danced along the swollen bit of flesh, his eyes riveted to her face, gauging her reaction. Desperate in her need, Ariss wanted to rip the robe off, but her hands were busy holding her up. The contrast between his silky soft tongue and the rough, scratchy fabric sent her senses reeling.

"Wait," Ariss breathed out, dropping back into the chair.

Kerrick's stunned look almost made her laugh. Almost.

"I want you to sit here." She stood up, pointing to the chair, hoping he wouldn't notice the straps. She'd carefully tucked them back into the scalloped design of the furniture.

With a curious half smile, Kerrick settled himself in the chair, oblivious to her true intent. When Ariss knelt before him, he moaned, anticipating the obvious.

Ever so softly, she trailed her hands along his thighs until she cupped the hardness of his prick through the loincloth. "I saved your life and you think I'm going to suck your cock, too?" she asked mockingly, making sure her hot breath caressed his twitching organ. One of the most wonderful properties of *astle* was its ability to conduct temperature. She knew her breath and his body heat combined would set him to the boiling point.

"No?" he asked, his face turning wistful and curious all at once.

Flashing him a wicked smile, she said, "Hold on." When Kerrick frowned, she added, "Grasp the back of the chair with both hands." Obligingly, he did. With two quick jerks, she bound his wrists with the thick, animal-hide loops.

Shocked, Kerrick yanked his arms forward. When he found them bound, his face turned thunderous.

Ariss automatically retreated, crawling back on her knees so that he couldn't reach her even with his legs. Her face must have conveyed her fear because his attitude diminished into speculation.

Softly, he murmured, "You naughty, naughty girl."

Nodding, Ariss stood, secure in the knowledge that he was now bound to the chair. The loops were sturdy, clearly designed to stop even the massive power of the Harvester from escaping.

"You didn't know about this chair?" Ariss asked, working the clasps of her robe apart.

"No, if I had, I would have strapped you to it." He tested the loops again, his entire body drawing taut, displaying the incredible strength he possessed.

"All that power now contained for my pleasure." With a flourish, she flipped the robe off her shoulders and let it pool at her feet. As his gaze ate her up, she stood straighter, lifting her face, enjoying the way his pupils dilated, and his breathing grew deeper and more ragged. Two cycles ago, she never could have even imagined herself doing something like this, but her provocative display felt almost natural with Kerrick. Having him bound, to do with as she pleased, was a heady experience. One she didn't intend to waste.

Licking his lips, Kerrick asked, "And just what will you be doing with me?"

Stepping near, Ariss slung her leg over his, settling herself on his lap with her sex tantalizingly close to his so he could feel her heat through the thin wall of fabric that separated them. "I haven't decided." Oh, yes, she had, but why tell him when anticipation would simply be another aphrodisiac?

Before he could ask her another question, she pressed her lips to his, kissing him deeply as she plastered her body against his. Where she was soft, he was hard. The contrast caused her nipples to contract. Playfully, she rubbed them against his, causing his to tighten and a low growl to rumble in his chest. Through the loincloth, she felt his cock—hot, hard, and oh-so-ready and willing. She resisted the urge to simply impale herself upon him. Instead, she decided that she would wait until he was panting and breathless with need.

Even though he was bound, he kissed her as if she were the one strapped to the chair. His mouth was aggressive, his tongue plundering, his teeth nipping her lips and coaxing plaintive moans to rumble from deep inside her chest. Kerrick tasted of wild passion and occult ecstasy. Wrapping her arms around his shoulders, she wriggled restlessly, her sex uncomfortably hot and tight. The longing inside became almost unbearable.

With a frustrated snarl, Kerrick commanded, "Take this damn loincloth off." And she did so without a thought, yanking and tugging the fabric off his hips. Once she pulled the cloth free, she tossed it aside and snuggled closer to him, unconcerned with him taking control even in his bound state. What did it matter when she wanted him naked, anyway?

After a rumbled expletive, he growled, "Gods, Ariss, you are so hot, so wet." He rested his forehead against hers and whispered, "Let me feel you." Tilting his head up, his gaze captured hers, the depth of his green eyes pleading his case with a frankness that astounded her. "I need you. Never in my life have I hungered the way I crave you." He paused for a moment, then added, "Please." Closing his eyes, he whispered, "Please."

Hypnotized, Ariss lifted up and slid herself down his length, watching as his eyes drifted almost all the way closed, and he exhaled one long, slow breath as if he'd been holding it for days. Her head went back as she took him fully within, his girth stretching her, his length pushing deeper until he pressed against the very depth of her body. Desperate to take more, she shimmied her body down in a useless effort.

Heeding her frustrated whine, Kerrick thrust up from the chair, forcing his cock just a bit deeper, just enough to make her utter a shocked gasp and clutch her thighs around his body.

Together, they moved, working their hips, rocking their bodies to a beat only they could hear. His lips found hers, kissing her with a commanding force that thrilled her and told her without a doubt who was in charge. She didn't care. She would follow his lead secure in the knowledge that he would not abuse her loyalty. With two quick flicks of her fingers, she removed the straps, setting him free, allowing him to do with her as he pleased.

To her shock, he stood, forcing her legs straight. He pulled out of her with a quick yank. Before she could react, he spun her around so that she faced away from him. He then pulled her back against his body, plunging his cock into her with startling accuracy. Carefully, he sat back down, taking her with him, so that now she pressed her back against his chest. She had no idea why the sudden change until he lowered his hand. Initially, he made wide circles around her clit, causing it to stand at attention, begging for his touch. The more she wriggled against him, the more he teased ever so close but never quite touching.

At her whimpers, he growled, "This is what happens when you try to capture the beast."

A shiver of sheer bliss shot through her. He would make her pay for her impulsive act. Of course, she knew that he would, which was why she'd boldly taken charge. Every cell in her body cried out for his possession, and she knew he wouldn't disappoint her.

Angling her hips down, he thrust into her several times with such aggression he almost pushed her off his lap. Only his hands on her hips held her against him, readying her for another wicked thrust. Gasping cries of pleasure were torn from her lips as she lowered her hands to the edge of the chair to help hold herself ready for him. He lifted them both up, snarling in frustration that he couldn't move the way he wanted. Balancing her against him, he stood, then strode toward the bed, placing her facedown against the edge.

"Much better," he moaned, pounding against her, causing the flesh of her bottom to shake with each hard thrust. His cock was a sleek tool, plunging, withdrawing, making her want more. In her haze of lust, she needed to feel everything he could give her. From the tenderest brush of his lips to the most brutal pounding of his hips, Ariss wanted all of him.

Each time he slammed forward, his balls slapped against her clit, striking her slick and tender flesh just hard enough to increase her pleasure and increase the pressure of an intense orgasm that longed to burst free. Her mind was awhirl with conflict; she wanted this, wanted him. She wanted all the pleasure he could wrench from her body, but she didn't want to lie to him, to trick him, to force him to become a father if he wasn't ready. Each time he moved against her was another chance for him to climax, and thus take the choice from her; but each time he didn't, he pushed her anxiety higher.

Making her choice, Ariss angled up, tilting her hips so that he could go even deeper inside. Each time he did, he pushed her into the bed, pressing the breath out of her body, causing her moans to burst forth in time with his movements. It began to feel as if he breathed for her, his body working hers like a bellows, blowing against the coals until the heat increased. All she needed was one little spark to ignite the blaze.

"Tell me you want more," he ordered, his voice a low rumble that pressed a primitive part of her brain, a part that wanted to give him what he needed just as much as he longed to do the same to her.

"More, Kerrick," she said, turning to look over her shoulder, catching sight of the sweat pouring off his neck and sleeking down his chest. He appeared to her as a god who walked upon the mortal world. Kerrick's body was perfection. His muscles bulged. Exertion caused him to glisten. "Give me everything you have."

At her words, his nostrils flared and his eyes narrowed, turning them into dangerous slits. Once, when she was very young, her father had taken her on an outing to see exotic animals from all over the Onic Empire. Most of them were caged, listless, all the fight beaten out of them, their eyes dull and their bodies listless. The pathetic beings had broken her tender heart and she cried, embarrassing her father to the point he strode quickly through the exhibits, berating her from out the corner of his mouth. But there was one, a sleek, four-legged creature with glistening dark fur that paced the length of his cage. So determined was his stride, the *otall* had worn a path into the wood plank floor. Kerrick's eyes reminded her of that caged beast—alive, glossy, waiting for a chance to run free. Her words had unlocked his cage.

He grasped her ankles, lifting her up, forcing the angle of her hips to deepen so that he could work more of his length within. She felt vulnerable in her exposure but also trusted the man who held her open for his pleasure. In his drive to mate with her, he became wild, untamed, and almost manic in his thrusts. Before this moment, she might have been afraid of his animal state, but not now, not when her own beast rose within, longing for more, needing more.

In a soft litany, she encouraged him to give everything to her, to shove his cock deeper, to fill her, to take her. She begged him until her voice grew demanding, desperate. Ariss grasped her fists into the bedclothes, tearing them in her frenzy to hang on, to keep herself wide for him. She imagined the silken fabric was his back and her nails were digging in, to force him to be more vicious in his possession. In the heat of her lust, she didn't want tender mercy; she wanted brutal punishment. Craving his discipline, she rent the fabric in a loud, long pull.

When Kerrick heard her tear the fabric, he laughed victoriously. "That's it, Ariss, show me how wild you really are." Leaning near enough to almost whisper in her ear, he added, "Tell me you want me to fuck you, you nasty girl."

That sinful word, *fuck,* was the spark that caused her entire body to burst into flames. Her cunt gripped around his cock, trying to capture him and force him to fill her, but he withdrew, holding the tip of his staff to her, teasing his finger along her clit, milking another series of orgasms from her still-spasming body.

Once the initial shivers subsided, he plunged so fast and deep into her that she gasped, clawing at the covers, pulling them down the length of the bed to bunch below her chest, which only angled her more for another ruthless plunge. In a rapid series of thrusts, she climaxed until she became a helpless quivering mound of flesh upon his bed.

She heard him catch his breath. He gripped his fingers around her ankles and a burst of short growls rumbled up from his chest. Glancing back over her shoulder, she watched him struggle to withhold his orgasm. He was determined not to tumble over the edge. He deliberately held himself back, demanding more climaxes from her before he would give her his.

Her conflict was overcome with her own dire need to feel his release within her body, and she knew, right down to her soul, that his passion to get deeper was his own primal need to fill her with his seed. Breathlessly, she obeyed, begging him to fuck her with the last bit of her strength. Later, she would worry about the morality of her actions. For now, all that con-sumed her was her duty and her primal need to mate, fully, with her chosen.

His breathing grew labored and the rushing air cooled her back. His fists to her ankles slipped from their combined sweat. He snarled in frustration, letting her legs go so he could slip his hands under her hips, holding her steady for a syncopated se-ries of thrusts that left her gasping and weak.

She knew his climax was imminent because of the way he struggled to keep his thrusts timed, but he kept increasing the beat. Ariss turned to look over her shoulder, longing to see his face become a twisted mask of pleasure denied, then the release that would allow his entire face to go slack as he rode out his pleasure.

What actually confronted her gaze caused her lips to part and a shocked scream to erupt.

11

Through Kerrick's red haze of lust, Ariss' scream penetrated, constricting his heart with panic that in his violent burst of passion he'd inadvertently hurt her.

Never, ever had that been his intention.

Kerrick thought Ariss wanted his wild, animal lust. She'd begged him for more, but now shock and fear twisted her stunning face. Before he could react, four strong hands yanked him off his knees, pulling his penis out of her with a violence that hurt him and must have hurt her, too.

Twisting his head wildly side to side, Kerrick was shocked to see two of his four palace guards. Meaty hands gripped his shoulders and brought his wrists together behind his back. Just as he opened his mouth to demand an explanation for them bursting into his room, for he hadn't pressed the panic button this time, someone clonked him on the head from behind. The last thing he saw besides a sparkly spate of bright stars was Ariss reaching out . . . but he didn't know if she grasped for him or the men she considered her saviors.

Kerrick awoke kneeling with his toes painfully splayed below his feet, the soles of which stretched to the limit of endurance and faced fully exposed behind him. Below his knees was a metal plate scattered with small seeds that dug into his flesh. His ass was high in the air since his forehead rested against the seed-scattered plate. He could breathe, but it hurt to do so, since his lungs felt lightly packed with sand from his awkward angle. Bound behind his back, someone had strapped his hands up toward his shoulders, stretching the muscles into the most uncomfortable position imaginable. He had no idea how long he'd been here, but it had to be a while given the various aches and pains that consumed his body.

Bare, bound, bruised, and at the back of his throat he tasted the bitter burnt wood of *umer.* Kerrick couldn't move his head, but he didn't need to look to know his cock was hard, his balls heavy from his denied orgasm. The guards interrupted him just as he'd been on the verge of filling Ariss with the most intense climax of his life. Once deprived of pleasure, his balls swelled painfully, demanding a release he couldn't provide.

When he took a deep breath, he tasted Ariss' scent upon his body. Even if he could get his hand wrapped around his prick, it wouldn't do him any good; the *umer* would prevent his orgasm for hours to come. Obviously, he was being punished for what he'd done to her. Kerrick despaired that he hadn't even been given a chance to plead his case, but worse, that he'd hurt Ariss.

The horrified look on her face filled his mind, tearing his soul to shreds. Never had he hurt a woman. Just the thought that he had hurt Ariss in any way tore his psyche apart and justified the punishing position he found himself in now. They didn't need to discipline him, for he would rebuke himself for the rest of life. He thought he was giving her pleasure as he took a full measure of such for himself, but apparently, he'd been wrong.

So wrong.

If his head weren't already forced to the floor, he would have hung it in shame.

"I told you he was in here."

The masculine voice commanded Kerrick's attention, but he was unable to turn his head to see who, exactly, was behind him. He waited for the mystery man to speak again in the hopes he could recognize his voice. Not that knowing who he was would do him any good. Or perhaps it would. Could he convince one of the recruits to set him free? Just from the scent alone, Kerrick knew he was near the training rooms. Sweat, leather, and the slightest tang of blood told him he was close to the practice floor.

"But he's the Harvester," another voice commented, wary.

Kerrick didn't need to see him to guess this second man darted his gaze around, seeking not permission, but the security of knowing that he would not be punished for what he wished to do. Just his sly, sneaking tone of voice caused Kerrick's heart to pound. In addition, this second voice was closer, and Kerrick realized they were coming toward him. Gulping in terror, he realized he was kneel-bound, his ass up, exposed, and there wasn't a damn thing he could do. Almost against his will, Kerrick understood exactly why they'd bound him like this and left him utterly alone.

Vulnerable.

The one word conveyed the truth and the dreadful knowledge of why he was where he was. In this place, he was just as exposed as he'd made Ariss. What was it they said on Tandth? Payback was a bitch. . . .

"How the mighty have fallen," said the first man, cupping his hand to Kerrick's right butt cheek. Caressing him possessively, with a clear intent to do so much more, the man teased the barest brush of his fingertip into Kerrick's crevice, the tip of his slender digit pressing threateningly against his puckered flesh.

It was one thing to feel the soft probe of a tongue, or the

playful finger of a lover in that defenseless area, but to feel the nasty invasion of a man's unwanted prick caused Kerrick to shiver in alarm and clench his butt cheeks together protectively. So tightly bound was he, that Kerrick couldn't even flinch. Instead, Kerrick whisper-growled, "Get your hand off me."

The second man laughed, and Kerrick almost recognized his voice. He was pretty sure it was Ninder, a pale recruit from Ries with his shocking white hair and disturbing pink eyes. They gave him something that protected his skin and eyes from the light, some kind of pill, because Kerrick saw him take it once and asked. He'd seemed a nice enough man, well, a kid, really. The pickings must be slim in Ries for them to select a skinny little thing like Ninder. But why would he come in here? Kerrick hadn't ever been anything but nice to him.

"And what are you going to do if I don't?" the first man taunted.

Raw panic consumed Kerrick. If not for the *umer*, his balls would have retreated into his body from horror. As it was, they hung limp and lifeless, utterly without feeling below his hopelessly exposed ass. These two were going to use his unprotected bottom to sate their lust. A burst of total dread caused Kerrick to fight his bonds with a violence that netted barely a quiver of movement. The device held him so tightly bound there was nothing, nothing he could do.

"I think the *gannett* has you completely bound, and utterly helpless, *phen'tabi.*" When he whisper-hissed the last word, Kerrick knew exactly who he was. Uad from Plete. The word he'd used was an insult that called Kerrick a pretty boy with big balls. In other words, Uad thought he was a man who looked good but didn't really have anything to offer because big balls didn't necessarily equate with potency. The other word, *gannett,* must be the device that held Kerrick so utterly immobile.

Kerrick considered issuing threats. He could swear to punish them both once he was free, but he quickly realized the folly of such claims. They would suffer no repercussions for taking advantage of him in this device. If he hunted them down later, he would be in the wrong, for they truly had only given him the punishment he deserved. The entire purpose of placing him this way was to allow the recruits to abuse him. Such was the retribution he would suffer: a rape for a rape.

Another hand joined the first, this one cupping his left butt cheek. Together, they caressed, sending shivers of terror through Kerrick's bound frame. He could easily picture Uad behind him, his copper hair glistening in the lights, his fathomless black eyes glittering with abusive lust. Again, Kerrick clenched his cheeks together as hard as he could, and actually succeeded in pulling them out of Uad's hands.

"Relax, Harvester. I'm told it only hurts for a moment."

Twin hands effortlessly pried his ass cheeks apart.

Kerrick bit back a cry of fear by clamping his bottom lip between his teeth. Cool air rushed over his sweat-covered flesh, but not enough to actually chill his burning anxiety. Nothing he could say would stop these two, not when they felt justified, not when his punishers left him so hopelessly bound and exposed. To protect himself, Kerrick wished his consciousness far away, into a safe place, but his mind refused to obey. Instead, his brain focused every bit of his attention on the exposed and vulnerable puckered flesh of his ass.

Thick, hard, and unforgiving, Kerrick felt the knob of a cock pressed greedily against his upturned bottom. In a horrible rush, he wondered if Ariss had actually wanted him to tease her in this place, or if he'd taken her acquiescence without due cause.

"Don't," Kerrick begged, his voice muffled against the metal plate at the bottom of his cage. Had Ariss begged him in such a plaintive tone and he'd ignored her? Gods, he'd been so determined in his lust, he honestly couldn't remember anything but her lovely voice begging for more, not less, of his ruthless possession.

The man behind him laughed, and pressed forward.

Bile rose in Kerrick's throat. If he vomited, he might choke on it, given his position. Moreover, he would be nose deep in his own filth, which only made him gag harder.

Kerrick braced himself for the worst but felt nothing. Confused, he thought perhaps the *umer* had dulled sensations in his ass, as well as in his genitals.

"I claim him," a voice rumbled, setting the hairs on the nape of Kerrick's neck to standing.

Kerrick recognized the voice immediately. His heart stopped beating, then hammered triple time in his chest. The two hands on either side of his bottom let go, but Kerrick didn't breathe a sigh of relief. If anything, he held his breath tighter.

With a series of subservient mumbles, Ninder and Uad backed off, leaving Kerrick alone with Sterlave.

A new and terrible shame filled his aching body. For his handler to see him like this, and then to have him use him was beyond what Kerrick thought he could endure. If nothing else, Sterlave could use this moment to assert his dominance. Kerrick had no idea what kind of man Sterlave was, but if he were anything like the men from Cheon, he would do anything to declare his authority.

"I swear I didn't mean to hurt her," Kerrick said, his voice muffled against the metal plate.

Sterlave uttered a noncommittal grunt.

Time stood still as Kerrick waited breathlessly for Sterlave to pick up where Uad left off. His heartbeat was loud in his ears, and his breath moved so quickly in and out of his lungs that he blew some of the seeds away from him, making them skitter across the metal with a sound that reminded him of the scratching feet of vermin upon slick tile.

Suddenly, the scent of Ariss rose off his body, enveloping his mind, twisting his guts, and he swallowed in abject misery.

"How is she?" Kerrick asked, trying to keep a desperate whine out of his voice.

Sterlave's utter silence hit him like a blow.

Kerrick sagged, but his body didn't move in the tight restraints. In his muddled mind, he couldn't remember how many times she screamed before he'd noticed. So deep was he in his rutting lust that he didn't even hear her cries. She must have been reaching out to the guards to save her, not trying to embrace him.

In one final indignity, tears pooled in his eyes and then fell straight down, splattering against the metal with silent shame. Kerrick did his best not to sob, because that would be the only way for Sterlave to know that he was crying, but his back quivered when he took a steadying breath.

Behind him, Kerrick heard the pounding of several feet that stopped short.

"Out," Sterlave commanded, his voice filled with irritation.

Kerrick heard the steps retreating amidst mumbled conversations.

"What were you thinking?" Sterlave asked, his voice a harsh whisper.

Kerrick drew a deep breath. "I couldn't wait for the next cycle."

"So you snuck some *yondie* into your rooms?"

Kerrick paused, his mind racing. Sterlave thought he'd brought a paid woman to the Harvester suite? Was that what he was being punished for?

"She's not a *yondie*," Kerrick defended, his anger replacing his terror and easing the pressure on his pounding heart.

"I don't care who she is; she shouldn't have been in your rooms!" Sterlave's voice rose in volume until anyone within the training room must have heard him. "Your *paratanist* was aghast when she caught you."

More confusion followed the first dose. He wasn't being punished for raping Ariss, but for having sex when he wasn't supposed to? Rather than speculating any further, Kerrick asked, "What, exactly, am I being punished for?"

"For being an idiot," Sterlave said, smacking Kerrick's bottom hard enough to set his balls swaying. "You are to mate with your female counterpart, and only her, and only during the new cycle!" Another slap landed; this one hard enough to wrench a cry from between Kerrick's gritted teeth.

"Stop hitting me!"

"Would you rather have me mounting you?" Sterlave asked, lowering his voice to a loud whisper. "If I'm not tormenting you in one way or another, someone else will. Do you get it now?"

No, he really didn't, but Kerrick kept his mouth shut. Let Sterlave spank him like a rebellious child. That was better than a cock up his ass any day.

"Just be thankful Chur hasn't come yet, because when he does, he's going to be furious with you."

Chur Zenge, the living god, the most mighty and influential Harvester ever. Just about the last thing Kerrick wanted was Chur coming into the room to see him ingloriously bound, especially when he really didn't know exactly what he was being punished for.

"I still don't understand what I did wrong. I was mating with the Harvester, just like I'm supposed to." Kerrick tried desperately to defend what he'd done in the hopes Sterlave would release him.

After a pause, Sterlave growled, "You idiot! You still don't get it, do you?"

Clearly, he didn't. "Spell it out for me."

"You are to mate with her at the beginning of each cycle, not whenever you feel the urge. The whole point is for you to be at your most potent."

"Potent?" The word rolled around in Kerrick's mind, seeking a meaning to attach to. When the word landed, his eyes went wide, and he gasped. Now he understood exactly what he was supposed to do with Ariss. Mate. And they wanted him to fully mate with her, not just fuck her. He was supposed to *impregnate* her. If he could have shaken his head, he would have; instead, he gritted his eyes at his own pathetic ignorance. Once again, he'd been thinking with his dick, pleased beyond the nothingness that he got to fuck the most beautiful woman on the planet. He hadn't thought beyond that.

But hopefully, it wasn't too late now.

"Chur risked his life to change the Harvest ritual back to the original form, and here you come, destroying it because you can't keep your cock in your loincloth for a paltry cycle." Sterlave leaned over the cage, placing his mouth fractionally closer to Kerrick's ear. "Do you know that before, a Harvester went the entire season without knowing the feel of a woman?"

Shock made Kerrick's eyes bulge. A whole season without sex would have made him mad with lust. Even his own hand simply wouldn't be able to pacify his passionate needs. "Wait, you mean you and Chur went a season without . . ."

With a laugh that was more a bark, Sterlave said, "Not me, because I knew exactly who I was going to choose when I became the Harvester." Sterlave's voice softened and became almost dreamy. "I challenged Chur to the death for her, so when I came to take her as my sacrifice, I claimed her as my bondmate."

Kerrick didn't need to see him to know Sterlave's face was a curious combination of pride, lust, and wry amusement. The tale about the passionate and rocky romance between Sterlave and the former empress Kasmiri was almost legendary despite the fact it had only started shortly after Kerrick became the Harvester.

"But if it was a fight to the death, then how are you and Chur still alive?" Kerrick asked, desperately trying to latch his attention on to anything other than his current precarious position.

"Again with your gossip!" Sterlave yelled, whacking the palm of his hand to the cage. The metal shook with the force of the blow, causing Kerrick's teeth to rattle in his head. "I have never known a man who cared so much for idle talk as you."

Chagrined, Kerrick clamped his lips together. Sterlave was right; now was not the time. "What will happen to Ariss?"

After a long pause, Sterlave said, "It speaks to your true character that you ask after her first, rather than yourself." Another long pause ensued, then Sterlave asked, "Are you in love with her?"

Kerrick did not want to speculate on that answer, not naked with his ass in the air, so he countered with a stern, "Now who wishes to engage in idle chatter?" But Kerrick knew that once the question had been placed in his mind, he would worry over it endlessly. Especially after the way she'd come to him, and he'd thought Fana had been under that robe, and he'd immediately said no to sex with Fana, preferring instead to wait for Ariss. Not once in his life had he turned down a willing woman for another. But that didn't mean it was love. Infatuation, fascination, even obsession, but not necessarily love.

"I do not know what punishment Ariss will suffer for her part, for each of you has violated the prophecy." Sterlave moved away from the cage, his steps crunching through the scattered seeds. Just hearing them *pop* below the thick hide of his boots reminded Kerrick of how they dug into his knees and forehead like tiny, dull swords.

Violating a prophecy didn't sound like a good thing at all. Kerrick guessed he should be grateful that they didn't simply kill him. A thousand thoughts collided in his mind, none of them good. If they'd put him in this *gannett*, surely they would do something similar to Ariss. Gods forbid, they did something worse.

Panic caused Kerrick to blurt, "It wasn't her choice." He hesitated, thinking what else he could say to take the blame off Ariss and onto himself. "I made her have sex with me." He gulped hard, and added, "I forced her against her will. I don't think she should be punished for what I did." It was a lie, but he didn't care. Kerrick couldn't bear the thought of Ariss being punished. Something inside twisted and almost died with the thought that they would allow others to rape her as they clearly allowed with him. His thoughts became a nightmarish swirl of horror that he would do anything to prevent. He would willingly let every recruit use him to avoid even one using her.

With a groaning sigh, Sterlave said, "And now you think that you can take her punishment by taking all the blame on yourself." Sterlave paced in front of the cage, his crunching boots telling Kerrick where he was in relation to his bound form. "You *must* love her."

Irritated that Sterlave insisted on returning to that, Kerrick bellowed, "I don't want her hurt."

Behind him a voice speculatively asked, "Would you take her punishment?" Commanding, and inarguably in charge, Kerrick knew without confirmation that Chur had entered.

His footfalls were almost silent, only the fact that Kerrick's head was pressed into the floor allowed him to hear the soft padding of Chur's bare feet. He'd only seen the man in passing, his eyes caught by the fact that Chur literally glowed golden just below his skin. Chur's intense azure eyes could hold anyone, male or female, effortlessly in thrall. They said he was a demigod, sent from *Jarasine* to bring Diola back to the righteous path they'd abandoned thousands of seasons ago. All Kerrick knew for certain was the man was huge. Thick muscles bulged all over his body. It was difficult to miss the perfection of the man's form since he paraded around in a low-slung loincloth. Damn it all to the nothingness, but even the man's cock seemed to have muscles. For some unknown reason, Kerrick had stared openly at Chur's crotch, amazed and shocked by the tremendous bulge below the black *astle.* When Chur caught him looking, he lifted one eyebrow, but Kerrick didn't know if it was in invitation or mockery. It did, however, cause him to jerk his gaze elsewhere.

"I am willing to take her punishment because she didn't do anything wrong." Kerrick closed his eyes against the red flush of embarrassment. There was nothing like meeting a demigod in such a demeaning way. Clearly, he was doomed to forever be doing something idiotic around Chur. Kerrick would offer out his hand in friendship, as they did on Tandth, but it was tied behind his back at the moment. Well, at least he was on his knees in obeisance. And with his head held immobile, he wouldn't be able to ogle the man's bulge.

Chur's steps stopped on the right side of the *gannett.* A moment later, Kerrick heard his voice almost right beside his ear. "Tell me, Kerrick, how did you force Ariss to come to your room clad in a *paratanist's* robe?"

Kerrick's mouth went dry. Lying to a demigod was obviously one of the more foolish things he'd ever done. Again, he acted without thinking beyond the immediate outcome. "I— I—" he stuttered, trying to think of a plausible explanation.

Chur's laugh rumbled like a landslide, rich and powerful, with a most dangerous edge. "I would suggest that you stop lying to me." Lowering his voice, he added, "For you see I already know the truth."

Kerrick heard seeds being brushed away and realized Chur settled in beside his cage.

"Becoming the Harvester wasn't at all what you thought it would be."

It was a comment, not a question, but Kerrick answered anyway. "Not at all." He'd never been so disappointed and shocked by the truth of anything. All the glorious tales were nothing but fancy lies to garner recruits.

"If you were given an option to walk away, unharmed, without any further punishment than what you have already suffered, would you take that opportunity?"

On the verge of saying yes, Kerrick held his tongue. He had to consider the likely outcome of such a generous offer. Here was a chance to leave the palace forever. He could finagle his way off planet and never step foot on Diola again. And all he had to do was simply walk away. From everything. Including Ariss.

"What will become—"

"I cannot tell you what will become of Ariss, so do not ask. She will face her own punishment, and perhaps she will be given a choice such as you are being given, but I doubt that very much." Chur sighed, conveying a genuine regret. "There is one who will refuse to let her go." Chur lowered his voice. "You see, Kerrick, there is a man who will do anything to possess Ariss. He even spoke at your Esslean tribunal, calling for your execution."

Kerrick wasn't surprised to learn that killing him had been an option. He didn't know what an Esslean tribunal was, but it didn't matter right now. Hesitantly, Kerrick asked, "Who is this man?"

"The man whose job you covet so greatly."

Kerrick didn't bother to ask how Chur knew, all he could do was blurt, "Ambo Votny wants Ariss?" Kerrick's voice was too loud against the metal, causing it to vibrate dully. He lowered his voice. "He is three times her age." As if that would make the man wake up and see reason. Kerrick's numb cock shriveled at the thought of Ariss with that ancient, blubbery excuse for a man. In his mind's eye, he saw Ambo flushed and sweaty from his several trips from the training rooms to the Harvest room. What would he be like looming over Ariss?

"So, do you still wish to simply walk away?"

12

Ariss screamed out a warning when she saw four guards rushing toward Kerrick, but he was so deep in passion that he didn't hear her. Two of the monstrous men grasped his shoulders, pulling him to his feet and out of her body with a violence that scraped the walls of her sex. Blind with panic, she reached for him, but they contained him so quickly she could do nothing. Before Kerrick could even think of fighting back, they had bound his hands and smacked him on the back of his head, knocking him senseless.

Trembling in shock and fear, terrified at the reason for their invasion of his privacy, Ariss clambered onto the bed, trying to get as far from the guards as she could. While two guards dragged Kerrick's limp form away, the remaining two followed her with their eyes, their expressions blank and unreadable.

"What are you doing here?" she asked, already knowing she wasn't going to get an answer. Just as she predicted, they stood mute, watching her with intense eyes that missed little.

The smell of lust filled the room like an accusation, exposing Ariss for the wanton woman she'd become. How had they even known what was going on behind the heavy Onic door? She and Kerrick hadn't been that loud . . . or had they? When she'd snuck along the hallway to Kerrick's room, his four guards had been at the far end of the hall, not right next to his door. Surely, they hadn't been able to hear her passionate cries that far away.

"Where will they take him?" Ambo asked another guard who entered the room beside him.

"They've convened an Esslean tribunal."

"As if a collection of recruits can pass judgment." Ambo halted midstride. His deep-set eyes widened slightly when they alighted on her, then narrowed with glittering appraisal. His gaze swept over her body, from her toes to the pebbled tips of her breasts. To her dread, his probing glare was almost physical. She practically felt his doughy hands following the trail of his vision, mauling her, forcing her to mold her body to his depraved desires. Even though she was nude, the sheet seemed terribly far away, crumpled up at the foot of the bed where she'd drug all the bedclothes in her passion. She was still too shocked to grab the sheet to cover herself.

The three guards in the room also looked at her, but not with the feverish perversion of Ambo. In his eyes lurked a darkness that no amount of light, not even the blazing power of the twin suns, could banish. Evil swarmed over his features, causing her to thank the gods that three other men were in the room to protect her from the fourth. Ambo was seventy seasons, but he possessed a strength that Ariss didn't know she could fight off. If he were determined to have her, she feared he would no matter what. Her only option would be to outrun him.

Licking his lips, Ambo turned to the guard without taking his eyes off her, and said, "Tell them I wish to address the tribunal."

The guard executed a modified bow and left. Now there were only two men to protect her from Ambo. Each man towered over him, their muscles thick and clearly defined by the mostly bare-chested nature of their uniforms. Short loincloth-like garments fastened about their hips exposed legs of hardened flesh. Tooled animal-hide cupped each man's left shoulder, crossing over the plate centered on his chest. A heavy belt held a short sword and other items Ariss could only assume were weapons.

Now that the initial surprise had faded, Ariss lunged down the bed, yanked the sheet from the clump of fabric, and wrapped the black *astle* about her body. Heat reflected back from the fabric, warming her. Protected by even this thin shell, she felt more confident. She lifted her shoulders and chin, refusing to cower under Ambo's intense scrutiny.

A snarl darted across Ambo's face that she'd defied him by covering herself up when he clearly wasn't done violating her with his gaze. His piercing eyes finally left her only to fall on the discarded *paratanist* robe. Lips peeling back in disgust, he waddled over to the pile of *mondi* fabric and yanked it off the edge of the bed.

"Is this how you came to him?" Ambo shook a fistful of the robe at her in accusation. "Dressed like a servant so you could be his willing *yondie*?"

Lifting herself to her knees with the dignity of an empress, Ariss responded, "I am no man's paid woman." She desperately wanted to add, *not even yours,* but held her tongue. The only way she'd be able to evade his clutches was to succeed in her duty. Sadly, Kerrick hadn't climaxed before they'd been interrupted.

"No?" Ambo stood at the foot of the bed, his face flushed with righteous anger. "I have never met a woman more eager to be mounted by an animal than you are."

His vulgar words shocked her, compelling a rude comment in turn, but she cautioned herself. Tilting her head, Ariss asked,

"You, who by law should uphold the prophecy, call the Harvester an animal?"

A small show of fear darted across Ambo's face as he considered the two remaining guards. Unreadable, they stood in silent witness to the exchange unfolding before them. Knowing they would keep their tongues, Ambo's eyes turned cold, his smile brutal and filled with malice. "You, who by all accounts has defied the prophecy, seek to condemn *me*?"

Appalled, Ariss sputtered, "How—how have I defied the prophecy?" She'd only been doing what her position demanded. "By my duty I am to mate with Kerrick."

Lips pursed as if to hold back an explosion of disgust, Ambo bellowed, "You are to mate with him only on the eve of the new cycle!" His gaze slid from her face to her neck. Triumphantly, he grinned. In that moment, she knew the stone was still black. Mockingly, Ambo snarled, "It seems the Harvester is much less a man than he appears."

One of the guards betrayed himself when the smallest ripple of anger scrunched up the end of his nose. Ire surfaced and disappeared so quickly Ariss wasn't sure she'd seen anything at all. However, her instinct was that he did not like to hear denigrating comments about the man he was sworn to protect. Even the mighty magistrate should show a measure of respect to the Harvester.

On the verge of telling Ambo that Kerrick was more a man than he would ever be, she held back. Antagonizing Ambo served no purpose. At the moment, he held her life, and probably Kerrick's life, in his hands. To survive, she had to find a way to appease him, and to avoid being alone with him, for if he got her unaccompanied . . . She didn't like what she had to do, but she saw no other choice.

Dropping her head in what she hoped was a show of submission, Ariss slumped her shoulders as if her entire world were lost. Through the thick net of her lashes, she peered up at Ambo to see if her ploy was working. When a greedy smile split his greasy lips, she knew she was on the right path. Holding dominion over others was what Ambo craved. Not being in the right so much as having power over anyone who dared to cross his path. That, that supremacy, the command of others, was what Ambo's ego craved.

"I beg the forgiveness of the gods," Ariss said, lifting her face up to the light and spreading her arms wide. The black sheet slipped a bit, exposing the very edge of her areolas. She made no effort to yank the fabric back because the subtlest hints of her body riveted Ambo's attention. Distracting him was her goal, and the one thing that always caught his attention was her body. In particular, her breasts.

Just as she predicted, Ambo's face went slack as his eyes fell upon the promise of her breasts' eventual exposure.

Determined to escape him, she knelt on the bed, letting her voice rise and fall in prayer to Varnatha, the goddess of the Harvesters. Prostrating herself, Ariss stretched her arms out before her as if she knelt before the goddess herself. Surreptitiously she glanced up at the three men before her; the guard who showed the flicker of anger at Ambo's denigrating comments had fallen to his knees, his head bent in prayer. The other guard stood but lowered his head respectfully. Nonplussed, Ambo stood glaring at both of them. Ultimately, he riveted his blazing gaze on her.

From her lowered face, she watched Ambo's lips quiver as he struggled to find something to say. He would have stopped her if he could, but as things stood, he couldn't. Manhandling the condemned as they sought the forgiveness of the gods was something even Ambo would not do.

When another guard entered to take Ambo to the tribunal, he issued a hasty order to the standing guard and departed.

Ariss stopped her prayers once he left and allowed the guards to take her from Kerrick's room.

To her surprise, they returned her to her suite. Inside, her *paratanist* stood waiting, a bundle of black cloth over his arm. Silently, he unwound the sheet from her and ushered her into the tub, where he proceeded to scrub her vigorously, as if he could scour the lust off her body. When her skin glowed pink, he dried, anointed, and perfumed her, as if readying her for the most exquisite celebration. Her heart sank when she thought he readied her for sacrifice. Would they ritualistically kill her for the gods she had so blatantly defied?

He proceeded to dress her in a curious black outfit. In the front, the fabric covered the length of her legs, but in the back, it barely swept the edge of her bottom. Worst of all were the twin curves of metal that imprisoned and lifted her breasts, leaving them completely exposed. Two straps rose over her shoulders, but there was no fabric to cover her chest.

"What do I wear over this?" Ariss asked her *paratanist*, covering her breasts with her hands.

Gently, he pulled her hands away. "Nothing."

Now she realized that was the point of the clothing, to leave her vulnerable and exposed. She settled at her mirror, allowing her servant to fashion her hair into a twist at the back of her head. Fastidiously, he set small white gemstones through her hair and along her cheeks, enhancing her gray eyes. The more he fussed over her appearance, the more her spirit plummeted. He was preparing her for execution. There was no doubt in her mind. He only confirmed her worst fears when he refused to answer her questions.

Numb, Ariss sat, wondering what would happen to Kerrick. If she could, she would take everything back. Had she known, she never would have risked both their lives to share his bed. In her effort to thwart her parents' wishes, she'd brought death to her and an innocent man. A man she only now acknowledged how much she cared about.

A lone tear escaped, and her *paratanist* wiped it away without comment, and without disturbing his carefully applied makeup. She cried not for herself, but for Kerrick. A wry laugh burbled up, because he'd wanted to turn her into a bad girl, and she'd far exceeded his wildest expectations.

"I'm so naughty I got us both killed."

Her servant ignored her remark. Lifting his hand, he pointed toward the door. Ariss stood. When she caught sight of herself in the mirror, slumping, she forced herself to stand straight. She would go to her death with pride. If she had the chance, she would plead for Kerrick's life.

In the hall, six guards, her normal four and the two from Kerrick's room, waited to escort her to her doom. Silently, two led the way as another two flanked her and two trailed behind. There was no escape. Her prominently displayed breasts did not distract them, so she didn't even consider running. She would only destroy her *paratanist*'s hard work and go to her death frazzled. Lifting her head a bit higher, she vowed to go to her execution with her pride intact. Whatever they would do to her, she would not give them the satisfaction of her fear.

After a time, they arrived at the temple, confirming her worst suspicion. Two white-clad acolytes held open the thick fabric drapes. Ariss entered. Behind her, the fabric fluttered closed with a soft *whump*, leaving her alone with a semicircle of male acolytes. Azure lighting crystals caused their white robes to glow and their faces to become frightening creations out of her nightmares. Cloyingly sweet herbs drifted in ribbons of smoke, making her dizzy. She tried to hold her breath, but that only made matters worse. When she gasped, she drew in huge amounts of smoke. In the end, she breathed in shallow pants.

The semicircle of acolytes parted, leading her gaze to a wall of blackness. Hesitantly, she stepped forward, terrified of what waited for her in the dark. Desperately, she widened and narrowed her eyes, trying to discern a shape out of the abyss, but she couldn't recognize anything. Her heart pounded so hard in her chest that she thought all those around her could hear it. Drums, far off in the distance, began to beat halftime to her heart, forcing it to slow. Something about the pounding of the drums and the smoke in the air relaxed her, culling calmness from her panicked mind and body. To her shock, she yawned.

With light steps, Ariss moved farther into the shadowy depths of the temple. She'd only been here once, for her inauguration, and everything was so overwhelming she'd hardly noticed the specifics of the place. Lifting her arm, she held it before her to feel for the wall, if there was one. For all she knew they maneuvered her toward a well that would plummet her to the bottom of the palace.

A blast of cold air hit her, tightening her exposed nipples almost painfully. Still, she didn't stop, just slowed her pace a bit as she continued reaching for the wall. After another few steps, a lighting crystal of pure white exploded into brilliance above her head, causing her to flinch back and shield her eyes. What she saw dropped her mouth open.

Carved of pure black Onic stone, the god of the Harvesters crouched, forming himself into the shape of a rough chair. His thick thighs formed the seat, his arms the sides as he clasped his hands around his knees. His handsome face leered suggestively. When she looked down, she realized why. Protruding from his hips was a thick stone phallus. How had she missed that when the lighting crystal struck it fully, the glow slipping over the smoothly polished stone like a caress?

Silently, two acolytes grasped her arms, turning her back on the grotesque statue. Now the cut of her dress became clear. As they forced her back, she struggled, but they were ready, clamping their hands around her wrists and upper arms with the power of ten men. Never had she known such relentless strength. Four more acolytes came forward, grasping her ankles, her knees, and her thighs.

Against her will, they lifted her, bending her body, forcing her to sit upon the statue. Without any fabric around her bottom, all they had to do was place her over the shaft, then slide her down. The Harvester god's cold phallus plunged into the slick heat Kerrick had created. Without such preparation, she knew the stone, despite the smooth contours, would have scraped her. Then she wondered if they had prepared him for her, for she sensed a great slickness over the rock. Once her thighs touched the statue's thighs, the acolytes released her, stepping back.

Ariss ordered her body to rise up, but nothing happened. Somehow, the stone god held her in place, forcing her to sit upon him, with his icy cock plunged so deep inside she felt the chill all the way to her heart. Her nipples, already tight and aching from the cold air, puckered even more as the mighty statue encased her within his frigid arms. In her mind's eye, she saw herself sitting upon him, his leering face triumphant as he plunged within her body, the moment of that first penetration frozen in time. The gemstones glittered along her cheeks, flashing dots of brightness into her eyes, clouding and confusing her vision.

The collection of acolytes bowed as they backed away. Ariss had no idea how long she was supposed to sit here, or what she would do while forced to mate with a statue, but she kept her mouth closed. As long as she lived through this, she would be grateful and suffer whatever punishment she must. She listened to the beat of the drums, feeling the same pulse in her sex. To her shock, her cunt grasped the phallus, cradling the contours, as if she welcomed the Harvester god's unyielding cock.

From her position, the rest of the temple glowed eerily blue, the shapes unrecognizable as the drugged air caused her to hallucinate. For all she knew, she was already dead and all this was nothing but a tangled dream of *Jarasine*.

Into her line of vision came the guard who had shown the flicker of anger at Ambo's rude comment about Kerrick. The same man who had knelt when she'd prayed. He kept his face lowered as he approached, stopping an arm's length away from her. His scent—spicy, male, but clean—penetrated into her primal brain. She wanted to lick him, to taste the salt of his sweat, then the heavier thickness of spice that lay under his sparse clothing.

"I have come to pay tribute." His voice was deeply timbered, causing a strange vibration in the rock she sat upon.

Ariss had no idea what he meant.

After a brief hesitation, he asked, "Will you accept my tribute?"

She nodded, then realized he couldn't see her. From the darkest recess of her mind came the correct answer. "I will accept your homage."

Tension slipped from his shoulders as he knelt. In practiced movements, he removed his loincloth, exposing his genitals. He was flaccid, but still impressively large, and Ariss waited breathlessly for what he would do. Clearly, with the statue plunged inside her, she wasn't supposed to mate with him. Although, there were other places he could put his prick.

"May I look upon you, Harvester?"

Again, from some forgotten place in her mind came the answer. "You may cast your gaze upon me."

Looking up from a lowered face, his eyes met hers, cautious and respectful. His gaze held hers for a timeless moment, then dropped to her exposed breasts. Without conscious direction, she thrust her chest out, lifting them, displaying them for his questing gaze. Her sex spasmed around the phallus, as if to draw it deeper inside. When she glanced down, she discovered the guard's cock had hardened, his strong hand helping the transformation.

"By my honor, it has been almost a season since I've given tribute."

Her body tightened another notch. He had not found release for almost an entire season? What was he saving himself for? Ariss let the questions loose in her mind, but not past her lips; she wasn't here to inquire of this man, but to accept what he would willingly give. When he looked up, she knew; he had been waiting for this. This man waited for a moment where his pleasure would have meaning, not just a climax to ease the pains within his body, but an ejaculation for a god.

Slowly, his hand worked along the length of his shaft, his movements calm and controlled. White light sparkled in his short hair and all over the hair that dusted his body.

Pinning her gaze upon the display before her, Ariss barely noticed the cold of her position. His passion, his sincere desire to pay tribute to her, warmed her from her core to the very tips of her toes and fingers. Ever so slowly, her body heated the statue.

Ariss wanted to ask his name, but refrained. This was not personal; this was what he wished to do for his god. All palace guards were once recruits. All of them once vied to become the Harvester. When they failed, they became enslaved to the empress, their might became hers, their bodies given up in service to her command, but Ariss had no idea some still worshipped the god that had abandoned them. How they reconciled their feelings, she didn't know; but this man, he truly believed in the prophecy, and the rituals surrounding the Harvest. By giving her his sincere and heartfelt tribute, he blessed her, and hopefully placed her back on the righteous path. This was not a tawdry exercise in lust; this was a blatant demonstration of sacrifice.

In a rush, Ariss understood her punishment. The stone phallus within her was the cock of the Harvester, in this case, Kerrick, and she could derive pleasure from him, as any healthy woman should, but she should not forget the meaning of their mating. Simple pleasure was not their goal. Procreation, the power of joining the male and female, is what ascended their passion beyond the mindlessness of the masses. Ariss had thought that was why she was seeking out Kerrick, but she wasn't being honest. He, too, should understand the meaning of their duty. Moreover, she should not use her duty as a tool to escape Ambo.

The guard's fist tightened over his shaft, turning the tip even darker despite the shadows. He tried to keep his face downcast, only looking up with his eyes, but rising pleasure lifted his face until the white light bathed his chiseled features. When he climaxed, jetting a stream of pure white into the air that arched gracefully to land near her feet, Ariss climaxed as well, her body pulling at the cold stone, heating it with her orgasm.

Spent, he lowered his head, drawing in slow, measured breaths. Without shame, he grabbed his loincloth and placed it around his hips.

"Has my tribute pleased you, Harvester?"

Filled with understanding, Ariss lifted her voice, and said, "You have pleased me greatly." For he had. Through him, she understood the nature of her duty, and the meaning of her punishment. All she could hope for now was that Kerrick would understand his.

A small smile of satisfaction darted across the man's expressive lips as he stood. With one last glance into her eyes, and a simple but subservient bow, he left her upon her sinful throne.

Before she could even recover her breath, another guard came before her. Scars riddled this one. He kept his face low with respect but also disgrace as he descended to his knees. She didn't need to be inside his mind to know that he didn't think he was good enough to offer tribute. His posture, the shameful slump of his shoulders, spoke louder than any words.

"I have come to pay tribute."

Despite his massive body, his voice was high and tight.

"Look at me," Ariss commanded.

Confused, he lifted his gaze to hers, his dark eyes made black by the shadows. Forcefully, he kept his eyes locked with hers even though he wanted to look down at the straining tips of her artfully displayed breasts.

"I want you to look at all of me." Lifting herself through the chest, she arched her back, thrusting her breasts out.

His breath grew labored, but each time he tried to look down, he winced his eyes closed. After several attempts, he whisper-hissed, "I am not worthy to behold such perfection." Clenching his eyes shut, he wrenched off his loincloth, exposing his semihard penis. Short, but shockingly thick, his cock was not the source of his shame as she had suspected. Very softly, so that only she might hear and the gods might miss it, he said, "I cannot stop myself. It has been barely hours since I . . ." His voice trailed off into nothingness, his shame apparent. He couldn't stop masturbating for his own pleasure. Apparently, the guards were expected to refrain and offer their climax only to the gods, but Ariss felt the wrongness of this ideal.

"When you find your pleasure, what do you think of?" Ariss asked, keeping her voice low even though her sense was that they were entirely alone. This was a sacred passage between her and these men; none would dare to eavesdrop on her exchanges. To do so would be to incur the wrath of the gods.

"Perversities," he growled, making his self-loathing apparent. "Men with other men, women with other women, all of them with me." He shook his head. "I cannot stop thinking of such debauchery ever since I watched over one of the empress's parties." His eyes sought her out, tortured and confused. "Before then I was strong, able to go an entire season without indulging. But since." He hung his head in shame. "The elite, they are . . ." He bit his lip, afraid to say the word, then whispered, "Depraved."

He hadn't told her anything she didn't already know. During her reign, Empress Clathia had hosted numerous parties that included plenty of secluded places for the elite to ply one another with erotic acts, drugs, and implements. The empress had disdained same-sex unions, which only made them all the more taboo to the iniquitous elite. The threat of censure simply compelled them to seek out such trysts with greater passion and more clandestine efforts. Clathia's daughter, Kasmiri, hadn't ruled long enough to continue the tradition; however, now that there was no empress, Ambo had stepped forward to carry on the custom of wild celebrations.

"It seems perverse to me that they would do these things before men they had forbidden to even touch themselves." Below her, the rock trembled as if in agreement.

The guard's gaze locked on hers.

"You have committed no sin." Only the *ungati*, those servants devoted to providing pleasure to their masters, but only allowed to climax alone with ritual *strocation*, should have to endure such austere restrictions. From her education, the god of the Harvesters was a lusty god. She sat upon clear evidence that the acolytes knew him best, portraying him as perverse throne. He would not wish his followers to suffer forced abstinence from pleasure. Just the opposite; he would want them to find release daily and in any way they could.

"You will accept my tribute?" his voice was awash with shocked wonder.

"The offering of such a virile man would please me greatly."

A relieved smile turned up the edges of his lips, softening the harshness of his scars. Lifting up onto his knees, thrusting his cock proudly into the light, he began by gripping his shaft firmly and squeezing several times in quick succession. His cock grew not so much in length but in thickness, causing her sex to quiver in response. This man would truly stretch her beyond endurance. Such a thought only caused her to squirm upon her tawdry throne. Lowering his other hand, he cupped his balls, squeezing them with the same pulsing rhythm until he grew fully erect.

He didn't ask permission to gaze upon her, but she didn't censure him. As a new and strange hunger filled her, she lifted her hands to her breasts, twisting her nipples between thumb and forefinger, pleased when he growled in response. He began to stroke his hand in fast, short strokes down his prick as he thrust his hips in time.

Tugging his hand down toward his rocking hips, he continued to arch back until the light bathed his entire upper body, showing off twisted white scars that crisscrossed his entire form. One of his nipples was gone, lost in the path of a knotted string of scar tissue. About the only place on him that was unmarked by weapons was his cock.

As he worked his prick in his hand, Ariss realized that he would not be as quick as the man before him was. This man knew his body and took his pleasure often, which allowed him tremendous finesse and control over his own climax.

Each time she thought he would ejaculate, he brought himself back from the brink. Only a small drop of moisture would pearl at the tip, a leak in the wall of desire waiting for the release of his masterful touch. He teased the slickness over the tip of his cock with his thumb, sliding it around and under the sensitive ridge until the tip grew ever darker.

Ariss discovered her breath matched his, and her hands grew firmer around her breasts, her fingers twisting almost hard enough to cause pain. When he climaxed, he bellowed, prompting her to gasp as her cunt clamped so tightly around the stone cock she feared she would snap the phallus off.

A powerful stream of pure white blasted from him, but he

angled his cock down, so his ejaculate splattered at her feet in a great gush. Several drops hit her bare feet, gratifying her need to have some type of contact with this most intriguing man. In the back of her mind, she speculated that if this deluge were after he'd climaxed once before, a delay of only a few days would make the volume almost overwhelming.

Falling back on his heels, curling in and bowing his head, he took a deserved moment to gather himself. Ariss realized her hands still cupped her breasts and she gently lowered them to the stone arms of the Harvester god. When she found him warm, she glanced down, stunned to find a slight grayish glow just below the surface. Convinced it was a trick of the light and the still-wafting sweet smoke, she shook her head. Once she dismissed the scar-riddled guard, another entered, dropped to his knees, and begged to offer his tribute.

She had no idea how long she'd sat receiving tribute, but her body grew weary. Her eyes were burning from the smoke and from gazing upon hundreds of men. Briefly, she let her lids settle, just to rest her eyes for a moment, and that's when she felt the stone arms of the statue lift from his knees and wrap around her waist.

Stretching up, he straightened his body, forcing hers to mold against his. Ariss relaxed into his embrace, allowing him to pull her higher until clouds swirled around them. Huge stone hands cupped her breasts with surprising gentleness as he moved his hips softly against hers. His mouth cupped her ear, whispering, telling her secrets and truths that she heard, understood, but only at the subconscious level.

He told her to call him Tavarus, and she did, pleased at the way his name rolled from her lips.

Trailing his massive hands down her body, he spread them against her hips, holding her steady for him, yet he didn't increase his rhythm. Caught up in the sensual movements, Ariss climaxed, lifting her hands up and back to wrap around his neck. He growled with the sound of rock against rock and climaxed, filling her with a stream of molten lava that didn't burn her, for she was living stone, too. As he released her, he whispered, "You will always belong to me."

Ariss blinked her eyes open only to discover a guard before her with a shocked expression on his face as he backed away. Cock in hand, he scrambled backward, falling, and then rising hastily to his feet. Within moments, a group of acolytes stood before her, their faces slack with awe.

With a halting voice, one said something in a language she didn't comprehend.

On the verge of demanding an explanation, Ariss looked down and realized the entire carved Onic statue that had been the darkest black, was now colorless. The lighting crystal of pure white that hung above shot bolts of brilliance clear through, then bounced back, lighting the room with shards of brightness.

Ariss sat in the center of it all.

13

Kerrick had surfed swelling waves of flame protected by the thinnest membrane. He'd jumped off plunging precipices with only a small parachute strapped to his back. He'd even dodged a spinning blade-covered puck. But he'd never really been afraid. Not until now.

Bent over with his forehead pressed into the metal floor of the *gannett*, Kerrick discovered that his lungs were slowly filling with fluid, making it ever more difficult to breathe. His head pounded. Every muscle in his body protested from lack of movement. He had no idea how long he'd been here, because time ceased to have any meaning. The only good thing was that because of Sterlave and Chur's interference, the recruits hadn't been allowed unfettered access to his exposed and horribly vulnerable ass.

"You can simply walk away."

Chur's voice was soft, but his offer sounded almost like an accusation. Kerrick had always disappeared when things grew difficult. Three times he'd been forsworn to various women, but in each and every relationship, he'd let himself be caught with another, so that his intended would reject him, demanding his departure.

Kerrick hated to admit the truth, but he knew the amazing coincidence of his chosen showing up at just the right moment, in just the right place, at just the right time to catch him with another woman was no accident. Always he exhibited shock and head-hanging shame, but in the back of his mind, he knew he'd carefully orchestrated his undoing so he could escape any responsibility.

The whole point of coming here and becoming the Harvester was to ultimately become the magistrate: a position with massive power and probably many nagging responsibilities, responsibilities that he could foist onto a subordinate. He could have all the prestige with little actual work. Mostly, Kerrick had wanted authority over his father. Even though he hadn't seen him in ten seasons, his rejection still rankled. As the magistrate, Kerrick could make or break his father. But what once seemed so important to him, now seemed pathetically juvenile. For all he knew, his father was deceased, or had long since retired from importing and exporting goods to Diola.

This whole mess really started one drunken night on Isela Five, when he and several other velto players engaged in a game of one-worse. Each man tried to give a more horrific story of life with his father. When Kerrick relayed his tale of a father who basically ignored him, except to tell him how worthless he was, and what a disappointment he continued to be, the others laughed. They said his experience wasn't that bad. Kerrick's father was cruel, but at least he hadn't beaten him. Or worse. Still, thinking of the past had stirred up long-buried memories of old hurts. That's when Kerrick became determined to repay his father for all he *hadn't* done for him. On a whim, he'd returned to Diola, a planet he swore never to set foot on again.

Several times, Kerrick had lamented that it was too late to turn back now, yet here was Chur, offering him the chance to depart relatively unscathed. There would be no revenge on his father, but he wouldn't have to live under the austere restrictions of his title, either. If he left now, Kerrick wouldn't have to fight to the death in the challenge. He wouldn't have to train into exhaustion. He wouldn't have to suffer the trauma of withholding his climax for only once a cycle. Given his history of taking the easy path, Kerrick should leap at Chur's offer, especially when he'd always acted without thinking.

What messed everything up was Ariss.

If he walked away, Kerrick could never touch her again. Worse, some other man, the one who became the next Harvester, would get to touch her, whether Ariss wanted him to or not. Kerrick didn't want to leave her to another, or to Ambo, either. He wanted her for himself. If he left, he would never again know the feel of her welcoming body wrapped around his, or her cool gray eyes turning hot with desire. If he stayed, he had to accept the depth of responsibility. If he impregnated her, he must bond to her. In this instance, he couldn't take pleasure without giving something of himself in return.

Gulping hard, struggling for each tiny sip of air, Kerrick realized he would have to make a commitment, something he had never done. His grandmother would be proud that finally he was truly considering the consequences of his actions.

"Are you going to answer me, or should I let the recruits in?" Chur's tone held a hint of mockery, as if he already knew the decision Kerrick had arrived at.

"I can't walk away." Kerrick's voice was harsh, almost strangled as he found it difficult to talk now. He would stay and finish what he started. If Ariss became pregnant, he would be the best bondmate to her that he could be. If she didn't, he would . . . and that's when his heart stopped. He thought he was staying to protect her, but to his shock, he discovered he didn't want to leave her, regardless of the outcome. "What happens if I don't get her pregnant?"

"You will face the challenge," Chur said. "If you survive that, you can choose a mate from among the sacrifices, or remain the Harvester for as long as you wish."

From bad to worse. If he didn't get her pregnant, he couldn't have her. "What if she chooses me?"

"She can't," Sterlave said. "As the Harvester, Ariss can only pick a free man within the palace walls. You are not free. Your position binds you to the ritual."

Kerrick would have laughed if he had the breath. Finally, he found a woman he wanted, but he couldn't have her unless he fulfilled some convoluted ancient prophecy. His grandmother must be laughing herself simple in *Jarasine.* Every woman he'd ever loved and left must be gleeful that he'd finally gotten his comeuppance.

Still, he had time to walk away. Kerrick stood at the crossroads of a momentous decision. Ariss stood at the head of one path and freedom stood at the other.

Pounding footsteps filled the room. When Chur and Sterlave didn't instantly dismiss them, Kerrick knew the person who entered wasn't a recruit.

"Release the Harvester."

Kerrick held his breath, wondering what was happening now. He'd never officially answered Chur, but this, whatever it was, might give him another option he hadn't yet considered.

"Under whose authority?" Sterlave asked, stepping toward the messenger, his feet crunching in the scattered seeds.

"By the gods, the Harvester has fulfilled her duty."

Kerrick's eyebrows rose. A smile tugged the edges of his lips wide. Ariss was pregnant with his child! He could not have been more pleased. In a way, he found the turn of events a relief, because now he had no choice. So what if technically they were forcing him to be her bondmate? He wanted her and she wanted him. The mechanics of the affair didn't matter to him in the slightest. Ariss was his for a lifetime.

Kneeling near to release him from the *gannett,* Chur whispered, "It seems the choice has been made for you."

For once, the thought that he couldn't turn back now satisfied Kerrick deeply.

Cleaned, anointed, his body nude under a heavy brown robe, Kerrick stood at the entrance to the temple. Before him two acolytes, one male, one female, both dressed in white, parted the thick fabric drapes, ushering him inside.

Vibrating with fury, Kerrick entered. Blue light and clouds of smoke greeted him, making him cough and cover his mouth with the sleeve of his robe. Rushing to his side, a female acolyte pulled his hand away, lowering his arm as she smiled up at him. Her teeth glowed weirdly blue-white, causing him to tug his hand from hers. Oblivious to his distaste, she lifted her hand, showing him the path he should take. On the floor were scatterings of what he could only assume were white flower petals as they, too, glowed in the dark.

Stepping carefully around them, convinced that they were as drugged as the air, Kerrick followed the path until he came to a raised dais of white stone. Upon an elaborate throne carved of the same white stone sat Ariss. Golden light tumbled around her hair and danced across small gemstones along her cheeks. She wore a black robe with gold trim. One hand covered her belly, the other lay limply along the armrest. Kerrick wasn't sure if it was the drugged air, but she appeared almost ethereal, her serene face calm and beatific. Her robe parted around her neck, exposing the stone necklace. No longer black, the *parastone* was now clear, confirming her pregnancy.

The details of this he'd been told as he was prepared by his *paratanist.* Fana had been almost breathless as she rushed around him, making him dizzy with her frantic hurry to ready him for the bonding ceremony.

Bonding ceremony. Kerrick gritted his teeth. This would not be a typical bonding. Every time he wrapped his head around one duty, they switched paths and he had to take another. He most certainly didn't want to go down this particular road.

Ariss' eyes met his, her lids blinking with graceful slowness, as if she literally blessed him by giving him her attention. Sympathy lay within the cool gray depths, but such did little to chill his resentment. How ironic that he thought he was teaching her, when she taught him the biggest lesson of all, one he thought he already knew: Always look out for number one. He'd stuck around because he felt sorry for her, or that's what he told himself now, anyway. The temptation to slap himself repeatedly was difficult to restrain, but he did, because breaking protocol in the temple would have him placed under the stone. In all honesty, he'd rather be alive than crushed to death.

Kerrick knew what he was supposed to do. He didn't want to, but Fana said that if he didn't, they would kill him, and another would take his place. That seemed to be their answer to everything: Do as we say or we will kill you. Unwilling to die just to escape the shame of his position, Kerrick dropped to his knees before Ariss.

Clenching his teeth to hold back an angry tirade, Kerrick unclasped his robe and slid the heavy weight off his shoulders. Cool air caressed him, peaking his nipples. Normally such a chill would shrivel his cock, but his *paratanist* had taken care of that, too.

Kneeling before Ariss nude, his cock hard and painfully sensitive because of some dreadful potion Fana had slathered all over it, Kerrick lowered his face, and snarled, "I have come to offer you tribute." They told him what to say, but they couldn't control the tone of his voice.

"What will you give me in tribute?" Ariss asked, her voice ringing through the temple in clear dulcet tones.

How about my cock in your mouth? That's what he wanted to give her, but he didn't say it, no matter how deeply his pride wanted him to say it. Damn it all to the nothingness, but he couldn't even bear to look at her as he said, "I will give you my body, my soul, my life." He drew a deep breath to bolster himself for the rest. No matter how shameful, he had to finish, because he'd cared too much about her to walk away. Worse, it truly was too late to turn back now. "I offer myself as your protector." He lifted his chin, letting the light illuminate his face, but he looked at a spot just over her shoulder rather than into her eyes. "I will protect you through this life unto the next in *Jarasine.*"

With those words, Kerrick offered himself as her willing slave. They were not bonding as mates. This ceremony bonded him to her for eternity as her servant. Not her partner, her mate, or her lover, but as her lowly, worthless slave. He could never leave her, not even in death, for he would have to protect her in the great beyond as well. He could never know the touch of another woman, but she could have all the lovers she desired. Should he displease her, she could have him executed and replaced with another. In her slender hands, Ariss now held his very life. To call him resentful was to call the twin suns bright.

The acolytes called Ariss the chosen mate of Tavarus, the god of the Harvesters. The child she carried was considered Tavarus'. Kerrick knew in his heart that he was the child's father. However, again, because of some convoluted ancient prophecy, he couldn't do anything. Kerrick became Tavarus' chosen lackey to watch over Ariss until she died and joined Tavarus in *Jarasine.*

All this Fana told him with exuberant excitement. As a slave herself, Fana thought becoming one to the carrier of a god's child was just about the highest honor possible. Kerrick didn't share her enthusiasm, especially not when he discovered what he was expected to do.

"Are you willing?" Ariss asked, her voice pulling him back to the present.

Looking directly into her eyes, Kerrick frowned, and opened his mouth to berate her a fool, but he pressed his lips carefully together. One did not mock the gods, not even the chosen vessel of the gods, not if one expected to continue breathing.

"I am willing." He impressed himself with the fact that his words sounded utterly believable even though he was lying right to her face. All he had to do was bide his time. Somehow, someday, there would come an opportunity for him to escape, and he would seize it without a second thought. Never again would he let concern for her sway his decision to look out for himself first. Just as the thought of fleeing from her gripped him, he knew he wouldn't, not when she carried his child. He might resent her, but he knew deep down to the sticking place in his heart that he could never walk away from his own child. No matter what, he would endure anything to protect him or her.

Ariss stood.

White light blazed around her head as she stepped toward him, forcing him to tilt his face back because he refused to look away in shame. In her hand, she held what he dreaded most, but he didn't move from his kneeling position. Leaning forward, Ariss kissed his forehead, her lips surprisingly cool against his flesh. With swift movements, she slipped the slender metal collar around his neck, locking it into place. It would be with him until the day he died.

She stepped back to admire him.

Kerrick gritted his teeth so hard he thought he heard them crack. At first, the collar felt cool around his neck, but the metal quickly heated to match his body's temperature. It felt unbearably heavy. In reality, the thing probably weighed little, but the burden it placed on him felt inordinately cumbersome. His shoulders slumped. All his life he'd lived for excitement and danger, but because he wanted revenge on his father for no very good reason, he'd become the possession of a demigoddess.

Ariss returned to her throne. "You may offer me your tribute."

He'd already heard details of how guard after guard had paraded before her, displaying himself, stroking himself. Now she expected him to do the same. Kerrick thought the entire process was degrading and designed to put him in his place. He was her pet. He was supposed to leap at the snap of her fingers to do her bidding. This did not hold the sensual promise for him as her request had in the mating room. There, he'd wanted to perform for her, to show her the power in his body as he worked his cock with his own hand. Here, he felt lower than low, a trifle, a plaything.

Wincing, Kerrick tried to will his erection away, but whatever Fana had put on him caused his cock and balls to throb in such agony the only way he would have relief was if he climaxed. How bitter that the seed he'd so eagerly wanted to pump into Ariss during their stolen tryst would now be splattered at her feet in a show of his submission to her.

Against his will, Kerrick wrapped one fist around his shaft. He recoiled in pain. He was so sensitive that even the softest brush caused untold agony. If he didn't give tribute, he would be executed, but he simply hurt so much he was afraid to touch himself. What the hell had Fana done to him in her blithering excitement? Whatever she'd put on him, she had obviously used too much. Even now, his cock glistened and the oil continued to run down to his balls.

Perhaps this was her revenge for catching him with Ariss. He'd been so enraptured that he hadn't even heard Fana enter his room. But she had. Shocked, Fana left and ran to the guards. She stood before them silently until one of them asked what her problem was. As soon as she had the right to speak, she'd spilled everything. As Kerrick knelt before Ariss, he wondered what would have happened if Fana had not returned to his rooms. Idly, he wondered what Fana had returned for. Not that it mattered. Not that he would ever get the chance to ask. Fana was at this very moment being given to the next Harvester.

Subtly, he knelt back on his heels, as if readying himself, but he actually used the movement to wipe the oil off his hands and onto his robe. He tried to touch himself again, but the contact was still too much.

Panic drew his body tight, causing his chest to constrict as he held his breath to do as she had bid. He tried again to grasp his cock, but just the heat of his hand caused him to yank his hand back. Desperate to show he was at least trying, he cupped his balls, hoping to remove some of the potent oil. Under the guise of teasing himself, he drew the slickness away, leaning back to wipe it on his robe.

"Stop."

His heart literally halted mid-beat. When he looked up, Ariss was standing. For the longest time she simply considered him, her head tilted fractionally to the side as if she were debating what to do with him. He swallowed hard. She moved toward him with dreamy slowness. As she drew near, she cupped her hand to his chin, lifting his face, then without words, she commanded him to his feet.

He took a deep breath, tasting the absolute ambrosia of her scent. Maybe she really had transformed, because she certainly smelled glorious. That sweet *valasta* was there but more powerful. Just her scent seemed to calm his frazzled nerves and reduced the sensitivity of his body.

"I'm trying," he whispered, in the hopes she wouldn't grow weary of him and call the acolytes to haul him away.

"Silence," she said, her voice seeming to drift right to his ear.

Looming over her, he peered down, causing her to lean far back to meet his gaze. She did so without any indication of anger. And why should she be upset? With a snap of her fingers, she could order a contingent of guards to crush him under the stone.

"I want your tribute within me." Ariss parted her robe, exposing her nude body, then stepped forward. She plastered herself against him. Deftly, she slipped his cock between her legs, wiping the oil away with her inner thighs.

Crying out, stunned by the combination of pleasure and pain, Kerrick grasped her hips. Expecting a horde of acolytes to rush in and yank him away, he held very still.

"They would not dare correct me," Ariss whispered, placing her hands on either side of his head to angle him for her kiss.

He thought of resisting, of turning his head away, but she'd taken pity on his pathetic state, perhaps she even understood what Fana had done to him. He saw a knowing in her eyes, an absolute certainty in her gaze. When he looked deeper, he saw her genuine hunger. Not for just any man, but for him. Apparently, her encounter with her lofty god left her unsatisfied.

Pulling her hips tight, feeling the welcoming softness of her thighs sliding along his shaft, he forcefully claimed her mouth. He might be a slave, but she would know that he was not a tender servant. To own him would be like owning a wild animal; at any moment, he could turn on her.

Matching his ferocity, Ariss kissed him back, her hands against his head, tugging at his hair. From a distance, it would appear she was the aggressor, but Kerrick didn't mind. Let her put on a show for the trembling acolytes. He didn't care what they thought. He tried to withhold his pleasure along with his climax, but his sensitized body wouldn't allow him even that satisfaction. She truly owned him in this moment. If she pushed him away, a part of his pride would die, and he feared he would never be the same.

Thankfully, Ariss gave no indication that she would do

something so cruel. Each small movement she made drove him mad with passion. Breathless, desperate, he pulled back, angled his cock to the sweet, hot entrance of her cunt, and then shoved forward.

Ariss gasped, pulling her mouth from his, twisting her hands against his head. Her head fell back, exposing her throat. Kerrick lowered his lips and bit her neck, drawing the tender flesh inside his mouth, marking her as he was now marked with her collar. In his own way, he laid his claim to her, and not as some pathetic servant. He would find a way to be her master, even if he was only so in private. Ariss would beg for him, writhe for him, spreading her legs eagerly to feel his strength and power.

Each thrust of his hips pulled another groan from her and sent another almost unbearable surge of pleasure through him. He thought at any instant he would erupt, but something held him back, something that waited for the right moment. Inside, he felt a power swirling from nothingness to grow larger, filling up every cell in his body until it oozed from his pores. When he looked down, he swore his body was glowing.

Ariss clung to his shoulders. Clasping him by digging her nails in, she lifted herself up, wrapping her legs around his hips, nestling his sex deeply inside. When he glanced at her face, he discovered her eyes were wide open, her pupils so large they ate up the colored portion of her eyes.

Losing himself in that abyss, Kerrick demanded, "Give me your tribute."

Her lips parted as her head went farther back. Tightening her thighs around his waist, she dug her feet into his buttocks, mashing her clit against the rough of his pubic hair.

Bouncing her once, twice, she let out a scream of pure satisfaction as her cunt clasped his cock. Then, and only then, did he offer his tribute in exchange for hers.

Kerrick climaxed with the strength of a god. He felt the pull from his toes to the tips of his hair. Everything in his body rushed out to fill her. All of that power that had pushed at the walls of his skin vanished with his orgasm. All of it was gone in the blink of an eye, causing Kerrick to stagger back. He fell to his knees so he wouldn't drop Ariss.

There was no question in his mind now about his true duty. Kerrick was not a servant to Ariss, but to Tavarus.

14

Ariss turned her back on the mirror, no longer caring what she looked like. She'd spent most of the day surrounded by a gaggle of servants who fussed over every strand of her hair, every minute fold of fabric, every tiny flicker of sparkling gems. Being a demigoddess was exhausting work. Whatever she'd become in the temple was changing her. Not drastically, but subtle changes occurred to the color of her eyes, the lift of her cheekbones, the texture of her flesh. Inside, she felt the same, but outside, she was changing. Slowly but surely, she was becoming the vessel of a god. When she placed her hand on her belly, she felt power below, even though the babe wasn't old enough yet to move in any way she could discern, she still felt him. Him, for she knew that her child was male. Too, she knew, that sacrifice and trauma shrouded his destiny. Ariss had no idea if he would prevail, only that she would not be there to help him through his strife.

"Are you ready?"

Kerrick's voice tugged at her heart. When she turned, she fastened her attention on his eyes. Beautiful clear green, like the darkest forest shade. His golden hair was longer now and perfectly straight, sweeping across his gaze so he had to flick the golden curtain back. Always she wanted to reach out and push the strands away, but the one time when she had, he clasped her hand and pushed her away. Not a big push, not enough to hurt her or even unbalance her, just enough to make it clear he did not welcome her touch. Such an action broke her heart. She knew in that moment that Kerrick would never forgive her.

Two cycles had passed since Kerrick had become her bonded slave. At the time, she knew the depth of his anger. On his knees before her, he'd clenched his jaw so tightly she thought he would permanently change the shape of his face. Repeatedly, she wanted to tell him that all of it was for show. She had no intention of keeping him as her servant. But she couldn't put his fears to rest in the temple. She had to go through with what was demanded of her. Placing the metal collar around his neck hurt her just as much as it hurt him. She didn't believe in owning other humans. And certainly, she didn't want to own Kerrick. She wanted him as her bondmate, not her bonded slave. Her joy at fulfilling her duty was lost amidst the pain of what she'd done to him, and the dread of not knowing whose child she carried.

Tavarus had embraced her through the tawdry throne, filling her with the molten lava of his seed. Yet, shortly before that, she'd been with Kerrick. He hadn't climaxed, but she knew he didn't necessarily have to. Besides, he'd later given his tribute deep inside her rather than at her feet. Not that it mattered to the acolytes. They said the father of her babe was Tavarus. Sadly, even Ariss herself couldn't lay claim to her own child. She was simply the vessel chosen to carry the issue of a god.

"I am ready," she said, extending her hand out to clasp Kerrick's arm. She needed his help to maneuver in her heavy robe. Once they entered the celebration, she'd be able to remove the unwieldy thing, but not until then. Part of her current duty included making grand entrances. The collar of the black robe rose high behind her head, forming a backdrop littered with gold and diamonds. Her hair was piled atop her head, elongating her neck, giving her a regal bearing. She looked every bit fit enough to be a god's consort. Her dreams of living a simple life in the forest seemed further from her grasp than ever. Because of her foolishness, her single-minded determination to escape her parents and Ambo, she'd placed herself into the grandest mess.

Often, in the dark of night, as she slept alone in her massive bed, she wondered if she could have changed anything, or if all of it, from becoming the Harvester to her willingness to do anything to feel Kerrick's magical touch, was all predetermined by the gods. How did one escape one's destiny if a god was determined to use one for his own ends?

Kerrick placed his free hand over hers. To those on the outside, the gesture would seem an offer of comfort and support, but she knew it was simply for show. By the prophecy, he was fated to be at her side until the day she died. On that day, he would be ritualistically executed, so that he could accompany her to *Jarasine.* The only way he could break free of his bond was to precede her in death. Of course, if he did, he was expected to wait in the nothingness for her to die.

Kerrick wore a simple brown tunic and loose brown trousers. The fabrics were of the finest grade, but the color indicated his station as a slave. Only a small black band of trim around his upper right arm indicated his previous status as a Harvester. Around his waist, he wore a thick animal-hide belt, also brown, that held several weapons. Normally a slave wasn't permitted to own weapons, but Kerrick was her protector. His status among the servants in the palace was unique. There had not been one like him ever in the written history of Diola.

She remembered the night she'd snuck into his room, and

his despair that he couldn't wield the weapons with much skill. Her teachings were immaterial now. Tavarus could possess him and his skill was unmatched by any mere mortal. Tavarus was the god of the Harvesters, a god of sex and war. If any dared to attack her, Tavarus would use Kerrick to inflict swift and sure retribution. So far, his skills hadn't been needed, as everyone in the palace avoided them but for when courtesy or protocol demanded interaction.

Already Tavarus left his mark on Kerrick by changing his outward appearance in subtle ways. His hair was blonder, his face stronger, his height slightly increased. However, the alterations that Ariss feared the most were the ones that none could see, not even Kerrick himself. There were times when Tavarus surged through Kerrick. When his eyes darkened and his pupils swelled to cover the irises, that was when she knew Tavarus possessed him. Ariss dreaded looking into his eyes and seeing fathomless black. Because when Tavarus took command of Kerrick, he made him do things that Kerrick would not wish to do. When Tavarus ruled Kerrick's body, he would throw her upon the bed, mount her in a fury, and then be gone as swiftly as he climaxed. Kerrick would awaken later, his expression bewildered.

Ariss did not tell him what Tavarus was doing.

Kerrick's resentment at being her bonded slave was bad enough. He didn't need to know that Tavarus was using him as a sex surrogate as well, especially when Kerrick was forbidden to touch any woman. The only way he could find release was once a cycle in the temple.

At first, Tavarus had possessed Kerrick with great frequency, often several times in the same day, but Ariss knew this was because she was new to him. After a while the novelty faded. Tavarus seemed to come less and less, which eased her mind. She thought at first he would move on to other women, using Kerrick to sample this mortal realm, but apparently the bonding ceremony literally bonded Kerrick to her; he could not fornicate with another woman, as far as she could tell. Sadly, Kerrick couldn't have her unless Tavarus was in his body.

Always, though, in her lingered the nagging question of what they would become. Where would they go once the baby came? Ariss feared the acolytes would tear the child from her arms and insist they rear him within the temple. Just the thought of his life there, shrouded in mystery and worshipped by those around him, made Ariss want to run. However, there wasn't anywhere to run to. If Tavarus wanted his son to come of age worshipped as a living god, then he could make it so. Even if she and Kerrick ran, all he had to do was possess Kerrick and return her to the palace. Should she dare to run alone, she feared he would do something to her through her child.

Once, when she stood on the balcony looking down at how far the land below was, and just the idlest thought of what would happen if she fell over crossed her mind, her belly clutched in such pain she backed away from the railing. The throbbing ache didn't stop until she returned to the room and closed the glass door. From that moment on, she hadn't been able to step onto the balcony. What hurt her more than anything was that she didn't want to harm her child, it had only been a passing thought, but Tavarus punished her for it. She hated him for not even allowing her the privacy of her own introspection.

When she'd been shaken by his violent sexual cravings, Tavarus had taunted her through Kerrick, chasing her around her rooms, ripping her clothing off in bits until she was covered in nothing but rags. He'd caught her, forced her to her hands and knees, and then brutally used her from behind. Fingertip bruises had lined her hips, and rug burns had marred her knees and hands for days.

Valiantly, Kerrick had tried to fight him. In his eyes, she saw the conflict as the god's possession turned his green eyes black.

Back and forth, his eyes changed from green to black, but ultimately the god was stronger, and Kerrick's resistance only fueled his anger. Things were easier for them both if they simply let Tavarus have his way. Kerrick remembered nothing of this encounter, but he'd frowned and raised speculative eyebrows at her injuries.

She knew he thought she was indulging another man; sadly, the only man she wanted was the one she couldn't have. The only hope Ariss clung to was that Tavarus would never hurt her deeply, only superficially, because he wouldn't risk the child within.

What made Tavarus' aggressiveness worse was that in the temple he'd been so unbelievably gentle. When she'd confronted him, he'd laughed, and said that was to waylay her into giving him permission to use her through Kerrick. If she'd known the truth of his sexual hunger, she never would have bonded to Kerrick.

"You are stunning," Kerrick said, ushering her from their lushly appointed rooms and into a clutch of guards. Four abreast in the front, four in the back, they made their way to the great hall.

Ariss smiled at him, pleased that he appreciated how many hours she had sat immobile to become the living statue she was now. She could barely turn her head less she muss her hair or ruin the line of the fancy robe. Behind the four guards in back lagged several of her servants. They carried extra adornments so that all throughout the celebration, Ariss would always look her best.

Kerrick's slave collar gleamed. She'd tried to remove the loathsome thing, but she was unable to do so. Even in death, he wouldn't be free from the band. To outside eyes, Kerrick willingly played his part of dutiful servant. Her heart took a dangerous lurch in her chest because his willingness to do this was to protect her from censure. Almost everything Kerrick did was to shield her from harm. But only in the public's eye. When they were alone, his anger was like a palpable force. Her heart broke when she discovered he could barely look at her without clenching his jaw. However, she realized he wasn't angry with her, but at the situation he found himself in. Deep inside, he still cared about her, but he couldn't stop resenting his subservient position.

She'd tried not to let her emotions grow, but she couldn't prevent herself from falling in love with him. Love was an emotion she could not afford, for she dared not cross Tavarus. But she'd only heard him laugh in her mind when he'd forced his way into the secret part of her thoughts, those she'd managed to keep hidden for a time. Tavarus said love was for poets and fools. The gods did not love. They merged to find pleasure, but there was nothing about love in their mating. Only foolish mortals considered themselves hampered by such delusions. If loving Kerrick soothed her, let such be so, for Tavarus didn't care. All he wanted was access to the plush, welcoming heat of her body when the mood struck him. Kerrick could have her heart, for Tavarus had everything else.

"What is this celebration for?" she asked, moving slowly but steadily down the hall. There had been so many in the last two cycles that Ariss couldn't keep them straight.

"The new empress has been crowned."

Ariss nodded absently, then immediately stilled her head. One more forgetful movement and her hair would tumble down.

At one time, she might have cared about the crowning of a new empress, but not now. The petty politics of the palace meant little when her world became that of the gods. The only thing that gave her pause was wondering if her parents would attend this party. She realized they likely wouldn't. Her sister had vied for the position along with every other girl from the elite Houses who was of age. Ariss didn't know who had won, but she knew her sister had lost. Mother said Father was so mortified that he'd wanted to return to Felton. She had no idea if he had, but moreover, she didn't care. The one time when she'd seen her father, he'd recoiled from her. He'd said all the right things to show obeisance to the god's vessel, but she could tell he wanted to get away from her as quickly as possible. It took Ariss a while to comprehend the fact that her father was afraid of her.

If he could have extracted some benefit from her position, he would have, but in this, she was alone. Her rise to the state of a demigoddess did not include her family, for her change had come as the Harvester, not as his daughter. Once Radox grasped that fact, he abandoned her. Her father was nothing if not practical. When he realized he couldn't use her any longer, he was gone, probably off trying to find a way to use one of his remaining daughters.

From what little gossip she heard among her staff, Ariss gleaned that Ambo refused to give her father the palace contract for raw *astle* fibers. All his work in making her the Harvester was for naught; she hadn't fulfilled her end of the bargain to become Ambo's bondmate, which voided his agreement with her father. Ariss couldn't even blame her father for her current misery. If she'd stuck to the rules of her position and clung honorably to her duty, she might have faired a far different fate.

"There's no turning back now," Kerrick said.

She startled, for she thought he'd read her mind, but instead, he meant they had arrived at the sweeping entrance to the great hall. Just beyond the arched doorway, hundreds of voices swirled in a cacophony as a thousand individual scents filled her too-sensitive nose. With a deep breath, she squeezed his arm and stepped inside. Glittering dresses of the brightest jewel tones littered the black Onic tile floor. Swirling to high-spirited music, the ladies and gentlemen of the elite were like beautiful flowers blowing in a gracious wind. Ariss' black clothing separated her from them. She was darkness in the sea of light that spilled across the expanse of the hall.

Heads turned in her direction and steps faltered, but only for the barest moment. Quickly they turned away to forcefully make merry, as if her dark presence hadn't disturbed their gaiety. Much like her father, the bulk of the elite granted her deference and the respect due her by virtue of her position, but below their forced smiles lurked hearts filled with fear. Only Kerrick looked upon her without terror skulking in his gaze. His eyes held a dull fury, but sometimes, far below, she saw his desire.

Tables laden with food dotted the room while potted plants offered secluded spots with chairs and couches so that guests could find a momentary reprieve from the festivities. Everywhere her gaze traveled, she found greater and greater excess. Servants were dressed elaborately and frozen in place like living statues. Ariss felt for them. Her own hideous outfit confined her movements. Huge fountains of red wine gushed into the air, burbling merrily. To her eyes, they seemed as huge, open wounds spewing blood. She clutched Kerrick's arm tighter as her stomach roiled in protest.

Sensing her distress, Kerrick led her to a raised platform with several layers, like widened steps. At the top rested the elaborately carved Onic timber throne of the empress. No consort throne sat by its side. Ariss thought that curious. Below the highest step rested another throne. This one was smaller and not as decorative. Was this one for her consort?

The protocol officer had drilled Ariss earlier, but she couldn't remember any of what she'd said. When Kerrick led her to the smaller throne, she hesitated, dread stealing over her. In a rush, she remembered. She would have fallen to her knees if not for Kerrick's strong arm holding her up. This was not a party for her to attend as a guest. This was a party for her to sit on high so all the elite could look upon her and see the vessel of a god. This show was to remind them that the child she carried would one day rule beside their new empress.

Turning her back to the throne reminded her of her punishment in the temple. She shivered, even though this one had no stone phallus. Carefully, as she sat down, her servants arranged her robes to fall artfully over the chair so that when viewed, she would be centered in the decorative folds. Feeling like artwork on display, Ariss sat very still, nestled in the golden fabric that lined the inside of her black robe.

Kerrick stood to her side. One hand dangled loosely at his side while the other rested lightly on the hilt of his blade. His gaze never ceased to travel over those below them. Now she understood another reason why they had seated her up high; such afforded her protector a wide view. Not that any would dare to attack her. She sensed that if any harbored her ill will, Tavarus would know. He would reach down through Kerrick and destroy them.

Once the music ended, the dancers babbled excitedly until a blast of fanfare drowned them out. All eyes, including Ariss', were drawn to the entrance of the great hall. Palace guards dressed in finery marched into the room, flanking into two lines on either side of the door. Their massive bodies created a hallway of protection for the new empress.

Ariss held her breath, curious as to which House had won the most coveted position in the entire empire. Crimson House had ruled the empress line for so long that none could remember a time when they didn't. Below her, the masses waited, too, their eyes gleaming, their mouths pressed tightly to hold back any excited utterances.

Sensing a problem, Ariss narrowed her eyes, as if that would help her see beyond the entrance. Her sensitive hearing picked up several voices whispering in fury. Suddenly, a sour-faced young woman stumbled into the path between the guards. Ariss sensed she'd been shoved by the way she struggled to keep her balance.

A collective gasp erupted.

Before she could stop herself, Ariss lifted a hand to her mouth, as if to block her strangled shock. Clad in crimson, the tawny-skinned girl with black hair was clearly related to Kasmiri. Older, but obviously her sister.

The whole reason for the empress challenge was that Kasmiri was illegitimate. As the product of an empress and an unofficial consort, Kasmiri had renounced her throne before Ambo could impose death or exile upon her. As an only child, Kasmiri's stepping down meant that Crimson House's claim on the throne ended with her. Yet, here was a young lady who simply had to be the sister of Kasmiri and the daughter of Empress Clathia. For her to even compete in the empress challenge, her claim must have been validated. She had to be the legitimate offspring of Empress Clathia and her official consort, but where had she been kept all this time?

Ariss scanned the crowd. They seemed as stunned as she did, with wide eyes and hand-covered mouths. The empress challenge was conducted in secret, shrouded in mystery, and obscured by ritual, so none here would have had foreknowledge of the outcome. Now that one had been chosen from the many, their daughters would be returned to them. Ariss' sister had failed early on in the challenge, as the competition was conducted in stages. Darabelle had survived the initial test of proving she was of an elite House; however, she'd failed the next round that judged them on beauty. Ariss felt a twinge of sympathy for Darabelle despite her petty behavior, but she'd not been allowed to see her sister before she'd left the palace in shame.

Similar in several respects to the Harvester competition, the apprentice empresses had to compete in a layered challenge involving six areas. The last level was the most secretive. The four who entered would have been secluded until one was chosen. Or so Ariss thought. She honestly had no idea, as her attention had been otherwise engaged in her own pressing issues.

Frowning at everyone, the new empress darted her pale blue gaze among the guests as if all of them were against her. Her enormous pile of black hair glistened in the light. Displaying an utter lack of grace, the extremely tall woman lifted her skirt and stomped toward the raised platform.

Ariss bit her lip not to erupt in laughter. Whoever she was, she was clearly upset about something. Probably the elaborate crimson dress. In her fists, she grasped handfuls of the fabric so it wouldn't impede her steps. Annoyance oozed from every glance, every breath, and every step she took.

Behind her, in the doorway looking on, the protocol officer, Undanna, openly cringed at the spectacle the new empress created. As the young woman threw herself into her throne, heedless of the way her dress twisted around her legs, the entire room of people fell to their knees. She might be a petulant, ill-mannered child, but she was still the empress.

"All hail Empress Bithia!"

A snarl darted across Bithia's face at the mention of her own name. Ariss guessed she preferred another name other than her given one. Although, with a name like Bithia, Ariss couldn't really blame her. Bithia was a name no longer used, as it harkened back to the time of the ancients. Perhaps Clathia had given her daughter such a name to show their lineage went back that far. Clathia's name was of the same era.

Everyone in the great hall called out her name as they lowered their faces for a moment of silence. Ariss followed suit, but cracked her eyes open to observe Bithia.

Upon her throne, Bithia glowered down at her people; then to Ariss' utter surprise, she rolled her eyes and exhaled a long, rather loud sigh as she tossed one leg over the armrest!

Small wonder there wasn't a consort throne; what man would willingly become this woman's partner? Another snarl twisted her face. Bithia lifted her hand to scratch at her hair. If the woman would stop scrunching up her face, she was actually quite pretty, especially with her light blue eyes set in tawny skin. As she scratched at her head, the mound of hair swayed dangerously from side to side. Ariss realized she wore a wig. What had possessed them to put this creature on the throne? Was it because she was a descendant of Crimson House?

Ariss' neck grew stiff from having to hold her head so still. As she longed to reach up and rub the knotted tension away, she appreciated Bithia's blithe dismissal of convention. If her neck were bothersome, Bithia wouldn't care about protocol; she'd do what she had to do in order to make herself comfortable. Ariss wished she had that much courage.

Once the moment of silence ended, the crowd lifted their heads, but none commented on Bithia's sprawled position. Eyes went wide, but none uttered a breath of disapproval.

"Oh, *grandathall*," Bithia said, swearing in a language Ariss didn't understand. Waving her hand dismissively, she bellowed, "Let the celebration begin."

Music blared into the room, compelling all to dance.

Kerrick leaned close to Ariss' ear and murmured, "She certainly knows how to make an entrance."

Ariss did her best not to laugh, less the woman hear her, but a small giggle erupted despite her best efforts. She hadn't laughed in so long, and sharing something lighthearted with Kerrick lifted her spirits.

"You, you there," Bithia said, snapping her fingers and pointing at Ariss. "Are you the god's *yondie*?"

Only those closest to the platform heard Bithia's comment. Ariss felt them straining to listen without appearing obvious.

Lifting her entire upper body, Ariss turned in her seat to face the empress more directly.

Staring straight into her eyes, Ariss proudly declared, "I am the vessel of Tavarus, god of the Harvesters."

Blinking back her surprise that Ariss met her challenge without flinching, Bithia shrewdly considered her for a moment. Her face broke into a wide and amazingly charming smile. "You, I think I will enjoy." Flicking her chin to the people below, which tilted her wig even more precariously, she said, "Them, I will tolerate."

Her grammar was atrocious, but there was something poignantly endearing about her. Ariss forgot all about why she was here, and instead, fell deeply into conversation with Bithia. Her life story was amazing, her spirit indomitable. She hadn't even known her origins until recently.

" 'Bout the last thing I ever wanted was to be tarted up and paraded around for a bunch of overdressed *peckards.*" She rolled her eyes again with a shake of her head. Ariss didn't know exactly what a *peckard* was, but it certainly wasn't complimentary. As Bithia's wig timbered to the side, Ariss reached out, even though she knew she was too far away to catch it. Growling in frustration, Bithia reached up and yanked at the pins holding it in place. Once she freed the enormous mound of hair, she tossed it into the crowd, knocking a man off his feet. His scowl of annoyance disappeared when he realized who had caused his downfall. Plastering a wide grin to his face, he bowed repeatedly as he brushed nonexistent dust off his deep blue clothing and melted into the swelling crowd.

Bithia's laughter rang through the room, causing several people to look up and quickly away. Her laugh was big, brash, almost a force of nature. Ariss had never heard its equal in volume or length. Bithia's real hair was extremely short. Black as ink, but the strands were no longer than the length of one of her stubby fingernails. Ariss had never seen a woman with such short hair, yet Bithia's face was strong enough to wear the odd style well.

She brushed her hands quickly through her close-cropped locks so they stood straight up from her skull. Then she leaned over, yanked her high-heeled shoes off, and tossed those into the crowd as well. "*Grandathall!* Now I can relax!" She snapped her fingers at a passing servant. When he approached, she snatched not one, but three drinks off his tray, settling the extras beside her throne.

A gaggle of female servants stealthily climbed up the back of the steps, carrying her wig and shoes, clearly determined to set her royal person to rights.

Bithia winked at Ariss conspiratorially, then lifted her hand, halting them in midstride. "One more step and I'll have you all . . ." she trailed off, trying to find the right term. "Put in the stone? Covered with stones?" She turned to Ariss, and said, "Help me out here."

"Put to the stone," Ariss supplied. Crushing wayward inhabitants below a massive stone was the preferred death sentence on Diola. Several times, Kerrick had been threatened with just such a horror. However, Ariss knew that Bithia wasn't serious, she simply wanted them to leave her be. And the threat worked; slowly but surely, the servants backed away.

Ariss admired the young woman's spirit, for most would be far too worried about appearances to ever be themselves around the elite. They would put on airs and demand the finest of everything. Ariss had a feeling the empire was in for quite a surprise with Bithia's rule.

"So," Bithia said, tossing back an entire glass of wine in one gulp. Pointing the empty glass at Ariss' belly, she asked, "That brat gets half my empire?"

Ariss darted a quick glance up to Kerrick's eyes, but they were clear green. If Tavarus heard Bithia's comment, he either didn't care or didn't understand the derogatory nature of the term.

Softly, Ariss returned, "When he comes of age he will rule beside you."

"Is that so?" Bithia grabbed the last glass of wine and swallowed her drink in one mighty gulp. Carelessly, she tossed the empty glass behind her. "What if I don't want to share?"

15

Kerrick stood still beside Ariss' throne, letting Bithia say what she would. None of her blather mattered. This child would rule beside her, or she would be cast aside. The most ancient of prophecy decreed that the very gods had chosen this child, which made him far more important than the empress herself. Nothing this silly girl did or said would change that. Bithia could no more alter the future than Kerrick could change the truth of his position.

In the temple, on his knees before Ariss, he'd been so angry that he swore he would master her. Visions of her on her knees begging for his touch fueled his passion and gave him the strength to continue. When she pulled him to his feet and wrapped her lovely legs around him, encouraging him to fill her slick passage, his heart relented, but only for a moment. He had no choice but to stay by her side. However, he would not become a slave to her body. She commanded him as her servant, but he refused to share her bed. He was her protector. To that end, he shared her rooms, but he slept on the floor. Ariss had tried everything to get him to share the massive bed, but he refused.

When she put soft pallets beside her bed to please him, he pushed them away, refusing to take her charity.

Anger still filled him that he hadn't walked away when he'd had the chance. He'd stayed to protect Ariss. Bitterly, he reflected that he truly was her protector now. In the temple, he knew that Tavarus commanded him to be her champion, not Ariss, but Kerrick found it difficult to focus his anger on a god without form. It was so much easier to focus his rage on the woman he was sworn to protect.

From his height, Kerrick scanned the crowd, but the elite gave little notice to him, Ariss, or even the new and startling empress. He didn't fear any would dare to attack because simply everyone was terrified of Ariss. To her face, they showed the deference a demigoddess was due, but behind her back, they whispered about her and the child she carried. None of their comments was complimentary. Besides, the elite were far too enchanted with themselves to bother with harming Ariss. They danced and drank, babbling about their worthless lives, gorging themselves on expensive treats and sexual perversities. Kerrick despised them. Even when Kerrick was at a greater height than they were, the elite still managed to look down at him. He noticed when they looked at him their gazes went through him, as if he were not worthy of being noticed. Kerrick speculated this was due to what he wore and years of indoctrination; brown was the color of servants. Ironically, the brown showed off the rich gold of his hair and enhanced the green of his eyes. He'd caught sight of himself in Ariss' many mirrors and was satisfied by what he saw; he might be a lowly slave, but he'd never looked better.

Kerrick turned his attention back to Ariss and Bithia, grudgingly pleased that Ariss managed to hold her own against the decidedly different empress. Kerrick didn't sense any ill will in Bithia, only a need to test boundaries, like a child poorly reared. Soon enough she would learn to share the mighty burden of her position, not only share, but also she would welcome additional support. Right now, everything was parties and pageantry, but very soon, it would be petitions and pacification. Once she realized that a thousand myriad details would demand her attention every day, she would welcome all the help she could get.

"Besides, you have eighteen seasons to get used to the idea." Kerrick hadn't realized he'd spoken aloud until both women stopped talking and glanced in his direction. Mortified by his breach of station, for a servant should never speak over his master, Kerrick hung his head in abject apology. His hair flopped over his gaze, shielding him from Bithia's penetrating glare.

After a moment, she laughed that massive booming laugh of hers, and said, "I think I will enjoy you, too."

Hesitantly, Kerrick lifted his gaze to her.

Her fingers smoothed against the arm of her throne, and he knew she wished to brush the strands of hair out of his eyes. He smiled inwardly. Even as a slave, he still appealed to women. In the greater scheme of things, this knowledge was immaterial, but to his battered pride, knowing lifted his spirits.

Flicking his hair back with a toss of his head, he bowed low but said nothing. He could only speak to Bithia if she asked him a direct question. Such was the case with Ariss, too, but he often broke that rule with no censure, which caused his slip in this situation. For the rest of the evening, he would have to be on his guard.

Bithia called for a passing servant. This time she took the entire tray of drinks. She offered one to Ariss, who declined with a shake of her head and a hand to her belly.

"*Tadenta fa!*" Bithia slapped her palm to her forehead. Slowly, she lowered her arm, considering their baffled expressions. She then translated, "It means, 'I'm stupid for forgetting' on Beserrah." She put the tray near her throne, then held a cup out to Kerrick.

By protocol, he wasn't supposed to drink, but Bithia didn't seem concerned with adhering to strict etiquette. After a quick glance to Ariss to confirm her permission, he took the offered cup. Before he could withdraw, Bithia stroked her finger along the back of his hand. He would have dismissed the caress as an accident but for the quick lifted brows she flashed him.

Ariss noticed but said nothing.

Without acknowledging her flirtatious behavior, Kerrick saluted her with his drink. In addition, he took a perverse pleasure in watching Ariss have to hold her tongue for a change. She noticed Bithia's interest but could do nothing to chastise her. One simply didn't correct the empress's behavior.

"To the child of the gods," Bithia said without malice, lifting her cup on high. "Long may we rule in harmony." She tossed back her drink, then tossed the cup over her shoulder, where it shattered. "Well, in eighteen seasons, anyway."

Her grin was infectious. Kerrick found himself returning her smile, which earned him a slight, almost imperceptible frown from Ariss. Bithia's face was unlike any he had ever seen. Sharp cheekbones lifted the oval of her face out of the ordinary and into something extraordinary. Her close-cropped black hair only accented the pale blue of her wide-set eyes and deepened the tone of her tawny skin. Someone had artfully applied makeup, but her constant wiping of her mouth with the back of her hand had smeared it, revealing the true dusky color of her lips. On most women, the effect would be comical, however on Bithia, such disarray echoed the honesty of her nature. Whatever trappings they slapped on her, she quickly eroded. Disorder made her far more interesting than studied perfection would have.

When she caught him staring, Kerrick dropped his gaze. If

he wasn't careful, she would take the absolute wrong meaning from his interest. Just about the last thing he needed was to encourage the attentions of the new empress. Ariss had been fairly tolerant about his breeches in servant behavior, but he didn't think she would forgive a tryst with the empress. Not that he would actually do anything with her. Bithia was cute in her odd way, but she didn't stir his lust. Not the way Ariss still did, despite his best intentions to remain aloof.

Kerrick had thought Ariss was staying true to him as well, but he'd seen evidence of her passionate encounters with someone else; rug burns marred her palms and knees, fingertip-shaped bruises dotted her hips. Whoever her lover was, he was unbelievably aggressive. Kerrick told himself he didn't care. Ariss could fuck every man in the palace if she wanted, and there wasn't one thing he could do about it. But the truth was, it chafed his already decimated pride. He thought that by denying her, she would beg for him. Still, he had visions of her on her knees in supplication for even the smallest kiss. Apparently, she'd turned to another rather than waste her time on him.

"Tell me about your home planet of Beserrah," Ariss asked.

"*Bes-er-rah,*" Bithia corrected mildly, giving the word three distinct syllables. Her gaze swept over the people below, then the entire great hall. "Beserrah is nothing like Diola. We have one season: scorching." She shook her head fondly. "It's always excruciatingly hot and very humid." She plucked at her heavy dress. "This would be considered a form of torture on Beserrah."

"What do you wear?" Ariss asked, leaning closer.

Kerrick grinned. He might love gossip, but Ariss simply adored fashion. Each time he'd accompanied her to official gatherings, she would endlessly discuss what each lady wore, especially the women from other planets. When she returned to their rooms, she would sketch ideas for her seamstress. Slowly, inexorably, Ariss was single-handedly altering Diolan fashion.

"Most wore little, if anything," Bithia said, her eyes flashing meaningfully to Kerrick before returning to Ariss. "Nudity was common."

Kerrick had been to a world like that once; one that was hot, not one filled with nudity. The name escaped him, but he remembered the game they had played. Each man in a low-slung vehicle fought to reach the summit of a long uphill expanse of sand. The first to the top won. Most tumbled backward or lost momentum in the deep sand. It had seemed to Kerrick that the real point of the game was to spend an inordinate amount of time standing around drinking and watching the other participants. When night fell, they'd sit around campfires doing basically the same thing.

"Your people walked about naked?" Ariss stifled a gasp.

"They were not my people!" Bithia rolled her eyes. "I didn't rule there, I only spent time in their . . ." she searched for the word. "*Natsuma*—court."

"Why did Clathia send you—" Kerrick cut himself off when he suddenly realized he was prying into the private affairs of the empress. Worse, he'd again spoken out of turn. Kerrick didn't think the warm feelings generated during this brief encounter were enough to ask the young woman why her mother had sent her away and never told anyone on Diola about her existence. How she'd been found and entered into the empress competition was another provocative question altogether. One that he swore he wouldn't dare to ask, even though he was dying to know. Sterlave's accusation, that Kerrick was more enamored of gossip than any woman, was a lot truer than Kerrick would willingly admit. His love of gossip could very well be the death of him.

There had been one redeeming aspect to becoming a servant; he was allowed entrance to the *tishiary*. In the lower level of the palace lay a vast set of rooms where servants gathered to bathe, wash clothing, gossip, and gather supplies for their masters.

He'd been furious the first time he'd been sent there to bathe. However, one of Ariss' other servants had to retrieve him because he'd been so caught up in gossiping he'd forgotten everything else. Rown was a servant to Sterlave and Kasmiri. He knew simply everything about everyone. Rown demurred about his master and mistress, but he eagerly talked about everyone else. Whenever Kerrick went to the *tishiary*, he looked first for Rown.

A sullen expression, filled with an age-old hurt, darkened Bithia's normally bright face. "You know, you are the only person brave enough to ask me to my face about why Clathia sent me away." Lifting her chin accusingly toward the entrance, where the protocol officer, the magistrate, and other assorted members of her staff stood deep in conversation, she said, "They speculate behind my back, talking just loud enough so that I can hear." A smile of malice twisted her lips. "I don't tell them because I know how badly they want to know." Bithia considered Ariss and Kerrick for a moment. "Well, that's what I tell myself." She took a long drink. "The truth is, I don't tell them because I don't know." Her face turned wistful and terribly sad. "I never knew my mother or my father. I have no idea why they sent me away."

In that moment, he saw that despite her proud carriage and her bluster, Bithia was still a very young girl with a tender heart. In fact, she was just barely old enough for the Harvest. And that's when he recognized her. No wonder Bithia looked so familiar; he'd harvested her only a few cycles ago. Someone had taken great care to obscure her features with makeup, and she'd worn a wig of blond hair, but those pale blue eyes . . . He would never forget that almost translucent color. But what he remembered most about her was that she was no virgin. Surely, Bithia had recognized him, too.

Softly, Ariss said, "Perhaps they did not send you away."

Hope filled Bithia's eyes only to be replaced with wary suspicion.

Shrugging delicately, Ariss said, "Sometimes, in a world such as this"—she lifted her hand to include all those below them—"a father or mother might have no say in what befalls their child."

Bithia glanced down at Ariss' still-flat belly. "You would not choose this life for your child."

"No." Ariss looked up as if she could see right into the mists of *Jarasine.* "I would choose a life far different."

"Maybe that's why they sent me away; they didn't want me to have to deal with all of these *peckards.*"

Ariss' laugh cheered him. She rarely laughed anymore. He knew that all her life she'd longed for a quiet home, surrounded by forest, earning her keep with the simplest of trades. Of all things, she wanted to sell medicinal plants. Ironically, she knew absolutely nothing about them, but she said that's why the whole thing was simply a dream.

Bithia tossed back another drink. With a low voice, she asked, "Are they keeping you here in the palace because of—" she pointed to Ariss' belly.

Ariss nodded.

"If you could send the child away, would you?"

Ariss' gasp said no louder than any words.

Despite his continued annoyance with her, Kerrick grudgingly admired Ariss for refusing to abandon her child. No matter what, Ariss would not walk away. Even if she herself became a slave, she would stay to protect her child. Although he knew in his heart that the child was his, he always referred to the babe as "her child" or simply "the child." Distancing himself was the only way he'd been able to contain his emotions.

For a moment, Bithia considered Ariss, then, no longer content to throw her glasses behind her, she tossed her current one onto the floor below. The fragile glass shattered with a delicate tinkle, almost like the peal of a tiny bell. Several people jumped, then danced away from the platform. Kerrick thought they were lucky she hadn't hit them. She might have, if too many drinks hadn't hampered her aim. He took note that as the evening progressed, the people below made a wider and wider path of empty around the platform.

Bithia reached beside her throne for another drink. She eyed the one in Kerrick's hand. He'd hardly touched the sparkly wine, but she offered him another, anyway. Kerrick tossed back the one he had, set the glass beside Ariss' throne, then took another.

Again, Bithia stroked her finger along the back of his hand. A wicked gleam came to her eye as she leaned close to Ariss, and asked, "How is he?" She kept her voice confidential, but loud enough that Kerrick could clearly hear her over the cacophony.

Confused, Ariss dropped her eyes to her belly, then followed Bithia's gaze to Kerrick. "He is a fine protector." She smiled up at him.

He nodded his head subserviently to her.

Ariss frowned slightly, clearly displeased that he wasn't more enamored of her praise.

"No," Bithia said, swirling her drink. "How is he with sex?" Before Ariss could sputter out an answer, Bithia said, "Some still talk of your encounters in the mating room. It is said he put on quite a show." Deliberately, Bithia let her gaze linger on his crotch. "Do you ever share him?"

Kerrick thought Ariss' eyes were going to pop from her head. Mainly because she didn't know the elite had observed them as they mated, but more so by Bithia's forwardness. Ariss blinked rapidly, as if trying to assimilate everything.

For once, he was pleased that his servant status prevented

him from speaking. He was going to relish watching Ariss squirm. However, before he could thoroughly enjoy her discomfort, he suddenly began to fidget himself. Without any lusty thoughts whatsoever, his cock hardened, pushing against his loose-fitting trousers in a prominent display since he didn't wear undergarments. He glanced down at the drink he'd so cavalierly tossed off and realized what caused Bithia's smirk; he'd just willingly consumed an entire glass of *illias*. Bithia had deliberately handed him the powerful, sparkling aphrodisiac; and he'd not only taken it, but quaffed it quickly. She must have taken his actions as an indication of his willingness.

Lowering her voice, Bithia said, "I would pay well to borrow him." Darting her gaze between him and Ariss, she added, "I promise I will not hurt him; however, I would like to use him with another, if that is permitted. Is he accustomed to that?"

Another? Kerrick considered what that might mean. Him, Bithia, and another man or another woman? Judging by the way her gaze lingered on anything and everything male, he was guessing two men. Or more. She might be young, but she clearly wasn't naive.

"You want to . . ." Ariss trailed off, unable to even speak of what Bithia suggested.

"You can join us if you'd like. I just thought that in your condition you would refrain from such vigorous encounters."

Ariss' mouth hung open but absolutely nothing came out.

Frowning, Bithia asked, "Isn't that done on this world?" She jumped her gaze from him to Ariss. "I thought it was proper to ask the owner of the slave."

"He is bound to me by temple rites as my protector, not my, my sex slave." Ariss glanced over at him as if seeking support, and that's when she noticed the bulge in his trousers. Her gaze flew to his face as an expression of disgust twisted her features.

Obviously, she thought he was intrigued by Bithia's suggestion. He wasn't, but he wasn't about to correct Ariss' erroneous assessment, either.

"You don't have sex with him?" Now it was Bithia's turn to be shocked. Her gaze traveled over him with the power of a caress. "But he was the Harvester, wasn't he?"

She knew he was. He saw the gleam of recognition in her eyes and wondered what game she was playing.

"He was, but . . ."Ariss trailed off, then lowered her hand to her belly. "I'm sorry, my lady, but I fear I must return to my rooms." Ariss stood. Her clutch of servants rushed toward her, but she stopped them with a lifted hand.

Kerrick grabbed her decorative robe, but rather than placing the heavy thing on her shoulders, he folded the fabric over his arm, using the massive thing to hide his bulge.

By the time they reached the bottom of the platform, their contingent of guards surrounded them with expert ease. As they left the great hall, Kerrick glanced over his shoulder. Bithia raised her glass to him, drank, and then tossed the empty behind her. A wide smile graced her face as she dropped her gaze to his fanny and lifted one brow.

"Will you stop staring at that audacious child?" Ariss whisper-hissed.

Chuckling, Kerrick turned his gaze forward. "Bithia isn't a child; she's a young woman. A very lusty young woman." They were out in the hallway, but Kerrick looked back just to irritate Ariss. "Someday we're going to have to visit Beserrah."

"If you look back again, I'll—"

"What? Have me beaten?" Leaning near enough that his breath caressed her neck, he asked, "Or will you beat me yourself? Perhaps with both hands. Maybe in a slow-up-and-down motion?"

Her face flamed red. They continued in silence. When they

reached her suite of rooms, Ariss dismissed her servants and slammed the door in the guards' faces.

Kerrick set her robe aside. Deliberately, he cocked his hip, causing the material of his trousers to stretch tight across his erection.

Striding forward, Ariss grasped his cock accusingly. "How can you be attracted to her?"

His erection had nothing to do with Bithia; however, Ariss' hand was only compounding his problem. Grasping her wrist, he snarled, "Why shouldn't I submit to the empress while you find your pleasure with some man who uses you so brutally he leaves marks?" He hadn't realized how angry he was about her betrayal until he flung the accusation at her. Here he was, trapped for a lifetime as her subservient slave, and she was finding satisfaction with another!

Ariss winced and tried to pull away.

Yanking her close, he dropped his lips a breath from hers, and asked, "Who is he?" He had no problem using his role as her protector to hunt the man down and beat the lust right out of him. How dare any man use her to the point he injured her, in her condition, no less? Just the thought of another with Ariss infuriated him beyond comprehension. Twice he'd fallen to his knees to give her his tribute in the temple, while she sated her needs with some brute.

Pressing her lips together, as if to prevent herself from speaking the truth, she tried again to elude his grasp, but he tightened his grip. Not hard enough to hurt, just tight enough to make it clear who was in charge. Her refusal to give the name made Chur and Sterlave flash instantly to his mind. Kerrick wondered if they had to grovel in the temple and give her their tribute. Chur was a demigod himself, so probably not. Sterlave, as the consort to the prior empress, probably got some special dispensation. But that wouldn't stop either man from sneaking trysts with her.

"Do you like it when he forces you down, then uses you so ruthlessly he burns the palms of your hands and the skin of your knees?" He twisted his grip, exposing her palms. Even now, the marks still lingered. "Did you think I wouldn't notice? Or perhaps that I was too stupid to realize what caused these marks?" Something about her allowing a man to maltreat her infuriated him. Such brutality wasn't about passion; it was about subjugation and violence. "How could you let any man abuse you?"

Breathless, she tried to pull away, but then, closing her eyes, she lowered her voice to a fragile whisper. "I didn't have a choice."

Stunned, Kerrick released her at once. Who would dare to rape the consort of a god? For that matter, when could such an event have occurred? He was by her side almost every moment of the day. The only time he left her was when he went to the *tishiary*. When he went there, a palace guard took his place. So when could any man have gotten near enough to harm her? As soon as he asked himself the question, he knew the answer.

"Tavarus."

Ariss winced at the name, closing her eyes tightly, as if she tried to block the images from her mind.

Kerrick stepped back, lifting his hands as if to ward off the truth. "Through me." His gaze dropped to the floor as a trickle of a memory took form in his brain. "I did that to you. Right here." In a hazy, jumbled vision, he saw himself tormenting Ariss, then forcing her down, forcing himself inside. Through his hands he felt her hips giving way below his fingertips, felt her body rock forward from his thrusts. If not for that damn drink, revulsion would have deflated his erection in a snap.

"You tried to fight him off." Ariss crossed her arms over her chest, hugging herself, holding herself. "But your refusal only angered him more." She couldn't meet his gaze. "I begged you to just let him do what he wanted." Her eyes darted to his, then quickly away. "I knew he wouldn't really hurt me. Tavarus wouldn't do anything to hurt his child."

Closing his eyes against the horrible truth, Kerrick sat down hard on a puffy couch. He dropped his head into his hands. His cock ached with a relentless need for climax, which he forcefully ignored. Right now, he'd rather suffer the torments of the ages than have Ariss assuage his lust.

"How many times?" he asked, hoping against hope that it had only happened once.

"It wasn't your fault." Ariss sat beside him, taking his hand into hers.

Her hand felt so small in his, so delicate and fragile. He opened his mouth to ask the question again, but closed it without saying a word. He really didn't want to know. One time was one time too many. Turning her hand over, he lifted her arm and kissed the center of her palm. No words would ever change what had happened.

"Do you hate me?"

"No." Ariss leaned into him, forcing his arm around her shoulders so she could press her head against his chest. "You were possessed by a god, Kerrick. There wasn't anything either of us could do."

Kerrick was overwhelmed by the feelings welling up inside. To be a tool for a god was bad enough, but for that same god to use him to hurt Ariss was more than he could handle.

"How can you even bear to let me touch you?" Her shoulders felt frighteningly fragile below his massive arm. Without any compassion or restraint to guide him, he could hurt her. A god such as Tavarus didn't care about mere mortals. He took what he wanted when he wanted it and damned the consequences. Terrified, because in a moment of god-fueled lust, Tavarus could make Kerrick kill her without meaning to, Kerrick suddenly wanted to get as far from Ariss as he could. How could he truly protect her when he couldn't stop a god from possessing him? He didn't know if he could trust Ariss' assessment that Tavarus would never really hurt her because of the child. If he was used to getting what he wanted when he wanted it, what would prevent Tavarus from lashing out, especially if using force gave him satisfaction?

Ariss snuggled closer, and whispered, "It wasn't you. I knew it wasn't you. When he fills you, your eyes swell black, eating up all the color, turning your eyes into fathomless pits." She shuddered, compelling him to pull her closer to his warmth. He kissed the top of her head, smelling that lovely *valasta* that seemed as much a part of her as anything. No matter what perfumes her servants placed on her, he could always smell that sweet scent.

"When was the last time he came?" Kerrick blanched at his own question. He'd meant the last time Tavarus had been here, not the last time he'd gotten off. Although, technically, they were the same thing.

"I think he has grown bored with me," Ariss said, trailing her hand along the opening of his simple brown shirt. "Right after the temple ceremony, he came several times a day, but it has been more than a quarter cycle since he's been here." Relief filled her voice. "Hopefully he has found another way to occupy his time."

Kerrick nodded, rubbing his chin against her silky hair. He hoped with everything in him that Tavarus would never bother either of them again. Gnawing at the inside of his cheek, Kerrick wondered if there was any way he could stop Tavarus from possessing him. Clearly, he couldn't creep into just anyone or the gods would be taking over mortals all the time. There had to be something that happened during the temple ceremony to allow Tavarus access to Kerrick's body.

When Kerrick glanced down, Ariss had undone every button on his shirt and pushed the edges open. She stroked her hand directly against his chest, teasing the smooth side of her polished nails along the rise and fall of his muscles. The contrast of her creamy skin against the fading bronze of his riveted his attention. Idly, she traced a circle around his nipple, causing the flesh to contract. His tormented cock twitched.

He took a deep breath. Mixed in with sweet *valasta* was the scent of her need. Gods be damned that he could smell her arousal. Worse, he could see her nipples pressed hard against the gauzy fabric of her dress. Twin outlines of caramel brown made his mouth water to taste and his fingers tremble to touch. Two cycles had passed since he'd felt the heat of her snug sex wrapped around his cock. For a moment, he let himself wallow in everything they'd done together in the mating room. As he turned to kiss her, the collar dug into his neck.

"Ariss, don't." Capturing her hand, he gently removed his arm from her shoulders and placed her hand in her lap. By the very vestiges of self-control he was able to stop her when everything in him wanted to beg her to continue.

Smoky gray eyes met his with genuine surprise and the smallest hint of hurt. "But I want you."

Kerrick resisted the urge to wrap her up in his arms and kiss that look of pain off her face. "I am only to give you tribute in the temple." He forced the words out even though he didn't truly feel them. If he had his way, Ariss would already be halfway out of her dress with her legs wrapped around his hips.

Her scoff was a light exhale of breath. "Since when do you follow the rules?"

Through lightly clenched teeth, he returned, "Since the last time I broke them I ended up a slave." Kerrick stood and took two steps away from her, desperate to put some distance between them before he lost his resolve. Damn Bithia and himself for stupidly consuming the aphrodisiac. His cock and balls ached almost as badly as they had after the Harvest. Every breath he took brought more of Ariss' unique scent into his mouth and lungs, but the weight of the collar reminded him what had happened the last time he broke the rules. Kerrick had a feeling that breaking this one would end in his execution.

"Stop!" Ariss' voice was cold with fury. "How dare you turn your back to me?"

Kerrick stood very still.

Ariss stepped before him. She cupped his face into her hand and forced him to look at her. Her eyes blazed with a ruthless determination he had never seen. At first, he feared that Tavarus had possessed her, but her eyes remained smoky gray. Intense and sharp, but not swelled black.

"You are my slave." She straightened her shoulders, tilting her head back so that even though she looked up at him, she held the power position. "I tell you what to do."

His nostrils flared in fury, which only drew more of her scent to his lungs and caused his cock to swell even tighter. If he didn't find release soon, he feared he would be permanently disabled.

"Do you understand?" She lowered her hand to her side, lifting her body throughout her centerline so that she stood in a most commanding pose. Her position also thrust her nipples firmly against the material of her dress.

"I am your humble servant." He didn't drop his gaze, as he should have, because he couldn't take his eyes off her. Not once in the last two cycles had Ariss flaunted her status over him. He couldn't believe she was doing so now. Was she looking for revenge on him for what Tavarus had done to her through him? Or was something else going on?

"Do you enjoy giving me your tribute in the temple?" She asked the question with some reserve. One brow rose inquiringly over her right eye.

Her curiosity wasn't surprising, given how he'd hung his head and masturbated as fast as he could jack his arm both times. Most of the other guards took their time, their eyes riveted to her exposed breasts. Kerrick just wanted the damn ritual over. What irritated him wasn't that she watched him; what goaded him was that she watched him and every other guard in the palace. How could he compete against all of those other men? He worried his cock wasn't big enough, that his moves wouldn't be erotic enough, so he didn't even try to compete. He just did what he had to do and walked away with his head hung low. Kerrick wasn't sure how to answer in a way that would please her, so he told her the truth.

Lowering his head but meeting her gaze, he confessed, "I can think of more pleasurable ways to give you my tribute." Right now, he'd like to bend her over her big bed and tease his hand along her sex until she begged for him. Kerrick would give anything to have their roles reversed. He would be a lustful but benevolent master. Never would he demand more from Ariss than she could give, but he would press her to test her limits. Kerrick's mind suddenly flashed on Tavarus and what he'd forced Ariss to do. He shook his head, for that was not him in charge, but a self-absorbed god with no concern for anyone but himself. Kerrick wanted to master her, not abuse her.

"I can also think of more pleasurable ways to receive your tribute." Her gaze dropped to his crotch. His erection pressed against the bland brown of his trousers. Lifting her gaze to his, she ordered, "Remove your weapons."

Now he had some idea of where she was going with her sudden need to boss him around. "How can I protect you without weapons?" he asked humbly.

She tilted her head to the massive Onic timber door. "Four stout palace guards stand beyond." Rotating her head back so that she faced him directly, she said, "I think I am well enough protected by them at the moment."

Kerrick glanced at the door. The last time they'd done something like this, palace guards had yanked him off her, beat him senseless, and then left him bound in the *gannett*. Only Chur and Sterlave had prevented the recruits from taking turns with his upturned bottom. Kerrick had no desire to repeat such an adventure. Still, Ariss was his owner. If she were ordering him to do something, he must obey. Further conflicted by the fact that he wanted to do what she asked only to waylay her into trusting him so he could turn the tables on her, Kerrick hesitated. True to form, he followed his initial impulse.

With a deep sigh, he removed his blade from his belt, setting the *cirvant* on the floor. When he stood, he removed the next weapon, placing each on the floor in measured movements. He could have just removed the entire belt all at once, but stripping down in increments was a curious sort of foreplay. Removing each weapon rendered him less powerful, in a way. No matter how stripped down, his sheer size made him more powerful than she was.

Ariss' gaze tracked his every action. Her tongue darted over her lips, licking in anticipation for the final reveal. Once he stood freed of his weapons, he rested his hand on the buckle of his belt.

Eyes wide, Ariss waited, holding her breath. When he only held his position, she blurted, "Why are you hesitating?"

Kerrick swore at that moment he wouldn't do anything unless she told him to do so. Lowering his face and his voice, giving up every last bit of his pride, he swore, "If you want to be my master, you must command my every move."

16

At first, Ariss shrank from Kerrick's challenge. She didn't want to master him, not in the full sense of the word, but she also didn't want to spend a lifetime receiving his tribute in the temple. Watching him stroke his cock in the mating room had been one of the most erotic moments of her life; however, watching him masturbate in a frenzy of shame in the temple only caused her indignity at her role. Given her druthers, she would prefer to feel Kerrick spend inside her, not at her feet once a cycle. She would much rather enjoy him finding release within her body on a nightly basis. Everything in her world changed after that moment in the temple when Tavarus claimed her.

She could never tell anyone the truth, not if she wished to survive, but in all honesty, she hated Tavarus. He was the god of war and sex, yet he was also the bastion of cruelty. Tavarus took. Never, ever did Tavarus give. Always his position was one of demanding accolades, demanding acquiescence, demanding humble obeisance. Ariss despised him.

However, Ariss enjoyed receiving tribute. How could she

not feel aroused by watching guard after guard stroke himself to fulfillment? The men chose whether or not to offer tribute. If they wished, they could refrain and give a greater tribute every few cycles or so, but most chose to give each cycle, releasing their tension in an acceptable forum.

As she sat upon her tawdry throne with Tavarus' crystal-clear cock buried deep inside her aching sex, she watched each guard come forward, fall to his knees, remove his loincloth, and masturbate while gazing upon her exposed breasts. Her nipples stood at hard attention, aching for the touch of not just any fingers, but Kerrick's. If only she could have him behind her, rubbing and twisting her nipples while she watched the men below, she would know the most profound orgasms. If Kerrick became her tawdry throne, she would climax in waves that would milk his cock dry. As things stood, she enjoyed her time in the temple, but her climax hovered just beyond her reach, elusive and frustrating.

What she wanted and needed was the one thing she wasn't supposed to have: Kerrick.

As her slave, he was to minister to her needs, mainly to protect her from those who wished to do her harm. Tonight, Bithia put the idea in her head that he could minister to her other needs as well. Since he was her servant, he had to do what she said. If she wanted him to pleasure her, she could demand his acquiescence. Ruthlessly, she pushed away the thought that she was just like Tavarus, taking and never giving, because she would give back to Kerrick. She wanted to pleasure him as much as she wanted him to pleasure her. The fact that suddenly he'd become a stickler for the rules was bizarre. Although his reluctance was more understandable after he'd explained about becoming a slave. But still, what would it matter if they indulged one another? How could anyone claim that Tavarus was not inside Kerrick when they engaged in their lustful encounters? Frankly, Ariss didn't think anyone had any damn say in anything she did. She was the consort to a god. If anyone dared to condemn her, he or she could take their complaints up with Tavarus directly.

Standing there, considering Kerrick, his silky hair obscuring his gaze, his massive hand hovering above his belt buckle, her body consumed with painful longings, Ariss knew what she had to do. Together, they had worked very diligently to turn her into a bad girl, and that's just what she wanted to be.

"Remove your belt."

From below the curtain of his hair, his brows rose slightly, but he did as she asked. Ever so slowly, he undid the metal buckle, then pulled the leather from around his narrow hips. At the end, he yanked hard, flicking the belt, making the end of the leather snap in the air. She jumped. Her nipples tightened. Somehow, the belt sounded just like the slap of a hand against flesh. Exactly like the way his hand had sounded when he'd playfully paddled her bottom. Right before he slid his tongue . . .

"Give me that." She yanked the belt from his hand.

"Are you going to use that on me?" he asked mischievously, his tone lightly submissive, yet oddly masterful.

Ariss considered the length of leather in her hand. Did he want her to spank him? Unsure, she said, "Perhaps I will." Slapping the folded leather to her palm, hard enough so that he could hear her motions, she added, "If you continue to defy me, I'll have no choice but to punish you." Her belly took a dangerous lurch. She wasn't sure she could actually do what she suggested; but she wasn't about to back down from a challenge, either.

"I would never defy you, my most sacred mistress." Submissively, he hung his head. In the same breath, he straightened his shoulders.

Now she realized he was mocking her. Kerrick as a willing, humble slave? No. Not in a thousand seasons would he bow down his will to another, and certainly not to a woman, definitely not to her. He was only playing. Well, she could play, too.

Walking behind him, she flicked the belt out as he had, snapping the tip against his right buttock. Kerrick shot into the air, clenching his cheeks together tightly, but he didn't turn around or speak. Using the belt, she fashioned it into a strong double loop that she placed around his wrists. Once she tightened the strip through the buckle, she yanked hard enough to convey that she now had him bound.

"Kneel."

After the slightest hesitation, Kerrick dropped to his knees in a graceful fall, difficult to do with his arms bound behind his back. He kept his head lowered, using his golden strands to obscure her view of his face. Without seeing him, she knew his face was one of probing interest. Kerrick would do as she ordered, but always he would hold a certain reserve, as if he indulged her, not the other way around.

Irritated by his continued indifference and subtle disregard, Ariss was determined to master him in this moment.

As she returned to the front of him, so that he now was on his knees before her, she cupped his chin, forcing him to lift his face and look at her. Like a good slave, he respectfully kept his eyes lowered. Clearly, he'd played this game before.

"Look at me."

His gaze shot to her face. Curious speculation lurked within his green-eyed gaze. He wondered if she could finish what she started, especially since she'd backed off last time she'd attempted such a scenario. She'd tried to control him but had ultimately given control back to him, which seemed to be what he was expecting now. Knowing she needed something to bolster her courage, she turned the crystals low, mimicking the ambient light in the temple. Carefully, she parted the bodice of her dress, exposing her breasts. Watching Kerrick's intent gaze, she cupped her breasts, flicking her thumbs over her nipples until they stood hard.

Kerrick swallowed. Into his gaze crept the smallest bit of uncertainty.

Striding toward him while undulating her hips caused her breasts to bounce. Once she stood directly in front of him, forcing him to crane his neck far back to keep his attention on her face, she lifted the gauzy fabric of her skirt. Below she was bare.

Kerrick held her gaze forcefully, but she knew he wanted to look down and see what lay hidden below her skirt. In that moment, she understood how power like this could be so arousing. He could not even dare to look unless she ordered him to do so. When she glanced down, his cock swelled so tightly with need it bounced in time to his heartbeat. His breathing had grown erratic, sharper, more labored.

Holding her skirt up, she peered right into his eyes and ordered, "Taste me."

With his eyes still open and riveted to her face, he leaned forward. Leisurely, he extended his tongue. Separating her folds, he drew his tongue down to the very core of her and then stroked up to the hard tip of her clit.

Flexing her knees, she parted her legs a bit wider to give him greater access. "Again."

Willingly, he continued and she tracked his movements, rocking her hips to help him tease along the full length of her sex. Building tension gathered in her clit. Holding her skirt with one hand, she used the other to bring his face to that hard little nub, and commanded him, "Wrap your lips there, draw my clit into your mouth, and flick your tongue across the tip."

He did exactly as she asked.

Each swipe of his tongue jolted her body, causing her to twist her hand in his hair, as if she could steady herself by holding his head. Waves of pleasure rolled, tightening her nipples even more. She knew if she told him to continue, he would until her orgasm exploded across her flesh in a cascade of desperately needed climax.

Stepping back, she released his head and dropped her skirt. The look that crossed his face was one of confusion, but he caught himself before he asked her why she'd retreated. Instead, he lowered his head but kept his gaze on her. Watching her intently, he deliberately licked his lips and lifted his hips ever so slightly, displaying his cock, encouraging her to use his most captivating asset.

Ariss considered how much she wanted to feel him inside. A thousand ways of placing him for her own greatest pleasure paraded through her mind. Still, she could do more with him. So much more that she hadn't even considered yet. Into her mind flashed an image of him with another as Bithia had suggested. Even in her thoughts, Kerrick was more powerful; he stood while the other man knelt before him.

Lifting her chin, she asked, "Have you ever been with another man?"

A flicker of apprehension crossed his face but quickly disappeared. "No, my sacred mistress."

Considering him, curious about his fear, she demanded an explanation.

Haltingly, Kerrick confessed that he did not find men attractive, not the way he found women attractive. He told her of what punishment he had suffered in the *gannett,* and his fear that if not for Sterlave and Chur, a series of recruits would have brutalized him. "I do not find the prospect of an encounter with another man at all appealing, my sacred mistress." He didn't hang his head, but he lowered his eyes a bit. In this, he was determined not to offer her any challenge.

"You would not even wish to have another man suck your cock?" That was the scenario she found most appealing; Kerrick standing tall, his massive hand cupped to the head of another man who greedily took his cock into his mouth. Ariss would want to watch. A man would know all the secret places and how to tease Kerrick into a frenzy of arousal.

Confused, Kerrick abruptly asked, "Why are you asking me this, Ariss? Do you want another man in here with us?"

She should chastise him for speaking without permission, but his genuine puzzlement compelled her to ease the rules.

"Perhaps." One thing she'd realized about being in command of another was that the master, or in her case, mistress, did not reveal the full of the desires within. Soon enough, their roles would be reversed, and she didn't want to give him too much power over her. Also, keeping him unbalanced took away a bit of his smugness. Humbling Kerrick was a difficult, if not impossible task. She was pleased that she'd finally found a way to bring him down a bit. When she looked closer at his face, she saw terror. That was not at all amusing or arousing.

"You think I'm going to make you do it, anyway, don't you?" Stunned that he could think her so cruel, she was on the verge of releasing him and stopping this entire charade.

"Wouldn't you?" He lowered his gaze to the carpet before her feet.

"Why would I deliberately try to hurt you?" She couldn't even believe she was asking. Hurting Kerrick or forcing him to do something he didn't want to do wasn't at all what she'd been after. She'd only be curious. Tavarus might enjoy such perversities, but she certainly didn't.

"To pay me back for what Tavarus did to you through me." He fell back until he sat on his heels, his entire body curved in as if to ward off blows.

Soundlessly, her mouth hung open; then she deliberately pressed her lips together. After a few deep breaths, she commanded, "Look at me."

Warily, he met her gaze without lifting his head.

"I would never do anything to hurt you. Just as I know you wouldn't ever hurt me, not deliberately. Tavarus compelled you." Once she moved near, she dropped to her knees. "You had no choice. I could no more blame you for that than I could blame myself."

"What are you going to do with me?"

She wasn't sure if he meant now or in the future. All the playful joy she'd felt at commanding him evaporated. Silently, she leaned forward, reaching her hands around to his back to free him from his belt. Both his arms were already free. He'd simply clasped his hands together. Somehow, the discovery hurt her deeply. Shaking her head, she rose.

"Ariss, wait." He climbed to his knees as if to come after her.

Spinning around and facing him, she said, "Don't bother. I can't believe that you didn't trust me enough to let me—" She didn't finish the thought. What was the point? He didn't trust her. That was enough.

"I'm sorry, but when you started talking about another man, I panicked."

When she gazed down, she discovered her parted dress still provocatively displayed her breasts. Ashamed, she tucked them back and straightened her skirt. Never again would she attempt such a situation. Apparently, in their relationship, the trust only went one way: from her to him. A relationship without mutual trust wasn't any kind of a relationship at all.

Turning her back on him, she took two steps toward her bed, but his hand on her shoulder stopped her. Without looking at him, she pushed his hand away.

"Ariss, please." He didn't touch her physically, but the plaintive tone of his voice did.

Keeping her gaze on the decorative folds of her bed, she took a deep breath before speaking. "I can't do this anymore, Kerrick. I can't play these games with you." Blowing her breath out sharply to waylay her gathering tears, she added, "It's all just a competition between us to see who can be the most in charge or who can be the most naughty." Lifting her arms, she removed the clever set of pins and twists that held her hair up, then tossed them on her bedside table. "Go play with Bithia. I have a feeling she would deeply enjoy such mischief." After fluffing out her hair, she pulled the blankets down. "I'll send word to her tomorrow that she may borrow you if you wish. I'll include a directive that you abhor other men."

Kerrick remained silent.

Without looking at him, she grabbed the nightshift her servant had left at the foot of her bed. Keeping her back to Kerrick, she undressed, slipped the simple *astle* dress over her head, and then crawled between the sheets. She should have washed her teeth and her face first, but she didn't think one night would cause any damage.

Kerrick hadn't made a sound.

Finally, she braved a look at him. He stood very still near the foot of her bed, his attention on the floor. His shoulders slumped and his hair hung over his eyes, obscuring his gaze. To her shock, his cock was still hard, pressing against the front of his plain brown trousers. How, after everything that had happened, could he still be aroused? The tears she thought suppressed returned when she realized the truth. "If you want to go to her now—"

"I don't want Bithia." He cut her off but kept his voice very low, controlled, but clearly full of fury. "I want you."

A shiver of fear ran down her spine. She couldn't see his eyes, so she didn't know if Tavarus had come. Her gaze darted to the door of the basin; he might not be able to bash his way in there. Slowly, Ariss slid across the slippery fabric of her bed, making her way toward the promise of safety. On the edge, ready to fling the covers back and run, Kerrick lifted his head, his green-eyed gaze pinning her.

He took a step toward her and winced when she flinched

back. "That's how it will always be." Flicking his hair out of his face, he said, "You're always going to think it's him. You say that you want me, but you're terrified of him. And I have no control over when he's in me."

Ariss swallowed hard, not sure how to react. He wasn't yelling or screaming, just standing and vibrating a terrifying fury. Worse, he was right. As soon as she had bound him, she relaxed, because she thought that if Tavarus came, he would not be able to harm her.

Even now, as he stood there, hurt by her fear, she was too afraid to go to him, because at any moment, the god could possess him, turning him into a lustful monster. She thought she trusted him, and she did trust Kerrick implicitly. What she couldn't trust was when the god would fill him with his greedy desire. Tavarus had destroyed something precious and rare. She hated him all the more.

Uncomfortable with the discovery, Ariss whispered, "What are we to do?" Without even thinking, she glanced down at his crotch. She couldn't believe he was still aroused.

Kerrick caught the direction of her gaze, looked down, then back at her. "For the love of—it's not me, it's that damn drink Bithia gave me." Defensively, he adjusted his penis. "I stopped being aroused a long time ago."

Taken aback by the realization, Ariss asked, "Bithia gave you an aphrodisiac?"

He nodded miserably.

Jealousy surged. Bithia might be the empress, but she was going to have to learn to keep her gluttonous fingers off Kerrick. Still, Ariss could understand why any woman would want him. Kerrick was magnificent. Golden hair, his compelling eyes, and the fact that he was practically a wall of muscle, combined with his humor and a sharp intellect made him a most intriguing man. Not to mention his other more prominent assets. Ariss did her best not to laugh, but she couldn't help herself.

Kerrick's head swiveled toward her, shock lifting his brows almost to his hairline. "You think that's funny?"

"I've been thinking she excited you, that all the things she was talking about aroused you, and that . . . well . . ." Unable to continue, she trailed off, shaking her head.

Chuckling softly, Kerrick sat down on the edge of her bed. "It seems we have been at cross-purposes most of this evening."

They sat in companionable silence for a long time. Kerrick reached his hand toward her. Tentatively, Ariss reached her hand out to him. They met in the middle, clasping each other's hand gently.

"I'm sorry," Ariss whispered.

"Me too," Kerrick said, turning her hand over and rubbing his fingers between hers.

"What are we going to do?" She'd already asked, but she asked again, knowing there really wasn't an answer. Not a simple answer, anyway.

"I don't know." Kerrick flopped back on the bed, his golden hair falling back from his face, exposing the intensity of his green eyes. Even in the low light, they glowed. "All I know is we can't continue like this." Turning his head to fasten his gaze on her, he added, "I don't want you to be afraid of me."

"I'm not afraid of you, but of him."

"I know. That's what I mean. That fear in your eyes causes my stomach to clench in revulsion." He shivered. "I've never had a woman fear me. It's not at all arousing." Lowering his brows ominously, he lifted his head to glare down at his erection. "My current state notwithstanding."

"My father says fear is the only way to make people do as you wish." She had no idea why she chose to share that information with Kerrick. Her father was long gone from her life now. She doubted he would ever wish to see her again. "He used intimidation on his workers, his family, everyone."

"And as soon as he wasn't looking . . ."

"They all turned on him." Ariss darted her gaze to the closet, even though she'd ordered the silver dress returned to Ambo. "My father worked out a deal with Ambo to make me the Harvester. I was supposed to select Ambo as my bond-mate."

Kerrick grimaced, but he exhibited no surprise. At her look of confusion, he confided, "Chur told me when I was in the *gannett.* He offered me a choice: I could leave and suffer no repercussions, or I could stay and protect you from Ambo."

"And you chose to stay?" It seemed she was forever on the verge of tears lately, but no matter what she did, she couldn't stop them now. He'd had a chance to leave, to go back to the wild, exciting life he'd left behind, and he'd chosen to stay. To be with her. Touched so deeply by his selfless act, Ariss moved across the bed, lowered her lips to his, and kissed him.

With her hand still entwined in his, he lifted his free hand to her head, teasing his fingers through her hair, holding her head softly as he kissed her back.

Long, deep, from sweet to passionate, they stayed on her bed kissing until her tears abated. In those moments, she had no fear that Tavarus would come. She was utterly alone, and completely safe, with Kerrick.

Letting go her hand, Kerrick rolled her over so they lay side by side. Cupping her chin, he kissed her again, and again, parting her lips with the press of his tongue while he wiped her tears away with his fingertips. He kissed her in every way a man could kiss a woman. Accepting, penetrating, giving and taking in such a way she knew they'd reached a new and remarkable moment in their relationship. He wasn't trying to command her. She wasn't trying to command him. They simply shared with each other. Each strove more for the pleasure of the other rather than their own. For the first time, she felt they were a team seeking mutual bliss.

"Tell me these are tears of joy." His eyes penetrated into hers with gentle ease.

Unable to speak, she nodded, then whispered, "I can't believe you stayed for me."

"Oh, Ariss," he rubbed his nose against hers. "How could I leave?"

Something in her broke free, spilling more tears that he wiped away.

"I was so angry at you." He spoke softly without vehemence.

Her eyes went wide.

"When I had to kneel as your slave and give you tribute in the temple." He shook his head. "In that moment, I hated you. I couldn't believe I didn't run as far and as fast as I could when I had the chance." He sighed. "Before you I always ran. Whenever anything became too difficult, I left. But I realized I couldn't leave you. Not just because of Ambo, but because"—he dropped his gaze momentarily, then lifted his eyes to hers—"because I wanted you."

Ariss thought there was more to his reason, but she didn't ask. Kerrick stood on the verge of revealing his heart. Pushing him would only make him withdraw.

"I wanted you, too." Her voice broke. "I still do."

A smile lifted up the edges of his mouth, infusing a beautiful light to his face. Never had he looked so handsome to her. "No more games."

She shook her head. "No more playing."

He shook his head. "Just you and I."

Each moving forward, they met in the middle, pressing lips to lips, hand to hand, heart to heart. When his erection pressed into her belly, she felt only pleasure.

Kerrick teased his hand along her back, pulling her tightly against him, carefully easing the straps of her shift away from her shoulders. Once bared, he lowered his head, kissing from the edge of her shoulder to the sensitive spot on her neck.

Ariss purred back with a sigh, loving how he knew just where to touch and how to arouse her the most.

Nuzzling the area right below her ear, he trailed his fingers up, drawing the fabric of her dress up. Cool air caressed her thighs; then his hand dipped back to tease along her back, causing small bumps to wash along her flesh. Delicately, he teased his fingers along the split of her bottom, exerting just enough pressure to make her shiver in response.

Even though the fabrics they wore were not that heavy, Ariss felt they were entirely overdressed. As she tugged at the drawstring of his simple trousers, she realized he'd knotted the string. Her pulling only tightened the knot. Without a word, he lowered his hand to help her unfasten them, but he, too, met with resistance. After fumbling with them for several moments, she couldn't take any more. Growling, she sat up, rolled him to his back, and then used her teeth to separate the knot.

Realizing suddenly that she knelt over him, gnawing her way into his pants, she glanced up. Kerrick watched with one brow drawn up in mild amusement. Together, they laughed. She continued to wrestle with the knot. Once she released the damn thing, she tossed back her hair triumphantly.

"In the future, I'll refrain from knotting the string."

"Yes." Ariss gazed down at the two flaps. All she had to do was push them aside and he'd be bare to her. "Or we could find trousers without such a troublesome fastener."

"I don't know," Kerrick said, stroking her hair. "I kinda like the way you bit your way into my pants." Leaning up, he kissed her shoulder and whispered, "All greedy and frantic and desperate-like."

A blush burned her cheeks, but she didn't look away. Everything he said was true. "It's been so long since I've been with you. With just you." Running her finger along the exposed flesh of his hips, she added, "And you looked so stunning tonight."

"Stunning?" He laughed.

"Stunningly handsome," she amended. "Your hair glowed under the crystals, and I've never seen your eyes so bright." Twirling her fingertip in a swirl of curly hair, she added, "I know brown is the color of slaves, but this particular shade makes you look like a god. No wonder Bithia wanted you. And I honestly don't think she was the only woman tonight who did." From the corner of her eye, Ariss had seen how the elite women, and some of the men, looked at Kerrick.

"I know." His face crinkled up. "Freeaal! That sounded arrogant! What I meant was that I noticed them noticing. And I noticed you noticing." Toying with the edge of her shift, he tugged the silken fabric up. "If we don't remove this quickly, I might just have to gnaw my way into it."

Grinning, Ariss pulled the shift up and tossed it off the bed. Kerrick's gaze roamed over her body, pleasure lighting his face. Not content to just look, his hands followed along the same path. Everywhere he touched tingled. When she reached out to clasp his neck, her hands touched smooth, hot metal and she withdrew.

"Ignore it," Kerrick said, wriggling his way out of his pants.

It wasn't difficult to ignore the slave collar once he had his pants off. His cock stood proudly at attention in a dusting of golden hair. Ariss caressed the heavy shaft, working her fingers across the ridge, and right to that sweet spot below the head that always made him groan. When he did, she smiled, cupping him more firmly as they settled side by side.

17

Kerrick lifted her leg over his hip, drawing Ariss close. When his cock nestled against the downy soft of her pubic hair, he thought he would die from the pleasure of it. He could have blamed his heightened senses on the aphrodisiac that Bithia gave him to drink, but he didn't think that had anything to do with his reaction. Finally, Ariss was in his arms again. He'd come so close to telling her the truth, but he'd felt the collar around his neck and didn't dare.

How could he tell her that he stayed because he loved her? His anger in the temple was because at that moment, humiliated and naked, he'd still loved her. In spite of everything, he knew that he would always love her. After hundreds of women, only Ariss embraced him for who and what he really was. She wasn't enamored of the mythical man who surfed waves of fire, or the man who slid down an entire mountain on one flimsy piece of carved wood. She knew none of that. Even if she did, he didn't think his outrageous stunts would impress her. Ariss wanted him. She wanted the man who couldn't handle weapons until she showed him how. She wanted the man who knew a thousand bedroom tricks but needed none of them with her. For the first time, he was *with* her. Not playing any kind of bedroom game, but honestly with her as she was with him.

At first, the intimacy alarmed him, because he felt she could look through his eyes and see right into his soul. Then he realized she wouldn't use the truth she found there against him. Ariss had no desire to cause him any harm or to lord herself over him. That fear, that a woman would be his master, was what had always compelled him to hold the real truth, the very core of himself, back. Revealing himself completely to another was something he swore he would never do; yet, here he was, giving himself entirely to Ariss.

What pleased him most of all was that she did the same. She held nothing back as she lay on her side, facing him, embracing him with her body and soul. One look into her eyes told him the truth; she loved him, too. He even understood why she refrained from speaking those words. Just like him, she was afraid of Tavarus.

Kerrick pushed the image of the ruthless god away. He didn't want him defiling this perfect moment. Ariss was in his arms. Warm, wet, and willing, she was with him. He wouldn't let anything come between them now.

Ariss still had her hand wrapped around his shaft. Slowly, she guided him between her thighs. Once she held him firmly with her legs, she let go, lifting her hand to his hip, rocking him back and forth along the slickness of her sex.

Lowering his head, he nuzzled her nose. "I can't even tell you how good you feel." Her skin was so much softer than he remembered, almost as smooth as *astle*.

Her laugh was light. "You don't have to tell me, I feel the same way."

Cupping her chin, he kissed her as they rocked together, teasing their bodies to create gentle friction. After every few strokes, Ariss would angle her hips, almost drawing him within, but then his penis would skim by. Waiting for the moment of penetration drove him wild. He knew by the way her breath grew labored that she was only making both of them crazy with longing. When he looked into her eyes, he saw smoky intensity.

"You are the most wonderful lover I have ever known."

He could see that she was going to immediately deny his claim, but something stopped her, perhaps the honesty in his expression. Whatever it was changed her mind, and she accepted his compliment with a smile and a soft kiss.

In this position, him on his side, her on her back with one leg over his hips, he was free to touch her everywhere, and he did. Everything from the nape of her neck to the swell of her bottom received caressing strokes. Cupping her breast, he twisted the nipple gently between forefinger and thumb, loving the way she arched her back, as if offering her breast to him. He lowered his head to taste and tease the bud with his mouth. Her sigh of contentment pleased him greatly.

Ariss splayed her fingers through his hair, holding his head, encouraging him with gentle pressure and subtle moans that drove him out of his mind. All the while, she continued to rock her hips, tracing the length of his erection with her sex. He'd never known a woman with such precise control over her hips. Ariss could finesse moments he swore were impossible. Just when he thought he couldn't stand any more delay, she moved her hips in just such a way to bring the very tip of him to the entrance of her passage.

"Wait." Holding her hip, he caused her to hesitate for just a moment, just until he could lift his head and look right into her eyes.

Ariss stared back at him with such longing, such beautiful yearning hunger, he thought no woman would ever be able to match her profound craving for him. His ego soared. He'd had women want him, but not like this. Not with Ariss' ardent enthusiasm. She didn't care what color he wore or what hung around his neck. To Ariss, he was a man, her man, not a slave, or a plaything, or something to be bandied about in trade with the empress. He was hers and they belonged together. Carefully, keeping his gaze pinned to hers, his lips close enough to almost kiss, he penetrated.

Her mouth opened on a slight gasp, drawing air from his lungs, causing him to exhale in time, as if feeding her his breath. Slowly, inexorably, he slid deeper, feeling her passage give around the girth of his cock, feeling the way her body quivered with want and something akin to shock at his invasion. No matter how slowly he went, he had to push his way in, which he found extremely exciting. He had to conquer. Lucky was he that Ariss not only let him, but also encouraged his triumph; she wanted him inside. Lifting her leg a bit higher on his hip loosened her entrance, giving him permission to press deeper, which he did. Now she gave him breath as he gasped at the enveloping heat of her. If he didn't distract himself, he would lose what little control he had left. Ariss didn't help matters by whispering about how hard and thick he felt inside her, and how she wanted to feel all of him sliding into her at once.

He lifted her other leg up, angling her legs over his hip with her on her back. He pressed his hand along the top of her hip, holding her steady, making her wait for him to catch his breath.

"Kerrick." She called his name with a breathless plea.

He answered with a roll of his hips.

"Oh, yes." Her head went back.

Angling himself above her, he slid his arm under her neck, supporting her head, so that he could kiss her deeply. "Say my name again."

She did, whisper-begging his name as she wrapped her arms around his shoulders, holding on to him. From her lips, his name sounded musical. Softly, she continued chanting his name in time to the rolling twists of his hips. Sliding his hand down from her face to her breast, he teased both nipples into tight peaks, then moved on to her waist, pressing hard so as not to tickle her, then down to her hip where he held her for a series of deeper plunges. Then, teasingly light and slow, he lowered his hand to the juncture of her thighs.

Ariss curved her body, as if to lift her hips to his hand, but he would not be rushed. Twirling his fingertips in her curls, he explored the triangle of hair above her sex. Tugging lightly elicited groans and growls, causing her to clench around his shaft. With his attention on his hand, he didn't notice that Ariss had reached out until she playfully tweaked his nipple, causing him to rock forward, forcing him to plunge all the way to the base of his cock.

Ariss exhaled in a sharp burst and then repeated the motion on his other nipple, eliciting the same thrust. Most Diolan women avoided touching him there, which was a shame, as his nipples linked directly to his pelvis. Fearless in her exploration, Ariss touched him everywhere, heedless of any societal semi-taboo rules. Once she realized the link between his nipples and hips, she couldn't get enough of twisting them.

"Is that what you want?" he asked, thrusting deeply with a quick flick of his hips.

Languorously, she nodded, then tweaked his nipples with both hands. Her wanton smile when he involuntarily thrust said it all.

Working one finger down between her thighs, he teased his digit against her straining little clit, then pumped in sharp bursts. Rocking her back and forth, he lowered his finger, pressing it alongside his penis, stretching her even further as his thumb smoothed wide, sweeping arcs along her tender clit.

Breathing raggedly, Ariss squirmed, each circle of her hips moving in a syncopated rhythm to his. When she hovered on the verge of a shattering orgasm, he changed the beat, throwing her off her tempo, bringing her higher.

Watching her face, his attention on her eyes, he marveled as her pupils dilated and her breath grew erratic. Knowing that a potent orgasm grew within her, Kerrick felt the inevitable rising up through his body. His breathing mimicked hers, each breath more labored as they moved relentlessly toward the final release. He'd been waiting two cycles for this moment and suspected she had, too. When the climax came, it would be profound. Moving within her, feeling her, taking her with him, Kerrick allowed his awareness to deepen until he felt every bit of his flesh pressed to hers.

His climax came first, a jetting tide that literally took his breath away as he plunged so deeply into her he dislodged his hand. Ariss' eyes went wide with panic, for he'd lost the beat of his thumb across her clit.

Fumbling, he lifted her left leg up high and pressed the other low. Parting her thighs allowed him to keep his cock plunged deep while he worked his thumb across her clit in a fast, steady beat, desperate to bring her back to that moment right before orgasm.

Alarm faded as her head nodded in time, encouraging him, catching her back up to the edge. When she tumbled over, such blissful joy filled her face he almost came again. Her cunt spasmed around his cock, holding him so snuggly he could feel each distinctive texture within her luscious sex.

Waves of pleasure washed over her, spilling into him, causing him to clutch madly at her hips to hold her tight. Ariss grasped his back, pulling him onto her, snuggling her body as tight to his as she could. His lips found hers and he kissed her as if he took life from her mouth. Again and again, she clenched around him, drawing him so deeply within he felt he was a part of her. In this moment, they were no longer separate beings, but one.

Cradling her in his arms, he lifted up to see her face. Peace suffused her features. Blissful, beautiful serenity glowed from her eyes. A delicate sheen of perspiration flushed her face, and when he breathed deeply, the fragrance of sweet *valasta* filled the air around her.

"I could lose myself in your scent."

Dreamily, she blinked up at him. "I'm not wearing any perfume."

"I know." Tracing his fingertip from her ear to her neck caused her to shiver. "You always smell like *valasta* to me." He wrapped the bedcover around them and she snuggled into his embrace.

"You always smell of the sky to me." She smiled up at him. "I know that sounds strange, but your scent is like air, like if flying had a fragrance, you had captured it somehow."

The notion made him echo her smile. "I always did like to fly."

Her smile faded. "And now you're stuck here." Her gaze fell on the slave collar.

"Ariss, don't." He cupped her face, forcing her to look away from his neck. "For now, forget all of it, everything. Just be here with me." Soon enough they would have to return to their respective roles, and all the rules and restrictions they operated under, but for now, they could lie here and pretend.

With a nod, she kissed him. "I love the way you look when you climax. Every time there is this stunned amazement, as if you thought it would never happen again."

"Truly?" He'd never seen himself in the throes of passion. The few times he'd been with a woman and a mirror, he'd been too busy looking at her to check out himself. "Maybe the amazement is that I'm stunned to be with a beautiful woman like you."

"Flatterer."

"It's not flattery if it's true." He meant what he said. Ariss was beautiful. All the other women he'd ever known paled in comparison.

"Wait until I grow large." She patted her hand to her still-flat belly. A frown twisted her face. "How long can we—I mean, before it hurts the baby?" Before he could answer, she asked, "How can we even—without smashing the baby?"

He placed his hand atop hers, rubbing the back of her hand and her stomach. "We can do this for a long time." Rolling her over so that he embraced her from behind, he curled up against her. "See? This way, there's room for the baby." He patted the empty bed before her belly.

"And how do you know all this?" She turned her head, looking at him over her shoulder. "Have you been with a pregnant woman?"

"Once." He thought back to that time with Nomi.

"You have a child?" The bottom fell out of her voice as she twisted in his embrace.

"No, no," he kissed the nape of her neck, settling her. "Another man did the deed, then left. Nomi was convinced no man would ever find her attractive again. I convinced her otherwise."

"Will you still want me when I'm huge?"

"Absolutely." He actually found the prospect of making love to Ariss while she was large with his child unbelievably arousing. With his mouth to her ear, he whispered, "Your breasts will be full and wonderfully sensitive." He teased the barest brush of his fingertips over the tips, springing them to life. "Every little touch will seem amplified. And your belly"—he slid his hand down to toy with her belly button—"will be round and proud, carrying life." He sighed. "We will have to be languid and slow, terribly tender and careful of the life within. How could I not find you attractive that way?"

She didn't speak for a long moment and he realized she was crying softly. He didn't worry over her rapidly changing emotions. Nomi had been awhirl of swift mental states from anger to sadness to unbearable giddiness. Kerrick wrapped Ariss tightly in his arms, rubbing his cheek against hers, murmuring endearments.

Ariss seemed on the verge of saying something, but forcefully held herself back, and he wondered if she'd been about to confess the truth of her heart. He absolutely understood why she didn't; he couldn't either.

"You don't have to say it, Ariss. I feel the same way."

Her sigh of relief said everything.

Entwined, his hand pressed protectively over her belly; they fell asleep with many things known but entirely unspoken.

Tavarus came early in the morning. He came with a swaggering arrogance and a mocking laugh that wrenched Kerrick from his pleasant dream. He and Ariss lived in the forest, not as humans, but as fluffy creatures that knew nothing of politics or power plays. They spent their time foraging for food and fornicating with lusty abandon. Leaving behind that blissful fantasy almost brought tears to Kerrick's eyes. More than anything, he wanted to give Ariss her heart's desire. Damn Tavarus for not even allowing him the briefest moment of success.

Never before had Kerrick felt Tavarus arrive. Instantly on guard, Kerrick realized Tavarus wanted him to know he'd come. When Kerrick felt him, he wanted to get himself away from Ariss as fast as he could, but his body was locked. In a moment of utter horror, he realized why Tavarus let him keep his awareness.

In his mind's eye, Tavarus appeared as a tall muscular man, draped in a black loincloth, with a straight nose, thin lips, bald head, and eyes of indiscernible color. Every part of his features was in perfect proportion. Deeply bronzed skin glowed with ethereal light. Around the upper portion of his right arm, a black band of sharp angles against a parallel line encircled his entire bicep.

Kerrick faced this god in his mind without any way to defend himself. In his vision, he stood as he was, nude, his blond hair gleaming, his green eyes positively glowing, a bronze collar around his neck, but Tavarus manifested multiple weapons in his hands with the snap of his fingers. When Tavarus tossed them to Kerrick, he dropped them as if oil coated his fingers. Tavarus laughed and laughed.

"I don't need weapons to defeat you." Tavarus made the blades disappear, then shoved him as he strode past.

Kerrick landed hard on his butt, humiliated, glaring up at the god who commanded his body.

Tavarus forced one of Kerrick's eyes open.

Mercilessly, he peered down at Ariss.

Sometime during the night, she had rolled over and now faced toward him, her features soft with sleep. Her eyelids fluttered and Kerrick realized she was dreaming. Her mouth curved in a soft smile, telling him her dream was a pleasant one, hopefully one like his.

His heart took a sickening lurch in his chest.

Ariss lay utterly vulnerable.

Cold, sharp fear infiltrated every muscle in his body, twisting him as tightly as a coiled spring.

"Isn't she beautiful?" Tavarus asked, forcing Kerrick's hand out to stroke her cheek. Her skin gave below the gentle pressure. "So soft, so sweet. But what's this? Dried tears?" Smoothing his fingertip over the tracks of sorrow on her face, his raucous laughter filled Kerrick's head. "Did you make her cry with your big, thick cock?"

Snarling, Kerrick verbally lashed out, but Tavarus silenced him with a flick of his finger. Kerrick didn't see his hand gesture so much as he felt the movement in his mind. He felt the promise of Tavarus' finger pressing against his lips. A frightening impotence made him hot with fury. How could he fight an enemy who had utter control over his body?

Worse, how could he protect the woman he loved?

Tavarus felt his conflict and chuckled. "Silence, you simple fool. You are lucky I let you have her uninterrupted last night." Tavarus forced Kerrick's hand to cup her breast, eliciting a soft moan from between her parted lips. "It pleased me to let you have that moment to waylay her into thinking I was bored with her. To convince her I had departed for good."

Disappointed with her show of pleasure, Tavarus pinched Kerrick's fingers to her nipple until Ariss whimpered. He let go before she woke. "How could I ever become bored with such a lovely, responsive creature?"

Kerrick tried to yank his hand away, but Tavarus only laughed, and forced his hand lower.

"I think with proper training, she will grow to welcome pain."

Kerrick struggled against him, but Tavarus easily bypassed his paltry resistance. Throughout his experiences, Kerrick had encountered those who found a curious pleasure within pain, but Ariss was not of that breed. She enjoyed the tease, the delay of gratification, but only by the darkest perversity would someone turn her into a woman who welcomed pain. Given enough time, and the manipulations of a powerful god, Tavarus could mold her to such a being. Just the thought destroyed a part of Kerrick's soul. Ariss was beautifully crafted for pleasure. The simplest touch, the most mild of erotic game, gave her tremendous satisfaction. Kerrick would rather die than be a part of perverting her innate response into something against her nature.

Slipping his finger between her thighs, Tavarus exclaimed, "Wonderful! She's still wet from last night." Rubbing his finger along her slick lips, Tavarus coated his digit with her juice, then lifted his hand to Kerrick's mouth. He forced him to taste her before sliding his finger back between her widely parted legs.

"Look. Don't you see how much she wants me?"

What Kerrick saw was her longing for him, not Tavarus. The

touches she felt she believed to be from him, not the wanton god who had hurt her so badly. Tavarus only touched her gently now to trick her into further submission. He wanted Ariss writhing and willing and then, and only then, would he wake her with the knowledge that he was going to hurt her. Kerrick could feel how much Tavarus longed for the moment when her face would change from welcoming enjoyment to frightened pain.

Knowing what pleasure Tavarus took in inflicting pain killed something in Kerrick. All his life Kerrick had sought out women to bed, but never with the thought of force. Each woman came to him willing, wanton, her needs meshing with his. Mutual shared bliss was what he sought. Tavarus wanted kneeling supplicants. He wanted Ariss terrified. He wanted her to part her legs in appeasement because of dread, not passion. The darkest emotions aroused Tavarus more than willing participation ever could. If Ariss wanted him, if she actively sought him out, he would not want her in return. If Tavarus succeeded in turning her into a woman who actually reveled in his abuse, he would leave her. How Tavarus had become a god Kerrick didn't know, but he wasn't a god of sex. Of war, perhaps, but not sex. Not when he used sex as a weapon.

Ariss moaned and spread her legs farther, giving him greater access. Her response was automatic as she anticipated more pleasure. To his horror, Ariss had no idea a maniacal bastard now ruled Kerrick's body. If he could have warned her, he would have, but Tavarus commanded him, forcing him to keep his lips pressed while he fingered her sleepy, defenseless body.

Slick, hot, and slippery with need, Ariss' body accepted his thrusting finger. When Tavarus jammed his digit into her passage, Ariss moaned and rocked her hips, accepting the forceful penetration, moving her body in time with his plunges.

Tavarus forced his other hand to his cock, stroking the flaccid flesh rapidly until he hardened. "Having her ready will make this so much easier. And see? She wants me. She feels my presence and willingly parts her thighs." Roughly, he thrust his middle finger deep inside her. Ariss bucked, riding his hand. "Willing little *yondie*." Another coarse laughed echoed in Kerrick's head. "I suppose I can't call her a *yondie* as I don't have to pay."

Forcefully rolling Ariss away, Tavarus settled himself behind her, angling his cock against the split of her thighs.

Ariss mumbled, then reached back, feeling along his hip, sighing as she nestled herself against him.

"Fast or slow?" Tavarus asked, holding himself at her entrance.

Kerrick begged him not to hurt her. Perversely, he felt her heat, and he wanted to press himself into that slick channel, but not with pain.

"Let us go slow and then, when she is on the verge of climax, I will roll her over and show her the truth." With that, Tavarus guided Kerrick's cock into Ariss.

She moaned, pressing her bottom against his hips, welcoming him within. Her hand came back, settling on his body, her fingertips pressing encouragement.

Kerrick hoped she didn't turn to look, because she would know Tavarus was inside him by the change in his eyes.

"Have you ever felt anything so tight and hot in your life?" Tavarus asked, rolling Kerrick's hips, swiveling his cock within her passage. Ariss groaned and curled a bit forward so that he would be free to make greater movements. "Even Varnatha doesn't possess such a greedy little cunt."

The name sounded eerily familiar to Kerrick, but he couldn't focus on that when every move Tavarus made raced amplified gratification through Kerrick's body.

"One of the perks of being a god is I can increase what you feel to mimic what I feel." Another jolt of liquid pleasure surged, causing Kerrick to scream emptily into his own mind.

Tavarus intended to make him the victim of the longest, strongest, most painful orgasm any man had ever endured. "Now you have a taste of what it is to be a god."

Tormented by his longings, because Ariss did feel good and he wanted to be within her, but not with a cruel god flinging rude insults, Kerrick struggled to keep his sanity. Every bit of pleasure Kerrick took, Tavarus managed to corrupt and turn ugly. After a lifetime of this, Kerrick knew he would become like Tavarus: aroused by vulgarity and force. He couldn't bear to become like the repulsive monster in his mind. Yet still, he lay passive, unable to do anything but what the god commanded.

Ariss rocked her body against him, uttering breathy sighs and growls. Tavarus forced Kerrick's hand between her legs and swirled his fingertips over her clit.

"That's what she likes; a strong, steady beat." Tavarus chuckled. "The look in her eyes last night when you lost the rhythm! I have never seen such a beautiful look of panic. How difficult it is for a woman to get back to that moment when her orgasm is inevitable." He forced his hand to make jerky motions that caused Ariss to fidget. "Let us see how long she will allow this fumbling."

Ariss squirmed restlessly against him, then placed her hand over his, guiding his movements, showing him how she wished to be touched. Tavarus complied, because when he hit the right beat, her cunt spasmed around Kerrick's cock. Each perfect set of strikes drew him deeper into her, snuggling the walls of her passage tighter.

In his mind, Kerrick saw Tavarus throw back his head and open his mouth, growling like a great beast as he made Kerrick rock forward in one mighty thrust.

Softly, Ariss whispered encouragement, angling her bottom to him, lifting her top leg so she could press his hand, still covered by hers, harder against her clit.

"It won't take much to make her a slave to pain." Winking lewdly at him, Tavarus forced Kerrick's body to thrust into her at a dizzying pace, but at least what he was doing wasn't hurting her. If anything, she enjoyed the rough, animal nature of their coupling.

"That's it, that's it," Tavarus encouraged, "make her come, make her cream all over our cock."

Kerrick struggled against Tavarus because it wasn't their cock, it was his cock, and he didn't want Tavarus to feel any pleasure. His struggles only amused him and compelled him to unleash another dose of concentrated pleasure. Lost in the grip of the most powerful orgasm ever, Kerrick was barely aware when Ariss climaxed, her legs clamping together, trapping their hands as her sweet sex did the same around his shaft. So tightly did she grip him he was unable to thrust. He simply held on to her as he rode out his mind-shattering release.

Panting, Tavarus stood in Kerrick's mind. He gave his semi-hard and glistening cock a quick shake. "Now you see why I will never, ever give her up."

18

Shaken by the strength of her orgasm, Ariss was unable to move for a long time. Behind her, Kerrick pressed against her back, his breath blowing like a bellows across her skin. His frantic lovemaking was in such sharp contrast to the gentle love they'd made last night, that Ariss shivered. Kerrick had handled her roughly, his passion so deep he took what he needed. If she hadn't guided his hand, he might have forgotten about her entirely. The thought gave her pause. Kerrick had never lost sight of her pleasure before. She closed her eyes against the truth. It wasn't Kerrick who'd shoved himself into her with brutal need, but Tavarus.

Afraid to move, lest he try something else, Ariss lay passive, gathering her thoughts, letting her heartbeat return to normal. Something was different about this time, because he usually delighted in tormenting her. Not once had Tavarus come without letting her know. Not just informing her, but rubbing his possession of Kerrick in her face. Her thoughts immediately turned to Kerrick. He would be devastated if he found out. Trapped between the desire to roll over and confirm her suspicions, and her longing to roll away to the safety of the basin room, Ariss stayed immobile, listening to Kerrick's breathing.

After a long time, his heavy panting slowed, but he remained still, as if he were stunned. Sweat covered his skin. With the covers tossed back, the sheen of moisture rapidly cooled, giving him a clammy feel against her flesh.

Shivering, Ariss clenched her teeth together for as long as she could, but in the end, she reached out and pulled the cover over her. Still, Kerrick didn't move. Worried now, she went against her better judgment, and called, "Kerrick?"

No answer.

Her belly twisted. Petrified that Tavarus had permanently damaged Kerrick's mind, she rolled over, dreading what she would see.

On his back, his eyes open and staring sightlessly up at the ceiling, Kerrick lay immobile. His pulse held steady, the vein at his neck throbbing slowly while his chest rose and fell with his breath. Against his hip, his semihard cock lay twitching, as if his orgasm continued long after he'd pulled away.

"Kerrick?"

One eyelid flickered weakly, but other than that, he was motionless. His eyes were beautifully green with a normal-sized pupil, so if Tavarus had been here, he'd since departed. All along she thought that Tavarus would never do anything to hurt her or the baby, but she didn't realize what he was doing might hurt Kerrick. He'd always been disoriented after one of Tavarus' visits, but not like this. Kerrick sprawled on the bed as if someone had beaten him repeatedly in the head.

Last night had been so beautiful. Tender and sweet, he'd loved her the way she'd always wanted her mate to love her. He'd soothed all her fears about what would happen to her when she grew large with child. Kerrick didn't tell her she would always be beautiful, he showed her. She'd wanted to tell him she loved him, but didn't because she feared Tavarus would come and ruin their perfect moment. They had left the words unsaid but no less clear. She knew Kerrick felt the same toward her. Sadly, it seemed Tavarus had waited and punished Kerrick for what they'd done.

Ariss wanted to rail at him, to scream out all her fury, but Tavarus wasn't here anymore, and even if he were, he wouldn't listen. He would laugh and depart once he'd sated his lust. For a god, he certainly behaved like a spoiled child. But why was it different this time? Why hadn't he announced himself, and what had he done to Kerrick?

"Kerrick?" She leaned over, cupping his face, peering intently into his eyes. His lids fluttered and she held her breath. As he blinked in slow waves, life returned to his gaze. Relieved, she pressed her lips to his, then pulled away. "Wake up, Kerrick. Please come back to me."

"Ariss . . ." he breathed her name between his parted lips.

"I'm here, I'm here." She pulled back so that he could see her.

Kerrick struggled to focus. His eyes crossed and his lids bounced up and down in confusion, almost as if he were relearning how to control his own body.

"Did he hurt you?" She hurriedly wiped her tears away before he saw them.

Kerrick shook his head slightly side to side. "Did I hurt you?"

"I'm fine." She didn't want him to remember any of it if he didn't have to. What caused her great shame was that she had enjoyed what they'd done. Somehow, Tavarus had tricked her into thinking Kerrick was responsible. Rough and wild, exiting, but not brutal as Tavarus usually was. What they'd done was mostly a picking up of where they'd left off in Kerrick's room two cycles ago. It wasn't much wonder she didn't realize until afterward that Tavarus had been present. Perhaps the purpose was to teach her that he could be sly. He could come and use her, and she would never know the difference, not unless he *wanted* her to know. "What did Tavarus do to you?"

Kerrick blinked several times. Wavering, he lifted his head to glance down at his body. Ariss followed his gaze to his still-twitching cock. Peering closer, she realized he was ejaculating in small dribs and drabs.

"It just won't stop," he said in gasping bursts. "I can't stop coming." His voice was as tortured as the look on his face.

She'd told him that he'd always looked surprised when he climaxed, but now he looked tormented. Worse, she had no idea what to do.

"Stop thinking about sex. Think about killing things." It wasn't much, but her suggestion was all she could come up with on short notice. Turning his attention away from pleasure might stop the torture from consuming him.

He laughed, then winced as he jostled his penis. "I'll try." Kerrick clenched his eyes closed and his brows drew together sharply as he concentrated.

To get his mind further away from sex, she hastily covered up with her discarded shift. In a burst of inspiration, she retrieved a small towel from the basin, soaked it in cool water, and then handed the cloth to him.

Gingerly, Kerrick placed the towel over his genitals, groaning out in pain until he had the fabric settled. After a while, the twitching finally abated.

Kerrick wiped himself carefully, then tossed the towel on the floor. Ariss frowned, scooped it up off the cream-colored carpet, and placed it in the basin room.

"Sorry."

"It's fine." She shook her head, a bit embarrassed that she was worried about damage to the carpet when a god had abused him. "What did he do to you?"

Kerrick let out a long sigh as he placed his forearm over his forehead. "He filled me up with this liquid pleasure to show me what it was like to climax as a god."

Ariss winced. "Why would he do that?"

"To punish me for being with you last night."

She felt horrible. All of this was her fault.

"He made me watch, too."

Swallowing hard, Ariss settled beside him, slipping his hand into hers. He squeezed gently, then lifted her hand to his mouth, kissing her palm. Tormented eyes met hers. For such a large man, he seemed suddenly, painfully vulnerable. His bewilderment broke her heart. Only by biting the edge of her tongue was she able to hold her tears at bay. In that moment, she would have given anything to go back to Tavarus' brutal bouts of vicious sex. If Kerrick remained oblivious to them, she would do whatever Tavarus demanded. She would suffer anything to take this burden from Kerrick's soul.

In halting bursts, Kerrick explained how Tavarus forced him to awareness but wouldn't let him move of his own volition. "I tried to fight him, but he just laughed. And then he kept hitting me with these massive doses of pleasure."

Ariss couldn't imagine being held captive within her own body, forced to do the bidding of a self-indulgent god, who, in turn, made her enjoy it. Also, she knew that this was Tavarus' warning; if she ever pulled Kerrick into her bed again, Tavarus would rape her while Kerrick watched. Tavarus would hold Kerrick impotent within his own body while he used that body to inflict pain upon her. Nothing would be more horrifying to Kerrick than watching Tavarus abuse her with his body while he was forced to take pleasure in the act. Ariss couldn't imagine anything more disgusting.

"I was terrified that at any moment he would roll you over, make you aware he was here, and then hurt you while I watched." Kerrick shivered. He clenched his teeth and then closed his eyes as if to block the images. "Repeatedly he threatened to do so."

The thought alone nauseated her. Her mind raced in a hundred different directions seeking a solution. How could she stop Tavarus from possessing Kerrick? She couldn't spend a lifetime with Kerrick and know him only when Tavarus decided to possess his body. She'd never be able to keep her hands off Kerrick, and she doubted he could do the same with her. Moreover, she had no desire to sate her lust with another.

Ariss wanted Kerrick. She loved him. More than her next breath, she loved the man by her side. Her heart curled in pain that she couldn't tell him. She knew he knew, but a part of her broke that she could not speak the words to tell him what lay deep in her heart. She knew Kerrick loved her, too. He couldn't say the words, either, not with a vengeful god over his shoulder. Just like her, he felt so much more than he could say.

Ariss wanted Kerrick as her bondmate, not her slave, and not as a convenient body for Tavarus to fill. If she couldn't have Kerrick, fully and utterly, she didn't want anyone. With great regret, she realized she might have to abstain from sex in order to keep Kerrick in her life. The perversity of that thought infuriated her; all her life she'd be taught to refrain from pleasure until she'd reached the bonding bed. Now that she'd found her ultimate bondmate, she couldn't have him without inflicting untold trauma on each of them. The gods had a most cruel sense of irony.

"He said that he would make you a slave to pain." Kerrick rolled his head back, pressing into the bed, covering his face with one massive hand. "He wants to make you addicted to pleasure-pain so that you will welcome his abuse."

Her eyes went wide as she considered what Kerrick said. There hadn't been pain involved in what they'd done, not really. Some of his hard thrusts had bordered on the verge of pain, but hadn't quite managed, not like what Tavarus normally did. Before, Tavarus has rammed into her so hard he hurt her passage and her cervix with his bashing. Clearly, Tavarus meant to increase everything until the pleasure turned to pain, and then he would make her welcome that. Her belly roiled as a new and far more terrifying thought occurred to her: What would he teach to her son?

"I would kill myself before that," Kerrick swore.

"Gods, no!" Ariss forced him to look at her. "I won't hear of that kind of talk."

"I won't rape you for him. I can't." He bolted up as if ready for a fight, but there was none there to grapple with.

"He won't let you." Ariss knew that for a fact. Tavarus would never let Kerrick kill himself. "He wouldn't let you because he uses your body to manifest himself physically."

Kerrick's shoulders slumped. "Then you will have to kill me."

The usual morning nausea she experienced turned worse. No matter what happened, she couldn't kill Kerrick. "He wouldn't let me do that, either."

Bloodshot eyes turned her way. "He has no control over you."

With a hand to her belly, she murmured, "He does through my child." She explained about the balcony and her thoughts of tossing herself over, and how her belly had hurt until she returned inside. "I can no longer set foot on the balcony. If I even go close to the glass door, my stomach begins to twinge."

Kerrick nodded resolutely. "Then I will find a way to fight him." He straightened his back, squared his shoulders, and lifted his head. His expression was that of the fiercest warrior she had ever seen.

A part of her wanted to caution him that such was folly, but he seemed so determined, so driven, that she didn't have the heart to warn him. All she could do was place her hand on his back, marveling at the heat of his skin.

Quietly, she said, "I believe in you."

"Do you?" He glanced over his shoulder.

"I do," she confirmed. "If anyone can solve this mess, I would put my faith in you."

Resolved, Kerrick stood, searching the floor for his clothing.

"Where are you going?"

"I'm going to find a way to fix this."

"Right now?" She thought she would have more time with him.

"Yes now." He yanked on his pants. "When do you propose I start? After he actually rapes you while I watch?"

Ariss recoiled from his vicious tone.

"I'm sorry." Kerrick released a tense breath and sat down beside her on the bed. He swept her hand into his, kissed her palm, and let go. "I'm not angry with you, but with him, and myself."

"None of this is your fault."

"I know." He nodded. "But you don't understand. He made me enjoy it." His voice fell to a whisper. "He made me want to roll you over and take pleasure in your terror." Kerrick took such a deep breath his chest expanded greatly. "Don't you see? He's going to turn me into him." Sheer determination overcame the revulsion on his face. "I'm not going to become Tavarus. I'd rather die."

Within moments, her staff of servants would arrive. Today was tribute day in the temple, which meant hours of preparation for her. When she reminded Kerrick, he nodded absently.

"You have to come," she reminded.

"I'll be there." He smiled ruefully. "I don't know if I'll be able to climax after what happened this morning, but I'll certainly try." Moving over to the couch, he grabbed his shirt and belt off the floor and slipped them on. "Do you want me to call Donlan?"

She nodded. Donlan was the guard who had fallen to his

knees when she prayed, the one who resolutely held to his tribute for over a season. Out of all the guards, Kerrick and she
trusted Donlan the most.

Once Donlan entered, Kerrick left, and Ariss gave herself
over to her servants. They washed, anointed, powdered, perfumed, and then slathered cosmetics over her face until she became almost a caricature of herself. They spent all morning and
most of the afternoon preparing her to receive tribute.

Donlan kept his gaze moving. He watched everything the
servants did, yet kept an ear on the door. His duty was to protect her from any harm while Kerrick was gone. Donlan took
his duty seriously. He was ever vigilant. However, she noticed
his eyes would linger a bit more on her once they fitted her into
the elaborate gown that covered the front of her legs, brushed
the edge of her bottom, and exposed her breasts. Donlan's
pupils dilated slightly and his cock hardened when he saw her
in her black ceremonial gown.

When Donlan caught her noticing, he blushed and forcefully looked to the servants. She honestly didn't think he had
anything to be ashamed of; Donlan was conditioned to become
aroused when he saw her this way. That was rather the point.
Ariss also knew he was looking forward to offering tribute. At
first, she thought he would wait an entire season, and perhaps
he was optimistic of doing so, but he found that being near her
was far too tempting. Donlan had given tribute at every opportunity just as every other guard in the palace had done since she
had become the consort to the Harvester god.

Prior to her becoming the vessel of Tavarus, the guards had
little opportunity to give tribute. Only during severely re-
stricted festivals were they allowed to enter the temple and
stroke themselves to fulfillment. At those times, they gave over
to their imagined consort of Tavarus. Mostly, they were expected to contain themselves and wait for the time when they
were allowed to bond. Sadly, most were not allowed that lux-

ury. Even if they were allowed to select a mate, only one child could come from their pairing. Giving the guards the luxury of temple tribute gave them the release they needed to truly focus on their job of defending the palace. If nothing else, Ariss knew what she offered these men mattered. She gave them a way to purge their lust. Without her, they often floundered and despised themselves for finding a release outside the strict confines of their roles.

Ariss had never confessed to anyone how much she enjoyed this part of her duty. Sitting upon her tawdry throne, her breasts exposed, and watching guard after guard fall to his knees to masturbate at her feet was profoundly erotic. Power filled her. They knelt for *her.* At times she pulled herself back with forceful regard, reminding herself they gave their tribute to Tavarus, but in her mind she knew they came for her. All these men willingly entered the temple to gaze upon her body and stroke themselves to fulfillment. She sincerely doubted that Tavarus ever entered their thoughts.

She had no idea if Tavarus could feel her through the throne, but she doubted it. If he could, he would have flung the information in her face when he possessed Kerrick. She wondered if Kerrick would be angry that she took such sinful pleasure in her duty, but given his erotic mind, she doubted he would.

She didn't think Kerrick would want to deny her pleasure. If the guards touched her in any way, she had a feeling he would be furious, but them looking at her, lusting after her, probably didn't bother him. Still, she was curious. She knew he did not enjoy giving tribute, because he didn't like being forced to do anything, especially not having to kneel to her power. Alternately, Kerrick wouldn't mind her bowing down to him, but as a man, he had a terrible time showing obeisance to another, in particular, a woman. He hadn't minded masturbating for her in the mating room. But this, in the temple, he found degrading.

With a sigh, she lifted her hand to Donlan. The time had

come for tribute. He opened the door and gave a series of sharp commands. After a moment, he ushered her out into the hall.

Surrounded by guards, she made her way laboriously toward the temple. Cool air caressed her breasts, peaking her nipples and washing small bumps across her flesh. The edge of the dress brushed against her bottom like a teasing caress. Silken *astle* washed down the front, smoothing against her meticulously shaved legs. Every step she took caused her outfit to stroke her, heightening her awareness of her own body.

Ariss lifted herself a bit higher, proud of the power in her form. Her family had spent so much time instilling shame in her, that she found a delicious irony in the fact that her entire existence now revolved around sex. No wonder her father took the entire family and ran back to Felton. He must be mortified. A wicked smile crossed her face. She had no sympathy for him. All of this began because of his ruthless greed. As far as she was concerned, he'd gotten his comeuppance.

Her mind flashed briefly on Kerrick, wondering what he was doing. She hoped he would be safe. If anything happened to him, she didn't know how she would continue. Her entire life had changed drastically, and she knew the changes would only continue. She wanted Kerrick there to help her. She now knew she had the inner strength to persevere on her own, but her life would be so much more bearable if he were at her side.

With a deep breath, she entered the temple, leaving her retinue behind. Smoke wafted in the air as the azure crystals cast their odd blue light over everything within. Stepping carefully along the path of acolytes, she made her way to the throne. Leering perversely, Tavarus' image hung over the seat where the clear phallus awaited. Carefully, Ariss sat, sliding the cool stone within her body. Anticipation caused a quiver along the inner muscles of her sex, clamping her tightly around the rock. It didn't take long for the heat of her body to transfer to the stone.

Lifting her hand, she nodded to the nearest acolyte, word-lessly instructing him to bring in the first guard.

The man was unfamiliar to her, but his large, wide-set eyes instantly struck her as unique. Curly black hair swept across his forehead, and a slight scruffy beard darkened his otherwise pale face. His nose hooked toward the end, possibly from a break. His lips were full, sensual, and parted in wonder as he gazed upon her.

He swallowed hard. He remained mute for a long moment; then his eyes widened in fear.

"Say, 'I have come to pay tribute,' " Ariss whispered to him.

Nodding vigorously, he cleared his throat. "I have come to pay tribute." His voice was so loud it echoed against the far-thest walls of the temple.

Ariss did her best not to smile. Waves of nervousness rolled off him, but she sensed that his heart was pure.

He stood very still, then cocked his head to the side, clearly unable to recall his next line.

Ariss whispered, " 'Will you accept my tribute?' "

He gave her a perplexed frown, then realized that was what he should say. After another very loud clearing of his throat, he practically screamed, "Will you accept my tribute?"

"You don't have to yell, I'm right here."

"You don't have to yell," he yelled, "I'm right here."

Ariss covered her face with her hand until her giggles abated. To his credit, he stood patiently waiting until she said, "I will accept your offering."

This part he understood. He fell to his knees so quickly she swore she heard his bones crack against the Onic tile floor. Ex-citedly, he yanked at his loincloth, but the fabric caught on his belt. Growling, he pulled until a sharp rent of tearing fabric filled the air. Once freed of the cloth, he tossed it aside.

Her eyes went wide. She'd never seen such an enormous cock. Long, thick, and to her shock, she realized he wasn't fully hard. Simultaneously she was aroused but also a bit afraid; a penis that big would be nothing short of painful, yet still there was something unbearably intriguing about considering the possibilities.

The man cupped his hand around his shaft. His fingers didn't touch so massive was his girth. He stopped suddenly.

So enraptured by his unusual genitals, she forgot the words he should speak.

He bit his lip and glanced up at her. Finally, he bellowed, "Can I look at you?"

It wasn't quite right, but it was close enough. "You may gaze upon me."

Eyes riveted to her breasts, he stroked himself with his left hand. After only a few rubs, his cock was fully erect. A deep blue vein along the top of the shaft pulsed dully in the azure light. Thrusting his hips forward, he eagerly displayed himself to her while increasing his pace. Back and forth, he worked his hand. His tongue crept to the edge of his mouth, making him appear to be in deep concentration.

Restlessly, Ariss squirmed against the throne, trying to imagine what he would feel like within her. Gods, she'd barely be able to move without crushing him with her sex. As if in answer, her passage clamped around the stone. Angling her hips back, she pressed her clit against the seat, but the polished stone offered no texture, only pressure, which wasn't enough to push her over the edge. A climax hovered just out of her reach.

The man before her was incredibly large, but he also had tremendous staying power. Each time she thought he had reached the peak of pleasure, he pulled himself back by exerting pressure to the base of his staff. Watching him move hypnotized her. Time slowed with each mesmerizing stroke. She knew the time was close as his face scrunched up. Clenching his eyes and lips together distorted his features, making him look slightly squished, which somehow only made his cock appear bigger. When he finally erupted, a beautiful pure white jet gushed from the tip of his cock, arched in the air, and splashed at her feet.

His body sagged with relief.

After a few moments to recover, his face unclenched and he gazed at her with curious pride. "Did I do well?"

"You have pleased me greatly."

He wasn't the most sophisticated man who'd ever come before her, but he would make some woman, some very large woman, extremely happy. Suddenly to her mind flashed an image of Bithia. Given her lascivious nature, she would find a man like this most welcome. While the man covered himself with his ripped loincloth, Ariss drew one of the acolytes near and suggested that he would find favor if he introduced the guard to the empress.

"Perhaps he can guard her at her next official function."

A baffled look washed over his plain features until he saw the still sizable penis the man covered with his cloth. The acolyte nodded slyly, then departed.

Ariss turned her attention to her next tribute.

As she enjoyed each man who came before her, she couldn't help thinking of Kerrick. What would he try to do? She hated to seem so pessimistic, but she didn't see a way out of their dilemma. Things would only get worse after her child was born. Once she healed, Tavarus wouldn't have to hold back in his pursuit of forcing her to enjoy the pain he dispensed.

As evening grew close, she thought that the ceremony was almost over. To her great disappointment, Kerrick entered, his shoulders slumped, his head hung low. Whatever he'd tried to do clearly hadn't worked. Visions of spending a lifetime with him but unable to touch him broke her heart.

Kerrick lifted his face and looked right at her. His pupils were so wide they ate up all the color of his gaze. Her mouth fell open and a scream caught in her throat.

19

As he strode away from Ariss' rooms, dull fury replaced the revulsion in Kerrick's gut. He would not become Tavarus' puppet. His demonstration this morning was to show Kerrick that at any time, he could command his body, force him to do his bidding, and worse, make him enjoy the atrocities he committed. Just the thought of getting pleasure from abusing Ariss was enough to make him consider suicide.

When he'd contemplated the notion, Tavarus trickled into the back of his mind, warning him that he would never allow him to take that option. Without Kerrick, Tavarus couldn't manifest himself physically. There was no way he would allow him or another to harm the body he considered his personal toy.

Kerrick wondered why Tavarus didn't just possess him outright and throw Kerrick's soul into the vast nothingness. After long consideration, he decided that doing so would render Tavarus a mortal, something he would rather not be. If by some bizarre occurrence Kerrick were mortally wounded, Tavarus would simply depart unscathed. Tavarus wanted the best of both worlds; all the lofty power of being a god in *Jarasine,* and yet he could still dabble in pleasures of the flesh on Diola.

Determined to find an answer, Kerrick had hastily dressed and left Ariss in the care of Donlan. Kerrick marched in great hallway-eating strides. He slowed when he realized he didn't know where he was going. At first, he thought of going to the training rooms and discussing the problem with Chur. The man was a demigod, after all.

Then Kerrick decided against telling Chur what was going on. If Chur thought Ariss were at risk, he would remove Kerrick from her side. Chur would do anything to protect the life Ariss carried. Kerrick decided he would seek out Chur only as a last option. Kerrick would rather spend eternity in the *gannett* than hurt the woman he loved. But until he was forced to make that choice, he had to remain free to find a way to solve their problem.

He wanted to be with Ariss. He knew she wanted to be with him. They were together, but not in the full measure each desired. What they'd shared last night had been a poignant reminder of everything they could have together, if only they didn't have a vengeful god destroying their plans. They would never survive with Tavarus inserting himself into their relationship whenever the whim possessed him. As Kerrick looked ahead to the future, he saw Ariss turned into a demoralized pain slave and he her abusive master. Shuddering with disgust, he swore he would find a way to stop that from transpiring.

Suddenly, the answer struck Kerrick so hard he halted in midstride. Like all gods, Tavarus had a female counterpart. He'd even said her name this morning. With his mocking smirk, Tavarus had said, "Even Varnatha doesn't possess such a greedy little cunt."

Varnatha was the goddess of the Harvesters. In her own right, she was just as powerful as Tavarus. She was the goddess of war and sex, which made her a formidable woman. A formidable woman who would be greatly displeased to find her counterpart taking liberties with a mortal woman. God or no, Tavarus was paired with Varnatha. Kerrick had a feeling that Varnatha, like any woman, had her pride. If she found out Tavarus were cheating on her, she probably wouldn't take the news well.

His purpose renewed, Kerrick turned sharply on his heel and headed toward the temple. Two acolytes eagerly held the curtain open for him, granting him entrance. He paused, confused for a moment, until he remembered today was tribute day. Ariss would sit on her naughty throne and watch every guard in the palace masturbate.

Personally, he found the entire process debasing. He didn't like having to perform for anyone, not unless it was of his own volition. However, he suspected that Ariss enjoyed her time in the temple. When he put himself in her place, it wasn't difficult to see why. If he got to lounge about while woman after woman fell to her knees to masturbate before him, he would jump at the chance to receive tribute. Unfortunately for him, that was never going to happen.

Many parts of Diolan culture had duality, but this was not one of them, mainly because a man couldn't carry the child of a god. Supposedly, the tribute was to Tavarus, even though on the surface, the act seemed geared toward Ariss. Still, Kerrick suspected that Tavarus hung close to Ariss during this time. Tavarus would enjoy watching her sitting upon his likeness with his carved cock plunged inside. Knowing him as he did, such a scenario would be extremely pleasing to Tavarus. It wouldn't surprise him, either, if Tavarus placed himself within the stone so that he could vicariously feel Ariss' reactions.

It was this notion that gave him the idea for how to reach Varnatha. If Tavarus hung near to his likeness, and surely, he did, because that's how he'd supposedly impregnated Ariss, then it stood to reason that Varnatha could be compelled to enter her likeness and possibly hear Kerrick's plea. Or so he hoped. Ariss had been involved in a form of punishment when her encounter with the god occurred. Kerrick was hoping he could achieve a similar result without having a portion of Varnatha's statue inserted into his body. If her stone likeness were big enough, perhaps he would have to insert his penis into it to get her attention. If that were what it took, he would do it, no matter how silly he looked or felt in doing so. One way or another, he would get Varnatha's attention. Of course, all of his speculation was moot if he couldn't find a statue of her.

Probably the only reason Tavarus allowed Kerrick the freedom of his own thoughts without censoring him was that Tavarus was otherwise occupied with Ariss. Today would be the only chance Kerrick would have to put his slapped-together plan into action. Once Tavarus returned to his mind, he would know everything Kerrick had even *considered* doing. He simply wouldn't have a second opportunity.

Once the fabric door closed behind him, Kerrick gave himself a moment to acclimate to the smoky air and odd blue lighting. Several acolytes motioned him toward the area where Ariss' throne sat. He headed that way. As soon as their backs were turned, he slipped behind the fabric-shrouded walls and worked his way around the temple.

Long ago, he'd seen a gilded picture book, one he clearly wasn't supposed to see given his father's reaction to finding him with it, but Kerrick would never forget one of the exquisite paintings within the pages. A tall woman with enormous breasts sat astride a warrior. She was dressed like a warrior, too, but most of her outfit seemed to be missing. In her right hand, she held a curved sword aloft, what Kerrick now knew as a *cirvant*, and in her left, she cupped the warrior's head to her breast. Her head was back, her mouth open in a triumphant battle cry. Some magical wind furled the strands of her long black hair in graceful curls behind her. Both she and the man were incredibly muscular. Bronzed flesh and glistening sweat made each muscle more pronounced. Something about the picture had intrigued him, but he'd only been ten seasons old, not quite mature enough to understand what was going on.

When he was older, he understood the woman was mating with the man, forcefully, but from what Kerrick remembered of the man's face, he didn't seem opposed to her possession. His eyes were open, gazing up at her almost worshipfully as he accepted her breast in his mouth. Even with her bulky, powerful body, the woman was extremely beautiful. For all Kerrick knew, she whacked the warrior's head off in the next moment, but in that captured image, she was a powerful, primal goddess.

Seasons later, Kerrick realized the woman in the painting was Varnatha. The picture in the book attempted to show her combined elements as the goddess of war and sex. What had upset Kerrick's father was the erotic nature of the book; certainly, it wasn't for children. Considering the rest of the images in that book, the one that had fascinated him had been fairly tame. When he'd grown older, Kerrick had tried to find a copy without success, but the mental image of Varnatha came instantly to mind. He was certain he could locate her likeness within the temple and plead his case to her.

As he worked his way around the statues in the temple, he grew discouraged. There seemed to be far more homage paid to the gods. The few goddess statues he did find were small, tucked into hollows at odd angles, and in some cases, dusty. He started to wonder if there was a different temple for the goddesses.

Just when he'd thoroughly lost hope, he stumbled across a tiny rendering of a woman with a blade held over her head. She was dressed as a warrior, but her full breasts were mostly exposed. Long hair pulled back from her face, then twined around her form. This had to be Varnatha. And there was no way his penis was going to fit anywhere in the tiny statue. The entire thing from base to the tip of her sword was about the same size as his erect cock.

Darting his gaze left and right, verifying that he was alone, Kerrick gingerly plucked the tiny black statue from the niche in the wall. A thick layer of dust obscured her features. So much was packed into her mouth, she appeared to be choking on the grime. Carefully, Kerrick wiped the mess away, using the edge of his simple slave shirt to clean every nook and cranny.

He couldn't help but smile as he rubbed the fabric over her incredible, gravity-defying breasts. Once he'd wiped some filth away, he realized that someone had spent a great deal of time rendering her in exquisite detail. She had individual strands of hair and delicate eyelashes lifting up from her compelling gaze. Her nipples were large and realistically pebbled. Her belly curved with a layer of muscles that drew his cleaning finger right down to her demurely covered sex.

Much to his chagrin, he became aroused. He would have blamed Tavarus for his reaction, but he was not within Kerrick's mind. He rolled his eyes, berating himself for letting a statue excite him. If he were still a young boy, he could understand such a response, but he was a bit too old for this. However, the more he cleaned, the harder he became, and the more his balls throbbed with a clamoring need for climax. After this morning, he didn't think he would ever be able to achieve orgasm again, but here he was, randy and ready.

Kerrick took a deep breath, hoping to steady himself, but that only drew more of the drugged air into his lungs. With a shake of his head, he glanced down and discovered Varnatha glaring up at him.

"You draw me from *Jarasine* into this puny vessel?" She shoved her sword into the scabbard at her waist, then placed her hands on her ample hips. Her breasts swayed with her movements as she looked over her tiny body.

Shocked, Kerrick almost dropped her. He fumbled his grip

on the base until he steadied his hand. Again, he darted his gaze around, but everyone was on the other side of the temple with Ariss.

"Forgive me, goddess Varnatha." Respectfully, Kerrick placed her back into the hollow in the wall, then knelt with his head lowered. "I humbly ask for an audience with you."

"That's better."

When he looked up, she considered her surroundings.

"This is where they've placed me?" Varnatha said something vulgar and tossed her hair back over her shoulder, fully exposing both breasts. Her eyes went wide when she glanced down at her ample bosom. Parting her lips in exasperation, she cupped her massive boobs, and snarled, "What is this?" She held them out, shaking them at Kerrick. Both big, hard nipples pointed right at him like tiny accusing fingers. "Mine are big, but this is absurd!"

Mesmerized by the undulating waves of her proffered breasts, it took him a moment to respond. "I did not carve your likeness, goddess Varnatha."

"What is it with the acolytes and their obsession with gigantic breasts?" She fondled her nipples. "Hmm. Well, they are nicely done. Very perky. Still," she said, removing her hands from them, "if my breasts were this large, I'd hardly be able to fight with such skill." Her gaze lowered to him. "Who are you?"

He bowed his head respectfully. "I am Kerrick. I have come to seek your aid."

"A favor. Of course. No one ever summons me to give me something." She sighed. "Stand up, let me look at you."

Kerrick stood with his arms held loosely at his sides.

"No, no, not like that. Disrobe. I can hardly see you through all those clothes."

Kerrick could just imagine what would happen if he were discovered alone in the temple, naked, before a statue of a goddess. This is how denigrating nicknames came about. But, she *was* a goddess. He had no idea what she could do to him if he disobeyed.

Kerrick slipped off his shirt.

Varnatha let out a long, low *oo* of pleasure. "Very nice." Her tiny eyes traveled over his chest. "Now the pants." She placed one arm under her breasts and lifted the other so her forefinger and thumb cupped her chin. Her pose was one of deep consideration, as if her willingness to grant him favors rested entirely on his body being pleasing to her.

With a fortifying breath, Kerrick worked at the drawstring knot. In his haste, he only tightened it. He didn't think she would chew the knot apart like Ariss had done.

"I'm waiting." Varnatha tapped her foot against the stone base of her perch.

Frantically, he struggled with the string.

"Get over here." She pulled her tiny sword.

He wasn't sure he wanted her hacking about around his crotch even though she was the goddess of war and probably very handy with her blade. What if her aim was off? Yet again, he didn't have much choice. Gingerly, Kerrick stepped forward. Varnatha lifted her *cirvant* and slashed at the knot, deftly splitting it in two without touching anything else.

She shoved her blade away, and commanded, "Off."

Kerrick slid down his pants.

Varnatha whistled. "You did enjoy polishing me up, didn't you?" Her voice was playful as she kept her gaze riveted to his penis. "Perhaps being this size has some advantages. I can honestly say I've never seen one as large as I am." With a flick of her hand, she motioned him closer.

His horrible nickname would only be more perverse if they caught him rubbing his penis on a little statue of a woman. Still, forward he stepped until his cock pointed right at Varnatha's tiny face.

She made several comments in a language he didn't grasp, but the rhythm of the words sounded similar to what he'd said during the Harvest ritual. She reached out and touched the tip with her tiny hands, making him twitch.

"What I could do with you if we were a bit more equal in size." Flashing him a lusty smile, she flicked her hand dismissively. "You may cover yourself."

Kerrick gratefully yanked on his pants and shirt. With the string cut, he had to wrestle the two loose ends of the pants together and tie them in a small knot that probably wouldn't last long. As Ariss suggested, he had to find pants with a different type of fastener.

"Tell me why you've summoned me."

Haltingly, he said, "Tavarus has been possessing my body."

One brow drew up. "I wouldn't mind playing with your body myself."

This was not the reaction he'd been looking for. Given her flirtatious nature, maybe the gods didn't bond as humans did. All his effort might be for nothing. Still, he had to try. Softly, he said, "Tavarus has been possessing my body in order to mate."

Varnatha went very still. "He what?" Her voice lowered dangerously. Her face became a controlled mask.

Now Kerrick was getting somewhere. "Tavarus is obsessed with my woman." His words sounded unbearably arrogant, and almost asinine to his own ears, but he gave up eloquence for succinctness. Ariss wasn't technically his woman, but he wasn't sure he could make Varnatha understand their complicated relationship. In an effort to curry her favor, he gave himself adequate ties to Ariss so that she would understand why he cared.

One eye twitched down as Varnatha gritted her teeth. After she peered intently at the floor, she shifted her gaze to him. Calmly, she asked, "And what, exactly, does he do to your woman?"

Kerrick wasn't sure what she was asking for. Hopefully not a blow-by-blow description of his mating technique. "Well, he says he's the father of her child, which is bad enough, but now he won't leave her alone. He abuses her with my body."

Varnatha withdrew her tiny sword. "Where is he?"

This was what he wanted: an angry, vengeful warrior woman who would rein Tavarus in. Kerrick pointed the direction of the throne. "He's with her now."

"Show me." Varnatha lifted her leg as if to take a step, then slammed it down. She bellowed another expletive. "I can't do anything in this form!" Her cool stone gaze swung to him. "How do you expect me to do anything when I only come up to your shin?"

Kerrick hadn't thought she'd need physical form. "I thought you could just do something to him in *Jarasine*?"

Waving her sword about, shaking her breasts with her motions, Varnatha said, "Do you want me to stop him or not?"

He did. "I don't know of any bigger statues of you." Just his luck. He got the goddess to come to his aid only to be stymied by her size. Life simply wasn't fair.

Eyeing him up and down, Varnatha said, "I could, with your permission, enter your body."

Kerrick considered. Having one god with a free pass was bad enough; was he seriously contemplating letting in another? What would happen to him if they were both in his brain at the same time? He considered finding a larger statue, but he didn't know how much time they had. She had to catch Tavarus in the act, or he would just deny Kerrick's claims and continue to possess him. Pressed for time, Kerrick realized he didn't have the luxury to consider all his options. Desperate to be with Ariss, willing to do anything he must, he granted Varnatha entrance.

A flash of light stumbled him back and then Varnatha was within his mind and body. She flexed his fist and looked over the surroundings from her new and far greater height. Lowering his right hand to his crotch, she cupped his shaft, giving him a strong squeeze.

"We don't have time for this." Kerrick tried to pull his hand back, but she continued her wanton exploration.

That's all he needed. How vile would his nickname grow if they caught him groping himself in the temple? If he were at Ariss' feet, that would be one thing, but standing around, idly fondling himself? No, that wouldn't look good.

With a frustrated sigh, realizing he wasn't going to get harder, she let go, and asked, "Where are they?"

Kerrick told her the way, and she moved his feet in the right direction.

"I need a weapon."

He frowned at her in his mind. "He's not actually in there, not physically. He's within his likeness."

Varnatha made a noncommittal grunt.

"This woman, does she know how to fight?"

"Ariss? No. Why does that matter?"

"Then she will be much easier to kill."

Kerrick's heart stopped, then started beating at three times normal. "What do you mean? I don't want you to kill Ariss!"

Varnatha laughed. "Did you think I would kill Tavarus?"

"I thought you'd scare him and get him to stop possessing me."

"Oh, that he will, when the woman with his child is dead."

To his horror, Kerrick realized he'd made a bad situation much, much worse. Varnatha had total control of his body. When he tried to push her out, she waved her hand dismissively, shoving him mentally back into a corner.

And like the story of his life, it was too late to turn back now.

Using his eyes, Varnatha looked to the short line of men and demanded to know their purpose. When he refused to tell her, she plucked the information directly from his brain. Just like Tavarus, she had complete power over him. Worse, he'd willingly let her in. Varnatha now understood that Ariss was within the room, sitting on Tavarus' likeness, receiving tribute. A sharp flicker of fury washed from her when she thought of the stone cock within Ariss' sex and Tavarus lurking within the rock.

"That soulless fiend!" Varnatha hissed under her breath. "Once when he did this I destroyed an entire village!"

Kerrick felt his hopes slump even more. He'd wanted a vengeful goddess, and he'd gotten one, but she was bitter at the wrong person. How many people would she kill before the guards cut his body down? All he could hope for was that Ariss' guards reacted quickly and killed him before Varnatha could hurt her.

Apparently, this wasn't the first time Tavarus had mated with a mortal through one of his statues, not if Varnatha's thoughts were any indication. From what Kerrick gathered, it was his preferred way to meet mortal women. The trick was in finding a suitable man to possess. It had to be a man who had an affinity for the woman, something beyond the merely physical. Kerrick fit that description perfectly this time around. The village that Varnatha spoke of was a situation long, long ago, back in the time of the ancients. Tavarus had been able to possess every man in the town to mate with every woman because of their religious rites. He'd turned the entire town into abusive sex maniacs.

Just as Kerrick suspected, having Tavarus possess him long enough would destroy who he was. His battered soul would depart, leaving behind an empty shell that Tavarus could use whenever the whim possessed him. To her credit, Varnatha did the villagers a favor; they were no longer in control of their bodies. She found it an abomination to let Tavarus keep them all as toys.

But that was not the situation here. Desperately, Kerrick tried to explain to her, but she ignored him. He struggled to regain control, but Varnatha ruled him with an iron fist. Her goal was clear in her mind and subsequently his: punish Tavarus once she sent him running back to *Jarasine*; but first, she would kill Ariss and the child she carried.

20

Ariss tried to scream, but all that came out was a thin, high whisper of air. Terror gripped her so tightly she couldn't move. The stone phallus that had felt sizzling hot just a moment ago was now shockingly cold, so deeply frigid the edges burned her tender sex.

Kerrick grinned at her, but she realized what he flashed wasn't a smile but a bearing of his teeth. The man she loved wasn't happy, he was snarling.

"I'm going to kill you with my bare hands. Something I haven't done in thousands of seasons." Lifting his hands, Kerrick held them out to her, clenching them slowly as if to show her what he intended to do to her neck.

Looking deep into his eyes, seeing the soulless black, she knew it wasn't Kerrick who threatened her, but Tavarus. He must have discovered that she and Kerrick searched desperately for a solution to block him from their lives. In retaliation, he would force Kerrick to kill her. As much as she feared dying, she couldn't bear the thought of Kerrick living on with her murder on his conscience.

"Kerrick, I know you're in there." She reached out to him, longing to touch him, desperate to hold his hand just one last time. "Please, know that I understand."

When he snarled, she pulled her hand back. Last night had been the most beautiful moment of her life. She was grateful that they'd been able to share that final, touching moment.

"What do you understand?" One eye twitched down, peering at her curiously as his brow furrowed.

"I forgive you." Using all her might, Ariss placed her hands on the arms of the throne and stood, pulling herself out of Tavarus' stone embrace. The phallus pulled free with a soft, almost inaudible *pop.* Her legs wobbled slightly, but she hoped he wouldn't notice. "I know you have no control over what he does."

Kerrick's eyes opened wide. "You're going to, what, stand there and *allow* me to kill you?" He plunked his hands on his hips in a curiously feminine gesture.

"If that's what he makes you do." Ariss considered running, but where would she go? If she screamed, she knew the acolytes and the guards, who always stood in attendance, would come to do her bidding, but they would be too late to save her, and she couldn't bear to watch them kill Kerrick in her last dying moments. Moreover, she clung desperately to her belief that Tavarus would not harm his own child.

"He?"

The one word question caused Ariss to furrow her brow in confusion. "Tavarus."

Kerrick tossed back his head and laughed. Again, his movements were oddly feminine. He took two steps toward her, stopping just short of the final step up to the clear throne.

They stood level to one another. Ariss gazed into his eyes and felt lost in the abyss of darkness.

"I am not Tavarus."

Ariss felt no relief at the revelation. Her mind was awhirl

with possibilities. Cool air washed over her, tightening her exposed nipples. Protectively, she crossed her arms, covering her chest. When she took a steadying breath, she tasted the combined aroma of her and Kerrick on his body. The rich, musky scent of their lovemaking calmed her despite her agitation.

Haltingly, she asked, "Who are you?" Had some other god possessed him? What kind of world were they living in if powerful beings could command them on a whim? Or was it a whim? Ariss had no idea what Kerrick had been doing since he'd left their rooms this morning. Just what had Kerrick tried to do?

Ignoring her, Kerrick, or whoever commanded his body, stomped over to the throne. He grasped the stone phallus in one mighty fist and snapped it free. Lifting his head to the leering face of Tavarus, he bellowed, "I will punish you, Tavarus! You can't escape my wrath!" Shaking the broken-off stone penis at his carved likeness, Kerrick added, "And this time I will do the same to your pathetic cock!" With a snarl of fury, he tossed the chunk of stone aside.

Ariss backed slowly away, angling toward the door, hoping that if she escaped him, the guards could protect her and capture him without bloodshed.

"Where do you think you're going?" Kerrick's voice was so low it rumbled toward her, caressing over her shoulders, holding her like a compelling whisper.

"Please, I don't know who you are," Ariss said. "I haven't done anything to you."

Kerrick thrust an accusing finger at her belly. "You carry his child."

Ariss hugged one arm tighter across her breasts but lowered the other to her belly. Desperately, she tried to determine who would be so angry that she carried Tavarus' child. Terror kept her mind a confused jumble, preventing her from thinking clearly. Every time she took a step toward the safety of the exit, Kerrick took one as well, flashing her a gleeful smile. Whoever was in there was daring her to run because he or she would enjoy pursuing her.

"Stop it!" Ariss cried. It was bad enough that whoever was in there was tormenting her, but that they used Kerrick to do so was beyond cruel.

"Stop it!" Kerrick mimicked, lifting his hands, spreading his arms wide, ready to grab her no matter what direction she went.

Frustrated, terrified, filled with such anxiety she could hardly catch her breath, Ariss demanded, "Tell me who you are."

"I am the goddess Varnatha!" Kerrick tossed his hands into the air.

Ariss jumped back, convinced that lightning bolts would descend from the sky. All that happened was Kerrick's pants fell down to his ankles. If she wasn't so frightened, she might have laughed.

"What the—" he bent over to yank them up.

Donlan erupted from the side, knocking Kerrick over. Lifting his blade on high, Donlan bellowed a battle cry. Light glistened off his dagger as Donlan's arm swept down.

"No!" Ariss yelled, diving toward their entwined bodies. She managed to knock Donlan's blade aside before he could plunge the metal deep into Kerrick's chest.

In a timeless moment, her eyes locked on to Kerrick's, hoping that the god within would depart. To her horror, his pupils widened until both eyes turned glossy black. No whiteness, no color; his eyeballs turned into fathomless pools of darkness.

"Kerrick?"

Donlan lifted his blade in one hand and tried to hold her back with the other.

"Don't!" she commanded. "He's not fighting you!"

Donlan stopped struggling with her. They both looked down at Kerrick. Perfectly still, he lay on his back, his sightless black eyes pointed toward the ceiling.

"They're in me," he whispered weakly.

"Who?" Donlan asked.

Ariss shushed him.

"Tavarus and Varnatha."

Placing herself right above Kerrick, so that without moving his head he could see her, she sternly said, "Leave, Tavarus. If you hurt him, you won't be able to have me anymore." To save Kerrick, she was willing to go back to appeasing Tavarus' lust.

A snarl darted across Kerrick's face. "I'll kill you!" Just as he reached up to place his hands around her neck, he stopped and bellowed, "I won't let you!"

Ariss could see the struggle between the god and goddess within Kerrick's body.

As his eyes slowly drifted closed, he whispered, "She won't let him have me." He drew a pained breath. "He won't let her kill you."

Tavarus and Varnatha battled for control of Kerrick and there wasn't anything she could do.

Kerrick lay on his back in the center of Ariss' bed, his eyes closed, his breathing shallow. His once gloriously golden hair lay limp, brushed back from his face in lifeless clumps.

Ariss sat beside him, tracks of tears dried on her face. Nothing had changed after a quarter cycle. Nine days and nights of utter agony. Neither Tavarus nor Varnatha would give up. While they fought, Kerrick wasted away.

The doctors wanted to force nutrients into him, but keeping him alive would only prolong the war within. Varnatha and Tavarus were tenacious. Both were warriors without mercy who never backed away from a fight. They would battle over Kerrick until he drew his last breath. Once that happened, they would simply depart and go back to *Jarasine,* killing the man she loved and leaving her life in a shambles as they found something new to battle over. How could anyone worship such childish gods?

"How is he?" Donlan asked as he stood behind her.

With Kerrick's condition, Donlan had become her protector. He was a good man, honest and steadfast to a fault. Ariss sensed there was more to his vigilance than his desire to be a good protector. At times, when she caught him looking at her, unaware of her attention, she saw something like love shining in his eyes. When he caught her looking, he would hurriedly glance away, guilt stamping clear lines on his handsome face. He'd made no overt overtures to her, and probably never would, but his longing was still there, lurking just below the surface.

"The same." Ariss kept her gaze riveted to Kerrick's face. "I thought I saw a flicker of movement in his eyes, but it might have been just wishful thinking." In his state, Kerrick didn't even dream. Neither she nor the doctors had seen any indication of eye movement. Or any movement. He lay so perfectly still he was like a statue.

Donlan placed a comforting hand on her shoulder. "You should rest."

She placed her hand atop his. "How can I when he lies here, alone, fighting against inexhaustible foes?"

Donlan had no answer. "I will have them bring you something to eat."

Nodding absently, she smoothed Kerrick's shirt for the thousandth time. She hadn't felt hungry since the confrontation in the temple, but she ate anyway, for her child. Because as she sat here, holding Kerrick's hand and smoothing cool cloths to his forehead, she continued to cling to hope that somehow, he would vanquish the selfish gods within and then they could be together.

Her deepest wish was that all three of them could find a small bit of happiness. She didn't care where they lived or what they did, she would be happy just to be together. All her silly dreams of living in the forest meant nothing if she couldn't have Kerrick there with her. As the days rolled slowly into one another, even that tiny hope grew ever more dim. Right before her eyes, Kerrick was disappearing.

One of her servants approached with a small tray of food. The young girl placed it beside Ariss, bowed, and backed away. Ariss ate absently. Bite, chew, swallow, repeat. Everything tasted the same, chalky and bland. All she could think of was how much she hated Tavarus. She hated him with a white-hot rage that no amount of cool reasoning could ever dampen. Never in her life had she wished ill on another, but if she could, she would kill Tavarus herself.

In spite of her loathing toward Tavarus, she loved her child. Tenderly, she cupped her hand to her belly. He was an innocent. A part of her wanted to join Kerrick and waste away until they were nothing but dust together, but she couldn't harm her child. Moreover, she realized Kerrick wouldn't want her to die to be with him. He would want her to live on, strong, raising her child to be a loving, responsible man, because if nothing else, Ariss would teach him how to behave. Her child would not be a self-absorbed spoiled child that would grow up to be a self-indulged god. Not if she had anything to say about it.

Briefly, Ariss had thought of appealing to Varnatha, but jealousy consumed the goddess. She would never let go of Kerrick so that Tavarus could use him to mount her again.

During her vigil at Kerrick's bedside, several people had come to pay their respects and to offer suggestions. Ariss had listened with great hope, but her optimism quickly faded when no one came up with a solution that would work. Several people suggested killing Kerrick to force the gods from his body. Once they departed, they could just bring Kerrick back to life.

Ariss pointed out that Tavarus would simply return once Kerrick was alive again. She wasn't sure about Varnatha; speculation was that Kerrick had invited her in to fight off Tavarus. His death would revoke her invitation, but that still left Tavarus. Knowing that Kerrick had brought Varnatha in to fight him off would only anger the childish god; Ariss couldn't even fathom what Tavarus would do in retaliation.

Another suggested trying to invoke the supreme god who ruled over all the gods in *Jarasine,* but Ariss didn't want any more gods involved, especially not one with more power than all of them combined. Orsolua was said to be both male and female, with all the powers of the other gods and goddesses combined. Still, who knew what Orsolua was actually like? Ariss had no idea what placing a third god in Kerrick would do. If two made him catatonic, three would probably kill him outright. Moreover, the gods and goddesses had minds of their own. Each had their own agenda that clearly didn't involve helping mere mortals. Adamantly, Ariss had insisted that there be no more divine interference.

When she had issued her edict, Donlan had grimaced, dropped his gaze to the floor, and turned slightly away. That's when she knew he had sought out a god, hoping to curry favor. She confronted Donlan and he fell to his knees, apologizing so profusely that she found his obsequious behavior embarrassing. She hurriedly forgave him, but warned him to make no further efforts along those lines. Donlan pleaded his case, insisting that he could reach Tavarus if only she would let him, but she put her foot down. In the end, Donlan relented, bowing to her wishes.

Scholars, acolytes, and even the empress herself had devoted countless hours to finding a solution, but they all came up empty. Bithia could not have been more kind; she gave Ariss leave to use whatever resources she needed to help Kerrick.

"He is far too fine a man to die so young," Bithia said, her rough-hewn hand gripping Ariss' hand with such compassion, Ariss felt the emotion right down to her bones. She had thanked her greatly, then turned back to her lonely vigil.

As night fell, her servants drifted away, and the guards left to their posts outside her door. Donlan was loath to join them.

"I wish to stay in here with you."

Even though she hadn't really done anything all day but worry over Kerrick, she was exhausted and far to weary to deal with Donlan's infatuation.

"There is nothing else for you to do, Donlan. Please, I ask you to return to your rooms until morning."

He looked to argue the point, but in the end, perhaps softened by her drained tone, he bowed slightly and left her rooms with his head hung low.

She and everyone knew that very soon, if they couldn't find a solution, Kerrick would die, possibly even this night.

In the silence of the room, Ariss could hear Kerrick's slow drawing in and exhaling of breath. Even, steady, almost like a heartbeat, he moved air into and out of his lungs. How much longer would he be able to do so? What horrors were happening to him within the borders of his mind?

Ariss curled next to him, snuggling her body close as she did every night, hoping that her nearness eased his pain in some way. Gently, she lifted his hand and placed his palm on her belly so he could feel the child within. Tavarus' or not, Kerrick loved her child. His great concern for her extended to the life she carried. As her protector, he'd been willing to die to keep her and the baby safe.

"I love you, Kerrick."

Each night before she closed her eyes, she whispered those words to his ear. Right afterward tears welled, forcing their way out from between her closed lids. She tried not to weep, but she couldn't stop. Ariss cried for what she hadn't done, for what she could have done, for what she should have done. As he had for the last nine nights, Kerrick stayed perfectly still, his breathing a soothing rhythm that ushered her into slumber.

Just as sleep tugged her down into blissful nothingness, she bolted awake, sitting upright.

She'd felt movement.

Filled with joy, she looked down to Kerrick's hand, but it just lay limply against her. While she was staring at him, she felt another tickle of movement.

"My baby."

Wrapping her hands around her belly, she hugged him through her skin, holding him as if she would never let go.

21

Kerrick existed in a nightmare world. Tavarus and Varnatha battled endlessly. He stood by the wayside, observing, unable to intervene, to speak, to do anything but watch them fight. Weapon after weapon manifested in their hands. Wound after blood-gushing wound appeared on their bodies. Nothing slowed them down. No injury was great enough to make them stop. They were immortal beings that would never tire, never die. Kerrick no longer thought they battled over him. Now it seemed to be fighting for the sheer sake of fighting.

Kerrick regretted every petty argument he'd ever had with Ariss. Had he known what little time they had together, he wouldn't have wasted a moment. What really devastated him was that he'd never told her he loved her. He was certain that she knew, but he'd liked to have said the words all the same. For once in his life, he wanted to say those words to a woman and mean them as more than pillow talk.

Sometimes, as he stood watching Tavarus and Varnatha hurt each other, he felt Ariss was near. He felt her tears, her pain, and her grief. In those moments, he tried to move, to reach out. He wanted to give her some indication he was still here. He wanted to comfort her, but the rage between the combatants held him immobile. They refused to release him until one of them emerged triumphant. Sadly for him, they were evenly matched.

Kerrick had all the time in the world to contemplate his life. He'd made so many mistakes because of his impulsive nature. In his haste, he willingly allowed Varnatha to possess him. His motive in doing so was pure, but no less stupid.

Still, he knew, given a second chance, he would likely make the same mistakes all over again. It was a hard lesson to learn, but he had to accept that his heart ruled him, not his head. He wanted to think of himself as an emotionless man who followed logic and reason, but he wasn't. Emotions had a greater hold over him than he wanted to admit. His need to connect his feelings to those around him fueled his interest in gossip.

Varnatha whacked Tavarus' arm off with a mighty blow. Before she could celebrate, he grew a new one.

Kerrick sighed.

"They won't ever stop."

Kerrick looked around, but he was alone in the misty whiteness. Great, he thought, now he was hearing voices.

"Of course you're hearing voices. Well, a voice. I am speaking to you, after all."

The voice wasn't one he recognized.

"That's because you haven't met me."

"Who are you?" Kerrick asked the air.

"I'm your son."

Now he knew he was hallucinating. He didn't have any children. He'd been with many women, but that was something he'd always taken great care with; controlling the birth of children was his primary focus just before pleasure.

"Until Ariss."

Kerrick wasn't sure if he said those two words or his hallucination had. Struck by the truth, Kerrick wanted to pelt this new speaker with questions, but he didn't dare. He didn't want the voice, hallucination or not, to leave. He was sick of being alone. And anyone, even a figment of his imagination, was better than nothing. Besides, he had a feeling all of this was just another way to hold out hope. What better way to pacify himself than to imagine he spoke to the child Ariss carried? He hadn't allowed himself to really see the child as his, even though he'd felt in his heart he was, because he feared what Tavarus would do in retaliation.

"They can't see me unless I want them to." A young man stood beside him, dressed in simple black trousers, his hands clasped behind his back. "Only you can see me."

Kerrick congratulated himself for imagining such a striking man as his son. He saw a combination of himself and Ariss in his face. If possible, his son had the best of both their features: gray-green eyes, high-angled cheekbones, a strong, square chin, and deep brown hair with golden highlights. Luckily, he'd inherited Kerrick's build: strong shoulders, narrow hips, and muscular arms. Shirtless, his chest was surprisingly free of hair. Around the upper portion of his right arm, a black band of sharp angles against a parallel line encircled his entire bicep.

Kerrick's stomach lurched. Darting his gaze between his son and Tavarus, Kerrick realized the mark upon each was the same.

His son noticed him looking at the mark. He laughed. "I am bound to Tavarus, but I do not follow him. I am bound to her as well." His son nodded to Varnatha.

Kerrick noticed that she, too, had the mark embedded into her skin, but not on her arm; her mark encircled her upper right thigh.

"The mark doesn't mean I am his or her disciple. Rather . . . the opposite, in fact."

Kerrick didn't know what the opposite was. "Tavarus and Varnatha are your disciples?" He asked the question in jest, but his son calmly considered for a very long time before he answered.

"In the future they are."

His son's voice was so composed and controlled, it caused a shiver along Kerrick's spine.

"Those two"—Kerrick pointed to the battling war gods—"worship you?"

His son laughed loud and long until tears ran from the corners of his eyes. "They?" He pointed. "Those two notice none but themselves. The only thing they worship is fighting."

"I don't understand." Kerrick reached out, expecting his hand to wash right through him, but he touched strong, solid flesh.

His son clapped his hand over his. Even in his hallucination, Kerrick felt the moist heat of his son's touch.

"I know," his son said. "It doesn't matter. What matters is that my mother needs you."

The most compelling thing about his son was the peace that emanated from him. He looked over everything with unshakable tranquility. Even when he spoke of Ariss, he remained calm, as if he were simply reminding Kerrick of something he forgot.

"I've been trying to get to her." Kerrick couldn't keep the frustration out of his voice. "But they won't let me go."

His son patted his hand and then released him. He cast his gaze upon the fighting duo, and called, "Tavarus? Varnatha?"

Whipping his bald head around, flinging off beads of sweat, Tavarus focused his gaze upon them. Varnatha lowered her blade, keeping her face toward Tavarus while darting a glance at them.

"I'm not your son. But you've always known that."

Tavarus' nostrils flared. Rage filled his eyes.

Calmly, Kerrick's son continued, "You just wanted Ariss. That's why you possessed her to make her mate with Kerrick, thus ensuring she would become pregnant." He turned to Kerrick and said, "In the temple, you noticed Ariss' pupils were wide. My mother wanted you, but he forced her to mate with you rather than just accepting your tribute as she had with the others. Tavarus needed your tribute within her to continue with his plans."

Kerrick nodded, just now realizing that Tavarus had subtly compelled both of them to bring about his desired outcome: a child that would be considered the issue of a god.

His son's eyes settled on Varnatha. "All along he's known the child is not his. He just wanted to make Ariss pliable to his demands."

Varnatha laughed.

Tavarus turned, swinging his blade, but she was already gone. Tavarus turned his attention to them. Anger in his steps, he marched over, his blade held on high. "I can still possess you whenever I want!"

His son didn't even blink. Calmly, he said, "No, Tavarus, you cannot. I won't allow it."

Tavarus' gaze fell on the mark encircling his arm.

Kerrick looked there, too. For the first time, he noticed gold highlighted the edges of the black lines around his son's arm, but not Tavarus'. His son's mark glittered with an inner radiance that was almost spellbinding.

Fear widened Tavarus' eyes. All during his battle with Varnatha, he'd shown nothing but aggression. Panic never crossed his sharp features. However, one glance at the mark on his son's arm turned his face pale and set his lips to quivering.

"Why didn't you use the power before?"

Kerrick realized that Tavarus directed the question to him, not his son.

"He didn't want to use his power against you," his son answered. "But he will if you return."

Tavarus narrowed his gaze, scrutinizing Kerrick, looking for weakness, anything he could exploit. Kerrick faced him without fidgeting, just as he had stood for the appraisal of the recruits when he stepped forward to claim the role of Harvester. Forcefully, Kerrick injected every bit of confidence he had into his posture, even though he didn't feel convinced. After long consideration, Tavarus gritted his teeth and mercifully vanished. Kerrick released a breath he felt he'd been holding forever.

"And just what is this great and mighty power I have?" Kerrick directed the question to his son as he considered the now vast empty mist around them.

"Love." His son said the word as if that answered everything. "That's your greatest weapon. Let your heart lead you, Father."

"But that's what has always gotten me into trouble." Every time his life went horribly wrong, it was because he'd acted without thinking.

"No, impulsively following your mind is what caused the mess. Follow your heart." His son considered him with a most engaging expression, then placed his hand over Kerrick's heart. "Your heart is what led you to Ariss."

Kerrick cupped his son's hand. He felt his own heart beating, then the beat below his son's flesh. Before Kerrick could ask any more questions, his son's hand melted below his.

Kerrick awoke.

Ariss lay beside him with her arms wrapped around her belly, holding their child, their son.

Protectively placing his arms around her, Kerrick pulled her into his embrace. She moaned in her sleep. He cupped a palm to her belly and swore he felt movement, as if his son acknowledged his presence. There were hundreds of unanswered questions, but for now, all he wanted was to hold his family in his arms.

22

"Derry? Where's your father?" Ariss called through the open window, but her son was too far away to hear her, or he pretended not to. When he was playing in the *galbol* trees, Derry became single-minded and oblivious to everything else.

Her heart plunged to her belly when Derry swung from one branch to another. No matter how many times she'd witnessed him scampering across the offset, spiraling limbs, she never stopped worrying. Kerrick assured her Derry was safe and knew his limitations, but that didn't make watching him flying through the air any easier on her heart.

"Derrick, I asked you a question!" Nothing got his attention faster than using his given name.

Derry turned his head her direction. Brown hair with golden highlights fanned out around his face. Almost thirteen seasons old, yet he had the eyes of an ancient. Once he riveted his gaze upon her, he rolled his eyes. She loved her son, always would, but he was at that age where he thought all adults were annoying. "Dad's at the hot pond." Jumping out, he reached for a branch, missed, but grabbed the next one down.

Ariss turned away before her heart gave out entirely. Gathering up her daughter, who slumbered peacefully in her satchel, Ariss left behind their neat and tiny home. Working her way across the yard, she took the well-worn path that would take her to the pond. Kerrick had discovered a hot spring on the property. With several cycles of backbreaking labor, he'd created a large, deep body of water that was surprisingly warm.

Despite the running water in the house, Kerrick preferred to bathe outside, even when the cold came and laid down layers of icy crystals. After his confinement in the palace as the Harvester, Kerrick had become obsessed with being outside. At night they slept with the windows open, even when it was freezing outside, just so he could smell fresh air. Ariss didn't mind. The chill gave her an excuse to snuggle deeper into his embrace. And they had plenty of wood to keep the metal stove stoked.

She emerged from the forest as he emerged from the water. Pushing up from the bottom, he shot himself out of the surface with great power. A large splash revealed his naked chest. He shook his head sharply side to side, flinging water in all directions. In the light of *Tandalsul,* his hair glowed brighter than gold, and the collar around his neck gleamed.

Again, her heart stopped, but this time at the sheer majestic beauty of her bondmate. Every time she saw him, she reminded herself how grateful she was, how blessed she was, how blissfully content she was to have him in her life. The time for a tremendous and painful change grew near, but with Kerrick by her side, she knew she would prevail. They all would.

Here in the forest, the question of his position to her ceased to matter. None knew of his past as her servant, so everyone they knew considered them bondmates. They thought Kerrick's collar was simply a fashionable accessory. When several of their neighbors emulated the smooth metal links, Ariss had to bite her tongue not to tell them the truth. If they knew the meaning behind it, they certainly wouldn't wish to wear something similar. In this case, ignorance was truly bliss. Kerrick chuckled when he saw them. He'd long since stopped worrying over what the acolytes had told him. They had crafted their own ceremony to bond themselves together. They exchanged words of love and fidelity, sealing themselves to each other as equals. That was all that mattered to them.

Kerrick saw her and smiled a greeting that turned into a suggestive leer.

Ariss playfully darted her gaze around even though she knew they were alone. The nearest neighbor was more than half a day away by foot. Usually they went to them, selling them the medicinal plants she'd learned to grow by trial and error. Ever supportive, Kerrick brought her books and seedlings, working by her side until she learned what worked and what didn't. Just like rearing her children, raising her garden was a labor of love.

Glancing down at her still-slumbering daughter, Ariss placed her near to the shore, but within the thick shade of the *merdica* bushes that grew around the *galbol* trees.

With Kerrick's attention riveted to her every move, Ariss slowly slipped off her dress, teasing him with the artful revelation of her body. Time and two children hadn't been too hard on her body, not if Kerrick's reaction was any indication. Once she was bare, he whistled appreciatively. He crooked his finger, calling her into the water.

Striding forward, Ariss entered the pond with her gaze held to his. Warm water sluiced up her legs, sensual as a lover's caress. As she drew close, he lifted his arm, offering out his hand to her. She grasped his hand and gave a blissful sigh as he pulled her into his embrace.

Hot, water-slick skin pressed against her, allowing her to slide her body against his. Her breasts flattened against his chest, her nipples hardening with the contact. Sliding her up, he took one firm bud into his mouth, suckling just a bit of milk.

"Not too much," he said, nuzzling one, then the other. "Just enough to taste." He took another sip. "You taste wickedly fine."

Rolling her head back, she wrapped her legs around him, clinging to him as he cupped her bottom. Bit by bit, he guided her down until he fitted his cock between her thighs. For a timeless moment, he held himself to her, ready to plunge within. Knowing her as he did, he knew how much she relished that moment right before penetration. Just when she thought she couldn't stand any more delay, he let her slither down and plunged his cock inside her.

They released a mutual sigh.

Ariss shivered from her toes to the tips of her ears. How could it be that after hundreds of encounters with him she still felt such powerful satisfaction whenever they connected?

"I've been waiting for this all day." He rubbed his nose against hers, his gaze holding hers in thrall.

"The day isn't yet half over," she reminded gently.

"Mmmm," he moaned, kissing her upper lip, then drawing it inside his mouth. Tugging on the sensitive flesh while flicking his tongue against the center of her lip instantly made her think of the same luscious movement much lower on her body. When she squirmed restlessly against him, he released her lip and grinned lasciviously. "My sense of time distortion must be from someone waking me up before the suns even broke through the clouds." Kerrick lifted her up, holding her while he made a slow swivel of his hips.

"You know she won't go back to sleep for me." Ariss wriggled against him, loving the way she felt strong and yet helpless in his grasp. He was so much larger than she was, yet his power never frightened her. Kerrick's strength only aroused her. What excited her was that for such a massive man, he was amazingly gentle. Even his tiny daughter recognized this basic fact about him. When she was fussy, only Kerrick could comfort her. Thankfully, their daughter slumbered peacefully on the bank, giving them this chance to be together.

"You just say that so you can sleep." Kerrick rocked her, plunging his cock to her in a series of quick bursts that rubbed her clit against his rough pubic hair.

Clutching his shoulders, Ariss moaned, "You know it's not fair for us to have a discussion while doing this." Because she had a tendency to agree to anything Kerrick wanted. To get his way, all he had to do was cloud her judgment with sex.

"I like it when you say yes."

"Kerrick—" she never got past his name. Smoothly, he lifted her up, withdrawing his cock. He spun her so that she faced away. He lowered himself in the water so that he knelt on one knee. "What are you doing?"

"Giving you a tawdry throne."

A deep shiver tightened her exposed nipples as her breasts bobbed at the surface. "You swore that you would never use that against me." One night, when they'd had a bit too much of *merdica* berry wine, she'd told him the truth about how erotic receiving tribute was. She honestly didn't miss anything about the palace but for that.

"I'm not using it against you." He bit her neck as he pulled her into his lap. "I'm using the knowledge to excite you." He slipped his cock inside her, forcing her hips down so that she sat upon him. Settling his mouth close to her ear, he whispered, "Picture a man before you, on his knees, begging for your permission to remove his loincloth and stroke his cock."

"I'm picturing you."

"Mmmm," he moaned, biting her earlobe. "Lucky am I to be both your throne and the man at your feet."

Ariss closed her eyes, clearly seeing Kerrick kneeling before her.

"I have come to pay tribute." His voice slipped into her ear, yet simultaneously curled around her nipples. "Will you accept my tribute?"

"Kerrick, I—"

"Say yes, Ariss."

"Yes, I will accept your tribute."

Kerrick moaned into her ear, but she could picture him on his knees at her feet, his hand reaching to the side to remove his loincloth. Once he'd pulled the cloth away, he exposed his genitals. He was hard, impressively large, and eager to show her what he could do.

"May I look upon you?"

Falling fully into their game of pretend, she said, "You may cast your gaze upon me."

In her mind, he looked up from a lowered face. His gaze met hers, briefly, and then dropped to her exposed breasts. Thrusting her chest out, she lifted her hands to tease her nipples. Her sex gripped tightly around Kerrick's cock, causing him to inadvertently moan.

"My throne never moaned before," she murmured over her shoulder.

"I can't help it." Kissing her shoulder, he nestled his hands to her hips. "You've never felt so tight."

"Perhaps it's because my throne was never so big."

He growled.

"So hot."

He groaned.

"Or buried so deeply inside me."

Snarling like an animal, he nipped her ear. "Stop, Ariss, or your throne won't last long!"

"I guess there is a clear difference between a man and a

rock," she teased mildly. Her laughter halted abruptly when he thrust his hips forward while holding her still. With his one leg placed between hers, she lowered her hands to his knee to hang on.

Once she settled, he asked, "Can you see me ready for you?"

In her vision, golden light fell upon Kerrick's cock as his hand wrapped around the shaft.

"I've locked my gaze to you," he murmured, warming to his description. "I'm working my hand along the length. A teardrop of moisture hangs at the tip and I palm it, pulling it down, stroking the slickness over my cock, lessening the friction so I will last longer."

Ariss saw him perform every move in her mind's eye. "You always did know how to put on a show."

He placed his lips to her ear. "Watch as my fist tightens over my shaft, turning the tip dark. All the while, my eyes blaze bright. Each stroke makes me think of my cock in your snug cunt."

That's exactly what she thought of, too. Each time she visualized him stroking down, she moved her hips, rocking upon him.

"I thought you were supposed to hold still?" he admonished.

"I can't." She'd enjoyed their game, but she'd gone as far as she could. "I want you. I need to feel—"

"Not yet." He held her firmly, forcing her to wait while he whispered, "Watch my fist fly up and down the length of my shaft. My breathing is erratic, my eyes closed, my head involuntarily goes back."

Ariss could see each movement he described. He lowered his hand between her legs and fingered her clit. Rubbing hard and fast, his voice in her ear was just as sharp and pointed.

"In a great gush I come, an arch of pure white jets from the tip of my cock to splash at your feet." His breath was ragged, blasting into her ear in great, hot waves. "Come for me, Ariss."

And she did.

She came so hard she fell forward, almost slipping below the surface of the water but for his arm across her waist, holding her up, and pressing her back against his chest. Suddenly, she felt him come inside her, his cock twitching, jetting a sweet, hot tide of pleasure.

Together, they stayed still, recovering.

With a soft brush of lips to her outer ear, Kerrick asked, "Did my tribute please you?"

Unable to speak, Ariss nodded.

"I love you, Ariss."

She never tired of hearing those wonderful words.

"I love you, Kerrick."

"Really?" He playfully nipped her neck. "Even though my name means chastity device in Felton?"

She laughed, turning to kiss him over her shoulder. "I will never forget the expression on your face when I told you." The first time he'd said his name in the mating room, she was certain it was a joke; a man who embodied sex as the Harvester named after a chastity device just seemed too ironic for words. Apparently, in Cheon, where he was from, the name Kerrick meant strength. In Felton, a kerrick was a complicated device that prevented the wearer from engaging in sex. There were different versions for men and woman, although it was now considered more of a novelty.

They laughed gently, holding each other. Even before he spoke, she knew he would say something she didn't want to hear. It wasn't anything in particular, just a general tightening of his body that gave her fair warning.

"We have to return to the palace."

She'd always known the time would come, but somehow the moment had arrived far too quickly. "He's still too young."

"No, he's not. He's thirteen seasons come this Harvest."

"I'm not ready."

Kerrick took a deep breath. "Yes, you are. You are so strong, Ariss. So much stronger than you give yourself credit for."

"We could run."

With a sigh, Kerrick rubbed his cheek against hers. "Derry has to go back. That was the agreement we made."

Ariss swore when this day came she wouldn't cry, but tears filled, then spilled over, falling down her face.

"Ariss." Kerrick snuggled her tightly. "Cry your tears now; then we will wash them away, so that tonight, when we tell our son, you will face him with clear vision."

She nodded, knowing that she owed their son that much. "You don't have to go."

"Don't even think it, Ariss. We're a family and we'll see this through together."

"But you hated the palace." Even now, he wore the mark of his servitude. The collar would not come off. Even on the day he died, it would hold fast. She hated the horrible thing and wished with all her heart that she could remove it. When she'd told him this, Kerrick shook his head at her, calmly explaining that it wasn't her fault. He'd gotten used to it so much so that he often forgot he wore the metallic band altogether. Later, when their neighbors naively emulated it, she'd tried to see the humor as Kerrick had, but she'd never quite been able to release her shame for placing it upon him in the first place.

"This time I won't be trapped inside, neither will you, or our children. We'll have our freedom."

"But Derry, he's—"

"Old enough to understand he will one day rule beside the empress. We have to take him now, so he can become accustomed to their ways." Gently, Kerrick lifted her, turning her around so she faced him. "We can't wait until his actual Harvest. Can you imagine what a shock it would be to go from this world into that world without any period of transition?"

Ariss knew Kerrick was wise to slowly indoctrinate their son to the ways of the palace, but she was loath to leave behind her peaceful world in the forest.

"For us, it's not for always. I've spoken to Ekker and he'll watch over the stead so that when Derry takes his rightful place, we can return."

Derry wouldn't take his rightful place for five seasons. "And what of our daughter? What world does she belong to?"

Kerrick's gaze darted to her satchel on the shore. "She can decide for herself when she's old enough."

Ariss opened her mouth to argue, but Kerrick kissed her quickly. Such was his preferred method of shushing her. Much to her chagrin, his ploy worked.

"When I became the Harvester and I stood there, gazing upon a row of exquisite women, do you know what I thought?"

Ariss shook her head.

"I missed my hair."

A great laugh burst from Ariss' lips.

"That's how unbelievably shallow I was." Kerrick chuckled, then draped her legs on either side of his knee. "I had no idea what I'd gotten myself into because of some petty desire for revenge on my father." He shook his head, which caused his silken strands to tumble around his head and obscure his gaze.

When she reached up to brush his hair back, he caught her wrist and kissed the palm of her hand.

"That was my signature move." Prompted by her confused frown, he explained, "Once I kissed the woman's hand, I would pull her near and kiss her lips. Once I did that, well, let's just say my kisses were rather persuasive."

"As if I didn't know." Ariss pulled him close and kissed him. "That's why you always save discussions for when we're intimate."

His smile was part bad little boy and part masterful man. "But you see, things are different now."

"They are? How?"

"Because I don't need any of that with you." Tenderly, he cupped her chin. "All my moves and seductive ways work on you, but I really don't need them." Placing his face very close to hers, he whispered, "All I really have to do is look at you." Before she could raise a fuss at his arrogance, he added, "And all you have to do is look at me."

For a timeless moment, their gazes locked. Ariss melted as Kerrick hardened. As he slipped himself inside her and she held firmly to his shoulders, she understood that together they could face anything, even a return to the decadent world of the palace.

"But Derry—"

Kerrick cut her off with another kiss. "Soon he will be a man. He will be able to look out for himself."

Ariss knew Kerrick was right, but letting go of her little boy was going to be much harder than she thought. However, as Kerrick often said, it was too late to turn back now. They'd only been allowed to leave the palace by agreeing that they would return when Derry was thirteen seasons old.

At the time they'd made the agreement, thirteen seasons had seemed like such a long time. Sadly, the seasons passed so swiftly it seemed they'd arrived only yesterday. Ariss wasn't ready to give up their private forest sanctuary.

Kissing Kerrick as they worked their bodies together a second and much slower time, she knew they would love each other no matter where they were. Always, they would be together. Nothing in this world, or even the world beyond in *Jarasine*, could tear them apart.